# Mary Gordon

# SPENDING

*A Utopian Divertimento*

SCRIBNER

SCRIBNER
1230 Avenue of the Americas
New York, NY 10020

Designed by Brooke Zimmer
Set in Perpetua
Manufactured in the United States of America

1  3  5  7  9  10  8  6  4  2

Library of Congress Cataloging-in-Publication Data
Gordon, Mary, date.
Spending : a utopian divertimento / Mary Gordon.
p.  cm.
I. Title.
PS3557.O669S64    1998
813'.54—dc21    97-40353
CIP

ISBN 0-684-83945-8

FOR NOLA TULLY

# Acknowledgments

Among the greatest of my good fortunes is the generosity of friends who have shared with me the fruits of their knowledge and experience: Susan Colgan, Noa Hall, Hayden Herrera, Gail Marx, Linda Nochlin, Andrea Pluhar, Roberta Berman Quinn, Elena Sistos. Most especially, for valor beyond the call of anything, I thank Helen Miranda Wilson, who has no aversion to stupid questions. I am indebted to Leo Steinberg's brilliant *The Sexuality of Christ in Renaissance Art and Modern Oblivion*. And, for superhuman endurance, I congratulate Eugene Sorenson, who put up with my utter ignorance about the commodities market and explained this foreign world to me with patience and grace.

# SPENDING

PART ONE

I must tell you, it was always about money.

The first important thing he said to me was this: "You work too hard."

Of course, it was also about sex.

And since I'm a painter and it affected my life and my work, you'd have to say it was about art.

Let's begin here. I used to be a moderately successful painter. Not anymore. Now I'm a very successful painter. He certainly had a lot to do with that.

It goes to show that sometimes doing someone else a good turn brings good results.

This is how it started.

I have a friend, an old friend from art school, who opened a gallery in Provincetown. In my opinion the last thing Provincetown needs is another art gallery. The idea of it made me feel I was going to drown.

My friend's husband has a software company, they live in Cos Cob, Connecticut, which is at least one too many C's for me. She gave up painting (well, she was never very good anyway) and he wants her to have a project of her own. Which he's perfectly willing to fund because he's a decent guy, and after all those years running PTA bake sales and giving dinner parties, she deserves it. I guess I shouldn't talk, I took money from a man. But at least it had nothing to do with cooking.

The idea of Louisa opening a gallery bored me to the point of vengeance. At times like this, my mind races. It must be that I'm so furious at the person boring me that I want to punish them. Which must be why I said to her, "Louisa, I have a much better idea. Why don't you open a restaurant in Provincetown instead of a gallery? You could call it the Inferno. You could have waiters and waitresses dressed as devils, and everything you served could be very high in fat and refined sugars. You could have a sign, 'No natural ingredients.' Just think how happy you'd make people. The air would be full of smoke! Whipped cream on every plate: mayonnaise in every bowl. . . ."

Then I looked at her. She's a very nice woman. She's a terrible painter, but I admire a kind of energetic patience that you could say is her approach to life. She's good to me; she's bought a lot of my work; she keeps trying to set me up with guys who are doing something really new with or on or maybe to the Internet. I could see in her eyes that I'd hurt her, and I was feeling so wretched I had to do something extravagant to make up for it. Just to avoid the accusation that people are always hurling at me: "You don't take me seriously. You don't think my work is as important as yours."

Which, of course, I usually don't, and what I want to say is, "No, I don't take your work as seriously as mine, but I think you're a much better person than I, which is why you don't work like I do. I mean, look how I live! It's crazy. You wouldn't want to live the way I do. Not everybody has to be an artist."

But I'm usually saying this to someone who *does* want to be an artist, so I'm hurting them, if I do say it, and if I don't it's just one of those wedges of silence—that grows until something happens like my outburst to Louisa about her restaurant, which I still think was a good idea.

I really envy brain surgeons. People aren't always coming up to them—on beaches, in coffee shops—and saying, "You know I do a little brain surgery myself. Maybe you could come over—you have a lot of spare time, brain surgeons are able to make their own schedules—and look at a brain I just operated on. I really think it's going somewhere."

Lucky, lucky, brain surgeons.

When I realized I'd hurt Louisa, I felt I had to make it up to her and

I told her that I really thought a gallery was a great idea and when she asked, I said of course I'd show some paintings with her. And when she said, "This is my idea. This is what will make it really unique [please, Louisa, put the knife just an inch or two higher, just below the breast-bone on the right, thanks]. I thought we could have the artists give slide talks about their work." I was feeling so wretched about what I'd said that I told her it was a superb idea and I'd be delighted to do it.

And you know, it happened, as it always does. When you say you'll do something in a year, you always think either there'll be a natural dis-aster, or a bankruptcy, or someone will forget. And then the time comes, and there you are: with something else required of you.

There I was in the Louisa Ryan Gallery in the middle of August, giving a slide talk. People did come. She was right to count on the critical mass of guilt that certain high-minded people feel on vacation. Having to sit through a slide talk made them feel a little bit punished.

I was with my work, in my work, but also with people, which is very unusual. Usually I'm in my studio, painting, and being quiet, so when I get a chance to talk publicly sometimes I get a little carried away. I was talking about a painting of mine called *The Artist's Muse*. In the background there's a lot of emptiness. De Chirico emptiness, that kind of spacy gray green. And a shadow of a table. In the foreground, a man wearing only his underwear, a very beautiful pair of green and white striped silk boxer shorts. I had a wonderful time doing those shorts, the pearliness of the white, absorbing that dim light, and the green stripes, the green of an Anjou pear, but waxier, relating to the empty green of the background. In the middle of that pearly white/pear green field of the boxer shorts, there's a lot of brush work, a swelling and then just the tenderest hint of pink.

In one hand, the guy's holding a black cast-iron frying pan. I enjoyed painting that very much—the blackness its own distinct black, with a touch of green, the circular shape, the hard edges of the handle. In his other hand, he's holding a white egg.

That night when I was giving the slide talk, I spoke a little bit about the composition of the painting, but I could tell no one was really inter-ested, what they wanted to hear about was painting an erection. Did I have a model, and who was he, and what did I do to give him one, was it just one, or a lot of them, and how did they last? Except, of course, they were too decorous to ask those questions right out—they did ask the one about the live model, though, which implied all the rest. But I wasn't going to dwell on that. In fact I didn't have a live model, which accounts for all the brush work. I did say that, and it got a big laugh. Also I said, "I was painting from memory. In the great tradition of Romantic landscape painting. The remembrance of things past." Another big laugh.

I'm sure there's an eternal punishment designed for people who are fed by "the big laugh," who'll say anything, almost anything to get it. Or maybe not. Maybe it's not worthy of damnation at all. Maybe it's a very pure act, a very generous act, you give yourself up to your audience, you're all together, carried up on a wave, and you really do lose yourself.

Sometimes, when I'm in the middle of going for the big laugh, or the next big laugh, the wave crashes and I look around me and see only flotsam and jetsam: old condoms, Tampax holders, empty bags saying Cheetos or Made in Taiwan. But that wasn't happening. The wave wasn't even beginning to crash. So I said, "You know, folks, there's a tradition that male painters get to take advantage of: the woman who's a combination model, housekeeper, cook, secretary. And of course she earns money. And provides inspiration. All over the world, girls are growing up dreaming of being the Muse for some kind of artist. Looking at their bodies in mirrors thinking, 'Maybe some man would like to paint that.' Reading French cookbooks that tell them how to make really succulent little dishes out of horsemeat with a lot of bay leaves and wine. Preparing physically and spiritually to carry his canvases to a hard-hearted gallery owner, their muscles straining, their eyes brimming with shed or unshed tears. Now I ask you, mothers and fathers of America, are your boys dreaming of these things? Where, I ask you, lovers of the arts, where are the male Muses?"

And he stood up, just there, in front of everyone, and said, "Right here."

I flipped on the light. That was the first time I saw him.

*    *    *

A few people stayed around to talk to me, but he was standing near the projector, and everyone seemed to feel they ought to leave us alone. When they did, he said to me, "Let me take you to dinner. We'll go to the most expensive place in town."

I said, "What's the most expensive place in town? I have no idea."

He said, "That's the kind of thing you'll get to know."

I suppose you want me to tell you what he looks like.

It's hard for me to remember looking at him as a person whose body I didn't know, a person I'd never seen without his clothes on. Thinking about his hair right now, what I'm focusing on is what his hair is like as I'm looking down on it when his head's between my legs.

How did I get to know what he looks like? How can anyone answer that question, as if that someone always appeared the same way, an image without a context. How did the knowledge of his body come to me? It wasn't all at once, it must have been gradual, in fragments. But in what way?

That first night, he was wearing jeans and a blue oxford cloth shirt. I remember because later that night I had my face against the shirt for a long time. He was a little less than six feet tall. I thought he must be around fifty. He was wearing white sneakers, but they weren't too clean. Not filthy, but not new in that way that makes you wonder if the guy's gay, or at least bi. Which in this day and age, the plague years, must give a person pause.

As we walked out the door, I said to him, "What's the difference what the most expensive place is? Don't you want to go to the place that has the best food?"

He said, "I'm trying to make a point. About myself and you. I want you to know that I'm a man who has quite a lot of money."

I've told you what he looks like, which is more than I wanted to do. I wanted to get on with the story. Now that's out of the way. But I'm not going to tell you his name right now. I'll just call him B.

We were walking up Commercial Street in Provincetown. Whatever my chic friends say, I love Commercial Street on a summer night. One of the reasons I love it is that it so relentlessly lowers the tone. All those tee shirt shops and saltwater taffy shops and fudge shops. All those places selling plastic whales. Irish families from Western Massachusetts buying sweatshirts and eating ice cream. Secretaries spending their two weeks' vacation at a guest house, sitting under umbrellas, eating their guacamole burgers, looking a little disappointed; it's dawned on them they got it wrong, there isn't a chance they're going to meet men here. Because, of course, Provincetown is a gay town, which saves this part of the Cape from being unbearably wholesome and full of family values—even left-wing family values like the Vineyard, and it's a little dangerous, a little over the edge—a drag show on every block, a pair of sequined shoes (size twelve) for every hundred full-time residents, so it's not quite decorous enough to make it like the Hamptons.

I'd been walking up Commercial Street for years, but this was new. Now I was walking with a man with a lot of money. He had his arm around me. No, not his arm, he had his hand on the small of my back, a little spot of warmth, delicious.

There's something about walking down a street with a man who's selected you, making his preference public and obvious. You don't have to indicate anything, because he's the one who's sure he wants you, you're not sure yet if you're going to take him up on it. You're walking as a chosen woman. You watch yourself being watched, you're being watched by him, yet already chosen, so you don't need to watch him at all. You can't possibly lose. He's watching you and you're watching yourself. And you know there's nothing you can do that he won't like. Your body weighs nothing. It would be quite easy to fly up, and float away. He would watch you, flying up, floating away, not at all surprised because the whole time he'd thought you were miraculous.

What an odd thing it is, this business of looking and being looked at. Being looked at is a bit like being tasted. It doesn't have to feel like being eaten up, so that there's nothing left of you. How can it be, though, that something is being taken from you—your manifestation—yet the consumption adds something? I have been added to by being looked at by men. Also subtracted from.

But he was taking nothing from me. I felt, as I walked by, that every time he looked at me I was getting wonderfully larger. But at the same time, my bones were being emptied of their fatigue, their heaviness. I was tall, but light, like a bird, without a bird's unsubstantialness. What kind of creature was I? Perhaps I wasn't a creature at all. Perhaps I was a great ship. Instead of two breasts, I had a prow. I was at sail. No obstacles. And in between my legs, occasionally, just a thrum, a little thrill, a little rolling joist from navel to knees.

A man planning to spend money on me was an experience rare enough to feel odd. I came of age in the sixties, when it was considered unliberated to have dinner bought for you. I've been earning my own living since I was fifteen, and I always thought it was ridiculous, even oppressive, to expect a man to pay for me when he had the same amount of money, or when I had more. And I've always been involved with artists, or intellectuals, so we always had the same financial woes.

But he had announced himself to me as a wealthy man. He had said that what he wanted to do was spend money on me. It would have been absurd for me to say something like "dutch treat." Besides, I didn't want to.

As we were walking, I was thinking about his hand on the small of my back, and the rolling between my legs, but I was also thinking about his money. At the same time that I was thinking of myself as a ship in full sail, I was thinking of the two of us being followed by a horse-drawn cart, full of bags and bags of gold. He had only to turn around, dip his hands (which I was beginning to notice were rather small for his body, with unusually short thumbs) into those bags and drip gold onto us. We could have everything we wanted. Or at least I could, for a little while.

I knew that he was looking at me but I didn't know what he was looking for.

He said, "Do you know that I own four of your paintings?"

"That's not possible," I said. "I know who buys all my paintings and I've never seen your name."

"I've bought them as a corporation. I had a woman who works for me buy them in the corporate name—for financial reasons—but also, when I started to be interested in you, I wanted to wait till just the right time to make myself known."

"Known as what?"

"You know," he said, "it's strange, walking with you, talking to you, looking at you from this close range. I've looked at you a lot."

"What do you mean?"

"First I looked at your work. Then I wanted to know what you looked like, so I put myself in places where I knew you'd be. Your openings. I've been to all your openings. And sometimes I've watched you coming out of Watson School, where you teach. I've stood in the lobby at dismissal time. Except that Irish lady that runs the switchboard was beginning to think I was a pervert. I'm convinced I saw her about to dial 911."

"There's a kind of man who hangs out at girls' schools."

"Not my thing. And I didn't ever want to look at you when you weren't with other people."

"How did you know I wouldn't eventually be abandoned by a crowd? Left alone?"

"I always took off before there was a chance of that happening. And I know how you look when you enter or leave a group."

"How?"

"You have a panicked look when you enter a group, and a desperate one when you leave it. I think you're afraid you won't be recognized at first, then you're afraid someone will follow you, and you won't be able to be alone."

"How do you know that?"

"I used to be with Interpol."

"Really?"

"No. Do you have any idea what Interpol really is?"

"No, only that I always wanted to be in it. Or to know someone who was in it. That kind of thing happened to me a lot in the fifties. Like I never knew whether I wanted to have a mermaid or be one."

"Why were people obsessed with mermaids in the fifties?"

"I think it was the tails."

"Yeah, the tails. They were cute, but they kept the girl in her place."

He moved his hand from the small of my back to my right shoulder. I wasn't quite as blissful as I'd been when I was thinking of myself as a ship or followed by horse-drawn carts. I was starting to feel uneasy. He knew about me and I didn't know about him. He could very well have been in Interpol. He could have kept a woman locked in a room dressed as a mermaid, locked in a room with a sensory deprivation tank. Why had he spent all that time looking at me? It seemed like a kind of theft. And yet I didn't feel stolen from.

Being stolen from. The worst thing about it is being taken by surprise. Being shocked. Then outraged. Then bereft.

I knew I wasn't feeling outraged or bereft. But I didn't know how I felt.

"I think you're a very, very good painter," he said. "I think one day you might be great."

"Oh, fuck that," I said, taking his hand off my shoulder. "I can't stand that kind of thinking. I do what I do. It's my job, it's what I do with my life, and what I do for a living. All this cult of the Master—which is just another game of who's got the biggest dick—it's all so beside the point. It's worse than that. It's destructive. It takes up a lot of energy. It makes people insane. I just do what I want to do, and I enjoy it very much. So don't talk like that."

I could feel myself building up a real head of steam. "Jesus," I said. "It reminds me of one of my openings.  I was walking around listening to what people say, which I should never do. I heard this guy saying to another guy, 'Well, it's OK, but it's not Matisse.' And I tapped him on the shoulder and I said, 'No, it's not Matisse. It's Monica Szabo.' And the guy wanted to die. Which I wish he had. It was the least he could do."

"I like a woman with a moderate disposition," he said. "Why don't you tell me what you want? Just so I don't have to fear for my life."

"I think I need to know what you want."

"I'll let you know," he said, and kissed me, sticking his tongue between my lips, cool, like a slice of peach, or mango.

*    *    *

We went into a restaurant with a view of the water. We were given the best table. I don't know what he did to get it.

That was when he said to me, "You work too hard."

"How do you know?"

He said I didn't sleep enough, that the lights were on in my apartment very late, and I was out of the house quite early.

"I teach early," I said, "but of course you know that."

"Interpol knows many things. But not how much domestic help you have. How much domestic help do you have?"

"How much what?" I said, and started laughing.

"Domestic help."

"A woman named Marta comes in once a week for three hours."

"That's not enough. And another thing, your studio is in a very bad neighborhood. I could change all that."

"And what do I have to do?" I said.

"Whatever you want."

It was the second time he said that, and I was getting scared, so I said, "I'm starved, let's order quickly." Which wasn't true at all. I was too scared to eat, and too elated.

But drinking seemed like a good idea. I rarely drink, particularly on the Cape, when I like to wake up early and go for a run with my dog. Did I tell you I had a dog, a mutt I found in the subway, named Mikey? He's physically undistinguished, that must be said. When I'm at home in the city and we're in the park and I let him off his lead, if he's in a pack of other black dogs I can't pick him out. Intellectually, though, he's very distinguished, and morally a hero. He can be still for hours when I paint and then in a second be ready for a run or a play. I've never found that kind of flexibility in a man.

As I was saying, in the summers what I love best is going for a run with Mikey and then the two of us jumping into the ocean to cool off. So I usually don't drink because I like to run and paint early in the morning. I like my body's lightness, or perhaps the loss of the sense of heaviness, the air and the light and the water taking all the heaviness away from having a body, leaving you only the best parts, the vital parts, the parts that love to move, that are with you in your desire to move, and do nothing to resist movement.

But that night wasn't one of those healthy nights. "A vodka tonic," I said, when the waiter came over. I started chattering about how I liked the clear look of the vodka, and the ice, and the green of the lime, how it always reminded me of summer. But he could see that I was chattering, and it seemed wrong to chatter that way when he already knew so much about me.

He said, "Do you like to dance?"

I said, "I love to. But I thought you knew everything about me."

He said, "After dinner, we could go dancing."

This is what we had for our first meal.

Blanc de blancs to go with the oysters, local. We each had half a dozen. Bouillabaisse, the tender shells, apologetic, knowing they're there for nothing, gray and black, swimming in the orange red broth, the taste of saffron, nonnutritive and granular, suggesting yeast or beer, the garlic, only amicable now, tomatoes and soft flesh of once-shelled creatures, melting, reminding me of what I know will come later in the evening. A salad of arugula and shaved Parmesan cheese. Eating each other's dessert: white chocolate mousse for me, pecan pie for him. Putting his fork in my mouth. All women want their mother. Coffee? Yes, thanks, I need it. For the dancing. Brandy? No, thanks, remember the dancing. Take my arm. Well, I could use it on the street, a haze around the edges of my body. Why is the street so crowded this late? What is the point of all those cars?

On the street, in the summer breeze, with the smell of the sea, or maybe it's the harbor, I am not myself, I am simpler than anybody I know well, and I am singing. Not out loud. I am thinking of him, and not thinking of him, what I am really thinking of is an old song. "I'm a sentimental sap, that's all . . . what's the use of trying not to fall?"

Hearing those words and at the same time going over what he said, "I own four of your paintings . . . You are a good, a very good painter . . . I have money . . . You appeal to my imagination."

\*       \*       \*

Imagination. I decided to sing right out into the open air. "Imagination is funny, it makes a cloudy day sunny. Makes a bee think of money."

"It's honey," he said.

"Money, honey, same thing," I said, letting my head loll against his shoulder, enjoying being stupid, why not be stupid, when intelligence is just so hard?

"Money can be like honey," I said.

"Oh, yes?"

"Sticky and dangerous. But I know very little of the subject."

"When you were younger did you think you looked like Hedy Lamarr?"

I laughed. "No, my problem was when I was younger, I didn't think I looked like anybody. I was longing for someone to look like. When I was growing up there wasn't anyone with a black bush of hair, without a button nose and little pink lips like a rosebud. Who was I supposed to identify with, Jane Russell?"

"No, as I said, if you were listening, Hedy Lamarr? The mouth, and your eyes are a little slanty, like a goat's."

"That's very flattering."

"Goats are very licentious animals. And Hedy Lamarr slept with every great artist in Europe. She was the mistress of many great men."

"Is that what you have in mind for me? To be the mistress of a great man?"

"No, you might be the great man yourself."

"Please shut up. I'm not a man."

"I noticed that. I told you I was with Interpol. We figured that out right away."

I kept thinking about the word "mistress," and all the things that went along with it. You know, walking around all day in peignoirs in various shades of rose pink, and in mules bordered in fur. My day made up of various ministrations to my prized and desirable body: massage, facial, nails, leg waxing, exercise with my personal trainer, whom I also screw on the side because my plutocrat's too tired to satisfy me. Little meals prepared by an ancient French maid, in whom I weepingly confide, who joins me in my tears or urges me to have patience because men are like that.

No work. No friends. No children. No travel. No connections to the larger world. Just pampered flesh in the pinkish light of lamps with bulbs of low wattage covered by satin shades. I thought I might be bored but I knew I'd always be rested.

I asked him how he made his money.

"Futures," he said. "Commodities."

"Which, futures or commodities?"

"They're the same thing."

"No, one is about time and one is about material objects."

"But they're the same thing. The futures market, the commodities market, what it's about is trying to predict the future of material objects, their future value in the world."

"You like that?"

"I like trading. I like the whole concept of trading. It's one of the very basic things human beings do. Like farming, and building, and making art or war. It's about movement. It's about trying to control the fate of the earth."

"And you think you can?"

"While I'm making a trade, yes."

"And you enjoy it?"

"I wouldn't do it if I didn't."

"Well, you might, you might just be addicted to the money."

"If I stopped enjoying it, I'd quit. You start making bad decisions when the pleasure's gone."

I wanted to tell him that I'd experienced a lot of the things he described when I was painting, but I didn't want to put us on a level. It was important to me that he think his work was inferior to mine.

"So what commodities do you trade?"

"They're called soft markets. Sugar. Cocoa. Cotton. Especially coffee."

"Do you think about them? Do you see them in your mind's eye? Do you imagine them in piles?"

"No, the last thing you want is to have the thing you own actually materialize in front of you. I mean, what would I do with fifty thousand pounds of coffee in my apartment?"

"And what about me? Am I a commodity? Or is my work? Do you want me to materialize or do you just like the idea of me?"

"I can tell you absolutely that my interest is not abstract." He took my hand and put my third finger in his mouth. Then he bit down on the tip of it, not lightly.

We went to another place by the water, for dancing. You had to have your hand stamped by the bouncer; I wondered how hard it would be to wash off the image of a hammer and nails. The music was pulsing and unmelodic, and every song went on for about ten minutes.

"Do you like this music?" he said.

I told him I thought it was dreadful.

He asked me what kind of music I liked to dance to.

"Motown," I said. "Sixties soul."

"Just a minute," he said, and then disappeared into a back room where you could see the disc jockey through plate glass.

I watched B look at some kind of list, then hand the disc jockey money. Just as he came out of the little room, the disc jockey announced over his mike: "Ladies and gentlemen, tonight we have a very special treat for you. Tonight at the Hammer and Nails is Soul Night."

Some people, younger people, groaned. But a lot of people clapped. And in a second, Martha and the Vandellas were blasting out "Heat Wave." Then Aretha Franklin's "Respect." Then Marvin Gaye and Tammi Terrell's "Ain't Nothing Like the Real Thing."

I asked him if he knew Marvin Gaye had been shot by his father. They were having a fight over a hundred dollars' worth of insurance.

He told me he knew.

Neither of us wanted to talk anymore. We wanted to dance. He was the kind of partner I'd always longed for, he was really a good dancer, but not a showoff about it. And he didn't bend his knees too much, or wave his arms around. He understood there had to be a limited range of motion, that all the exuberance in the world could happen within that range. I'd never been involved with anyone who could dance. Who could dance as well as I could.

I was almost afraid to meet his eyes. What we were doing was so much about sex, so clearly a pantomime of sex, that I couldn't begin to pretend it was anything different. I had to understand that I was giving in. I had to understand the exhilaration, and the danger and the loss. I had to look right into his eyes and relinquish something. I had to say: "All right, yes, all right." I had to move my hips knowing exactly what I meant, let my shoulders relax not as a completed gesture but a prelude, acknowledge that my breasts weren't bouncing for nothing. I'd danced before as a kind of free-play, danced by myself whomever I was dancing with, danced to express abandon, not attachment, giving the message: Look at me, not to desire me, but to admire my moves, as you'd admire a basketball player on a court. Now it was a different kind of court. I wasn't being judged, but a sentence was being passed down. It was exciting in that way, like the silence before a sentence.

Then I just wanted to let everything go. I looked at his lips. They were very full, a bit reddish. I saw that he had a heavy beard, he was the kind of man who probably should have shaved twice a day, and I was wondering if it would chafe. I let my eyes fall to his crotch, which revealed, unfortunately, nothing. I let him put his arms around me and bring me close. Our hips ground together, like the kind of teenagers I at least had never been. Scandalous people: she'd get pregnant, he'd have to work in a gas station the rest of his life. Of course they would, you couldn't dance like this and not have a life of disaster. Dancing with him like this I was a girl with no prospects. Just the prospect of being taken home and being fucked.

But I was too old now to lose anything by it. I almost certainly couldn't even get pregnant anymore. One of the things we could both count on was that we were past many things that once might have been at stake.

Johnny Mathis was singing "Misty." I knew there was a movie called *Play Misty for Me,* about some woman stalking Clint Eastwood, before he became middle-aged and sensitive, but I didn't feel like thinking about it. I wanted to think about that insinuating sax. We kissed as we danced; we were scandalous, or we should have been, except that no one was looking at us, no one cared. He had his hands right on the base of my spine and was pressing me against him and we moved in slow circles that felt like a whirlpool. I let myself be taken up in it, or down.

I guess we were a little tight, but just a little. Or he probably wasn't at all. A vodka tonic, two glasses of wine, had loosed my pelvic hinge. When the music stopped, I could just float beside him, let him lead me to the car. I figured I would leave my car in the driveway of Louisa's gallery. I'd get it in the morning, I said to myself.

"How much did you give the disc jockey?" I said, as he paid the parking lot attendant.

"Five hundred."

"Jesus," I said, "I live on that for two weeks."

"Did you enjoy yourself?" he said.

"Of course."

"Then you might think of shutting up about how much it cost."

He had his hand on my knee and was moving it up between my legs. We'd danced so hard that my skirt was damp, my legs were sweaty, and between them was a swamp. But he didn't go that far. Traveling up and down, a five-inch path beginning with my knee.

I didn't notice what kind of car we were in. I never notice that kind of thing. We drove a while. The sky was very bright; the moon was full. We drove up a hill. I couldn't tell where we were. I could have been in danger, but I didn't think I was. We made a turn; he stopped the car. "We're here," he said.

The house was behind a hedge, and I could hear the ocean, I could smell it. He told me to wait in the car till he opened the door. He said he couldn't stand someone watching him fumble with keys.

The house was mostly glass, and I kept hearing the phrase "people who live in glass houses shouldn't throw stones," and I thought that was a good sign for me, a sign of potential safety. Then I dwelt on the idea that the phrase was "shouldn't throw stones" not "don't throw stones." From the side of the house where we stood I could only sense the ocean; I could tell that it was calm. Then I went into the house.

One wall of it, or what would have been a wall, was completely glass, so you could look right down onto the ocean. My eye followed the silver track the moon made on the black surface of the water. He

stood behind me, his hand on my shoulder, and seeing that I was enjoying looking out at the water, he turned the lights off so I could have the
full pleasure of the light of the moon. He asked if I wanted anything to
eat or drink. I said just some cold water.

I followed him into the kitchen, completely black, except for the
appliances, which were white. I became absorbed in the identity of
being a thirsty person. He opened his white refrigerator and took out a
pitcher made of cobalt blue glass. Ice cubes clinked against the glass and
when he walked toward me, holding the pitcher, I could see shadows of
lemon slices. He poured the water for me. I have never had anything so
delicious. Beads of moisture collected on the cobalt skin of the pitcher.
More than anything I wanted to put my cheeks, which seemed so hot,
against that cool glass surface. Then I said to myself: "Why not, why not
do it, this is the kind of situation in which you're meant to do anything
you want." So I took the pitcher from him and held it against my
cheeks, then moved it down toward my clavicle, and stopped at my
breasts.

"Are you warm?" he asked. "Would you like a bath?"

I said I'd like it very much.

"I'll draw it for you."

He showed me into the bathroom. It was huge, with a stall shower
the size of a servant's room, and a movie star mirror surrounded by
lights. The tiles were white and large and cool, the bath mat was white
too, made of some kind of fur. Across from the sink with the fancy mirror was an enormous white bathtub. He took his shirt off and bent over
to turn the water on. Then he took his jeans off. He was wearing light
blue boxer shorts. He filled the tub with green salts from a clear bottle
with a long, thin neck. He twirled the water with his hand and this
made visible the movement of his back muscles below the skin. His
shoulders were broad, there were a few fine hairs. I thought his back
was beautiful; I followed it from shoulders to waist; the inverted triangle, the lively muscles of the scapular. I knelt behind him and ran my
tongue up and down his spine, lingering at every vertebra.

I didn't want a bath. It seemed right to be sweaty. It was only my
clothes that were the mistake, so wrinkly, and the way they stuck to my
skin. I took off my skirt and blouse, and then my bra. I kept my green

silky underpants on. I stood behind him and I pressed myself against his back. Then I sat back on my heels and he tipped me onto my back, and onto the cool tiles. They felt wonderful against my hot skin. His fingers were inside me very soon. I kept moving my hands over him, back to front, then back again, then forward. It made a nice variety, the smooth round globes, and then, after all, bringing to mind more vegetable shapes than anything, but so unvegetable in its texture, the velvet head, the bulk. I felt wrong to be so open and so empty. I splayed my legs as if I'd just been shot.

It's always a bit of a shock, isn't it, not to be empty when you've been so empty. He made his way inside. It was relief, nothing but relief to be filled up, to be touched in such a deep place you're sure it never existed before, it only came to be at just that minute. But after a few minutes my skull grinding against the hard white tiles was uncomfortable, and I said, "Can we move inside now?"

It was so sad to be without him for the walk into the bedroom. Just a few steps, but I felt bereft. And after such a short acquaintance.

He put his head between my legs, nuzzling at first. His beard was a lit-tle rough on the insides of my thighs. Then with his lips, then his tongue, he struck fire. I had to cry out in astonishment, in gratitude at being touched in that right place. Somehow, it always makes me grate-ful when a man finds the right place, maybe because when I was young so many of them kept finding the wrong place, or a series of wrong places, or no place at all. That strange feeling: gratitude and hunger. My hunger was being teased. It almost felt like a punishment. I kept think-ing of the word "thrum," a cross between throb and hum. I saw a flame trying to catch; I heard it, there was something I was *after,* something I was trying to achieve, and there was always the danger that I'd miss it, I wouldn't find it, or get hold of it. The terrible moment when you're afraid you won't, you'll lose it, it won't work, you won't work, it is unworkable and you are very, very desperate. At the same time, you want to stay in this place of desperation, tantalized, arching and leaping for the fruit just out of your mouth's reach, and yet you don't want the arch, the leap to be quite over. You want to go on having it forever—

the arch, the reach, the desperation—at the same time, you're saying to yourself, you're almost there, you're almost there, you can't possibly lose it now, keep on, keep on a bit longer, you are nearly there, I know it, don't give up, you cannot lose it. Then suddenly you're there.

I was so wet from my own desire, and his tongue, that my need to be filled up became enormous. But I held off. I lay him on his back. I explored his shoulder, his flanks, the line from neck to pelvis, following it with my tongue.

He swelled inside my mouth, a fruit that has to burst its skin. Comfort me with apples for I am sick of love. And it is a comfort, isn't it, the root, growing so solidly from its mossy bank, the bounty of abandonment, the cry that means full stop.

We were riding each other now, perhaps not kindly, like twin animals. I gave over first. He waited a while, then joined me. On top of me, he was all weight. His head was on my shoulder. My arms were around him, and my legs. I joined the soles of my feet together. We must have slept.

When we woke, or came to, I really wanted a bath. We walked into the bathroom. We had left the tub with a quarter of an inch of water in it and the salts, unmelted, collected near the closed drain. He turned the water on and the salts turned into green suds.

The bath was large enough for both of us. I felt I had to comment on its size.

"Did you get a bath this big so you could bring people into it?"

"What people did you mean?"

"People like me."

"There are no people like you."

"I mean women you've fucked."

"Do you like the scent of these bath salts? Calendula. From nasturtium."

"You're changing the subject."

He took a thick, pinkish cloth and washed between my legs. Then he put the cloth down and with the lather he'd made between his hands, he soaped me, as if what he really wanted was to clean me, but we knew that was a dodge, a trick. I reared up out of the water, held myself up, then sank down.

He helped me out of the tub and dried me, chafing me with the roughness of the towel. He brought me back to bed. He lay on his back. I knew what he was expecting.

Why does being sucked make men look so overwhelmed? There's a kind of surrender to it—maybe because their legs are so big—that's unlike anything I can imagine a woman conveying.

He moved my head and put me on my back.

"I won't be up to much for a long while. I could when I was younger, but not now. I'm delighted, though, to be at your service all night long."

"You're on," I said.

We fell asleep and it was serious this time. I felt I could sleep forever. The fan overhead lapped my exhausted skin with fresh air. Fresh, as if no one had used it before. I loved the feeling of his warm skin, but after a while I had to roll away from him; his body was a furnace. I wanted to hold his hand, but at the same time to feel alone, so I could sleep, next to him but not too close.

I didn't sleep for long. I could see that it was four-twenty by the digital clock. I could concentrate only on my own hotness so I got up and went into the kitchen. I opened the refrigerator door looking for that blue pitcher, hoping he'd refilled it. And he had! I stood naked in the kitchen, which was dark except for the moon. My feet looked very white and thin on the black tiles. I took the whole pitcher of water and poured it over my head. I admired myself for the gesture. I stood in the middle of the floor, letting the icy cold drip onto my shoulders. When I opened my eyes, I noticed him in the doorway. He came over to me and touched my wet hair.

"Do you know you have slices of lemon on the top of your head?" he asked.

I felt a little foolish, how could I not, but he laughed as he took off a couple of the slices, he was still laughing as he put his face on my breasts, nicely cool from the ice water. I knew he wanted his rough cheeks cooled. He led me back into the bed. He opened a bottle of

lavender oil and oiled my breasts and stomach, paying particular attention to my belly, which he covered in circular motions. He used a
shockingly wasteful amount of oil to stroke me: I could see waste was
the point. I was the most voluptuous thing in the world, more fluid
than solid; I gave in to my own liquidity, and to the thrumming motion
of his middle finger, which traveled up and down as if there were a
string it was plucking, a string I now understood must have been there
all the time. We fell asleep.

But soon I was awake again, and I noticed that the pillow was sopping
wet because my hair, which was so thick, was wet from the water I had
poured onto it, and was oily now as well. The pillow was a little disgusting; I didn't want it anywhere near me. I took it into the living
room and put it on the deck that led to the trail out to the beach. There
was no light, except from the bedroom, and when I walked to the other
side of the living room to get a fuller view of the ocean I saw that
moonlight had fallen on the pillow, which was shining like a marble
lozenge on the deck. In the emptiness of the night, the rectangular
shape and the whiteness of the pillow captivated me. I looked around
the room for paper and pencil, to make some sketches and some notes.
I sat on the wooden floor—the wood was light colored, probably
pine—in combination with the light of the moon it provided illumination. I made sketches on a lined pad, and some notes about the quality
of the light. I made three rectangles: the frame of the glass door, the
rectangle of the pillow and the barely visible horizon.

I realized that he was standing behind me. It was annoying. I hate having anyone watch me work. He could tell he'd annoyed me; he disappeared into the kitchen. But he'd already disturbed my concentration. I
didn't know him well enough to be able to work, even to sketch around
him. I could hear him go to the freezer and I assumed he was getting himself some ice cream. I don't know why I assumed that, but I was right.
He came into the living room eating coffee ice cream from a yellow bowl.

"I'd like to take a shower now," I said. I felt sticky and dirty again and I
resented the fact that he'd seen me working. I felt like I'd had too much
sex. I didn't want to be near him.

But after a while in the shower, I began to miss him, and I walked into the kitchen, half soaped, and asked him to join me. We showered together chastely like companionable athletes. He dried my back and patted my shoulders, but left the rest of me alone. From some dark closet, he brought me a new pillow. I was thinking that when I did the painting of the pillow on the deck in the moonlight, I'd have to include the figure of a naked woman in the room, and all I could think about was the problem of the proportions. Thinking of that, and not of him, I fell asleep, and that time I knew the sleep would last.

In the morning when I woke up, I was shocked, I didn't know exactly where I was for a few seconds. Seeing the pile of our clothes in a path to the door, but feeling myself alone in the bed, I imagined he was disgusted with himself and me, furious that I was so distant with him before we went to sleep. I could imagine the note for me on the kitchen table. "I'll be in touch."

I wondered how I'd get home. I had no car. I calculated that I could walk it; I could walk five miles. I decided it was five miles we'd driven, although I didn't exactly know where I was. Then I began to be afraid. Suppose it was ten miles? I told myself I had enough money for a taxi. There were taxis at the airport; I could call the airport for a taxi to take me home. I could look in the phone book. He would have to have a phone book, I told myself. No one would have to know what happened. No one saw us leave the gallery. Except Louisa, who'd keep her mouth shut. I hoped no one had seen us dancing.

But he hadn't left the house, he was in the shower. He walked into the room, his hair slicked against his skull, his body warmer than mine. He lay against me, took my hair out of my eyes, and said hello, as if we were in the middle of a shopping mall. He was wearing a white terry cloth bathrobe; his skin, which I was seeing for the first time in daylight, was tan. His feet were also tan, but the arches were lighter than his legs. His feet looked so beautiful, cool and sculpted. I kept thinking of the biblical phrase "How beautiful are the feet of the messenger of the Lord."

I put his cool foot between my legs, then right into the cleft. A parenthesis filled up. I rocked myself against his foot. The bottom, a bit calloused, was a surface I could only be fascinated by. I rocked and rocked, arousing myself, but just a little. I didn't want a full-course meal, just an hors d'oeuvre. Then a shower. I thought of the number of baths and showers we'd taken in the past few hours, and all that water seemed like a part of the luxury of the whole event. I moved his foot and told him that I wanted a very long shower on my own.

"I want to be as lovely and cool smelling as you," I said, kissing his forehead. "The soap is lemon, isn't it?"

His bathroom was stocked with a stupefying array of conditioners and oils and powders. They were all from the same place, Hifongers, Covent Garden. White labels trimmed with gold, inscribed in black calligraphy. Thick yellow and green liquids in bottles shaped like scallop shells, or plain, straight-sided soldiers. "I can't believe you have all this stuff for baths."

"I'm an intermittent voluptuary," he said. "This is one of my intermittencies. I found this shop, near Covent Garden. Dark Victorian wood. Silver-handled shaving brushes. Pigskin shaving kits. I love bubble baths, but I only take them here. In New York, I take two-minute showers and shampoo with Liquid Prell."

"And how do these intermittencies apply to me?"

"I'm considering reformation. Think of yourself as the Martin Luther of the voluptuary life. Think of my body as a cathedral on which you nail the ninety-five theses."

"Wittenberg," I said.

I walked into the shower and closed the door. He sat on the floor, cross-legged, like a tailor, so he could watch me. He didn't approach me; he was respectful, detached, scientific, businesslike. He watched me soap, then dry myself. He watched me put my hair up in a towel. He watched me looking at myself in the mirror. Did he know what I was thinking? That I was appraising my fifty-year-old body favorably, acknowledging that my breasts didn't have their old spring, that I had a little belly and my ass could charitably be called crepey, but that I was looking at myself from the front, so it was all right? Did he know that I turned sideways so that neither of us would be looking at me from the back?

He watched me pull the beautiful tortoiseshell comb through my hair. He watched me put on the white terry cloth bathrobe, trying to not think who it might have belonged to, convincing myself it was brand-new.

He sat on the bathroom floor, his arms over his head. The hair under his arms was rough looking and abundant. I wanted to nuzzle it. I wanted its coarseness against my mouth and lips and tongue.

I looked at his watch. It was nearly nine, the sun full in the sky, a yellow white disc I could see over the tops of the trees. He asked if I'd like breakfast on the deck. I said I wanted something light, only fruit.

"Yes, I have a beautiful melon. Jesus, fruit's expensive up here."

"I thought you didn't think like that."

"Only intermittently and only in small things."

I saw my clothes in that derelict pile near the door to the bedroom. It was impossible to think of putting them on. I considered going into Provincetown in a white terry robe. I decided to think about it later.

He laid the table on the deck with the yellow pottery. The table was cast-iron and glass, the chairs, cast-iron. They didn't look very comfortable. He brought in royal blue place mats and napkins. The silver was Vienna Secessionist, I thought. There was coffee in a white pot, and a platter with slices of honeydew, cantaloupe and Persian melon arranged alternately.

"No wonder you're complaining about prices. Who would buy a Persian melon in Provincetown during the month of August? You must be crazy."

"Actually, I didn't mean to buy it. Then I saw this guy with a cellular phone about to reach for it. There was only one and the minute I knew how much he wanted it, I just had to have it."

When he said that, I realized there was no need for me to apologize for being rude when he'd come in on me sketching. That made me feel marvelous, knowing that I didn't need to apologize for not having a thoroughly nice nature. We were sitting in the sun, the ocean was silvery blue.

"We have things to talk about," he said. "I hope you don't think what happened last night complicates any of it."

It was an awkward moment; his words—"what happened last

night"—made it seem there were no words able to contain the event. I felt it was up to me to break the tone. So I put my feet in his lap. This made him smile, a grateful smile, the smile of a good boy who's just been told the vase he accidentally knocked over isn't valuable at all. I couldn't find in that smile anything of the man who'd grabbed the Persian melon just because someone with a cell phone wanted it. He tucked his chin like a duck before it's about to step forward, and his smile, because it was made up so largely of relief, conveyed such a sense of movement that I felt that he'd actually taken a step forward. Toward me, or something having to do with me.

He took my feet in his hand and squeezed them, as though the idea of them gave him a simple comfort. In his hands, they seemed nourishing and simple, two plain loaves of bread.

I hardly knew him, so each of his gestures was fresh to me, and therefore exciting. We sat and smiled at each other, because we weren't used to each other's faces yet.

It's the prospect of learning a whole repertoire of new gestures that makes taking a new lover so exhilarating. No lover can replicate the gesture of another. That's why it's always seemed ridiculous to me to say, "This is what I like," naming a series of acts or gestures. You can't separate a gesture from a gesturer. Something one lover does that drives you wild means nothing when someone else does it. I had a lover who used to rub his knuckles back and forth against the front of my shirt, and it was fantastically arousing. So I asked my next lover to do it but since it hadn't been an idea that originated with him, since he was trying to accomplish something, to follow a set of directions, to perform a task, the whole thing fell flat. We both felt we were doing something hollow, or, rather, dim, like one of those carbons that's so far at the bottom of the pile that no impression is made, or the impression is illegible. A real gesture has to come from someone's history, which is why when sex is good it's always in the present: the past has been absorbed.

I kept my feet in his lap even though he took his hands away so we could hold hands on the table.

"I'm happy to be here with you," he said.

"Me too," I said, although it made me feel shy to say it and the word "happy" seemed at once too general and too extensive to fit our situation. And yet, it did fit, because there was such a sense of animal well-being, and such a sense of being pleasing and pleased, such a delight in novelty and yet such a sense of security based on desire that is absolutely congruent—the right feeling of a fine fit—that what else could you say except you were happy. It was hard for me to look into his eyes after we'd both acknowledged how simple our responses were—but it was easier because I liked his eyes. They were dark brown, monochrome brown, without flecks of gold or undercurrents of maroon. They were a little doggy. They reminded me of Mikey's eyes. I thought it would be a mistake to tell him that, "Your eyes remind me a lot of my dog's," but I found it quite reassuring. He had unusually long lashes for a man, the kind that made my mother say, if she saw them on a little boy, "They're wasted on him."

Looking at him like that and having him look at me was making me feel thirsty, giving me a little bit of a sore throat. I took a drink of orange juice but the feeling didn't go away. Then I realized my throat was constricted because I needed to be physically near him. I walked to him and sat in his lap. The terry robe seemed ridiculously heavy, and it was all wrong to have that much fabric separating us when what was giving me a sore throat was the need for contact with his skin. I let my robe fall to the floor and took his off so it fell on top of mine. I put his hands on my breasts and offered my neck to be kissed.

"We're supposed to be getting down to details," he said.

"We are," I told him.

"As I was saying," he said. "There are a lot of things we need to talk about. I want to do what I said. I want to give you what you were asking for in your lecture."

"I was really only kidding," I said. "It was just a riff for the audience. I say a lot of things in public just for the sake of saying them."

"You meant everything you said. And you're not the only one saying it—a lot of women artists have said the same thing. If it's possible for you to do something, not for the verbal effect, keeping in mind that there's no one here, the TV crew has left for the day, tell me what you think you'd need to do the best work you possibly could."

I got off his lap and moved back to my chair. He was frightening me.

"What would make you want to do something like this?" I said. "What I mean is, who are you?"

"You mean you want my history."

"Yes."

"I'm forty-eight years old. I was a teenager in the sixties. I wanted to go to Selma but my parents wouldn't let me."

"Where are you from?"

"The Bronx. And you're from Queens."

"Astoria."

"I know."

"We're not talking about me. So you're in the Bronx, it's 1964, 1965, you're all hopped up on Martin Luther King, and then the Vietnam War, and you're in the protests. And now you've got all this money. How did we get from there to here?"

"Would you believe me if I say I don't exactly know? I'm in college, then I graduate, then I'm doing street theater, but nothing ever lasts. Nothing works out. While I'm doing that, I'm driving a cab, but I'm going nowhere. I decide to get what we used to call a 'straight job' for a year or so, so I could earn money to go to Europe. This friend of mine got me a job on Wall Street as a messenger. Pretty soon I could see that I was a lot smarter than most of the people I worked for and then—it was a little insidious because I went there thinking I'd use the system because money and capitalism were evil—I realized I was very good at what they did. Which became what *I* did. I made money. Making money—you do get the illusion that you're creating something, making something exist where it hadn't. I kept getting promoted. Then I went into business for myself. I've made what might in another time have been called a fortune. And I've been very absorbed in it. Or it's absorbed me. For too many years it's been my whole life."

"You were never married?"

"I was married for fifteen years, to someone who wanted to be a dancer but never quite got it together. She left me for an orthodontist; she lives in Tenafly now. Three kids. She doesn't think about dancing anymore."

"So I'm supposed to make up for her?"

"No one could make up that much. My wife was to marriage what

Torquemada was to free speech. What about you, you're divorced I take it?"

"There's not that much to say. It was painful for a while, of course, how could it not be? We'd been together eighteen years, since I was twenty-seven, and we split up when I was forty-five. I can't even remember anymore how we drifted apart. But drifted was the right word for it. Like two boats. Except that I was always very irritable, and you can't imagine a boat being irritable. The irritability is part of the explanation for the drifting—although the two feelings are quite different. I guess I felt him drifting away, doing less and less of his share, both of domestic things and earning money. He's a scriptwriter, which is an insecure profession, if not a delusional one. I was furious that I was doing everything I could to make money—teaching at the Watson School where my girls went so I could have a salary and free tuition for them—and he was lying around waiting for inspiration, not wanting to do anything lowering or compromising. Which implied that it was fine for me to lower and compromise myself, because I wasn't as pure a soul as he. So of course I could teach and then come home and do the laundry. Resentment about household tasks is the strongest anaphrodisiac in the world.

"My husband—Roger was his name, still is, he's not dead—was getting vaguer and vaguer and more and more depressed and I was getting more and more irritable. We just started moving away from each other, spending more and more time apart. So by the time he met Merrill, it wasn't like a flourishing organism was being cut down in its prime. Merrill is a very nice woman; she's a social worker with a very good pension. She works with disturbed teenagers. I think that's why she likes my ex-husband, because he really is like a teenager, but a charming one, rather than a disturbed one. He has that sweet faith that everything will work out, and it always does, because some woman makes it happen."

"I believe, as they say, we were talking about us," he said. "How can I put it? I wish I were an artist, but I'm not. I'm a trader. And a trader is a gambler. I love your work. I'm attracted to you; I'm interested in the problem of the woman artist, but I'm sick of dead-end discussions about why there's no female Picasso. I've seen the way you live, it's too hard. I'd like to take a gamble. Or perform an experiment."

"And I'm your guinea pig?"

"Say you are, and let's get it over with."

"My kids had a guinea pig. They pulled it by the tail once, and the whole goddamn thing fell off."

"How old are your kids?"

"Twenty. They're twins. Rachel and Sara. Rachel's at Brown, Sara's at Smith. Rachel's doing anthropology and making the revolution, Sara's doing music and trying to revise large-scale interest in the viola da gamba."

"At any rate . . ."

I'd learn that the phrase "at any rate" was something he'd say when he wanted to change the subject. Or bring the subject back. I've often wondered if the sense of money, or good value, was something he got from his work, or was part of his nature, and his nature had dictated his work.

"What do you think you need that would give you the optimum conditions for work?"

I answered quickly. "Space and time."

"Go on."

"Well, time is obvious. I'd like not to have to teach. Or just to teach a little bit. There's too much of it now, and it's exhausting me."

"All right, that's time. What about space?"

"My studio in New York is hot in the summer and cold in the winter. It's too small. The light stinks. It's too far away from where I live. I can't stay there late at night, because it's too dangerous, so I often have to stop work before I'd like to. I like my situation up here, I rent the little house from my friend Larry. It's a hundred yards away from what's called the big house, down in a hollow, backed up against a little hill, so it doesn't get much sun. There's a largish room with a stove and a sink and a refrigerator. A tiny bathroom with a shower—no tub, but that's all right in the summer. I wouldn't be able to live without a bathtub after Columbus Day. One small bedroom in the back. And a loft, where I paint, when I'm not painting outside. It's hard to work there on rainy days."

"So, you'd like a bigger, safer studio in New York, and something bigger up here."

"Right," I said.

"How easy would it be for you to take a leave from your job?"

"I don't know. I couldn't do it for the fall."

"The spring?"

"I'd have to see."

"As soon as you do, I can write you a check for your year's salary."

"Just like that? And you would?"

"I said I would, and I will."

His doggy eyes narrowed a bit. "What about the other part of what you were saying in the lecture? You know, young girls standing in front of the mirror wanting to be the artist's object of desire. What do you think is the relationship between inspiration and desire?"

"Do you mean do I paint better if I'm getting it regular?"

"I'm actually interested."

"Well, I can't stand talking about sex. I'm really very fond of having it."

"I like talking about it."

"You mean you spend a lot of money on 900 numbers?"

"No, I mean there's a kind of conversation that can be as arousing as certain kinds of touch, and then there are other things. For example, I'd like to know what you like."

"Can't you tell? What's wrong with trial and error?"

"I just want to know."

"I thought we were talking about space and time?"

"We are."

"Well, why don't you start?"

"No. You."

"I'd rather talk about what I don't like. I don't like talking. Most words that connect up with sex have one kind of bad effect or another. Either I laugh or I want to become a Carmelite. Slang is no good. Scientific names are no good either. They make me think I've been given a terminal diagnosis. And I can't stand people naming things. George and Martha. Héloïse and Abelard. Then there's the visuals. Most pornographers lack a sense of both humor and variety. The same is true of inventors of sex toys. Tricky condoms that are supposed to drive women wild. How can you be driven wild when something makes you think of antlers? I think it's important that the notion of antlers not enter a sexual moment. And I don't like being called mama. I've had entirely too much of that.

"Then there's all the stuff I don't understand. Shoes or rubber suits. Whips and chains. I want to feel good, not be hurt, although I'd rather hurt than be hurt, if I had to choose. I can't imagine a situation in which I'd have to choose. I guess I'm stuck in the oral-genital phase. No pain, all gain."

"I think we're going to be very happy," he said.

We went back to bed. "We'll talk some more later," he said.

I woke after a nap and it seemed late, too late to be in bed on an August morning. I was worried about my car, my clothes were too wrinkled to wear, and Mikey had been out all night. He'd been fed and I left him water; it had been a warm night and he had a place under the house he went to if he was cold—but he wouldn't be cold in the middle of August. At that moment, though, all I could feel was guilt about having left my dog.

"I have to go home," I said.

I felt horrible. What did I think I was getting involved in? I went to bed with a man who challenged me to accept his money because he admired my work. I couldn't remember how many times we'd had sex, and it wasn't even eleven o'clock in the morning. I kept telling myself this wasn't the sort of thing I did. And it wasn't. I've been careful about men since my divorce. In five years, I hadn't met a man I'd been tempted to take seriously enough to get involved with. I never lost myself. I wanted to keep myself for work. To keep myself to myself. With B—probably it was just the sex, but I suspected it might have been more than that—I felt like I was letting go of something. And I wasn't sure I wanted that to happen.

"I don't know you very well," I said.

He'd put on jeans and a work shirt, and he'd rolled up the sleeves. I wanted to tell him that my favorite part of his body was his forearms. I didn't want to leave those forearms. They had exactly the right amount and texture of hair. I focused on them. I didn't feel like worrying about the money, and everything it implied. Not right then.

"Do you like dogs?" I asked.

"I love dogs. Except little yappy ones. But I know Mikey's not like that."

"How do you know his name is Mikey?"

"From your painting, *Mikey and Michael.* I own it."

I thought of that painting. I wanted to call it *Women's Best Friends,* but that seemed corny. I'd painted my best friend, Michael, sitting by a window reading, with Mikey asleep beside him. I really liked the rectangle of the window, and the trees behind it. And the aqua cushions on the couch. I'd worked on it when I was staying with him for two weeks after he'd broken up with that little creep Jeffrey. Michael was so devastated he'd decided to read *The Man Without Qualities.* Which I told him at the time no living person had ever finished. Probably that was why he finished it. It wasn't a book you could talk about, he said.

"I don't know who Michael is," B said.

I didn't feel like telling him Michael was gay right at the moment. I was enjoying the little flicker of anxiety I heard in his voice.

"Michael's my best friend. He's an analyst."

"Financial?"

"No, not financial. Psycho."

"Married?"

"Not right now."

I couldn't stand that look on his face any longer, like he thought he might have left the oven on back in New York.

"He's gay," I said. "And don't say something fabulous like 'I have a lot of gay friends myself.'"

"Actually, I don't," he said. "I don't have very many friends. I've done nothing but work for fifteen years. My life is a bit of a shambles."

"And you want me to tend your garden?"

"I don't know exactly what I want. Only that it has something to do with you."

"And sex and money."

"And your work."

I sat in the chair and tipped it back, like I was a cowboy in a saloon.

"So tell me," I said. "If I looked exactly the way I look but you didn't like my paintings, or if I painted exactly as I paint but you didn't like my looks, would we still be here, talking about what we've been talking about?"

"No, we wouldn't."

"And which is more important to you?"

"Which is more important to you?"

"Work, of course," I said. But I knew I was lying. I took a certain ignoble pleasure in feeling superior to other women painters who never got a haircut, never wore makeup, came to their openings in overalls, or in some terrible sweater that was supposed to hide the extra fifty pounds. I wasn't proud of that, but I like that he'd guessed it.

I let the front legs of the chair hit the floor with a bang. "Look," I said. "I need to figure out something to wear into town so I can get my car. Do you have anything unisex that I can put on for a little while?"

"I'm much bigger than you."

"You don't have anything with elastic?"

"You're free to look in all the closets and the drawers."

The closets in the bedroom were very big, but he didn't have many clothes there. A pile of shirts from the laundry. A pile of sweaters. Trousers hung in rows. But as I walked into the closet, I got the smell of him, the clothed man, the public man, but the man I'd made love to left a lingering trace in the air and the fabric. I went over to the pile of sweaters and rubbed my cheeks against them. I buried my nose in the wool. It was enormously comforting. It reminded me of one of the things I like about men: their clothing doesn't change much from year to year, they're always the straight man, the fixed pole of the compass, Fred to Ginger, the tux against the feathered gown. I unfolded one of his white shirts and put it on. It was very big, and reached almost to my knees. That solved a lot of the problem.

"Do you mind if I look in your underwear drawer?" I asked.

"I said you could feel free."

"People say that, but you never know what line they're secretly drawing."

"You're a suspicious character."

"I'm usually right."

"And vain."

"I prefer to call it a highly developed sense of justice."

There was an unopened package of Fruit of the Loom boxer shorts. I liked it that with all his money he still bought Fruit of the Loom. My father's brand. I remembered sticking Fruit of the Loom stickers on my dresser as a child. I was glad he had a fresh package of boxers. Wearing his shirt was fine, but putting on underwear he'd worn seemed a little weird. I walked out onto the deck, sauntering falsely.

"You look adorable," he said. He pulled the material of the shirt tight so that my breasts were very visible. He touched me between the legs, putting his hand through the fly front. I didn't even have time to sit down.

We sat on the deck, drinking coffee. I had forgotten my anxiety about the car and the dog. The sea was a bluish silver; there were thin clouds in the sky, and the wind was moving the branches of the larch up and down like a fan. Occasionally we would bring our hands together on the deck railing. It was so pleasant I kept wanting to close my eyes. At the same time, I wanted to look at the sea, the sky, the leaves of the trees. And at him. The doggy eyes. The reddish underlip. The delicious black hair on his forearms. The place on his arches that was lighter than the skin on his limbs.

"You need to drive me into town."

"Will you come back and stay a few days?"

"Let me be alone in my own place for a while to think about it."

I said that more gently than I normally would have. After everything, all the work, the shows, the teaching jobs, I still half expect people to fight me when I say I need to be alone. But I knew he understood, because he'd come to me first through my work. The fact that he'd invested in it, although it created complications, meant that he considered it, literally, valuable.

I heard a beeping in the other room. I asked what it was.

"A fax."

"You have a fax machine this close to the ocean?"

"Oh, moisture won't hurt it," he said.

"That's not what I mean. Aren't you supposed to be on vacation?"

"Like you, I'm never on vacation."

"Oh, but it's not like me at all," I said, and then I was embarrassed.

"You mean because I make money and you make art."

"Well, yes, I guess I do mean that. There'll always be more money. One piece of money is very much like another. But if I don't get that particular image, it's gone. Gone forever."

"And if I don't make a particular deal, not only is it gone, but it could lead to a lot of other things going too."

"Hmm," I said. I wasn't really interested. Because suddenly, I realized there was a problem with shoes. I was wearing his shirt and boxer shorts. And my shoes were black satin three-inch heels.

"I'm going to have to go barefoot," I said, holding my shoes like they were pieces of meat that had gone rotten overnight.

The problem of my shoes cast a cloud over everything. The cloud that had appeared then disappeared because of sex. Now I wanted to be away from him, and back in my own place.

"Come and look at the house, quickly," he said.

"No," I said, walking toward the door. "I want to go right now. Just describe it to me in the car."

Sometimes looking at things is so taxing for me that I just can't stand it. And now was one of those times.

He spoke as we drove. "There are three more bedrooms, one with a view of the ocean. The other looks out into a kind of arbor. You could set your painting things up in any one of them, or you could paint on the deck. Whatever you like. One of the rooms has a phone with a separate number. And Mikey can have the run of the house, but can we keep him off the white couch?"

"Well, I don't know, I hate to curtail his freedom."

"Think of it as good for his character. And for yours. Making an effort might be something of a novelty. For you I mean. I wasn't speaking about Mikey."

"I'm not very interested in changing for any man."

"If you take my offer, your life will definitely change."

"I know," I said. "That's the problem. I like my life."

"You work too hard at things you shouldn't have to spend time on," he said, putting his hand on my knee.

I didn't like the fact that he could make me soften toward him so easily. But his hand felt so warm on my knee, I didn't have the heart to tell him to move it. I would have had to whip up resentment, or the impulse not to be close to him. I'm perfectly capable of doing it, it's something I've done with men when I need to be alone. But right then, it didn't seem like it was worth the effort of all that whipping up.

He left me in the parking lot of Louisa's gallery. Thank God she hadn't arrived yet, so I didn't have to have a heart-to-heart with the duenna of Cos Cob. The asphalt felt warm and comforting on the bare soles of my feet, and the feel of the gas pedal against them made me feel like a girl.

He closed the car door for me and leaned down to kiss me through the window.

"Call me," he said, handing me a slip of paper.

I drove away.

Finally alone, I kept losing and gaining spirits.

Space and time. Money and sex. Money and sex, that was the problem.

I wonder how old you have to be—when I say you I mean, of course, girls—before you learn the connection. That there is one, at least. I wonder how long the gap is between knowing that there's such a thing as sex and knowing that some people get paid to have it. And that those are people that you don't want to be like. I wonder whether there has ever been a girl so numbed or blasé or abused that the first inkling of this knowledge doesn't make her feel sickened for what she shares with every woman. The potential to be called a whore. Whore. The fixed pole representing whatever it is that isn't good. There's no similar fixed pole for men; no word that gets called out at a man on the street, hissed out between the closed lips of an enraged or disappointed lover, no single vessel for everything loathsome about his sex. It had never occurred to me that I might travel anywhere near the other pole.

The bad one. If I'd rejected the madonna and the virgin, it was for something better, something self-invented, something that smashed icons and cast off old ties. But now, because he'd offered me money and had sex with me, I had to question things—ancient things, there seem to have been whores as long as there's been history—I'd never imagined questioning. It seemed to me that at my age I'd questioned quite enough, what was the point of learning anything, when learning usually had so much in it of humiliation?

I imagined myself in all sorts of costumes. Draped like a Greek temple prostitute. My golden hair braided closely to my head: one of the medieval consorts of priests, who were the ones executed when the priests had to adopt celibacy. High-waisted, garbed in velvet: a Renaissance courtesan. An eighteenth-century tart in an Empire gown; an opium-eating Victorian on a dark London street, Irma la Douce, Kiki's brilliantined girls in Montmartre, Louise Brooks as Lulu. None of it seemed to have much to do with what had happened last night. But what had happened last night? That would take me some time to figure out.

I pulled into the sandy driveway and Mikey greeted me with antic enthusiasm; I could hardly get out of the car. He followed me into the house and I filled his aluminum bowl with kibble. I sat down on the couch and put my knees to my chin, then began rocking back and forth. Mikey looked at me in a censorious way. He joined me on the couch. I buried my head in the fur around his neck. It didn't make me feel any less lonely.

My two best friends were both out of the country. Michael was in Venice and Theresa was in China. This wasn't something you could talk to just anyone about. At this historical moment, and at my age—fifty—having good sex or even the prospect of it is like having a lot of money and living among people who are barely getting by. Most of the people I know aren't having a lot of sex. Either they've been married a long time and sex isn't that important in the marriage, so they've put sex into a very minor place in their lives, or they're not married and getting any kind of sex at all is a real problem. A friend of mine, who looks just like Gene Tierney, went for three years without having sex. It's never been that bad with me, but I've had long periods without sex and for seven years I haven't taken anyone I've slept with seriously.

I knew that I could talk to Michael and Theresa about it. I didn't have to worry about Michael, because he often makes great mistakes for good sex—and I've been very sympathetic, we've talked about it for hours. And although in some moods I find this annoying, Theresa is happy in her marriage and they seem to be having good sex. But because she's been faithful for such a long time she's curious and sympathetic about the irregular sex lives of her friends. It's a little voyeuristic, but everyone involved knows it, so it's fine. With neither Michael nor Theresa would I feel like I was showing up at a party for homeless people in an Armani suit. I felt relatively easy about the sex part; I still wasn't sure whether I could talk to anyone about the money.

And I didn't know whether spending a week with B in a house that was so much more luxurious than mine would make things better or worse, clearer or less clear. I was pacing the living-room floor. The living room's about twelve feet long, so it was a pretty confining experience. Every step I took, Mikey followed. When I realized how ridiculous both of us looked, I sat back down on the couch.

My dominant feeling was anger. I decided to call B and accuse him of bringing tincture of whoredom into something he claimed was about women and art.

"Tincture of whoredom? What's that, something from the health food store? Three drops on your tongue, and you hit the streets? Can you just tell me whether you're coming over or not?"

I said I'd be there in half an hour. Then I said that I wouldn't come to his house, he should come to mine.

HE DROVE UP and I walked out to meet him, a hostess now, no use pretending I hadn't been waiting for the sound of his car. It was 7:00, the twentieth of August. Two weeks before there wouldn't have been even a suggestion of dusk, but now there was and with it the slight anxiety of coming nightfall, or the end of one more precious summer day. The grass was damp and the air had a peppery smell. My skin had lost the smoothness it had had in the morning when I'd given myself over to well-being. I felt the strain of trying to hold myself back. I didn't want to hold myself back, although, considering all we had to talk about, I thought I should. But I simply couldn't do it; my impulse to be near him was too strong.

In his arms, my accusations lost some of their edge.

"Look," he said, "there were a couple of choices, none of which are pure. Once I became interested in you and began watching you, I began to desire you. Following that were only a few options. I could have kept it from you that I desired you—which would have put things on one kind of false footing. Or because I desired you, I could have dropped the idea of giving you money. Which could keep you from certain very real benefits. I could have given you money first and then tried to make love to you. But then neither of us would have known what place gratitude played. And gratitude is the end of good sex. So why not spend a week with me? My house has much better light."

"I like this house. I've been very happy here."

"It's very sweet. It's very dark. It's very small."

"But it's completely mine. And your house wouldn't be."

"Are you suggesting that I sign my house over to you? Because I'm not prepared for that."

"I don't know what I'm suggesting, or what I'm prepared for," I said.

I offered him a cup of herbal tea. I don't know why I did that. I kept herbal tea for menstrual cramps.

I couldn't think of any more reasons not to spend a few days with him. I packed all the clothes I could think of, and my easel and brushes and paints. I packed a drawing pad and pencils. I took the dog's bowl and his leash.

When I drove up, he came to the front door. There was a wonderful garden in the front of the house. I particularly noticed the cosmos with its feathery, fennel-like greens.

"I like your cosmos," I said.

"What other cosmos is there?" he said.

"I mean your flowers."

"Yes, sweetheart, I know what you mean."

I think the most important thing to say about why I did everything I did was that I always felt he liked me a great deal. That the sight of me pleased him. One night, he said, "I just want to look at you." I was awfully glad he used the phrase "look at *you*." Instead of any of the names. All of them are terrible. Vagina seems like a gum disease. Pussy sounds like it was invented in the men's room of a bus station. Twat reminds me of a Rorschach. Snatch is a felony between your legs. Cunt is probably the best—it sounds older, more agricultural, but it's been said with so much hatred that it's impossible to bleach the hatred from the word. Cock, on the other hand, is still perfectly all right: a bouncy, early morning creature, full of a slightly comic pride.

I was glad he didn't use any proper nouns and I'm not going to either. My daughter Rachel can refer to her pussy as easily as she does her elbow. But I can't. Too old, I guess. And I'm telling you all this for my own pleasure, so why not please myself.

He propped me up on two bluish gray pillows. He sat on a chair a few feet away from me. Then he came over and opened my legs wider. He stared at me, and his eyes began to look so heavy I thought he was falling asleep. I thought, what will I do if he falls asleep? But he wasn't falling asleep.

His stare became a kind of touch, a vector. As his eyes moved up and down or became static, I felt the arousal travel as his eyes traveled, stop when they stopped. When he shifted his focus, I felt as if a search-light had settled where he stared, a circle of heat and illumination focused on the spot. For the first time I believed a man really liked looking at me.

I asked him then, what was it that he liked, what was it that he saw?

"Home sweet home," he said.

"You could put it on a needlepoint," I said. "It might be a big hit at craft fairs."

"Do you do needlepoint?"

"Shit, no. I'm a painter. Needlepoint is for wives."

"You were a wife once."

"I only went tourist."

"Never again?"

"Never again. As far as I'm concerned there are only two reasons for having a husband: to carve large slabs of roasted meat and to be with you the first ten minutes of a cocktail party. But it's too big a price to pay."

That week was almost wholly devoted to pleasure. We made love. We took baths. We swam in the ocean. We put suntan lotion on each other's backs. We went shopping for groceries; we'd meet each other, surprised, in one of the aisles, and kiss, delighted with the sight of each other. We fed each other fresh peas in the car. We made cioppino. We listened to Dinah Washington and Schubert. We chopped vegetables and scrubbed mussels and clams. We made a recipe with monkfish and ground almonds. We went out for ice cream. Sometimes we went out for ice cream twice a day. We didn't talk about money or the future. I wasn't working; I thought he wasn't either.

Once, though, at three in the morning I went into the living room and saw him in the bluish light of his computer screen. He was rapt, his eyes looked a bit maniacal. He was clearly having some sort of E-mail conversation; he would aggressively pound the keys and then impatiently wait for a response, which seemed instantaneous to me, but clearly wasn't fast enough for him. He'd press a button and the screen would switch from showing words to displaying some kind of chart that moved instantaneously. I felt I couldn't go any nearer to him; I was almost afraid of what he'd do if I approached. I went back to bed and pretended to sleep.

When he came back, I asked him what he was doing.

"Talking to this guy who's a journalist in Rio. There might be some unrest and it could affect the harvest."

"So will there be unrest?"

"The putz can't tell yet."

"What's the unrest about?"

"How do I know? The whole country's insane."

"And you don't think about that?"

"There's nothing I can do about it. I don't think about it, no."

"But you're profiting by it."

"I'm not profiting by it, for Christ's sake. I'm not Adnan Khashoggi. I'm trading coffee, not Uzis. There's a difference. Besides, it's possible to argue that we have political leverage in these countries because of economic influence."

I wanted to say I didn't buy it, but I decided to shut up, since I was taking his money.

"Do you often get up in the middle of the night to work?"

"There's always some market open somewhere."

"So, potentially, you could be working twenty-four hours a day?"

"Just like you."

I wanted to tell him that it wasn't at all just like me, that the images I was working with came from my mind, not a computer screen, not from some market someplace I couldn't even make an image for. But I didn't feel like fighting. He seemed tired, and I was tired too. I liked sleeping with him; I liked fitting my body into his. I thought that meant something; you don't always like to sleep with everyone you're sleeping with. I liked sleeping with him and I liked the way he looked when he slept. I drew him sleeping. That was, really, how I got my idea.

We'd been sitting in the living room, reading. I can tell you exactly what we were reading because I always remember; I was reading *The Idiot*. Every summer, it's my project to read one big novel and I was almost through with it. I wasn't going to put it down because I was in the middle of a love affair. He was reading a book about Jews in Spain. Did I forget to say that he was Jewish? Being Jewish was a very important part of his understanding of himself and the world, although he was completely nonreligious. At any given time, he might be reading a book about Jews in Spain.

It was about ten o'clock at night; we'd grilled swordfish and made a sauce with a lot of garlic, olive and lemon. I was very happy, reading. The light was falling beautifully on his silvery hair. I wanted to be near him. So I went over and took his book out of his hands and took him in my mouth. Then I climbed on top of him. Afterward, he held me on his lap for quite a while: I rested my cheek on his head.

I wanted a cup of coffee, an espresso, and he said he'd love one too, but would I make it. "For some reason," he said. "I'm completely spent. I can't think why."

The armchair he was sitting in had a very high back; it's a wing chair with an apple green slipcover. When I came out with the coffee he was sitting with a towel draped over his crotch, his arms on the arms of the chair, his head leaning against the back. He'd fallen asleep. His knees were spread apart, his feet a little separated; the end of the towel hung between his legs. I kept thinking I'd seen that posture before, it reminded me of something. Then it occurred to me what it was: he was sitting like Jesus in Carpaccio's *Meditation on Christ's Passion*. That relaxed weight, the heaviness. The loss of regard. The position of the limbs, the hands and feet. The relative unimportance of the head, except as another weight-possessing object. The face unexpressive. No, not unexpressive, empty of expression.

I began thinking about other dead Christs. Pontormo's. Mantegna's. The Rosso Fiorentino at the Boston Museum of Fine Arts. They were all dead, but they didn't look dead. Not in some way that meant the final loss of life. I picked up my pencil and pad and started to draw. I drew B. Then I tried to draw the Carpaccio from memory. Both of them emptied of something, but without anguish. And suddenly, I had an idea. Suppose all those dead Christs weren't dead, just postorgasmic?

I sat in front of him, drawing with a kind of fever. He never woke up. I knew what I wanted to do: a series of paintings of postorgasmic men based on the great Italian Renaissance portraits of dead Christs. I even knew what I'd call the series: SPENT MEN, AFTER THE MASTERS.

I started walking up and down the room. Soon I realized I was hopping. And I guess my hopping woke him up.

I jumped onto his lap and began covering him with kisses. I told him I had a fantastic idea, but that I couldn't talk to him about it yet, but yes I would take him up on his offer, because I did have a project that required time. And money for travel. Did his offer include money for travel?

"Anything you need."

"A trip to Italy. But right now I need to go to New York."

"Well, it's midnight, but I'll drive you in the morning. Unless you'd rather go alone."

"No, I hate driving. I hate that shitty rental van I have. Would you really drive me?"

"Of course. It's part of my job description. I'm your Muse."

I couldn't sleep. I watched him sleeping, and all night I sketched his body as he slept. As the dawn came up, I could smell my body. It had that particularly rank smell it always has when I'm working hard. I took a shower and brought him coffee and toast in bed. He could tell I was too anxious to be on the road to think of making love.

I hadn't noticed that his car was a convertible. Cars aren't the kind of things I notice; as far as I'm concerned, a car is a pocketbook on wheels. Something to not have if you can avoid it. He was pulling and attaching and folding the canvas top down. I could see the look of rapt joy on his face. "What do you think of this beauty?"

"It's very nice," I said.

"Nice? That's like saying the Sistine Chapel is nice. Don't you know what this is?"

"I have absolutely no idea."

"It's a sixty-five GTO convertible. Beautiful in itself. More beautiful for what it represents."

I started singing, " 'GTO, you're really lookin' fine. Three deuces and a four speed. And a four eighty-nine.'

"The Beach Boys wrote almost as many songs about cars as women," I said. I never had any idea what they were talking about. Which was not to say I didn't sing those words with my whole heart, like they were the pledge of allegiance or the litany of the virgin.

"You've got it. A sacred text. And do you know why I spent a fucking fortune on it?"

"In honor of the Beach Boys?"

"When I was a kid and I used to schlep all the way to Jones Beach on the train and then the bus and I'd be walking off the bus onto the parking lot, stinking from the commute in my chinos and madras shirt. I was kidding no one, and I'd see these blond guys with blond girls in GTO convertibles with the radio on—77 WABC—blasting the Beach Boys through the parking lot, jumping out without opening the doors, and I felt like such a loser compared to them."

"Don't worry, they're all dead. They all cracked up their GTOs because they were drunk on beer, or they were conked on the head by their surfboards. Or they're beach bums in Laguna. Wherever the hell Laguna is."

"I certainly hope so. I certainly hope they went from failure to failure. And I've got the car. The best of both worlds. The look of the six-ties. The sound system of the nineties."

When we got onto the highway, he put his Beach Boys tape on. I hadn't been in a convertible for thirty years, and I was having a great time letting my hair blow, not worrying what it looked like, singing "Catch a Wave and You're Sitting on Top of the World." Then I noticed the speedometer. He was going eighty-five.

"Could you possibly slow down?"

"I'm an excellent driver, I drove a cab for four years, as you recall. Besides, the majority of accidents are caused by people driving too slowly, not people driving too fast."

"Where did you get that statistic?"

"It's very well known."

"I never heard it."

"I'll look it up for you sometime. But not right now. Right now, I'm driving eighty-five miles an hour."

We were singing "When I Grow Up to Be a Man" when the car phone rang. I'd never been in a car with a car phone. He said, "I can't talk now," and then some numbers and then something like "go long." I felt like I was listening to one of those football plays: 22, 24, 26, 28, hike. It made about as much sense to me. He kept trying to get off the phone, but whoever was on the other end was giving him a hard time about it.

When we got to New York, he left me at the museum. I ran up the stairs like a movie star, or royalty, stopping at the door to wave at him, thinking how great I looked.

But the minute I climbed the stairs to the European wing, I had no more consciousness of what I looked like. I was a worker, working.

I knew I had to calm down: there was so much that excited me, so much I wanted to reproduce or render. I wasn't sure then, I'm not sure now, what the right word is.

I found the Carpaccio, right next to Bellini's Davis *Madonna*, possi-bly the greatest sky, the greatest skin tone in Western art. The blue of the sky, the pink of the sunset, the pink flush of her cheeks, her skin sil-very and bluish, taking up the tone of her veil. I allowed myself the luxury of looking for nothing: I wasn't trying to learn anything from it, I wasn't trying to reinterpret it, or get anything from it that I could use. I was just looking. When I turned from it, it was with the reluctance of leaving the boudoir for the factory bench. I was here to look at the Carpaccio, not innocently, not freely, but to use it to make something of my own.

First, I made some drawings of the legs. Then I looked at the other figures in the painting: three men, including Jesus. The other two were Job and St. Jerome. I knew I wasn't going to use all three of them, just the figure of Christ. All of them made triangular carvings of space with the angles of their legs and thighs. I allowed myself the fun of drawing their shoes. Job sits cross-legged in a loincloth and a pair of soft black leather sandals that tie in the middle, the laces making another triangular shape in the middle of his arch. St. Jerome has wooden sandals that remind me of those Dr. Scholl's sandals we all used to wear in the sixties; we thought for some reason they were good for our health. I didn't wear them much, they were too uncomfortable. Poor St. Jerome; Job was doing much better in the footwear department.

I was entranced with the prospect of painting the stony foreground, each pebble lovingly created. And an excuse to paint the Northern Italian landscape freed from the demands of realism. A permitted leap right into allegory: half the landscape is brown rock, symbolizing death, half is flourishing Italian campagna, full of mild, innocent cultivation and buildings with triangular roofs. And there are a few nice allegorical animals: a pheasant, a leopard and a deer, a rabbit. Tawny grasses, tender pink flowers, luminous olive leaves, with a touch of pinkish silver.

And the MAN himself, the Redeemer, whom the inscription on the seat where Job is sitting assures us LIVETH, is really worn out. Despite the wounds he'd inflicted, a crescent shape on his left breast, a deep horizontal cut on his right hand, he doesn't look dead. He's just had it, for now.

The loincloth covering his shame is again a triangle, an inverted triangle above whose base flourishes a really impressive efflorescence of pubic hair. His lips are open in a sensual gasp. One hand is relaxed, the other gripped, one finger points upward, stopped in midgesture, the imparting of delight.

The separation of his legs is beautiful, the gap of desire. The tail of fabric between them, a reminder of the animal beneath the skin. The body is thin and gently muscled. He's not a bruiser. His neck is stronger than his legs. The sinew, falling between the bones of the clavicle, shows he's capable of real hard work.

At his feet a crown of thorns, to the right a skull, a jawbone and a hammer. In the background tiny figures, perhaps dozing. One on horseback in a red turban.

One of my decisions would have to be: of all these smaller infinitely engaging things, which, if any, would I reproduce? I wasn't going to deny myself the initial pleasure of rendering them. But all the time, I knew that, however wonderful they were in themselves, however well I'd done them, they might have to come out of the finished painting.

It was a quarter to five when he tapped me on the shoulder. "I'm not ready," I said. I'd been there six hours, but it wasn't nearly enough time, I hadn't even begun. I felt that his presence was stealing something from me. And yet, he was the one who'd driven me down and was going to drive me back.

"I think I have a good idea," he said. "Why don't I try to get us a room in one of the hotels on Madison Avenue? Then you can stay here till nine o'clock, when the museum closes, and be here first thing when it opens."

"But we both live in New York. We could both go back to our apartments."

"I thought yours was sublet."

"How did you know that?" I asked suspiciously.

"You told me."

"Oh."

"And mine's being painted. But even when it's not, it's sort of uninhabitable. Besides, at a hotel, we could have room service. And all those wonderful towels. And the little refrigerator with those little bottles. You don't have anything moral against towels and refrigerators and room service?"

"On the contrary, I morally distrust people who say they don't like room service."

"I'll arrange everything. I'll be back, just to tell you where to meet me. You come whenever you're ready."

"What will you be doing?"

"I don't know, it's a hotel, maybe I'll read the Bible."

"You're not a religious freak?"

"You're losing your sense of humor."

"When I'm working like this, I don't necessarily have a sense of humor." I nuzzled his ear. "But to make up for it, when I'm done work for the day, I'm sex crazed."

"That's my idea of a good aesthetic."

When the museum finally closed at nine o'clock, I was shocked again that I had been there for so many hours. Painting, that is painting from life, or copying something does such strange things to time. It takes so long to make something appear that time goes very slowly and doesn't seem to pass as it ordinarily does. And you lose yourself when you're copying. You pay attention to what's in front of you. You lose yourself in order not to lose your focus.

He'd gotten us a room at the Westbury, thirteen blocks away from the Met. The room was only tasteful, not unusual, not spectacular: colonial wallpaper, a four-poster bed. On the chintz spread was a shopping bag, a fuchsia so bright it looked enameled. Instead of a handle, there were loops of black braided yarn. It was from one of those shops on Madison Avenue that I'd always looked at when I was at the Whitney or the Met but had never gone into.

"It's for you," he said.

Wrapped in paper that felt wonderful—rice paper with the name of the store woven in—was a pair of silk pajamas. Striped men's tailored pajamas that looked like Myrna Loy had worn them in *The Thin Man*.

"You looked so marvelous in my shirt, I thought these might suit you."

*      *      *

I couldn't remember the last time a man had bought me clothing. Something in me wanted to refuse the gift: the fear of being bought, of being paid for sex. And what that meant about my being owned, about my time being at the disposal of a lover. A lover with money. My time in sexual thrall to a man. But I couldn't help being excited by a man going into a store, an expensive store, carrying the image of my body in his mind, the costliness of the gift a sign of my power. It was happening to me, a woman who had refused the idea of belonging to a man because she'd wanted work and freedom, also because she'd feared that in the game of allurement and desirability, the winning of which got you things like the pajamas, she didn't measure up. Being glad about the pajamas wasn't a position I admired, it certainly wasn't a heroic position. It was more like knowing that bitter chocolate is superior, but going for a Mallomars.

Sometimes, there's nothing like a Mallomars.

I spent the next day at the museum in front of the Carpaccio, drawing. I spent hours in a universe that was triangular; I lived among triangles. The position of the legs, the loincloth. I'd worked very hard to make the universe a world of triangles. It was difficult work. My body felt used, worn out, fatigued, dirty, and yet overwrought.

I needed a kind of sex that felt like rutting. A little unclean. Grimy. Matted hair, the suggestion of the overripe, something on the point of going off. Going to seed. When I work the way I'd been working at the museum, I feel like I've been in a filthy cellar with little puddles where God knows what might be breeding, hidey-holes inches thick in sooty dust. I have to go rooting in; I have to come on all kinds of things. Bottles half filled with unrecognizable liquids, potatoes going soft, the carcass of a bird or rodent, then at the bottom, I see the thing I was looking for. The thing itself.

After working like that, I feel I have filth all over my hands, and at the same time I'm incandescent. Everything fleshly has been burned away. I'm bluish, a pure spirit. I'm pulled down to the stink of things and yet ready to be turned into air. So you can see why sex not based on tenderness seems like the only way out. Like the whistle of a train that you hear in the distance and long for because it might eventually stop for you and take you where you're meant to be.

When I got back from the museum, he was lying in his jeans, asleep. He must have been out walking. I looked to see if he had another wonderful expensive bag for me, but there didn't seem to be one.

He hadn't shaved that morning and his beard was coarse. I ran my face along it, liking the abrasion. I began undressing him without so much as a hello, how was your day. I didn't see the point.

I put my nose into his armpits and smelt his rank oniony smell. A sweaty animal. I loved the pelt. I sniffed and licked him. The hair around his cock smelt like mushrooms before you've washed the soil off. He tasted vinegary. I climbed on top of him. There was nothing sweet in what I did. Then he wanted to be on top. He tried to roll me over. I wouldn't give. I hunkered down onto my haunches; he could wrestle me if he wanted, but he'd have to win. I wasn't succumbing. He pushed against my arms. I leaned down on my hands. He put his hands on my waist and tried to turn me off balance. I was firm. I felt his strength and I used mine against it. Then I didn't care who won, I liked the struggle. Pitting myself. Feeling my own force, then his.

He'd bought me another present, after all, an expensive art book. The paintings of Carpaccio. I didn't even wash before I fell on it.

I turned the pages like someone who knows her taste in pornography. I knew what I was looking for: Dead Christs. And I found another one, called *The Dead Christ*. Jesus is in the desert, the same landscape as the painting in the Met. But this time he's lying on an altar. I thought of a guy I'd slept with once whose bed had reminded me of an altar. Did he think that fucking him was the ultimate sacrament? Or the ultimate sacrifice? Or was he the victim?

This Jesus is on top of his altar, or slab, or marble bed, and he doesn't look anymore dead than the other Jesus does. Just taking a nice postcoital snooze. A cluster of ideas was in my head: the man laid out, the bed as altar, sex as sacrifice. But I wasn't focusing on any of that. I was really in love with the greenish sky.

B was awake now, looking at me. All I could think about was green skies, skies with small, dingy, disengaged smoky clouds in them, like smudges underneath an eyelid. Mascara the morning after. I was making notes about the colors I could use. But it wasn't enough. I needed to be near a green sky. I thought I was lucky that it was late August, and that, if conditions were right, the sky would get greenish on the Cape just before the sun went down, and that if I sat by the bay at around six o'clock, I could see it. I wanted to go.

I felt full of greed for the green sky, the late summer, and all that was contained in that watery light. I looked at B, and something like hatred came over me. Because I wanted what I wanted and he could let me have it. Why should that make me hate him?

I hated myself because he was telling me that if I wished, I could live in service of my greed for an image, to live as if that image—going after it, pinning it down, not letting it get away, not letting life get in the way of it—was the most important thing. Which was the way I'd said I'd wanted to live. But when I was confronted with the possibility, it seemed horrifying.

"Don't you think there's something a little disgusting about your compliance? Doesn't it make you feel like a freak?"

"No, feeling that I needed to wear your brassiere would make me feel like a freak. This doesn't. I know what I'm doing."

"What are you doing? If you're not getting sick, I don't know why. It's making me feel a little sick."

"Maybe you have a weak stomach. This is an adventure, a gamble. The gamble that if you're given the right conditions you can do something really good."

"It's not your business."

"I'm making it my business."

"I'm not a business. I'm not yours."

"You can get out of this any time you want. If you stay in it, you get what you say you always wanted. If you don't, you go back to what you had. Which, as you've often said, was perfectly fine. Now I'm happy to drive you back to the Cape. Or put you on the plane, if you prefer."

"Yes," I said. "Yes, that is what I prefer. I prefer not to be with you. Because thinking about what I'm doing is making me sick. Thinking about being a whore."

"Why aren't I the whore?"

"Because you're paying."

"It depends on what you think the currency is. There's money. And there's giftedness. And then there are works of art."

"Is this all about your being bored?"

"Why can't you think of this as an adventure? I'm a rich man. You're a fine artist. I want to be part of the making of art."

"Because you're also fucking me. You've wrecked everything by introducing that."

"Only if you misunderstand the currency."

"Why didn't you just make a big contribution to an art school? For the support of needy, promising young women. Why do you have to put your body in the middle of it?"

"Say I wanted a stake?"

"And your stake is right between your legs."

The whole time we were talking, we were both naked. Like Adam and Eve, we both realized it at the same time, and neither of us liked it. Not looking at each other, we dressed.

We made it to La Guardia in time for the seven o'clock shuttle, so I could get the last plane from Boston to Provincetown that night. I called Larry to pick me up, and he said he'd bring Mikey in the car. I didn't tell anyone where I'd been. Maybe they thought I'd needed same-day surgery.

All the way home I thought about not liking B, about the fact that I couldn't think of one thing about him that pleased me. Occasionally, I had to remember that he understood the paintings, and he seemed to understand me. Like the time we were lying in bed quietly, and he began laughing. "I just thought of a situation that would completely paralyze you. I challenge you to a race. But I tell you the loser gets seven straight hours of oral sex."

Every time I thought about the time and attention he'd lavished on who I was and what I did, I began to get aroused. And a little grateful. But I wasn't going to let myself be grateful. If I did, I'd feel guilty, or I'd worry that I wasn't nicer to him. And if I worried about being nice to him, the whole thing wouldn't work. It had to be about not being nice. Who would worry about being nice to the Muse? The Muse is there to serve the artist, not to be considered by her. So when I started to feel grateful, I thought about all the male artists I knew who treated their wives like shit.

It was great to be with Larry and Mikey. We stopped off for pizza; he bought a slice for the dog.

When I got home, I fell right to sleep. In the morning, I took out my drawings, I took out my Carpaccio book, I took out my new silk pajamas and hung them over my white chair. I went to the beach to collect some stones that might look like Carpaccio stones. I spent the morning drawing stones. I was really waiting for the green sky.

But at three o'clock it started to rain.

I knew there were other things I could do. I could prime the canvas. I could sketch. I could underpaint. I could do a lot to begin the thing, so I'd know I'd stopped fooling around. But I was in that moment of paralyzed shock that always precedes something new. I wonder why I ever wanted to do it. Then I want to fall asleep. Or eat till I feel nauseated, or walk up and down wringing my hands. Or think about the global economy, or global warming, or something that makes it useless even to contemplate beginning a new painting. I am filled with dread, and I feel loathsome to myself. My hair feels filthy; my nails belong to a witch; my lips are cracked; my breasts flat dugs. This is the time when anything in the world seems preferable to work. The time when refrigerators are cleaned out, bathroom tiles scrubbed, alliances made that spell disaster to the next five generations. This was when I wanted him. If I could be in bed with him, I could forget about the disgusting prospect of trying to make an image come to life.

I phoned his number in Provincetown. A man with a Southern accent, who told me he was B's assistant, said B had stayed in New York and wouldn't be back till late this evening.

"Did he say what he was doing in New York?" I asked in an irritated voice.

"No, ma'am, he didn't."

Don't "No, ma'am" me, I wanted to say. What do you think this is, fucking Dodge City?

I was very annoyed that he wasn't there when I really wanted him. Hadn't he said he'd be at my beck and call, like all those women who live with male artists, lying around just for moments like this? This was when I needed him near me naked, or barbecuing chicken at 3:00 A.M., telling me I was brilliant and beautiful, that there was not the slightest reason to doubt myself. And what was he doing? Selling pork bellies or platinum or coffee beans or soy? I wanted him here, with me.

I wouldn't let myself leave the house. I insisted on remaining a colonist of the filthy cloud that had visited the region. At least I could do that. I tried to read the book on Carpaccio. I read about his taking a trip to Constantinople with Gentile Bellini, brother of the more famous Giovanni. I started thinking about Constantinople in the fifteenth century. Then about Turks and turbans. Then I thought of the man on horseback in the background of the Carpaccio. I began seeing a turban in red silk. I began drawing turbans.

And somehow—I can't explain why—drawing the turbans made it possible for me to begin the canvas. I sketched in the chair and the man sitting on it. I made marks for the rocks.

I worked for six hours straight, and then I lay down on the bed, exhausted. It was ten o'clock; I could hear the rain drumming on the roof so close above my head in the little house. Then the phone rang. It was B, calling from the car.

"Where are you?" I said, feeling free to sound annoyed.

"I stayed in the city. For some strange reason, I thought you'd rather be without me."

"I did at the time. But later I wanted you here. But as it turns out, it's good you weren't here, you would have gotten in the way. I started it."

"That's wonderful," he said. At that moment I liked him. I liked him because I knew he did think it was wonderful that I'd begun the painting. And I had a sense he knew how hard it had been.

"I'm about two miles down on Route 6. I have a picnic basket from Balducci's. Smoked fish. Three kinds: tuna, bluefish, trout. Fabulous tomatoes. Two kinds of bread: pumpernickel and onion rye. Champagne, which you probably won't want. Three kinds of biscotti: almond, pistachio and chocolate hazelnut. I'm happy to leave it at your door and go away. Or I'm happy to have supper with you. But I can't do both at once—which given the way you're talking, is your first choice."

I didn't like this grateful feeling. But there it was. It was something to do with the food.

"Please," I said, probably so pleasantly I was surprised at myself. "Come over and we'll have supper. That would be very nice."

I didn't let him stay the night, because I knew how much time sex takes from a working morning. I told him that there would be very little sex in the sunlight while I was working, those were my best hours, and we could do whatever we were doing just as well in the dark.

The last week of August was glorious. Warm days, and the tide was high in the morning, so I could start my day with a swim and end my day with a run and a dip in the bay to cool myself and Mikey off. I'd take off my bathing suit and sit in sweats, watching the sky, which had obeyed me and taken on Carpaccio's green. That lovable twinge of autumn was in the air, the first cold, chilling my still-wet skin and lightening the sky with silver, so that every twilight is shot through with yearning. Too beautiful almost to fix on, when the moon rises out of a turquoise nest. All that yearning, that sense of longing, I would put into my picture. If only I could solve the problem of the triangulation, get the posture of the legs, the shape of the loincloth I had made into a towel. If I could convey heaviness, resignation, rest.

I worked until late every night. He never phoned me. Sometimes I would fall asleep in my clothes and wake up, surprised, at three or four o'clock. But sometimes at eleven, I was physically lively, and I would begin thinking about the difference between the texture of his body where there was all that hair and then, only inches away, that smoothness that seemed immature. I would call him up, he would come over; stay for an hour, an hour and a half. I never let him spend the night.

He would take shopping lists for me and his assistant would leave the bags of groceries on the kitchen table, putting the perishables in the fridge. Often, when I came back from the bay at eight or eight-thirty, there would be supper waiting for me, without even a note.

In that week, I made great progress on the painting. I was ready to put it down, go back to New York, begin teaching and not be afraid that I would lose it. It wasn't like being interrupted just as you're approaching orgasm, it was much more housewifely than that. More like you'd made the stock and it could stay in the refrigerator till you were ready to get on with the soup.

I hated packing up on August 31. I always hate the idea of having to give up my wonderful leisure to go back to teaching. I like teaching and I'm very good at it, but when I'm doing it it's what I do all day. And in the winter, it's too dark to wake up early to work. I try to do a little each day, even if it's just a drawing, or a few strokes on a painting. But the months of uninterrupted work are gone. And as September approaches, I go into mourning.

I'd told him that, so he asked if I'd like help packing up. I said that would be great, thinking he'd send Bobby, his assistant. Bobby is another of his investments. He's writing his dissertation on cross-dressing in Renaissance drama, but apparently everybody is, and he's run out of grants. So B hires him to keep an eye on the house in Provincetown—he gets to live there all year, except when B wants to be there, then he stays with friends. He's a great house person; everyone's happy. I thought he'd send Bobby over with some empty cartons from the liquor store, but he came himself. With a tape of Rosemary Clooney singing World War II songs, and Django Reinhardt and Stephane Grappelli. He said it was impossible to be sad listening to them.

We sang and packed my things. It went much faster with his help. It was almost as if we were friends.

He said, "Next year, if you want, you can stay at my house instead of coming here."

I didn't like the idea, but then I never like going to new places. It always feels as if I've put my hand on a freezing railing and when I move it, I've left some skin behind.

"I'm sorry," he said. "I shouldn't have brought that up now when you're starring in *The Cherry Orchard*."

It was the first time I'd heard him apologize. Or half apologize.

He kissed me good-bye through the car window and said he'd see me in New York. I felt a kind of panic: I hadn't thought of that. How was I going to incorporate him into my already overfull life? I wasn't sure I wanted to.

I tried to think of what was really wrong with what we were doing, in the sense of causing harm to someone else or debasing myself. It wasn't as if I didn't like the sex. It wasn't as if he was treating me contemptuously. But there's something about money that muddies whatever water it touches. And the fact that he was trying to be part of art without doing the work of the artist was a little creepy. When I thought about it that way, I wanted to phone him and tell him it was impossible.

But then, I thought about what I'd always said I needed for my work: space, time and money. He could make things happen.

I told myself I should have kept sex out of it. Even if he wanted it, I should have said no.

But I hadn't had such good sex in twenty years.

All the way down the Mass Pike, over to Route 84, in the traffic of Hartford and through the art deco fantasy of the Merritt Parkway, I tried to imagine how I'd tell Michael about it. Because we always had dinner together the night I came back from the Cape.

If I were part of a couple, it wouldn't be so easy to go out with a friend my first night home. I didn't like what that implied.

I double-parked the car in front of my building—well, in front of the deli—ready to make a million trips up the three flights of stairs. Mr. Kim, who owned the deli, said he'd keep an eye out for the cops. I wrote recommendations for his daughter to get into Columbia, which she did, on a scholarship, so he's happy to help me out in things like this.

I always called Michael the minute I let Mikey in the house. He lives a block away; it's why I got this apartment—he, Theresa and I all live within ten blocks of one another. I live on Eighty-sixth and Amsterdam, on top of a deli. Or I did live there, but you'll hear about that later. I moved there when the kids left for college. I sold the apartment Roger and I had until then; we were lucky, we'd bought it for $20,000 when the place went co-op, and I sold it for $250,000. Roger and I split the selling price; we'd agreed he'd use his half for the girls' college tuition, to make up for my having worked at Watson all those years and his lying on the couch waiting for inspiration. My share gave me a little nest egg, to do things like rent Larry's house on the Cape.

The place on Eighty-sixth was a two-bedroom apartment—room

for the girls when they came back on vacation, cheap enough so I could rent the studio on the Lower East Side. Which was horrible, but had the virtue of existing.

I liked the apartment, I didn't love it. I was grateful to it, though, in the way you are to dwellings, because it was the first place I'd lived alone in since I was a student. The first place I wasn't a mother. The nest I made so that I wouldn't have an empty nest.

When the girls went away to college, I was lonely for a while. I kept buying too much food. I had rolls and rolls of toilet paper in the closet that never seemed to get used up. I bought three times too many Tampax. I'd make soup that I'd never get around to eating; it would grow mold and I'd have to throw it away. Off and on I was seeing the guy who had the bed like an altar, but there was nothing in it. Michael had Jeffrey, and they were in the midst of nouveau-domestic bliss. Theresa has been married to Robert for so long that we could do things alone, or with Robert, whom I like very much, except that he worries about me. I saw some colleagues from school. I'd thought I'd get a fantastic amount of work done with the girls gone, but it didn't happen. I spent a great deal of time roaming around the new apartment. I didn't sleep well and I used a great deal of my work time taking naps. But eventually, and much more quickly than I thought, I grew to like living alone. I liked entering a dark apartment that I could light at will, that I could fill with color or sound, or not—according to my desires.

There's a savor to an empty space that you and only you have created. A delicious quality to the quiet—especially if you've been a mother—that's as desirable as food or sex. Each time I opened the door of my apartment, I thought how hard it would be for me to give that up.

I felt different than I usually did when I came home after the summer. This time I was reluctant to call Michael. I didn't know how I was going to tell him everything that had happened. Suppose he didn't understand? Suppose he told me I was being horrible? I didn't want to have to give it up—but if Michael made me feel like a pig, I knew that I might have to.

I stood in the doorway and watched Michael walk down the hall, holding a bottle of wine I knew he'd brought back from Italy. The sight of his face was pure joy to me. My friend. My very handsome friend.

Living your life as someone who bears witness to the visible can have its bad points. Because the visible is only itself; beauty isn't truth, truth isn't beauty. Beauty certainly isn't goodness. Some of the best people I know, including my parents, have taste that would make Jesus weep. And I've always thought that collectors, in the very attentiveness of their eye, are on morally thin ice.

Was B collecting me? Collecting my making of art? Collecting my essence as an artist? And what about my sex? All these thoughts were crowding out my pleasure in Michael's thick black hair (I saw he'd got a great cut somewhere in Italy) and the new loafers he'd bought there. What I was starting to say was that, whereas being a witness to the triumphs of the visible has its problems, because I live my life with such emphasis on what the eye can see, the physical beauty of someone I love seems like a particular sign of the world's goodness.

I could smell his shampoo: eucalyptus. I figured he'd just come from the gym. He'd probably put on five pounds in Venice and was determined to get it off in an hour and a half.

"You're very beautiful, as usual," I said.

"And you look eighteen. You're happy. But how's my godson?"

"Mikey was not named after you. That's a very narcissistic belief you seem unable to give up. Have you thought of getting professional help?"

"I wonder if you think it's part of your Bohemian charm living in a third-floor walkup. You might consider moving on. Or out."

"I may be."

"You're getting me really worried. It's essential to my mental health that I can be in your living room within five minutes of waking up. And I mean no more than five."

We unloaded my boxes. I took a shower. We drank his wine. He'd bought me violet bath salts in a beautiful art nouveau bottle and thirty postcards of the Venetian artists. Ten Bellini, ten Titian, ten Carpaccio.

"Speaking of Carpaccio," I said.

He was sitting on the floor, wrestling with the dog. "Were we speaking of Carpaccio? Mikey, were you speaking of Carpaccio?"

"I have an idea for a whole series of paintings. My idea is that many of the deposed Christs aren't deposed Christs at all, but just your ordinary postcoital Joe. You know, the little death, not the big one." I showed him the sketches for the Carpaccio.

"It's fantastic. You're fantastic. You're utterly brilliant. And you'll have a great time. If only you had enough time to give yourself to it full out. The bad luck is that it's September and you have to go back to the overprivileged of the Upper East Side."

"Shut up, my girls are wonderful. And I may be able to take off some time."

"What do you mean?"

"I don't mean that I don't have to go back next week. I do. But I may be able to take quite a lot of time off. Like two years."

"You're going to marry a rich man?"

"No. Although I am sleeping with one."

"I can't leave you alone for a month without something like this happening."

"Something like what? If I knew what it was like, I might feel better."

I told him everything. Or everything except the sexual details. I did tell him the sex was great, but sometimes a little mean, a little untender, because I partly wanted to punish B for the money. And I told him I couldn't figure out whether I liked B or not.

"What I need you to tell me, Michael, is whether this is a degrading and immoral thing. Whether I've turned myself into a whore."

"You know in my line of work we don't use that kind of language."

"Well, the language of your kind of work sometimes drives me nuts. So just tell me as a friend, a good friend, someone who grew up in an Italian neighborhood. What would your mother think?"

"I don't think we should bring my mother into this. What do you mean by a whore?"

"Someone who has sex for money."

"Is that what you're doing?"

"I don't think he's paying me for the sex. But he may be paying me so he can be fucking an artist. He knows he doesn't have talent, but he thinks art is important. What he's good at is money. And he's got a lot of it. And he's bored. And he'll turn fifty soon. He's got no kids. He thinks I'm really good."

"I think you're really good, too. I'd give you money and a new apartment if I could."

"What would you be getting out of it?"

"I'd be feeling that I was a part of something marvelous. What about all those donors in the Renaissance paintings? They got themselves painted into the pictures, right next to the Virgin and Christ and all the saints. Probably their motives were not 100 percent pure. Not even 99 and 44/100 percent pure. But what they did with their money was a good thing."

"Suppose they were fucking the painter?"

"Maybe they were. We'll never know. Does it matter?"

"I'm not sure. But I wish I hadn't slept with him. It makes it murky. On the other hand, we were fantastically turned on to each other, so if we hadn't it would have been false, something we were purposely not saying or not doing."

"You've always gotten yourself into trouble doing things because not doing them would be false."

"You know what I mean, Michael. If I didn't sleep with him, then I'd be not sleeping with him to keep some sort of purity intact. But what is the purity? If you don't think sex is bad, if you don't think having sex with someone means having something taken away from you, what's wrong with it? I wish I knew whether I liked him."

"Why don't you like him?"

"Because he can make so much happen. And he knows that. And that makes him different from any man I've ever known."

I felt better, talking to Michael about it. But I wasn't ready for him and B to meet.

I lay in bed and thought about B. I realized I sort of missed him. But I wasn't sure whether I missed him or the sex. Then I asked myself, what's the difference? I convinced myself to call him up.

He was still in Provincetown. The phone rang four times. I would

have been upset if he'd been with someone else. But it's always embarrassing, creating that scene where the two of them say, "Let's just let it
ring."

He came to the phone on the fifth ring. He said he'd been thinking
of me. He said he wished I was there. He described the moon on the
water. Only a quarter moon now; we'd met, he said, when it was full.
Did I remember that? Although it wasn't a forgettable event.

I liked it better when he was a little harsh, a little spiky. I didn't
quite know what to do with him when he brushed the sentimental.
When he started talking about the moon on the night we met.

He asked if we could have dinner when he got in.

"Yes," I said, "I think that would be nice."

He took me to restaurants I'd never gone to and never would have
gone to without him. I was uneasy at first, but he said if I enjoyed it,
why not. Once, he took me to Petrossian and we spent hundreds of
dollars on caviar. Dollops of it were brought to us on silver platters. It
seemed like something you'd only do once, so I thought, why not, why
not, a bit of old Russia, Pierre and Andrei and isn't that Natasha? You
were paying to pretend you were in another time and place. "But hundreds of dollars for a meal," I said, "it isn't worth it."

"Worth?" he said. "What's worth?"

"You have to have some sense of worth."

"To the person who works at a hospital, a nurse's aide, minimum
wage, the Argo Luncheonette on Ninetieth and Broadway is out of
sight. Not worth it."

I had to think about money in a new way; it was simultaneously
more abstract and more real than it had ever been. How much was too
much when you had more than enough? In a world of desirables, what
did you say no to? It was easy for me to make the decision for myself: a
good use of money bought time for work, education and freedom for
my children, a certain amount of pleasure, attractive food, someplace
to live that didn't look like Lee Harvey Oswald was brought up there,
an occasional new item of clothing. I've never been tempted by purchases that were supposed to announce who I was in the world: the
right brand of this or that. But of course, everything you buy says some-

thing about who you are. The fact that I like pure cotton instead of polyester blends makes some point. But a point only up to a point.

I started trying to understand the idea of luxury. Something chosen beyond question of need. Something possessed for its own qualities, because you want it near you, not necessarily to be used up but to be savored. The pleasure of excess. The love of what is not required. The appreciation of it for its own sake. For its excellence in relation to its own—what?—construction, fineness, superiority of material. How much beauty is enough, too much? How much pleasure?

I began to resent him when I started thinking like that. I felt that, in trying to free me from the burdens of earning money, he was forcing money to invade my mind as it never had. As an idea. Every time I saw my cleaning woman and I realized the kinds of calculations she had to make—whether or not to take an extra bus, could she afford a cup of coffee—I'd consider the grapefruit he'd had delivered from Balducci's. I just didn't know how to think. I'd take the grapefruit out of its basket filled with straw. I'd look at the perfect blush of its outer pink against the sunny yellow. Then I'd slice it open—he also bought me a fine set of knives, German steel, and I would look at the shape of them, feel the heft in my hand, see how purposefully they did their work, and a kind of love grew up between me and my new knives. I would thank them as I held them in my hand, prepared to slice excellent grapefruit with an excellent knife. I split the sunny globe directly in two. And I wondered if these grapefruit hadn't come uptown in their basket of straw, if I'd picked them up at D'Agostino or even at Fairway, would I have taken the time to notice them quite so closely, to honor them in quite the same way?

Money slowed me down. I was becoming surrounded by things that were there for their fineness. They required, therefore, my attention. I was becoming a citizen in the world of things deserving of attention. Grapefruit. Knives. Silk pajamas. Caviar, or *caviars*. But I kept telling myself that that was what I did, as a painter; I did honor, paid homage to the physical world. It was part of my work. That's what he was telling me by giving me so much money. That anything was good if it enriched my work. So I had to think of my work in a new way too, and even that took time.

Theresa said to me once, "It must be frightening to have to consider whether your work is really as important as you believed it was."

The clean slate. The clear field. There it is: the work. Nothing to keep you from it.

Sometimes, usually just after waking up, I would be overcome with dread about what was happening to me. What was expected of me.

Then I really disliked him. I saw him standing at a doorway, peeking, waiting for me to produce. I didn't want to be a producer. I didn't want to have to come up with something. I didn't want someone standing, waiting for it. I didn't know if there was anything there, if anything would ever come again.

When I started thinking like that, I had to get myself right out of bed. I had to rush into the shower. There's something about warm water that makes you feel hopeful. Sometimes I'd phone him in the morning and he would call me "sweetie" and tell me to describe the day ahead. I would tell him I couldn't; it was an enterprise so full of dread.

"I understand," he said, "having to send thousands to their deaths, downsizing major corporations, dealing with the debt of Latin America. I think of your work as right up there with all that."

"Nevertheless I'm full of dread."

"Draw something. Draw the cup you're drinking from. Draw the spoon."

And I did feel better.

Sometimes, on Wednesdays when I didn't have to be in till ten, he'd come up for coffee and we'd have a quick dive into the mattress, two executives, pressed for time.

Then I would go off to teach. I had no idea what he did. I never asked.

Whereas with most lovers, I've always felt I had a special skill in getting them to reveal themselves—this is who I am, who are you?—so that part of foreplay was a game of self-revelatory double solitaire, with him, there was very little I wanted to know. It was as if I were with someone whom I insisted on seeing only in a half mask. I never went to his apartment. I didn't meet his friends; I didn't ask about them. I knew a bit about his ex-wife, but I particularly didn't encourage him to speak to me about her.

I took him at his word; if he was really most interested in my producing my best work, I would accept what he offered in the way that was the best for my work. And what felt best then was not worrying about him as a full human being. Using him, as a Renaissance painter did his patron. This habit of mind entered into our sex. I didn't worry about saying no to him if I wanted to get down to work. I didn't have to tell him that at my age, I'd had rather a lot of sex and I didn't have endless time to do all the painting I wanted to. I could only make love freely to a lover who understood that sometimes I wanted work more than love.

By November, we were seeing each other only two nights a week. We'd go to movies, to dinner, to concerts. He was still new enough for me to feel the excitement of sitting in the dark of a theater or a concert hall, feeling his leg against me, or his hand on my knee. Once, during a particularly boring Polish film—the theater was nearly empty—he lifted my skirt and stroked me silently, stealthily in the dark. At every moment I wondered if one of these cultivated people—mainly women in their late sixties—was going to turn around, look at us, and scream for the usher. Of course it didn't happen. My eyes were fixed on the screen ahead of me: apartment houses in Eastern European cities. I focused and didn't focus. The dark became voluptuous, a fur I wrapped my aroused flesh in. Mouth open, I stared at the screen, where I was not. I followed his lead; I let him bring me off. Now, that's another strange expression. Bring me off. Off what and to where? Whatever it was, I did it for the first time in a public place.

Those fall months were strange, because I didn't actually do a lot of work on the painting I'd started in August. It was odd going back to school, telling my chair I'll be gone for five terms. Two and a half years. Suggesting a rich relative had died, not wanting to go into it. To others, not connected with the IRS, others to whom I didn't have to put things in writing, I mentioned a grant. For women in their middle years. Last chance at the Laurel. Theresa suggested we call B the Last Laurel Foundation. Theresa, by the way, thought I was mad ever to have questioned it.

She pointed out that if he'd said he wanted to marry me it would have seemed fair and square and I'd have had much less freedom and no way of getting out of it. Think of it as a blow to the right wing, she said. Think of it as striking out against family values, for sexual freedom, and the demands of art.

I agreed to try.

That fall, I went to the Columbia library every night after school look-ing in books about Renaissance painters, seeing which dead Jesuses really looked dead—like the Holbeins—and which were just faking, like the Rosso Fiorentino, who was slyly grinning. When I read about Mantegna there was a reference to a painter I'd never heard of, Sodoma. The name also made me curious. Sodoma had a bad reputation because he liked a young man named Giovanni Sbarbati. Vasari accused him of "bestialità and pozzia." He had a private zoo. He rode in the Palio. Vasari thought he wasn't really serious about art, just in it for the money. The pre-Raphaelites thought he had profundities.

Columbia didn't have much about Sodoma, but one image caught my eye. A Pietà in a private collection in Rome. I'd never get to see it. But even the lousy reproduction excited me. The dead Christ is leaning back, supported by two women, probably his mother and Mary Mag-dalene. His mouth is slightly open—there's no agony there, he's just zonked. And the line of his upper lip suggests that there's a cigarette hanging out of his mouth. Maybe it was just a bad reproduction but I didn't care, I wasn't writing my dissertation, just stealing ideas. So I got an idea for a boy with a cigarette in his mouth but so lazy or stoned that he falls asleep with it that way, he's too far gone to take it out of his mouth and stub it out.

I found five paintings that I Xeroxed and took home and pinned up on my wall. The Pontormo, for the sense of weight, the Rosso Fiorentino, for the grin, the Sodoma, for the bad boy's exhaustion, a Bronzino, because of the fabulous feet, and a Mantegna, which I'll tell you more about later.

The nights or weekends after I worked at the Columbia library, I'd walk back home, carrying my notebook and sketches in a leather bag I'd had for twenty years. I'd think about what I was trying to paint. My subject was the sexual male, the stilled male, the weighted male, the non-

SPENDING    - 79 -

dynamic, postdynamic male. I was thinking about how much male sexuality had to do with action, or the possibility of action, and female sexuality just didn't. I began feeling sorry for men: all that responsibility on their shoulders, or between their legs. Only the spent male suggests desire without the responsibility of fulfillment. He's about recollection, not promise. He can't do anything for you. He seems in need of comfort. I realized that what would be missing from my paintings, what was there in the Renaissance paintings, was the female comforter. My males would be alone, in the landscape. Forlorn.

As I was thinking about desire and desirability in the abstract, I was very caught up in desire for the body of one man. B. Desire connected to response. I loved, for example, the fold where his thighs and his pelvis met, but I loved it because he was so aroused by my tracing the line with my tongue. I wanted to paint that fold, that line. I loved the various textures of his bodily hair. I loved the surprising whiteness of the buttocks and the groin. So, although I tried to think about other male bodies, and I even had Michael buy me some gay porn magazines so I could look at a lot of them, only the body of B inspired me. What I wanted to paint couldn't be simulated by a model. It had to be the heaviness after love. The complete repose. The utter relaxation that is not quite sleep.

I wanted to paint *him*. I wanted my desire to be part of the subject of the painting. And in wanting this, I felt I was flying in the face of the masters. I thought of the Brassaï photograph of Matisse contemplating a nude model. She's beautiful, of course, unusually muscular, with the thighs of a Greek discus thrower and the round unpliant breasts that suggest the height of young womanhood, with middle age not outside the lens's outer reach. Her arm is in an arc over her curly head; her gaze is over at the floor. You can't imagine what she might be looking at. Certainly not at the painter. And he, an old man, bearded, in a white coat like a lab assistant's or a pharmacist's, looks at her like someone about to make a purchase. Coldly, as if her desirability were nothing to him.

I'd always been taught—but by whom I do not know, so let me say that I always believed—this was the ideal relationship between artist and model. That cool, distant appraisal. It's possible, of course, that

Matisse might have fucked the model fifteen minutes before or fifteen minutes after Brassaï took the photograph. But with his pencil in his hand, she was his material, no different from the goldfish or the fruit. Rilke praises Cézanne for not loving his apples. For going past love. But going past love into what? Whose idea was it that there are a series of rooms and that the real room, the room of vision, is the one past love?

Certainly I'd believed that if a woman painter was going to be serious, not an embarrassment, not a painter of chocolate box or calendar art or her own menstrual or menopausal nightmares, she had to be distant. That, because she was a woman, she had to work extra hard to prevent the hot fluid of desire from steaming up her glasses. In the school I wanted to belong to, the one presided over by the austere, modernist fathers, there was no space for female desire. Picasso's Marie-Thérèse, with her hypervoluptuous buttocks and breasts, was something else.

"Stupid girl," I imagined these men saying to me, these men in their beards and their baldness. "You can be one or the other, a woman who desires and is desired or a painter. Choose."

Was it their voices I was afraid of, or another voice, a chaste older sister warning: "Desire has weakened women, it is only by denying our desire we have had what little place we have"?

I walked down Broadway, raving. "I want to paint a male body desired by a woman. I want to paint a body I desire. I will not remove myself. I want to paint a body I've known through my eyes and my fingers and my tongue. I want to paint that sense of weight that I know because I've felt it on my own body so that I had the sense of resting under a mountain. I don't want to pretend, a distance I don't feel so that you—whoever you are—will take me seriously."

It's at moments like this that I feel the foolishness of the way I've lived my life. Who was I to be raving at Picasso and Matisse? Coming after the Titans, everyone feels a failure. To be postmodern is to deal with the temptation to be apologetic; many choose to deal with the inadequacy by jokes. Warhol, Lichtenstein. Cindy Sherman. But I didn't want parody. At the same time, I've never had any ideas about changing the form of painting, only, perhaps, of introducing new content. If you introduce new content—a new liquid—the shape of the bottle changes because the light in which it's seen is new. But I've never begun by imagining a different-shaped bottle. I called upon my beloved painters, masters of the minor shift: Vuillard, Ingres. I asked them to forgive me for lacking the torrential energy to wish to change the form.

Sometimes the smallness of what I do shames me. I say to myself: the world needs people teaching poor children to read, dealing with disease in Africa, caring for the old and the homeless, restoring moldering paintings in dark churches in Europe, saving classic buildings in the minor cities of the U.S.A. It does not need new daubs on canvas. Then I tell myself: but that's what I do. And then I tell myself that it would be perfectly possible for a very bad painter to say the same thing to herself. In fact, they do it all the time.

My only way out is to be interested in the process. Which gives me pleasure, the kind of pleasure I get from a good meal. To know I'm taking the risk of being ridiculous. The risk of self-delusion. But to forget that in solving the problem. How shall I place that figure? How to create the roundness of that stone?

I was arguing with dead men when my daughter Rachel introduced a new voice—a living one, one that wasn't mine—into the conversation.

Rachel is my daughter with the dyed black buzz cut, the pierced eyebrow, the one at Brown doing postmodernist anthropological work on Latin America. She's the one I can count on to be, if not harsh, certainly not tender in her judgments. She's the one who told me her father was right to leave me because I was a work-crazed bitch. I thought she'd give me the toughest line on my arrangement with B.

"I'd say you're a whore," she said to me. "Of course I don't get freaked out by sex workers like you do. Just call yourself a sex worker."

"Sex worker? Is that a new category, like blue collar?"

"It just means that they're wage earners, and sex is their job. No judgments attached. It's just a job description like any other."

"Rachel, I think there's a difference between calling somebody a stevedore and a prostitute."

"Just a difference in language."

"No, Rachel, I don't think so. Whores give up something very personal. Their sexuality, their privacy."

"So do waitresses and secretaries."

"It's different."

"It's different because you think it is. That's why you're feeling bad about your arrangement, because you're calling yourself a whore. If you call yourself a sex worker, you don't have to get freaked out."

"Rachel, I am not a sex worker."

"I didn't bring it up, Mom. But since you did, you might as well call it what it is, then live with it."

It seemed an unusual conversation for a daughter and a mother to be having. But maybe I'm wrong. Maybe it's more common than I think.

Rachel has a way of looking at me that makes me feel like a treeless plain; unprotected and entirely visible. At the same time, there's the pleasure of unencumbered light, the absence of obscurity, diffusion. No daughter, of course, likes to think of her mother having sex. I'd never made my girls my confidantes. There are some doors that should remain closed. But it didn't really matter what I told them or what I kept back. It almost didn't matter what I did. They saw what they needed. It was essential to Rachel that she prove she wasn't me; she had to feel she was passing me on the road, passing me or surpassing me. The first step in all these tasks was judgment. Nevertheless, I knew that between the level of judgment and the one of a determination to surpass, there was a spongy middle layer of well-wishing. I always felt clarified when I looked at her clear gray eyes, her remarkable thick eyebrows—remarkable even though pierced—which I'd seen knotted in anguish, straight in understanding. The day we spoke they were neither knotted nor straight; she didn't know quite what she thought; she was trying something. Trying it out on me.

And I was trying something out on her. Because I knew she'd give what I was doing the most rigorous analysis possible, and yet we'd go on. We'd have to, we were mother and daughter.

But my first instinct, when she called me a whore, or rather a sex worker, was to say, "Mind your own goddamn business. What I do in bed is up to me."

I didn't say that. But I did say, "I like sleeping with him, it makes me happy."

And saying it to her, I knew, as I hadn't before, that it was true.

I said, "I like him. He's a person I enjoy. He wishes me well. You may be too young to know how rare that is."

Rachel said, "A lot of whores like their johns."

I found, as I often had with Rachel, that I was being sucked into the argument on tempting but shaky intellectual ground. "But whores wouldn't sleep with their johns if money wasn't involved. And I would."

"All right," she said. She'd begun smoking. Merit Ultra Light, blue.

Seeing her light up, I pictured her once-pink, fruit-textured lungs turned black and carbonated. I knew I should say nothing, but I convinced myself I'd have said something to a friend. "Do you have to smoke?"

"Is it your body?"

"Is it your body that was the subject of our discussion of my sex life?"

"Jesus, Mom, it's a little different."

"Yes, what I'm doing won't kill me."

"Just corrupt you."

"You mean it won't corrupt a sex worker but it will corrupt me?"

"It'll corrupt you because you don't admit you're doing it."

"Doing what?"

"Taking money. People shouldn't take money for fucking. No, I don't mean that. I don't care if they do, but they should be up front about it and call themselves what they are."

"I'm taking money for painting."

"And for fucking."

"That's not what the money's about."

"How do you know what you're getting money for?" she asked, flicking her Bic, I knew just to annoy me. "How can you ever tell?"

"I can tell."

"Well, good for you."

What is this thing between mothers and daughters, this primitive compulsion to make totems of each other so that we can appear before each other's eyes as the larger-than-life caricature of everything we hate and fear? Pendulous breasts, jutting buttocks, lidless eyes, the teeth of the devouring monster spitting blood through lips that close over the helpless prey. Hi, Mom. Hi, honey. That you? Yeah, it's me, is that you? Then we kill the creature, and we're done with it. Until the next time, when it can rise up and be killed again.

When I heard Rachel telling me all the things I told myself, but the pulp fiction version, with the lurid overcolored illustrations, I could name the exaggerations. I could mistrust her accusations as I didn't dare mistrust my own.

Talking to Rachel made me feel it was all right for me to ask him for a trip to Italy. The one painting that fixed my imagination was Mantegna's *Dead Christ,* in the Brera Gallery in Milan. I arranged to have a younger teacher cover my class for two days, and we went the week before Thanksgiving.

It was the kind of thing that money could make happen. It wasn't necessary. I could look at reproductions. It was the opposite of necessary: it was luxurious, extravagant.

I hungered for proximity to the original. Why? What did that mean? Magic? That something would leap from the thing that had been touched by the hand of the Master, straight into my brain, and then out my hand? Magic, perhaps, but I wanted that.

I had to see the foreshortening, the magnified feet, so vulnerable, what one critic had called "the livid light." Livid light. It was imperative that I see livid light.

A triangle of ribs. A broken tent of crooked fingers.

And in the center of the picture, at the place where all lines meet, the half hard and plainly visible cock of the Redeemer.

I convinced myself that it was necessary that I see this picture. Without B's money, I would have convinced myself of exactly the opposite.

Now I could say: "I have to see this painting," and it would be possible. He would call Alitalia, or his assistant would call, only a few days ahead of time, buying first-class tickets at the highest possible rate. I'd never flown first class. Always before, I'd pass the stocky, overupholstered men, the women in their stiff hair, and contemptuously take my seat in virtuous coach. But now I was settling back in a wide leather chair that bent back completely so I could sleep almost horizontal. I was drinking champagne. I was being handed steaming towels. The stewardess gave us thick plaid blankets, big enough for a double bed. They gave me an idea. I went into the bathroom and took off my panty hose and underpants. I came back to my seat and decorously spread the blanket over both our legs. I took his hand. "I have a surprise for you," I said. He was surprised.

A car and driver met us and drove us to the four-star hotel, in the Magenta, a fashionable neighborhood near the Brera. A hotel in a kind of grove, set back from the street, art deco beds and a bathroom of white marble. Definitely not a fleabag near the station where I'd normally stay.

I was with a man who knew who to call for the name of the best restaurant in Milan, although I was the one who spoke Italian and had to press the buttons of the gray Balthus telephone to make the reservation.

For the first time, I didn't have to ask, "How much?" I didn't have to live in the shamed fear of being cheated, because if I was cheated nothing was at stake. And I'd know that if I was cheated, it was done out of envy, not out of contempt. This made a very great difference.

We walked down streets where everything we saw was spectacle. The city of Milan, capital of the world of fashion as theater. We walked by windows full of clothing no living woman could possibly wear. Shoes made of glass and metal, skirts of feathers, jackets of acid green or kumquat leather. But then we saw the pearl gray camisole that turned us both on. He bought it for me; we didn't look at what it cost. He bought a belt. I bought a scarf, the color of blue hydrangeas. He bought a wallet. I bought a box of stationery. We sat by the window in one of the overpriced cafés in the Galleria; he had gin and Campari, I had Martini Bianco. It was early, and we watched the people stroll, their beautiful hair, their beautiful shoes. We saw *carabinieri* patrolling in long capes and boots with spurs. I said, "I would like to dive under this pink tablecloth right here behind this glass, right here where *tutto Milano,* including *carabinieri* in boots and spurs, are passing by, and get down on my knees, unzip you and have my way."

He called for the bill pronto, pronto, and off we went in a taxi, pronto, pronto, back to our expensive hotel and had each other, throwing our clothes on the floor. Then after all that haste, we let ourselves be taken over by the dove-colored Italian sheets. The afternoon had a feeling of doves about it; I don't know whether I really heard them cooing outside the window, or whether it was the jet lag, or the afternoon's aperitif, or the languor after all that haste, that made us seem like faithful, gentle creatures, not creatures of hunger but domestic, monochrome.

The next day we went to the Brera to see the Mantegna. I'd thought about it so much that I was a little afraid to see it. It was like meeting a movie star or the president of a country.

I kept saying to myself, "Be calm, you might be disappointed," as we walked down the corridor to find the painting—mentioned on the municipal map like a building or a monument. My heart was racing: I had to give B the gallery plan, I was too agitated to make sense of it. Then, almost surprised (but I couldn't have been surprised, I know), I came upon it, hanging modestly, in modest light. Brownish, crepuscular, the orangey marble on which the body lay the most vivid thing about it. The beautiful head, slightly to one side, lying on its pillow of marble. The beautifully drawn bluish feet, the bashful toes.

I couldn't have known from seeing only reproductions how radical the foreshortening was. Up close, the legs were nearly dwarfish. Did I want to paint dwarfish legs like that? I knew that I did, for the sake of the feet, the chest like an unexplored continent, the cock in its beautifully draped cloth, quietly drawing all eyes to itself.

I'd have to think about the problems raised by that foreshortening. I'd have to consider how to create the livid light. The vulnerable desirable feet.

I'd walk away from the painting from time to time because there were other great things to see: A Bellini Pietà with a storm-filled brownish sky, Raphael's young boy, maybe a Cupid, breaking a stick over his knee. The Piero della Francesca of the heavenly court in a monumental Roman space, one of my favorite pictures because of the egg hanging over the virgin's head, suspended by a string from the elaborate ceiling.

I can't tell you how happy that egg makes me. Probably because I love painting eggs myself. My first still life was a bowl of eggs, so I have a sentimental attachment to them. What's great about painting eggs, or even drawing them—and it's hard, it once took me an hour just to draw the outline of an egg properly—is that they're completely defined, but unlike a lot of things that are completely defined, the scale is human. They're geometrical, and yet organic. And there's that wonderful horizon that your eye is always traveling around when you follow the shape. I looked at the Piero and thought that it was certainly right to say that he put the egg there for its symbolism—the hope of the Resurrection, I'd guess. I envied painters who operated out of a symbolic universe because it gave them an excuse to put in such wonderful, yet nutty objects: who would think of hanging an egg from a ceiling when you're painting something high class and serious like a heavenly court? But say it's a symbol of the Resurrection, and you get the fun of painting the shape and the texture, and you get narrative to boot.

Saturating my experience of looking at the Mantegna, or surrounding it like an envelope of vapor, was my sense, in the presence of all these beautiful paintings, that I was doing something worthwhile, that this was a sensible way to spend my life. We stopped in front of masterpieces by people I'd never heard of. A severed head of John the Baptist by Palmagerano. The head is carelessly discarded, stark on a plain brown table, against a background of midnight blue. And someone named Altobello da Melone, who lived in Cremona in 1517, painted a strange virgin martyr standing in a treeless space against buildings that could have been done by de Chirico. Cherries in the foreground of a painting by Carlo Crivelli, whom of course I *had* heard of, with flesh like silk or jewels, but silk or jewels for the palate, the roof of the mouth. All these people doing what they did beautifully, fully. And I was with them. I wasn't measuring myself against them. What they did before me buoyed me up in the ocean of a shared labor in which we, separated by hundreds of years, yet breast to breast, dove, were overwhelmed, clung to the sides of a boat and had our hands beaten by oarsmen, and then, sometimes, occasionally, confidently, swam.

The relationship of my work to the Masters who'd gone before me wasn't hostile. There was nothing I was making fun of, no fault, either in execution or in interpretation, I was trying to show up. There was only the one thing that, as a woman artist, I was occasionally stunned to remember: for most of history, no woman was allowed to do what they did. All those beautiful images, all those wonderful efforts at form and effect, none of them were done by anyone who had a body like mine. I don't know if it made a difference—I don't know how it could not—but who knows what kind of difference it made. I wasn't trying to settle a score. How could I settle a score with Michelangelo? Only to say this, calmly and with amusement: I will paint what I have seen, which is something you didn't. Even if you had a man's body on top of yours there's something I, having a smaller body, smaller bones, different morphology, know about this feeling of weight that you don't. It's not the whole story. Just a part of it. My part. And not the whole of that. Because you and I, I'd say to those who'd gone before me, are another part of the story. I speak to you over centuries, a conversation made up of accidents of time and cells. Just that. Not everything. Not nothing either.

I didn't feel I had to rave and shout at the Mantegna or Bellini the way I had to at the Picasso and Matisse. They seemed older, more gallant. More avuncular. Less mean.

I made sketches for hours. I came home to rest on the dove-colored sheets and went back to the Brera and sketched some more. I was hardly with him. I was distracted during marvelous meals, wanting them to be over, resenting the time it took the charming waiters to bring our food. Every pleasurable distraction seemed a snare. I wanted to be working. Because of this, I could see that compared to him, I wasn't a very good traveler.

It wasn't only because I was distracted by my work. I'm not a very good traveler because I can't stand feeling ignorant, a legacy of my abashed and law-abiding father. And in Europe I often suffer cultural shame for what America has done to the face of the world. Each McDonald's is my fault, each poster of Sylvester Stallone plastered against the stones of a palazzo. I believe that America has made the world uglier, and it is a sin I find unforgivable.

He didn't feel that way. Perhaps it wasn't only the difference between my living by the eye and his not. Our first experiences of Europe were different. I came first in 1968, and everywhere I went, every fellow student I talked to, I felt I had to apologize about Vietnam. "It's my country, but it isn't me. It's the government, not the people," I'd say, over and over, my backpack on my back. Even though I knew that wasn't true: my parents, my aunts and uncles, most of the people in my neighborhood in Queens were committed to the war. Their sons were there.

He came first in '73, a bandanna around his forehead, carrying James Brown records and nickel bags. He sat in the Dam in Amsterdam for a month, stoned, and knew that all the Dutch kids were trying to copy him and his friends. Five years earlier in Amsterdam I was in the Rijksmuseum, apologizing to the boy who'd brought me to see the Vermeer.

"Everybody wants to be American," B said. "We're not forcing them to copy us."

"We seduce them with speed and convenience," I said.

"We seduce them with freedom and honesty. And what were we doing in Vietnam but following the French? I'm not going to apologize to a continent that put millions of Jews in ovens and invented Fascism."

"And also Gothic architecture and perspective and easel painting."

"That was a long time ago. What have they done for us lately? Except give asylum to terrorists and reinvent nationalism."

I couldn't stand him when he talked that way. When I had to think of him as the Ugly American. As I did in front of the lacy façade of the Milan Cathedral. We were standing at the doors admiring the stone saints. A Gypsy woman pressed herself against my side. Her face was a mask of desperation, but obviously just a formality, a mask put on for an audience. Underneath that mask was coldness and calculation and indifference to the fate of anyone not hers, a deep disconnection from those she walked among, a knowledge that anything could happen to her, no one would lift a finger, so that anything she thought of doing was all right, one thing was as good as another, since she had a belly empty as a drum and children with empty bellies who could be used for what she needed. And for what they needed. Underneath that layer was a genuine desperation, so habitual she probably no longer knew it was there.

She was pulling on the bag I carried at my shoulder. She was telling me she needed money for her baby, whom she held in a shawl at her breast. Her older child, who stood beside her, crying, coughed deeply; it was a wet cough I knew from my own children. Only in this case I was afraid it was tuberculosis.

Oh, I was frightened. I felt her will to harm. I felt she had a right to harm me. The whole expenditure of this journey suddenly seemed as rotten as a luxury hotel that crashed because of a decrepit beam. The money I had spent, that he had spent, on a teddy that reminded us of the color of the Hudson in winter would feed her and her children for two weeks. The money that had been spent in order for me to look at a five-hundred-year-old painting, in order to create one more painting in a world already overfull of paintings, could have allowed her, perhaps, to have shelter instead of a life on the street for, maybe, a year. And she was only one of hundreds of thousands, millions.

I was frightened; he was angry. He considered her a thief. I thought she was the face of justice. I told myself that if I could do anything to relieve the world's poverty, I would do it. But I didn't allow myself to speculate very long about what that might be.

Like a Victorian with a Baedeker, I concluded that the poor were impossible. I wished they could be kept out of sight while I was seeing what it was I'd come to see.

I couldn't think about it. I had to tell myself that, for the present, it was better that I did my work.

I have to keep telling myself, but I never quite believe it. I believe we will all be horribly punished by the angel of justice, who will not be exalted, shining, carrying a sword, but filthy and vengeful, with closed, hard eyes.

He believes that the most important thing for me is to do my work. I don't know what he believes about the poor. I never want to ask.

I saw that his failure to feel inferior to Europeans gave him a freedom I couldn't have. He bumbled through on his ten words of Italian; I was paralyzed if my nouns and pronouns didn't match. He was more naturally curious than I. Being in a new place itself delighted him. He could walk forever. He didn't care where he ended up. And he wasn't afraid of being lost.

I was a good walker, but it was impossible for me to simply walk. I was always walking *somewhere;* I was always afraid of missing THE REAL THING, the thing the right people had seen—those connoisseurs of travel who wrote those books and knew what there was to know, those learned men with the proper things in their luggage and the names of the good people to call in every city, every village, every jungle outpost, every cluster of mountain huts. I was so terrified of missing the real thing that I often missed a sight on the way to the real thing. He was interested in seeing anything he hadn't seen before. I would walk like a rhinoceros to the church of St. Ambrogio; he would point out a pot of flowers on a balcony. He would make me stop. I didn't know whether I liked stopping or not.

We had very different responses to being lost. I always feel that if I'm lost I'll never be found, I will be disappeared. And then there's the difference between living in a male and a female body. A female wanderer stands for terror; a woman on a city street alone at night makes us feel in danger. A man alone has the possibilities of adventures and romance.

So I guess it's a combination of all those things that made me so crazy when we got lost that night walking from the restaurant to our hotel. When, suddenly, we found ourselves on the verge of what had turned from a metropolitan avenue to a four-lane highway with no notice. Was it shame or fear that made me say to him: "How can you have gotten us into this situation? How can you have done this to me?"

I'd never have talked that way to another woman. I would have behaved well, thought rationally, dealt with it, worked as a team.

If often occurs to me what a morally weakening thing it is to be with a man.

That night, I was so angry at him for getting us lost that I slept far away from him at the edge of the bed. In the morning he stroked my belly while I was still sleeping, like a cat making circular motions. Padding around. I wanted to be punitive, but I was aroused. Sometimes I resented not being able to hold a grudge against him because of my desire.

I don't think he was tempted to hold grudges against me.

I don't know if this had to do with nature, gender or money. Or none of them. Or all.

He was very good to me in Milan. We made love. We ate two spectacular meals a day. Between meals I spent my days in front of the Mantegna. We did this for a week, a week only. Long enough for me to feel I knew the picture, but not so long that we'd lose the effect of the frame: this extravagant surround we'd made just to see one painting. A time that was devoted to one thing only. A pilgrimage with a beginning and an end, made possible only by money.

But because of the money, I always wanted him to believe he had no automatic right to sex. I always liked to feel that I was on the verge of saying no.

That was very rarely the case. But I wanted him to consider it.

I know the importance of the look of things. So, naturally, I was tempted to suggest to him that he find someone younger. One of the thousands, millions of young women with perfect breasts and thighs and—in the words of a video I once spent twenty bucks on—buns of steel. I thought that if I were a man I'd do that, I wouldn't be able to resist, because the visual bombardment of beautiful female flesh is constant. Why not an eighteen-year-old with honey-colored arms and dark pink nipples, with no legible marks of childbirth, without the inscriptions or incisions of fifty years?

He said he knew all about it, he'd done that, and he wanted me. He said it got boring, and above all I should understand how terrible it was to be bored. I said, "But can the visually beautiful ever be boring?"

He said, "Weren't you ever bored by your kids?"

And I remembered that I never found them unbeautiful but that sometimes I felt that if I didn't have an interesting conversation with someone, I would die, that after a while the touch of that beautiful skin wasn't enough.

"Is that what it's like?" I asked him.

"Yes," he said. "Now do you understand?"

I did, sort of, but I didn't quite believe him. I didn't want to talk much about it, though. I was afraid I'd change his mind, that I'd make such a good case I'd lose, whatever else, a lot of fun.

And the sex did make the work better. I was a lively body, looking at bodies. The rind that covers the sexual underskin when you're not having sex, the one that keeps you from despair, was pulled back. The fruitlike flesh was exposed, palpable and porous as the skin of an orange. A blood orange, a mixed color, orange bleeding into red. After sex, I was free of anger and bitterness. What others did, how they'd moved ahead of me, how I hadn't got what I deserved and they'd got so much more, all that was melted. What's it called when something disappears on brass or copper, and the fresh plate is there, ready for impressions? That's how I was after we'd been together; a peeled fruit, a fresh copper plate. That was how I worked when I left his bed and went to the Brera. It almost frightened me to feel so alive.

We got home on the first of December and I was determined that nothing would interfere with my work. I'd give Christmas two days, and I'd go out with B on New Year's Eve. But that was all.

We settled into a routine. We spoke every morning, we saw each other two or three nights a week. He asked me a lot of questions about teaching, and knew enough to keep his mouth shut about the painting. I never asked him anything about his work, and he never volunteered anything.

We never talked about it because if we did we'd be talking about money. And we both felt there was something a little unseemly about that. Or maybe only I felt it. But isn't money supposed to stand for shit? Doesn't everyone believe that?

Like shit, money is to me simultaneously boring and terrifying. Something all of us think about more than we admit, find really interesting as an object, but don't talk about, because we think we're too refined. People who have no stake in refinement will talk about both. Money and shit. Like my mother, who asks what everything costs, and is genuinely fascinated by the relationship of what she eats and how she shits. I'd hear her say, "You know I have to stay away from things like romaine lettuce because the whole leaf just comes out in one piece."

Or, "I was terrified because I saw all this red in the toilet then I remembered I had beets for supper." It was the kind of thing that made my sister and me cringe, the kind of thing that made us want to go far away to college. To another continent. I think we would have signed up for space travel if NASA recruiters happened to be around when my mother started talking about shit. Or if we'd been alive in the Age of Exploration we'd have tried to get a place on the *Niña*, the *Pinta* or the *Santa Maria*.

And of course, we would never have admitted that we found our own shit interesting, would never have had the courage to come out on the occasion of a bathroom visit, after a light breakfast, with the day ahead of us, a few simple pleasant tasks, and say, "I've just had a very successful shit. I am very proud of myself. I feel like I've really accomplished something." It would be the truth, but we'd never dream of saying it.

People who think of themselves as cultivated say that money is abstract, but they forget the pleasure of counting coins or bills, making piles of them, putting them in order, looking at the faces of the presidents. They think that money is only symbolic or only material.

They think it's the root of all evil, or the most desirable thing in the world. They wish it didn't exist, or they wish they had unlimited amounts of it. They say they wish it didn't exist but probably they're lying because if it didn't exist there'd be a terrible hole, as if you'd uprooted an oak from your lawn. They say all kinds of terrible things or untrue things about it. But at least, whoever said those stupid things was willing to talk about it.

I never was. I never spoke about it to B. Was that insulting, not to speak to him about what he did all day? I suppose so. But it was better than what I would have said if I'd told the truth. "I think what you do is boring, probably a bad thing for the world, and a bit disgusting. Nevertheless, what you do enables me to do the things I want to do, which I believe to be fascinating, important and beautiful."

I couldn't have said that to him, could I? It was much better to say nothing.

But I knew he knew what I thought.

*        *        *

I was preparing to call the girls to tell them they wouldn't be able to count on my company during winter break. If they wanted to stay in the city they'd have to stay with their father. Roger was perfectly agreeable; he loved his role as the "new man," and Merrill said something nice about blended families. I was happy to let her deal with everything until Sara's call.

The first sentence wasn't promising. "I just got back from the infirmary."

I panicked. She'd been in a car crash. She'd taken an overdose. She was going to die.

"I've got mono, Mom."

I knew she'd been tired all semester; she'd complained of it every week. I'd put it down to Sophomore Slump. I'd sent her expensive vitamin C from the health food store and lectured her about staying up late. When she told me she was sleeping a lot, I thought she was just humoring me.

Why hadn't I listened to her more closely? Why hadn't I phoned her more often? Why had I accepted the Health Service's verdict that there was no need to test her for mono? Why hadn't I insisted that she come back to New York and see our internist? Why hadn't I gone up to Northampton to spend a day with her? Why had I concluded that her fatigue was based on depression and not an organic cause?

I knew that the answer to all those questions was: work. If you asked me, I would have said my daughters were the most important thing in the world to me, but I hadn't behaved that way. In my own defense (and I definitely wanted someone to defend me) I'd come to think of them as independent women, women whom I'd launched into the world. Of course the launch is never complete.

The doctor at the Health Service suggested that Sara not take her finals, that she postpone them until she was stronger. I blasted him.

"Why didn't you give her a test for mono when she asked for one in November?"

"It was a judgment call," the doctor said.

"What the hell is that supposed to mean? What would the obverse of that sentence be? It wasn't a judgment call? Like you could stick her in an electron microscope and get a computer printout?"

I had no idea what an electron microscope did, but it sounded scientific and dire. My sister is a doctor with the World Health Organiza-
tion in Geneva; I was planning to have her call the doctor and make him
feel ashamed.

"I don't think this conversation is productive," the doctor said. "I
understand that you're distressed about your daughter's condition, but
we need some information from you now. Do you want me to put her
on the train or will you come and get her?"

That is what he said. What I heard was, "Are you going to come and
get her, or are you an even more shamefully neglectful mother than we
had imagined?"

This call took place at nine in the morning. I said I'd be there by suppertime. There was a small problem in that I didn't have a car. If
Michael couldn't lend me his, I'd rent one. I had that extra financial mar-
gin now. I could do it without thinking twice. I wouldn't even have to deal
with Rent-A-Wreck, as I had when I rented a van in the summer.

Thinking of that made me think, of course, of B. I wanted to hear
his voice. It wasn't that I needed his advice, but I longed for the sound
of him, the voice of someone who didn't think I was remiss, who
thought of me as desirable. I wanted this before I called Roger to tell
him about Sara, or Michael to see if I could borrow his car, or Theresa
for assurance that I wasn't a monster mother, the objective correlative
of every antifeminist diatribe against the unnatural effects of work on
any kind of maternal instinct. Theresa's kids are ten years older than
mine, and they'd all prospered, even though when they had the flu, she
sometimes left pills in little cups with taped instruction about what
time each should be taken. She often said: "The secret of successful
motherhood is benign neglect."

Of course, her Robert was a better father than Roger; in a way he
was more traditionally maternal than Theresa, and she was the first to
admit it. I knew Theresa would point out that it didn't occur to me to
share the blame with Roger, and that Sara had some responsibility, at
twenty, for her own health. But I wanted to hear B's voice before I
heard Theresa's slightly impatient reassurance or Michael's reluctant
willingness to lend his car.

I'd had children and B hadn't; it was the reason I rarely talked to him about Rachel and Sara. For one thing, I wasn't sure he'd be interested, and for another, I didn't want him thinking it was too bad he hadn't gotten around to fatherhood. I didn't know what I wanted him to say when I called. That it didn't matter if I'd failed my daughter because I was a great artist and the sexiest person who ever lived? I wanted to hear his voice.

He told me that he'd had mono in college, that it wasn't so bad, that Sara probably just needed her mother. Then he said, "It's sort of a blow to your plans for full-out work."

I denied it vehemently. In fact, I'd forgotten all about those plans: I'd been too busy feeling worried and guilty.

"If I remember," he said, "she'll mainly want to sleep. She won't need much attention. It might be sort of cozy, having her warm and covered up right near you. Maybe it will make it easier to work, remembering there are other parts of your life."

"You say that because you never were a mother," I said.

"That's perfectly true. And I've come to terms with the fact that I never will be a mother. It's one of those instances of midlife reconciliation."

He was right that I, however ambivalently, wanted Sara near me. I could have gotten Roger to pick her up. I could have gone through Merrill, told her I understood that Roger was at a crucial point in his work—which would have been bullshit, he was always, or never, at a crucial point in his work, since he didn't really know how to work—but I needed his help. But I wanted to gather up my wounded bird. I was broody: I could feel the emptiness of the empty nest.

The old ache came back: desiring, needing my children, along with the fear that whatever I did was wrong. Being with the children, or even missing them, meant I wasn't really a serious artist, and thinking about painting, being distracted, wanting to paint when I was with the children, meant I wasn't really a good mother. These feelings had disappeared pretty much, since the girls had been at college, but they came back, like an old injury.

I'm not even sure whether I really wanted to nurse Sara or whether I didn't want anyone else to. Sara was a very satisfying person to nurse.

If Rachel had come down with mono, she'd have hitched to New York, refused to see my internist, consulted a homeopath and worked on convincing her that smoking wasn't incompatible with homeopathic treatment. Sara didn't have Rachel's independence, or her cunning. She was more fragile, but then anything's more fragile than a Mack truck, which is how Rachel always seems to me. Except those times when she collapses (usually because someone's hurt her feelings by telling her she's a Mack truck) and she becomes my baby again, trying to sit on my lap although she's twenty and three inches taller than I am. Sara is more tolerant, more comforting, and more susceptible to comfort. When they were little, I used to hold myself back, not ask too much from Rachel, not depend on her; I used to hold myself back, from going to Sara for comfort.

B offered to lend me his car. I hesitated; I was a little nervous taking the Beach Boys special onto the highway. If I racked up Michael's '87 Honda, it wasn't that much of a loss. But I convinced myself that I was borrowing the GTO for Sara. It would be more comfortable, and there was a terrific sound system. Sara's a music major; I thought it would be soothing for her to hear her favorite CDs and cassettes while we drove.

All her friends were sitting in her room. She was dressed, but lying on the bed wrapped in her comforter. Her friends looked at me as if I were taking the czarina to Siberia. They hugged her and cried. They told her she was incredibly lucky to be missing finals. I told them to visit during vacation, though I hoped they wouldn't because already, even before the desired caretaking had begun, I was worrying about my work.

"Does this car belong to the man who's giving you the money?" Sara said.

"You've been talking to your sister," I said. "She thinks I'm a sex worker."

"Well, that's Rachel."

"You don't agree?"

"Mom, I don't think you could do anything bad that was related to your work."

"That's not true, Sara. I could kill someone and say it was for my work. That wouldn't be good."

"You sound like Rachel, Mom. But think about it. That wouldn't be possible. It wouldn't be in your character to murder someone. Anything you would do that would be in your character and about your work would necessarily be a good thing."

I was touched by that, and comforted. I squeezed Sara's hand, but she'd already drifted off to sleep. It was wonderful to be in the luxurious closed space of the large car with my sleeping girl, listening to Handel, watching the gray stubble of the harvest corn on the gray brown fields softened by a dusting of light snow.

For three days, I devoted myself to making soup and custard, to juicing not only oranges but tangerines and mangoes. I worked for an hour or two a day. It wasn't that Sara was demanding; it wasn't like having a toddler you couldn't take your eyes off of. But my awareness of her shattered my concentration.

And people kept coming to visit. Roger and Merrill and Kerry, their five-year-old. Theresa came by to play Scrabble. Michael brought his entire collection of *Thin Man* tapes. A friend of Sara's from Watson, at Columbia now, seemed to come by at all hours. I found it hard to go to my studio, and when I got there, I spent a lot of time wringing my hands over my lack of focus, then castigating myself for wringing my hands.

And I didn't feel I could leave her to spend time with B. He'd sent a box of Florida grapefruit for Sara, and she was very nice about it. She said maybe she could meet him soon. I told her I wasn't ready. She laughed. "This is role reversal, Mom. Those are supposed to be my lines."

"Speaking of which, who is this Jeremy who keeps calling?"

"I'm not ready to talk about it, Mom," she said.

Which was fine with me.

One night, when she seemed pretty much on the mend, I suggested that her friend from Columbia stay over, that I give myself a night with B. I told him I was in a state of self-pity. I needed to be pampered. I was practicing the sentence "peel me a grape."

"What exactly do you think that grape was peeled with?"

"Teeth," I said. "Lips and tongue. You remember."

"They ring a bell."

I'd never gone to his apartment before. Because of the money. I'd always wanted sex to be on my turf, so I'd feel I could ask him to leave in the middle of the night if I wanted to. If I were at his house, on Forty-seventh and the East River, I'd have had to worry about getting a cab.

But I needed to be with him too much to be making that sort of point.

His building was modern and it had one of those circular driveways that makes you think a lot of limos might be pulling up. The lobby's walls were some variation of stucco; there was a horrid abstract sculpture that I think was supposed to represent the sun—thousands and thousands of dollars' worth of brass that could have been made into something perfectly useful.

Compared to mine, his apartment was empty. In the living room were two of my paintings, and a sculpture made of terra-cotta in the shape of a wreath, with animals inside that looked like goats and maybe lianas. The furniture was black leather; the coffee table, glass and chrome. Except for the paintings, the place could have belonged to anyone.

On his CD player, clearly worth my children's college tuition, was a solo violin passage. The music was yearning, haunting, climbing, climbing up; then another violin joined it. The conversation promised no cessation of yearning, only yearning with the ante endlessly upped, no satisfaction; no end of loneliness.

"Whose music is that?" I asked.

"Telemann," he said.

"I can't believe it, Telemann does all that hyperactive court stuff."

"Sorry, it is," he said, and showed me the CD case. "How much does it annoy you that you were wrong and I was right?"

"How much does it please you?" I asked.

"Very, very much."

We were still at the stage when kissing seemed a worthwhile effort, not just something you began with. He happened to be just the kind of

kisser I liked. Some people just stuff their tongues in your mouth and
flop them around like a beached whale; some people can't keep their
teeth out of the business. But his tongue was quick, never too heavy,
never too insistent. We sat on his couch and watched the boats go
down the river. The music rose and fell. It reminded me of that invisible string that he was playing, fretting it, as the violinist fretted the
string, pressing down, letting up, traveling, arriving, repeating the gesture till the moment was complete. As the notes climbed, reached,
strove, his finger moved and I gave myself up to the movement of the
music, tensing when it tensed, then losing it, traveling past it, but followed by it, till I fell back on the couch and listened to the andante
that no longer had anything to do with me.

I spent Christmas with Roger and Merrill and little Kerry and the girls.
We escaped going to Florida to be with my mother because of Sara's
mono. I convinced her that Sara was highly contagious; my mother's
too narcissistic to expose herself to infection.

The day after Christmas, the rest of them, including Sara, drove
down to North Carolina to be with Merrill's family. There was nothing
in my way. I had no more excuses. It was time for me to ask him to
pose.

I had to ask him for something that might be more difficult than the
things he'd given me: sex and money. Something that wasn't his idea. I
was asking him for his presence—to look at him, observe him, then
present him. Re-present. That's what representation means, doesn't it:
presenting again.

I'd have to ask him to give me the right to the image of his desired
body, for which no other could be substituted. ACCEPT NO SUBSTI-
TUTES, I heard a stern voice saying, not a TV voice, an older, more official voice, a voice from radio. I'd have to ask him to be simultaneously
absent and present in his life. Of course I'd be there, looking at him in a
way that would be impossible to ignore, but I wouldn't be there with his
body as he knew it. I'd be there with the image of his body that was in
my eye and that I would be trying to bring into the work.

I could understand that it might be lonely for him, that he might
feel morose, or even mad. He'd have to be able to accept himself as

himself and as my creature, he'd have to lose himself and yet inhabit himself fully so that I could make an image of that thing that indicated HIMSELF to the world. And all the time, he'd have to know that the woman looking at him, stealing from him, consuming him, erasing then re-creating him, would be someone whose body he would later look at and then enter, whom he would lose himself to and who'd lose herself to him. I thought it might be too much to ask.

But then I thought, too fucking bad. Women have been doing it for their artist lovers for centuries. What's your problem, I wanted to say to him, your cock?

Of course it is a problem, isn't it? A problem or a case. The case of the cock. Not a problem in the sense of acid rain, but for a painter, a formal consideration. No other body part changes so dramatically, so quickly and in such a fickle way. You can say, for example, that the skin changes with age. It matures or it degenerates, or it alters with disease or mutilation. But with these changes there's no going back. You can't have the skin of a child one minute, then the skin of a forty-year-old, then back to the child.

So you have to ask yourself, when you're thinking about a cock: which is the true one, which is the false? Is one a mask for the other? Limp, there's something of the abashed little animal about it, peering out of the brush, blinking in the light. Then, suddenly, something much more like a divining rod, or a branch in the wind, or a long-legged bird. There's no way of painting the transformation. No middle ground that represents a change, in the way that the head of Vermeer's girl in a turban gives at once the impression of turning toward the viewer and turning away. No way to express the delight a lover feels when it's in her hand or mouth: proof positive. Delight, like the expression on the face of the Vermeer girl looking at her strand of pearls. And disappointment when it goes down. The pearls purloined.

The hardening cock as pearl of great price. The softening cock as lost treasure.

No wonder men are so reluctant to be looked at. They don't know what to show.

More and more I began to think of what an unusual thing it is for a woman to be looking at a man's body.

Looking at women's bodies was something men have always been told was a good thing. "I will lift up mine eyes unto the hills." And we know what hills were meant. "Standing on the Corner Watching All the Girls Go By." The wolf whistle. The strip tease.

But women have been told to live with our eyes cast down. Warned against male beauty, warned to keep our eye on one ball only: the ball of the good provider. When women were first allowed to study painting formally in the nineteenth century, they couldn't look at the male nude. For them, marble and plaster. Statues. Casts.

Of course, in some way, I've been looking at men all my life.

I remember that when I was fifteen my best friend Diane Milano's aunt drove up from Florida. She had dyed red hair and drove a Thunderbird convertible. Also, I think, red. She took us out for ice cream one summer night. I guess she was bored. She said, "Girls, the first good-looking guy we see, we're going to follow him to see where he goes." I remember giggling in the dark with Diane, being scared about what would happen. What would we do if he turned around? Came over to us? Tried to get in the car?

I know we did follow someone, but I have no memory of what he looked like. I think I forgot it because it was too peculiar, too frightening: three women looking at a man.

I have clear memories of being struck by the images of men. One was when my cousin Frank came back from Korea in his soldier's uniform. The story was that I took my first steps to Frank. I don't know whether that was true, but one of my earliest visual memories was of his hard oxblood shoes—later when I learned the word oxblood I was excited by it, it seemed to match the thing so perfectly. Afterward when I learned the same color could also be called cordovan I was momentarily elated, then let down. I remember another man, who dated my aunt Linda. His name was Jack and they called him Black Jack: his hair was wavy and sticky, and it seemed more like a food than something growing from his body. And I remember being disturbed because when he took his shirt off on the beach his nipples seemed too dark against his white hairless chest.

My father was barely visible. When I say I hardly saw him, I mean it in two ways, both of them literal. He was always working, always at the bakery. He left the house at four in the morning and got home after nine. He was also a man who didn't think of himself as visible. Or even audible. He was kind, but he did almost nothing but work. He died of it, at sixty-four. Died happily, shoving loaves into the oven.

As I was thinking all these things about looking at men, seeing men, I called B to ask him to pose. I knew I was incapable of asking him if I could use his body unless his body was, at that moment, a thing I couldn't see.

I spoke rapidly, like a teenager. Like a Valley girl, really. I sounded foolish and guilty.

"Can I think about it?" he asked.

"Yes, but not too long. And you really need to bear in mind that you have a responsibility to do it. It's part of your bargain, remember. Think of all those women taking off their clothes for all those men. Think of all you have to make up for."

"The way you put it is so subtle, so full of possibility. I suppose I have no choice."

"Right. Thanks," I said, and hung up.

I didn't tell him I wanted to paint the way he looked just after he'd come. I wasn't going to make him pose in postorgasmic triste right away. I wasn't going to be that insensitive. I would have liked to, but I was afraid it wouldn't work. I'd have to lead up to it.

I was feeling anxious and irritable waiting for him that night. I knew I wouldn't be able to concentrate on anything important, so I made myself do things that needed doing. I answered three letters and sewed a button on my brown jacket. I went through my pocketbook, in which two days earlier the cap of my Advil had come off, paving the bottom of the bag with rose brown pills. Or caplets, as they're called.

I played back the eight messages on my answering machine. I felt overwhelmed by the number and the variety of my connections. My friends. My children. Ex-students. My mother. Someone who owned a painting. The pharmacist. The man who does my taxes. My dentist, also something of a friend. There were days when I couldn't face the machine's blinking red light; I threw a shawl over it, or I put the whole contraption in a drawer. Some weeks, I didn't look at my mail either. I often missed important information. But when I was working hard, I didn't care.

I didn't want to answer the eight calls. And then, I turned that disinclination into an anger against B. Often, in the middle of nowhere, I'd get angry at him. Something would bloom up, a dark Georgia O'Keeffe iris—not that I'm not sick to death of Georgia O'Keeffe—and I'd start feeling rage against him, against the fact that he was giving me money, that he had something I needed, and that he could stop my having it anytime he wanted.

Now he was giving me something else I needed, something he could also take away. He was going to pose for me. My gratitude needed to be doubled. I had to think about the nature of my obligation.

Gratitude and obligation are not sentiments that (in my case, but it must be that way with most people, mustn't it?) soften the tarlike layers of the heart, or anyway its moral chamber. When I feel I ought to be grateful, when I feel a sense of obligation, I turn into a rebellious slave. I will destroy the cotton gin or set the plantation on fire. I will overturn the galley, I will incite my fellow rowers to bloody revolt.

I was ready to pick a fight with him the minute I heard the buzzer ring downstairs. I stood in the door frame, looking belligerent. But then, the sight of him was always pleasing to me. As he came into the light, closer to me, I had to work to feel antagonistic. And then there was his smell. Sweaty or fresh, out of the shower or after six hours of driving in the sun, on an airplane flight, lying on the sand after a swim in the ocean or in his best suit, wearing his English lavender—the sight and smell of him gave me pleasure. The minute my nose hit the collar of his coat, my objections to him melted. I was a happy animal. I couldn't help smiling. I guess animals don't smile, but mine felt like animal instinct. Before I saw him, I was planning to give him a long lecture on what was wrong with his life. Instead, I put my face to his shirt, and sniffed.

\*     \*     \*

"I HAVE something for you," he said.

I was hoping it was something delicious to eat, not sweet. Smoked mussels. Parmesan cheese we could have with red wine. Something to eat, rather than something to wear, because I was hungry. The day before I'd made a tomato sauce with black olives and I'd been thinking of it all day, the dark olives like a Morse code of serious flavor in the hyped-up red.

But he didn't have food for me. He opened his briefcase and took out a copy of *The New Yorker*. "It's an article about Stravinsky's wife, Vera," he said. "She used to be married to a painter. This is the list she made of the responsibilities of the Muse. I couldn't help identifying."

I opened the magazine to the page he'd marked, and read what he'd highlighted in yellow.

1. Force the artist to work, even with a stick.
2. Love his work no less than him.
3. Welcome every burst of creative energy. Kindle him with new ideas.
4. Keep the main works and the drawings, sketches and caricatures in order.
5. Relate to new works as if they were surprise gifts.
6. Know how to look at a painting for hours on end.
7. Be physically perfect and therefore his model forever.

I felt a great number of things reading that list. First, I was amazed that Stravinsky's wife, standing for all women like her, had actually written it down. More amazing was that she had consented to live that way: that we had to understand that living like that was an act, of volition, of understanding, not an instinct.

After that I felt angry: on behalf of the woman who'd set herself a task of such idolatry, then for myself, because it would be so impossible for me even to formulate such a list of demands. Demands for all those different and specialized forms of self-sacrifice, all those skills: dominatrix, courtesan, aesthetician, secretary, actress, scholar, model.

Then I was angry at B for assuming that all this self-effacement was what I wanted from him or anybody. All the pleasure I'd gotten from looking at him and smelling him disappeared.

"Let's just get a few things straight," I said, waving the magazine in front of his nose.

"Can I get a life vest first?" he asked.

"No, you just listen. I don't need to be forced to work, I don't need any new ideas from you or anybody. I don't need someone I fuck to keep my drawings in order. You don't have to look at my pictures for hours, I have Theresa for that, and my painter friends. I can trust their criticism, and I can tell them they're the stupidest people who ever lived—particularly Theresa. I remember saying once that it was astonishing that she was allowed to speak to students— more than astonishing, it was bordering on the criminal. I can be as childish as I like with friends. I can't with a lover."

"You could have fooled me," he said.

"And furthermore," I went on, not interested in listening. "I don't need you to make a life for me. I had a fine life before I met you. I enjoyed it. I can get downhearted and irritable and overwhelmed. I can get annoyed, I'm constantly annoyed at the attention and prosperity that people who are definitely my inferiors seem to be given. But underneath it all, and don't you forget it, Daddy Warbucks, I've had a good time. Do you know what was under my picture in the 1965 St. Augusta's Yearbook?"

"Astonishingly, I seem to have missed it."

"Well, I'll tell you what it said, it said, 'No one can be bitter who can lie in the sun.' "

"You were a little ahead of your time. Say two years. Sounds like something right out of the summer of love."

"This list is 85 percent bullshit," I said. "The only part I really agree with is the last. The one about the great body. I want your body in the shape it is now so I can go on drawing it. So watch the saturated fats."

I unbuttoned his shirt and pulled if off him. I threw it on the floor. I pulled his shoes off. I unzipped his fly and pulled his trousers quickly off his legs as if they were filthy. I took off his socks and threw them across the room.

"Now just stand there and let me look at you. Don't move. I'm going to get my pad."

I began sketching him. That sounds like a simple sentence but the two pronouns, I and him, were actually very complicated when they were connected to my sketching. I was his lover, someone who knew something of his life—the part of his life that could be called his biography—but I was looking at him merely as a series of planes, a series of angles, a series of shapes whose relation to one another I was trying to make manifest. He was a form that I would try to reproduce.

But that's not really true either. I'd wanted the image of him because his form was saturated in desire. I wasn't Matisse in his white pharmacist's coat.

It was because of what I felt for him as my lover that I'd asked him to pose.

Posing. Position. Deposition. It's about place, about putting someone in a place, his place. Or yours? And what's your position in relation to the sitter's? And what's his position in relation to you and to the world? I was copying a series of paintings whose formal name was *Depositions*. Christ was being de-posed. Did that mean his being on the cross was a pose? If he was being de-posed or displaced, where was he, or what was the painter painting? One of my interests was precisely the absence the figure represented, the absence after death or after sex.

I had a chance to think about those things quite a lot, because his posing for me went on for several months. So there were many phases. Sometimes, even in the course of a single day.

In the beginning, despite his tough-guy, I-don't-want-to-make-this-too-easy-for-you feints and dodges, I could tell he was excited by the prospect. Like a lot of amateurs, he would strike aesthetic postures: dreamy, thoughtful, or because he thought he knew what I was looking for, amorously dazed. I'd worked enough with inexperienced models to know that this was something I'd simply have to wait out, although I praised my saintly patience for not telling him to, for God's sake, knock it off. I believed that, eventually, boredom or fatigue would take over and something real might emerge. In his case, it was anxiety. When he stopped trying to be the defunct Savior, he became a man who was unable to let go of certain gestures of alarm. His shoulders naturally wanted to climb up around his ears, his eyes seemed most used to an expression of alert, terrified watchfulness.

At the beginning, I was most interested in him as a form, and in the formal prospects he created. While the process was new to him, he didn't seem to mind it. He kept telling me how exciting it was to feel he'd be the subject of a work of art, and how eager he was to see what he looked like. He said that people are always afraid they don't really know what they look like, that they're always waiting—hopefully or fearfully—for some new information.

During this period, he didn't seem to mind my absence from his life, my relating to him as an object rather than a person.

But the honeymoon, of course, ended. I knew it was over when, during one session, I became aware of a low rumbling noise. At first, I thought Mikey had spotted a cat, but I realized that was probably not possible in a closed apartment on the third floor. Gradually, I understood that it was B.

"What are you doing?" I asked, afraid that he was having a heart attack.

"Growling. I've been doing it for ten minutes. I couldn't stand the fact that you didn't know I was here."

"Of course I knew you were here. I was drawing you."

"You were drawing something. Some THING. But not me. It was making me feel panicky."

"Just don't get analytical. Take a break."

I tried to say this pleasantly, but since I wasn't ready to take a break, I really wanted to tell him what a self-indulgent, insecure child he was. But after a minute I had to understand that what I was doing to him was kind of awful, a theft, or perhaps a slow embezzlement. I offered him a back rub. Pretty soon it turned into a front rub. Our work was over for the day.

Sometimes, though, I'd get annoyed when he didn't tell me he needed to take a break, and I'd look up and see a tormented expression on his face, or, later that night, he'd ask for a massage because he'd suffered such terrible cramps.

"Why didn't you say something?" I asked.

"I didn't want to disturb you."

"You're my model, not my slave," I said.

"Only because you have no other options in this political system."

"That's not true. You know I hate slavishness. A good model knows how to be most truly himself when he's posing."

"I thought you wanted me to be the image in your mind."

"Just stop thinking about things you don't know anything about."

"Now, there's a real First Amendment position."

Some nights, we'd part angry with each other, a simple annoyance making us very glad we had separate addresses. Some nights, I could tell the experience had frightened him, and he wanted to get away from me so he could get his soul back. The soul he felt I'd eaten up. He said that sometimes he felt like one of the disappeared, one of those people in Latin America who are made to vanish without a trace. He said sometimes he felt I'd made him vanish, that he could walk on the earth without leaving a footprint.

Sometimes, though, this was mostly later, when I felt the formal problems weren't uppermost in my mind, my desire for him would become part of the process, and there would be a moment when our eyes would meet, our old eyes, the ones we'd seen each other with before we'd become painter and subject, and we would come together as we used to, remembering who we'd been.

Eventually, we worked out a system that was actually pretty efficient. I used a timer, as I did with a professional model: it rang after twenty minutes, we'd break for twenty, then go back. I didn't make him pose for me for any more than two hours. I would have preferred more, but I realized more than two hours was useless. And, really, I was grateful to him, I understood the magnitude of his generosity. After a while, he actually became quite good at it. He figured out that listening to Mahler created the possibility for the right level of zoning out. He asked me once if we were having sex so I could get him in the position I really needed afterward. I told him absolutely not, and it was true. Almost.

*        *        *

IT WAS SPRING. I was drawing a lot, copying details from Mantegna, Carpaccio, Sodoma, Pontormo, Caracci. And also drawing B. His lines were growing familiar to me as the lines of a vase I'd painted when I was doing still lifes, a chair, the spines of a leaf when I was absorbed in a world of leaves. And then the focus would shift and the lines would disappear, he was no longer a form marked by its exactness, I would dive down into the blurry world of yearning, my eyes half closed, my interest no longer in what he was in air, in space, in relation to other objects, but in relation to myself and other things invisible to me.

I was having a very good time. I love drawing. In my painting, the lines of the drawing are very clear, very defined. I think that's because using line to describe the world was my first love. I remember being nine or ten, it was winter, and I drew everything I could see out the window, every branch of every tree, a beech, a maple, and the lilac bush so large it could have been a tree. Knowing that I liked the winter trees better because the lines of the branches were more visible.

Theresa once said to me that I require my line to take a lot more responsibility than most artists do. I like my line to make a kind of clear sentence. So that, for instance, if I'm painting a tulip, instead of saying, "Beautiful tulip," it's saying, "Apricot parrot that budded three days ago and is now half open with the light hitting it at two o'clock on an April afternoon." I like that complete clarity. Clarity, not precision. Precision implies painstakingness, but that's not what I mean. For me, that clarity is like pure sex, when you give yourself up to knowing something that's not yourself, to doing something far beyond anything you really ought to be able to do. That feeling of impossibility. It's not a negative feeling.

I was doing other things than drawing that spring. Or one thing, and it was utterly absorbing. It wasn't directly connected to my work. I was looking for a new place to live.

Now, indulge me, because I'm going to talk about one of my favorite subjects: my new apartment. The apartment he bought for me.

We kept looking for places downtown. In Soho, in Tribeca, those neighborhoods where artists are supposed to live and work. And I wasn't happy. We kept looking at lofts that had a tremendous amount of what all those real estate people called square footage. Lots of light, lots of everything you'd think I'd want.

But nothing seemed to suit me. I couldn't stand everyone on the street looking so young, so well-dressed, so fit. I couldn't stand the postmodern stores that didn't carry anything in a size larger than a three. I kept being noncommittal about all the places the agents showed us. The woman who was "handling our file" was getting impatient, though she tried not to show it. When I think of her, I can only remember her drumming her candy red nails on a lot of flat surfaces; I felt she wanted to rake those nails over my uncooperative face, but she was thinking about her commission.

I don't know what would have happened if he didn't, one day, get straight to the heart of things. I think it happened when I said there was no good place to walk Mikey in Soho or Tribeca, and I began to rhapsodize on and on about the dog-walking culture of Riverside Park.

He said, "You know, I don't think you want to be downtown at all. I don't think you want to leave your neighborhood."

It was the first time I kissed him publicly. There is something remarkable about being understood, as if you were in a foreign country, and someone finally got the fact that you'd been asking for the bathroom. I began to say how important my pharmacist was to me, the dry cleaners, the stationery store. The filthy coffee shop where Michael and I had talked over everything. The fact that I could be at his or Theresa's in a couple of minutes.

B was right: I didn't want to leave the place that felt like home. I just wanted more room. It was as simple as that, but I hadn't thought of it, or I was too embarrassed by it to let it surface in my brain. I thought it was both unhip and unserious not to want to move downtown. I was afraid of what it said about my need for ordinary comfort. I don't mind admitting to the need for luxury but the importance of Joe and Tilda in the dry cleaners (she once sewed up a hem on my long skirt when I caught my heel in it on the way to a Watson fund-raiser: I was panicking—those East Side mothers—and she just knelt and stitched the hem while I was still wearing the skirt). I was embarrassed to say I didn't want to move out of the neighborhood because of things like that.

We changed realtors. We said we were interested in properties with a view of the river between Seventy-ninth and Ninety-sixth streets. Only there, we said.

When we walked into the first building with an apartment we were being shown, I knew it was exactly right. I loved the lobby; it looked like a semieducated teenager's fantasy of a castle. Twenties faux, but lovingly cared for. And I was crazy about the smell of the hallway when you got off the elevator; a smell of lumber, maybe cedar, almost a nursery smell, clean, but not antiseptic, and a suggestion of something from so far back in your memory that it probably couldn't be named. Only connected to other things from the same time: the smell of picture books with English illustrations of girls wearing capes or cloaks of ochre or burnt sienna or teal.

And when we walked through the door and I saw the view, I knew I was at home. The building was situated at the place where the river turns, so you could see water from the north, south and west windows. And as you walked into the living room, the Soldiers' and Sailors' Monument appeared. I would live with the words "The Brave Soldiers." From one window you could see the George Washington Bridge. From another, next to the monument, was a paving of red-and-white tile, very Italian looking, formal, in geometric patterns: a gathering place, a public location, where people would naturally meet. So that, before my eyes, any time I wanted it, I'd have the monument, the square. They'd be important parts of what I looked at every day, like one of those Masaccio frescoes, where people walk in and out of emptiness marked by monuments and good public design.

From the other window, there was a mansion that had turned into a yeshiva. I could see little boys with side curls playing ball and I knew there would always be the sound of children. Next to the mansion, on its property, was a huge tree that took up all the space where another building might have stood, stealing some of my view of the water. A zelkova, I later learned.

I walked into what I knew would be my studio. The light didn't feel like light coming through glass, light that was part of an interior. When you stood in the room, the light fell on you as if you and it were both outside. It was southern light, it would be best in the afternoon. But it wouldn't matter what time it was best. I knew that, however it felt, the light in that room would always be good. Good for me. Useful and inspiring. Nourishing light.

Going into what would be the bedroom, I realized that I could lie in bed and see the water. And off the bedroom, there was a decadent, wonderfully vulgar bathroom. Gray marble floors and walls. A mirror in the ceiling. When I sat on the toilet (which I thought I should do: there was a lot of money involved, after all, suppose I didn't like the toilet) I could see upside-down people walking their upside-down dogs in the ceiling mirror. The bathroom was a voluptuous place. Of course you'd sit in the bathtub for hours, making or getting ready to make love.

There were details I adored. The arch going into the living room. I decided I'd put a mirror on the opposite wall so I could have, reflected, an Alhambra of illusory arches. And in the kitchen, a blue ceiling, robin's egg to turquoise, which had been dropped two inches so that it seemed like a slice of floating sky.

"That is it, isn't it?" he said.

I couldn't stop smiling.

Then I realized there were only two bedrooms. The studio and the master bedroom. My girls couldn't live with me. It was impossible that it would be their home.

I had already decided, impulsively I suppose, but I always make important decisions a little wildly. I convinced myself that it would be good for them not to have the option, as so many of their generation did, of crashing back into the nest. I had to live in that apartment, I just had to. I knew it was a place where I would live fully and joyously, would fully and joyously work.


I was having fun, drawing a lot, picking out furniture, getting the apartment together.

I guess it was more than fun. Maybe a sense of the goodness of life, a sense of prosperity, of a world like a generous sun, illuminating, and providing warmth without a hint of future punishment. I could keep what I liked of my old furniture and get rid of what I didn't like. Don't think I'm too stupid to understand this was a metaphor. But it was more than that; I hadn't had a dining room, now I had one. I bought a Shaker table, pine too, green base, and six green Shaker chairs. I spent weeks deciding on a couch: a couch is an anguishing purchase; it can make or destroy a room. And I hadn't lost all maternal feeling; I knew I had to have a foldout so the girls could stay if they needed to.

The trouble with couches is that they can suggest so many bad things, discomfort being only the first among equals: evil burrowing into their upholstery, misery beneath the cushions, disease lurking in the frame. They can be too big, like a fat lady in a dress too small for her, or too little, like her pathetic, pint-size husband. Finally, I decided on two art deco love seats: one for each girl: rounded armrests, rounded legs (suggesting mother love, even if your real mother hadn't made a room for you), a ruby-colored linen. It seemed more resistant to TB or other debilitating plagues.

Packing up my old apartment, I was saying good-bye to my old life, or part of it. A part that was difficult, hard won, and yet satisfying: I'd done everything myself. I was saying good-bye to an incessant, bred-in-the-bone fatigue; but also to the pride and the self-love that kind of fatigue signals. I was bidding farewell to darkness and small rooms, but also to the sense that I had to be grateful to no one. Now I had light, and space, paid for in the currency of gratitude. And by what else?

I packed and then unpacked my linens and my dishes, memories of meals and sex and children's sickness. Travels. Reluctant, ambiguous or ecstatic acquisitions. I walked around my nearly empty new living room, marveling at the view that I could, properly and even legally, call mine. Can you own the sight of something? I felt I could. Sometimes I wanted to flap my arms; I felt I could fly through my new, light apartment.

And even when everything was moved in, even when the space was filled, weighted down, with my possessions, I had that feeling of lightness, the sense that I was just about to hit the road.

All that was easy. The gratitude was hard. Because I began to let myself feel grateful to him.

It happened in a moment, at a banquet where Theresa was getting an award. She's always getting awards. Robert's tired of being the only one he knows at the ceremony, so he usually makes me come. We sit together and clap outrageously. And sometimes there's good food; this time, very beautiful filet mignon sliced thin, and very cold. I couldn't wait to have it in my mouth. You know how wonderful steak can be when you've been too virtuous to have much of it.

An old student of mine served the salad. We said hello. Afterward, she came up to me. "You were a wonderful teacher, you were very important to me. I want to give you this." And she took an enormous branch of cherry blossoms that had been on the table and put it in my arms. Then she kissed me.

I felt purely happy. It was a spring night, late April. It had just rained and the air had a wet chill, but a suggestion of warmth at the same time. The air was wet and silvery. The Calgary pears were blooming and the moon was white on the blossoms and the leaves. I suddenly knew that I wanted to give the branch to B. I phoned him. I said, "Come down to the street, I have something for you."

I wanted to present it to him, outdoors, in the open.

He was waiting in front of his building. I gave him the branch, the flowering branch, and I kissed him very lightly. I felt very girlish giving it to him, and I ran away like a shy girl. I wanted him to be alone with the flowering branch. I wanted to think of him in a dark room with the pink-and-white flowers on the black branch. Then I would draw it.

I didn't want to be in the room with him. I wanted to imagine him. I didn't want to be part of the scene. I wanted him to be alone in a room with my gift. I wanted to think of him in a room alone without me, holding a flowering branch, the sign of my gratitude.

Later that night he called and said, "Come and spend the night here with these wonderful blossoms."

The apartment was, of course, itself: anonymous, and lightly tenanted. There was the black leather, glass-and-chrome furniture. There were my paintings on the wall. The computer terminal. The desk with papers spilling onto the floor. And in a brass wastebasket, full of water, the blossoming branch.

It was the first time I'd spent the night in his apartment. I'd stayed with him in Provincetown, but that had a holiday feeling to it; this seemed serious. I felt like a bit of a stranger, and the girlishness that had accompanied my feeling of gratitude reemerged when I undressed for bed. Bed in both its senses; we were going to make love, and we were going to sleep. I was reticent, a follower; my passivity intrigued and then aroused him. I kept my hands at my sides. He was the host; the leader.

In the morning, I pretended to be asleep while he made coffee in the kitchen and brought it in on a tray. He buttered my English muffin and asked if I'd like marmalade or jam.

"I'm surprised at how much I like being served," I said.

"Oh, really?" he said. "No one who knows you is surprised."

"Shut up," I said, and put his hand between my legs.

The next week I moved into my new place. I allowed myself four days of housewifery, or property-owning reveling. Then it was the fifteenth of May.

It was time to get to work.

PART *Two*

I stayed at his house that summer. It wasn't an easy decision. Nothing touching money ever is.

I'd known I was going to do it for a long time, I guess; he'd suggested that I stay there when we first met. But it wasn't until March, when Larry called, supposing he was nailing down the usual arrangements for my renting his little house, that I realized this year was different. I wasn't going to the little house, I was going to the big house. When I said that, I kept thinking of "the big house," as in prison, and "the big white house," as in plantation. You can see the element common to both.

I felt bad about letting Larry down, so bad that I kept putting it off. This is the kind of thing I often do: I make everything worse for everyone in order to spare them the pain I know I'm going to cause them eventually. I'm like a doctor who lets a patient die of gangrene rather than amputate a toe.

B saw that the question of Larry's house was driving me crazy.

"I have an idea," he said. "Why don't we rent Larry's house and you can offer it to your daughters? What are they doing this summer?"

"Rachel's working in a lab in Boston and Sara doesn't know what she's going to do. She was thinking of waitressing."

"Why not suggest that she get a job in Provincetown and live in Larry's house?"

"She'd need a car."

"She can use yours. We can both use mine. I don't really need it when I'm in the city."

"What about driving back and forth?"

"I'll fly, you can pick me up in Provincetown."

"You'd do that?"

"Well, I'm hoping it will encourage you to let me spend more time in my own house."

"It's your house," I said petulantly. "Which is why I don't like the whole plan. Maybe I should stay at Larry's as I always have. I can just see the whole summer going down the toilet."

"And I'm the automatic flush."

"Don't do this to me. This is what I was afraid of. You put me in an impossible situation. You provide the money. And now the house. And we're lovers, but I'm also your employee. As your lover, I should want your company. But as your employee, or your investment, or whatever it is I am, I need to be alone to do my work. I need to have days that don't have someone's shadow in them. I need to think that I can eat whenever I want, sleep whenever I want, shut up or talk whenever I want. Your presence casts a shadow. I'm not saying it isn't a desirable shadow, and that it isn't good at absorbing the glare."

"Then maybe we'd better forget Sara and leave Larry's house for you to go to when my presence gets intrusive."

"Then I'd have to keep moving my things. I'll just stay in Larry's house as I always have."

"I don't know whether you're being purposely exasperating, but you're succeeding. Why don't you try staying in my house? If you have to move things, we'll hire the seven Santini brothers. All seven of them. Vito, and Aldo, and Tony and Sal and Sneezy and Grumpy and Doc. I'll leave you alone for a few weeks."

"Two weeks," I said. "After that you can just stay in the city during the week like a normal red-blooded American . . ."

"Husband?"

"I would never say a thing like that to you. I happen to have too much respect, to say nothing of affection."

"All right, so I leave you alone for two weeks, then I come up on the weekends. Am I allowed an extended vacation?"

"Yes, but not for a while. How about August? That's what you used to do."

"All right."

"And if I don't like having you there, I'll move into Larry's."

"Or you can even go for most of the weekends if I'm too much."

"Well, you might be. You don't know what it's like to have to fight your impulses to be a bimbo or a domestic servant because the person you're sharing the bathroom with has a cock."

"I missed the part about your impulse to servitude."

"But you got the bimbo part?"

"Absolutely," he said, unbuttoning my shirt.

On June 10, I packed up everything at Watson, and on June 12 I packed my rental van. Michael helped me, as he always did. Only this time, I could invite him to come for a visit. I had a place for him to stay.

It was hard for me to get used to having something luxurious that I didn't pay for by a kind of hardship that proved how high-minded I really was. Some austerity that suggested I was really roughing it. The problem with the Cape is that I always think it's too good for me. It's THE REAL THING—no, more than that, it's the best, and I always think the best things are for Protestants. Or Europeans. Or American Catholics educated by the Jesuits or the Mesdames of the Sacred Heart.

B and I shared an interest in class and its implications, we talked about it a lot. We both came from working people; his father owned a laundry. We grew up among people whose idea of a vacation was taking the train or driving a borrowed car to Jones Beach every day, then driving back at night. When we were young, it never occurred to us that we wouldn't always be the ones who waited two hours in an over-heating car or bus to get into a beach parking lot. That we wouldn't be lying on our six inches of sand next to fathers too abashed to take their black wingtips off. In those days we wouldn't think about ordering a hot dog or a hamburger; we ate our gritty sandwiches instead because it was cheaper. We grew up among people who planned all year to go to the Catskills for a week, swimming at a ratty little lake with a ratty dock, and who were grateful the whole year. They didn't think of it as automatic; they worried they might not have it again. Sometimes he and I would walk on the empty beaches of Truro, surrounded by protected and protecting dunes, no sign of cars, or blasting radios, knowing we could lie down on the beach and do all sorts of things with each other, with or without clothing, and no one would come along.

Once, when we were actually on an empty beach watching the sun go down and then staying there to look at the stars, we pretended we were teenagers on Jones Beach. It began when we were talking about how exciting it was to neck for hours in the dark next to several thousand other necking couples, but knowing you were never going all the way. Moments of high frustration when you ached from desire and your legs cramped from keeping them squeezed together.

"What was it like for a boy? Did your balls really turn blue like we heard?"

"No, but it was physically painful. Then you went home and brought yourself off. Although there were ways of bringing yourself off and the girl pretending she didn't know."

"What kind of morons did you go out with?"

"Judy Himmelfarb."

"She must have been left back."

"No, she went to Mount Holyoke."

"On an athletic scholarship."

"She's an endocrinologist now."

"Tell me about you and Judy."

"Ah, Judy Himmelfarb, how the name comes up, mixing memory and desire."

"Just get to the hot stuff," I said. We were feeling well fed and comfortable; we'd just had lobsters, which I'd cooked. He can't do it. He can't stand to hear their little claws climbing up the side of the pot, but it doesn't bother me. I believe it's their fate and they should give in to it gracefully.

We lay on an old army blanket on a part of the beach you could get to by walking down a stairway that leads from his house. He'd brought a bottle of Orvieto and two glasses. We lay and watched the stars, so thick they seemed almost dim, and the sea, ruffles of waves like twitching moustaches. Comic and provisional, not ancient and awe inspiring at all.

"Tell me about Judy. I'll do everything she did."

"Please don't," he said. "I'm in no shape for a hundred choruses of 'The Times They Are A-Changin'.' Judy was a very serious girl."

"OK, then, I'm not Judy. I'm a very frivolous girl. But not so frivolous I'm going to forget I have to be a virgin on my wedding night. So I'm telling you right now, nothing below the waist."

"And I know you mean it now but I'll be able to talk you into it."

"Never."

"Wait."

I let him touch my breasts but every time he tried to take off my underpants I jerked away violently. I moved my leg to where I could feel his hard-on, and I shifted my leg, up and down, back and forth pretending we were just kissing. Then I had second thoughts and pulled away.

"No more," I said.

"I just want to do this one thing."

"No."

"I'm not doing anything wrong."

"Don't take anything off."

"I promise."

And like the brilliant boy he was, the boy about to win every scholarship, he found what he was looking for without taking off my panties. He didn't say a word. Just did his job.

He began to insinuate his finger into the elastic around the crotch of my pants.

"No," I said.

"Shh," he said.

He put his hand inside my panties. "Look," he said. "I've been thinking about it and I think we know each other well enough to go all the way. I really respect you."

"Really?"

"Really a lot."

I took my own underpants off. He unzipped himself and entered me and finally I was the kind of girl I never was, and Judy Himmelfarb wasn't either.

"Do you know," I said to him once, but it was daylight and we were on our feet. "Even the sand here seems more expensive than Jones Beach. Less used."

"They probably paid retail for it," he said. "Goyishekop."

He'd explained to me that goyishekop, meaning, literally, the head of a goy, indicated the inherent stupidity of the goyim. I didn't tell him that my mother thought that "Jew you down" was a perfectly good synonym for the verb "to bargain." I hoped she never said it to Mr. and Mrs. Cohen, who ran the butcher shop next to my parents' bakery, and who were probably their best friends.

I asked B once if he could give up luxury. Or if it were taken from him, could he do without it. Go back to taking the train to the beach, standing in line in the bathroom to change into your bathing suit, your shoes picking up the wet sand that had fallen from somebody else's bathing suit, or that maybe someone had pissed in, then coming home, sandy and sticky, to sit in front of your fan.

"You're saying that because you think I couldn't live without it and you could."

"No, I'm saying it because I'm afraid that if I had to give it up now I'd turn bitter. I have the seeds of bitterness in me and I know I've learned to like good things too much."

"What's too much?"

"So much that I know I'd be unhappy without them."

"I think I probably want them too little. I have it in me to be one of those men who never shaves and sits all day in the dark. Who doesn't fix the broken furniture. Who has a filthy little fan he puts on a chair so it'll be the right height for the television. Your appetite for pleasure is more connected to things than mine. You could never disappear from sight."

I saw him disappearing, like an image on a TV screen, into a gray field, becoming a white dot, then nothing.

"But if you became one of those men, what would you do for sex?"

"Well, I guess that's what would drive me out of the lair."

"So you believe that however reclusive you became, if you eventually stumbled out in your dirty shirt and three days' growth of beard, you could still get laid."

"I guess so."

"Jesus, I feel like if I gain another ten pounds I'll be off the market for good."

"My God," he said, and he put his hand on me, cupping me as if he wanted to shield me from something. "You don't know much, for all you think you know. Don't you know the incredible power of what you've got there? Of the appeal of that endless responsiveness, and all its variety? There are things I'd like you to know about the way you are, about the way women are, but I'm afraid to say them, because you'll get pissed off."

"Try me. But I don't promise not to get pissed off."

"Do you understand how I adore it that you're always open to me, always generous almost beyond your will, that sometimes I want to fuck you endlessly, partly out of tenderness, partly out of gratitude, partly out of the awe of your being always open. And you're talking about ten pounds?"

I suppose I could have objected to the suggestion that I was doing things without or against my will, but I didn't feel like it. His hand, cupping me, did feel like a solace. I thought: what a solace our bodies have become to each other. And I felt, as he put his face to me, the absence in him of anything like recoil. It was an act of appetite and attention. Sometimes I forgot how fortunate I was.

When he would leave on Monday mornings, I was able to develop a routine. Each morning I stood on the deck—his deck—with my first coffee and looked at the ocean. It would rise out of its envelope of mist, of confusion, and become distinct first, and then splendid. I would walk down the steps to the shore and try to make my mind empty of everything but color. Sometimes it actually happened; language stopped and I would lose myself in pure color, pure expanse. The silence itself took on color, and sometimes I was afraid of two things, absolutely opposite to each other. I was afraid of not looking enough, both in the sense of not doing enough homage to all that it was and in the sense of not getting sufficient knowledge from it, not having the patience to have looked enough so that it would, as a kind of acknowl-edgment of my attention, give itself to me, give up the visual informa-tion that I needed as an ordinary human being and as a painter. At the same time, I was afraid of looking too much, of losing myself in look-ing, of forgetting myself and being absorbed, time going by and my being fixed in a paralysis of visual absorption so complete that I would pass directly from seeing into death.

So although I felt freed in a way I never had been, with an expanse of time I had ahead of me—no man or children to be fed or tended, no needy friends, no teaching to go back to before I was ready—I was always torn by two simultaneous and conflicting wishes, born of the very luxury of time: the desire to look and the desire to reproduce what I was seeing. It was always with a bit of hunger that I gave over the state of looking to the state of activity, a little emptiness, a little sad-ness, as I walked back up the stairs onto the deck where I would set my things up for the day's work.

After all those months of looking at the Masters, copying them, mak-ing drawings based on them, then drawing B, I had to make certain decisions about how I was going to place myself, my own representa-tion, my own marks on the canvas, and in what relation to the Masters. Over and over again, I kept asking myself the same question: "What do you want to do and how do you want to do it?" The simplest ques-tions in the world, aren't they, and after all the only real questions about style. Or what all questions of style boil down to.

With this project, the question of when and where I entered had a lot of possible answers. One was simply to efface myself. To adopt entirely the style of whatever Master I was referring to. I'm not talking about a kind of Sheri Levine thing; I wasn't interested in copying to make some kind of postmodernist point about looking. What I mean is that for a while I thought I'd create a modern scene, modern clothing, architecture, furniture, but use the palette, brush work, the posture of the figures in the painting of the Master I was looking at. But that didn't seem right either. That kind of half imitation wasn't what really interested me. Or only part of it. I was interested in the weight and repose of the male body, which I could render by copying the Masters, but I was interested as well in the way that we who love the past see the sights of the present through a veil or scrim created by our visions of it. A ghost vision overlaying our own.

I played around with techniques some people are using now, mechanical techniques that can add interesting layers. I worked with a video studio in Provincetown. First I projected a photograph of the Old Master's image onto some kind of gauzy material and made a literal scrim through which you'd see my image. You could move the scrim away or look through at your own discretion. Then I thought people would get so caught up in the gimmick of the thing, all the pulling and pushing, that they wouldn't really be paying attention to my painting. The idea of which I simply couldn't stand. I thought of projecting negative photographic images of the older paintings onto my canvas, tracing them there in black and white. Something about the difference between memory and vision. About past seeing and present vision.

They were all nice ideas, but none of them worked. They all seemed too thought out—which I wouldn't mind, I'm not a primitive or a romantic. But there has to be a kind of electric connection between the thought and the body—mine, in this case—that executes the image. And there wasn't with any of those ideas. For almost two months, everything I did seemed dead.

You can imagine how pleasant I was to be around. I'd invited Michael up for the first week in August, but I canceled the invitation. B suggested that I put Michael up in Larry's house. But I said it wouldn't work, there were too few creature comforts for Michael. I'd hear him sighing about the bathroom from six miles away.

Looking back, I think I only allowed B to come near me so I could be sexually rejecting. Those months tested his loyalty. He'd phone from New York and ask if he should come up. I'd say yes, but I'd try to make him feel like I was doing him a big favor. All the time, mind you, I was in his house, but I wanted to make him feel like an intruder.

When we did have sex, I had trouble coming, which was unusual for me and made me wildly impatient. I felt like I wanted to kick in the television screen. Very kindly, he'd say that we should stop.

"It's not the Olympic shot put," he said.

We had very different attitudes toward orgasm. For me a failure to come was a sexual failure. I felt angry at both myself and my partner.

He said that for him everything was a continuum. One gesture led to another gesture, perhaps the gesture wasn't finished right away, or you didn't even know what the final shape of the gesture really was.

I said, "It's very simple for me. If I don't come I feel like Margaret Thatcher at the Falkland Islands. Search and destroy. Slash and burn."

"Try relaxing and enjoying whatever it is that's happening," he said.

"There's nothing that makes me more furious than someone telling me to Try and Relax. Try and Relax is a three-word oxymoron."

He learned how to break through whatever it was I was throwing up between me and him, between me and my own satisfaction. He took a lot of time. He'd touch my chin, my neck, behind my knees. He'd deliberately keep himself away until I felt starved for his tongue or his finger, and then he would come near me, grazing, moving away, coming back, brief, almost careless touches, barely making contact. When I came it was strong and shuddering, and I needed him inside me to bring me to ground. Sometimes I would weep, involuntary tears that felt like sweat, because the relief was so great it felt like the end of a fever.

You'd think I'd be nice to him after that. I was, for a while, but it didn't last. You see, I was really miserable. I'd set myself a problem that I didn't know how to solve. Everything I tried seemed dead, and it gave off the shameful stink of the dead. And I felt sickened, as if I were look-ing at a corpse that looked back at me with direct, accusing eyes.

I felt sick, also terrified and ashamed. I wasn't any good, after all. The voices that had named me as a fake and a fraud were right. I could hear them telling me what an embarrassment it had been all along, my pretending to be an artist when I was just a third-rater. Worse than a Sunday painter, because my pretensions were so vast. The idea that I once believed I could create something of value seemed like an insult to every great painter I'd loved.

And it was even worse: I'd taken money on the grounds that what I did was of some worth. When I felt ashamed in relation to B, the shame grew and spread. It became sexual; I felt I stank. I couldn't bear to have him around me. Every time I talked to him, I apologized. I said he should take the apartment back, and I'd find some way of repaying him for everything he'd given me.

"You're making me long for the days of narcissistic sharp-edged abuse," he said. "What happened to me, the imperialistic colonizing capitalist pig, feeding off the tender flesh of the vulnerable artist? What happened to the automatic flush?"

"I'm sorry," I said. "I hope you'll forgive my arrogance someday."

"I can deal with arrogance. It's craven abjection that's hard to take. Craven abjection is not a turn-on."

"I'm sorry," I said.

"Get back to work."

"OK."

"Aren't you going to tell me to fuck off and not to tell you how to run your life?"

"No."

"Jesus, you're in a bad way. Do you want me to come up?"

"No, I don't deserve your attention."

"Oh, for God's sake, shut up and get back to work."


I wish I could tell you how things changed. I stopped all my technological experiments. I just kept looking at the Masters and doing drawings from them. And then I allowed something to surface that I'd buried the whole time I'd been thinking about what I wanted to do. It was something both frightening and embarrassing, but something I knew finally had to be taken into account. It was the nature of the figure of Christ. I wasn't dealing with an anonymous figure, a man with no associations. Nor were the associations merely mythical or historic. I wasn't painting Achilles or Charlemagne. I was painting someone people had given their lives for or dedicated themselves to.

I was painting a figure I had once prayed to, whom I had believed was the repository of power and goodness. Someone I'd believed had died for my sins and risen from the dead. Someone I'd believed was the embodiment of love against which all other love could be measured and found wanting. Particularly my own.

Like most serious-minded Catholic girls, I'd wanted to be a nun. Once, when I was six years old I'd come into St. Hyacinth Church and seen our first-grade teacher, Sister Imelda, whom I now understand was very young. She was in her black and white habit, kneeling in front of the monstrance. Oh, maybe you don't know what a monstrance is. A gold vessel in the shape of a sunburst in the center of which rests, behind glass, a consecrated Host. Called monstrance from the Latin *monstrare*: a vessel for the purpose of enabling looking.

Sister Imelda's hands were perfectly folded. Her spine was perfectly straight. She was aware of nothing; she had become her prayers. She had no self and there was no world around her. A beam of light filtered through the light blue of the stained-glass window commemorating the Immaculate Conception. The light struck her and bounced off the lenses of her eyeglasses. What I saw in her was an image of perfect concentration, perfect self-forgetfulness, and I knew it was the life I wanted for myself.

The object of my attention isn't what Sister Imelda's was. I tried to make it, for a while, the same as hers: God. It didn't work. The object of my attention is the visible world. Whenever I feel I'm working the right way, I know it has something to do with that self-forgetfulness and attention I saw when I looked at Sister Imelda in the beam of bluish light.

The life of the spirit. That would have to be part of my project, too. It would have to be in my paintings. The ghost of a spirit. The coming together of art and faith in the hands of a woman—me—whose life was no longer shaped by belief. The light presence, not oppressive, of a former impression, something traced, but lightly, barely visible. I thought of the light presence of the Risen Christ, so light that what Thomas doubted was his corporeality. All of that needed to be in the paintings. After I understood that, the way of doing it came to me.

I would paint my spent men in the posture and with some of the surroundings of the Italian Masters, but in my own style, that is, something informed by modern departures from classical balance, influenced by the Masters, but not effaced by them. And then, overlaying the figure, I would trace a white outline, drawn, but in white paint. On top of, but skewed in relation to the colored figure, I would trace the outline of the figure of the Master.

My paintings would include the relation of the past—art and

faith—to the present; the working female artist. Touched by the past but not shaped by it entirely. A light, indelible impression. Not a crushing hoof.

For a while, the work went quickly. I blocked the shapes on the canvas, drawing in pencil. That's a terrifying thing to do: so much is at stake and when you're working in pencil or charcoal everything is provisional, and yet what you lay out will have consequences that are very hard to change. A time of dizzying possibility and sickening responsibility.

I was much happier the minute I began touching tubes of paint. Because what's more delightful in this world than color?

When I give myself over to color, I'm back in a time before words, a time of childish delight. Who understands green better than a baby crawling through grass, surrounded by green grass but without the words for either green or grass. When I'm working with color, I become that child without words. Everything is more alive; everything seems saturated with and by color, and I'm saturated. I understand Rothko absolutely, although I could never be an abstract expressionist because I'm too interested in drawing and the relationship between subject matter and line and form. But when I'm going back to color after a long time away from it—away from thinking of it intensely and away from the substance of paint, its textures and smells (I love linseed oil's smell, I can't stand turpentine's)—the world seems transformed.

Like the time I went swimming with B in one of the Wellfleet ponds. Let me tell you what "pond" means on Cape Cod. It's one of those New England evasions, a strategy by which people who own the world try to convince you or themselves that they don't. A pond is really a small lake. Some of the Cape ponds are public, but some are restricted—or at least the beachfront is—to people who own the adjacent houses. Of course, B knew people who owned a house on Slough Pond and weren't using it that summer because they were traveling to Turkey. Or buying it. I was never really sure which with some of his contacts.

No one was around and we could swim naked, which, next to sex and painting (please don't ask me to state my order of preference), is my favorite activity. My breasts float; between my legs a cool and open sluiceway, I can feel the shape of my back as it folds in and out of the water. Movement is utterly easy; you're working against nothing, what you're in wants you to move in it, with it, it offers no resistance, only help. The colors of those ponds suggest, embrace, encompass blueness: blue influenced by sun on top, sand on the bottom, the greenness of the surrounding trees, blue that gets darker, lighter, purpler or more yellowish, in layers or in patches and in clots. Swimming next to B, I saw the whiteness of his body taking its place in all that blueness as if it were a shape made of milk.

He seemed so abstract, and yet so personal. It was probably the fact that he'd posed for me and made love to me as well. I wanted to keep away from him so I could look at him, so that the shape would remain intact without my intrusion. Then I wanted to feel his solidity, reassure myself that he wasn't, in fact, milk. And I wanted to touch his cock, floating so innocently, so florally, so purposelessly, like one of the lilies on the surface of the pond. I swam up behind him and I put my hand on his shoulder so he wouldn't be startled. He turned to face me; I wrapped my legs around him and clung like a baby animal to this sleek, wet creature, so cool, so borderless.

In the middle of August, he arrived for two weeks. It was a perfect time, as I pointed out, for him to pose for me. I was painting the figures, and, although strictly speaking, I could have worked from the drawings, it was much better to have him there. He gave me an hour a day; the rest of the time, or the rest of the time that there was light, he left me alone.

On August 19, my sister called me. She had to give a lecture in Boston: would I come to see her.

I was delighted. She lives in Geneva. I don't get to be with her nearly so much as I'd like to. You see, despite all the terrible press sisterhood gets—rivalry, resentment, two female cats scratching each other's eyes out, begrudging each other, eaten up with jealousy—with Helena and me it simply isn't the case. I love my sister; I have always loved her. When I'm with her, I always feel I'm exactly where I belong and together, the two of us can go anywhere, do anything. Being with my sister is like having a letter of transit to anywhere in the world.

We're eleven months apart. In the parish, this was called "Irish twins," although we weren't Irish. Helena and I both had twin daughters. We think we did it so we could reproduce our own situation. Freudian ovaries, Helena calls it.

Somehow the closeness of our births gave my mother, although she's a devout Catholic, the excuse to use a diaphragm. She claimed the doctor (which doctor she never quite specified) told her she had a weak heart from a bout of rheumatic fever as a child and that having two children so close together had weakened her heart even further: she mustn't have any more. She told herself—and later, her two daughters—that using birth control was an order from her doctor, and therefore not a sin, but she never mentioned it in confession because it would just "put the priest in a bad position." Have I mentioned that my mother was pleasure loving?

All through school Helena wrote poetry and I drew. That was how we went through the world, fearless, convinced we were "artistic," therefore special and not required to live by the rules. We started a literary magazine in high school; she was the literary editor, I was the arts editor. She was senior class president the year before I was. I followed her to Cornell.

In her junior year—my sophomore year—she fell in love with Science. She thought she was an English major, just taking biology as a requirement, then she was seized. But she felt guilty about it, in relation to me. She was no longer the Poet to my Artist. So she was a little mean to me for a couple of years, a little condescending. And I was mean and condescending to her. I kept suggesting that all her new premed friends were really boring, really straight. They weren't interested in stopping the war, just getting an A in Organic Chem. This made her, out of spite, move even closer to the premeds, further from the artsy crowd. I was sure she was doing it out of spite when she began to spend time with a really fat blond girl from Iowa who made a specialty of helping Asian freshmen lose their virginity.

Helena went to medical school in Michigan and for four years I didn't see her much. Then she did her residency at New York Hospital and we developed a new relationship. I'd say more mature, but there's always something a little girlish and a little wacky about what we do. Spur-of-the-moment trips no one else would think were possible. A weekend at the Grand Canyon. An hour and a half at the beach. And then there are the things that make us laugh that no one else gets. Like the time we were sitting on a plane and lost it over some of the items in the airline catalog. Mottos carved in "realistic-looking stone," seventy-five bucks a pop. Things like "Teamwork is everything," and "When the going gets tough, the tough get going." We took turns being the executive and his secretary, saying to each other, "Myra, this says everything I feel."

I got married and had children before Helena because she was off in Africa studying contagious diseases. When she came home for holidays, she would buy my kids shockingly extravagant gifts, take them to expensive places. They adored her. Then when she moved to Geneva, she married Hans. Her twins are twelve now, lovely European children, much more polite than mine. And blonde! I can hardly believe it, but I don't know my sister's husband and children very well.

But I know her very well and she knows me. So of course what we both wanted was a room at the Ritz, twin beds that were really double, and room service.

I told her everything about B. She didn't ask me about the sex. I knew that I could always assume Helena's first response to anything about me would be to wish me well. I decided that, of all the people I knew, she'd be the first to meet B in the flesh. What a stupid expression. As if you were ever going to meet someone *outside* the flesh.

I asked B to come to Boston.

"I want you to meet my sister," I said. "We'll have dinner at the Ritz."

"Do I have to wear a ski mask? It could be a challenge getting my dinner through that little hole for the mouth."

"It's much too warm for a ski mask. A simple domino will do."

"I'm a little afraid of meeting your sister."

"Don't worry, she's much nicer than I am."

"Do you want me to say 'Impossible' or 'I'm not surprised'?"

"Why, of course, I want you to say whatever you like."

"Such a coarse lie should be beneath you. We both know that you want me to say whatever *you* like."

Helena and I had an hour between lunch and her meeting, so I invited her to come to the Museum of Fine Arts with me to look at the Rosso Fiorentino. I always like to hear my sister, the doctor, talk about bodies.

"First of all," she said, "this guy is not dead. He's not at all rigid and those coy crossed ankles are just not possible on a dead person. He's trying to hide his cock from those dirty little girl angels. Fingering that wound like that. The sluts!"

Helena looked a little angelic herself; she has huge gray eyes—really gray, an extremely rare color—and they're set quite wide apart. The wide-apartness and the lightness gives her a guileless look, which is misleading, and which has often served her quite well. Nevertheless, it's a bit shocking to hear words like "cock" and "slut" come out of that angelic mouth.

"Do you think his nipples are erect?" I asked.

"As a physician, I can absolutely certify it."

She went back to her lecture. I stayed at the museum, in front of the painting, making sketches. I focused on the massive chest and thighs. I did a drawing of the two candles, held by angels in the painting, but I wasn't going to use the angels. I'd use the candles as some kind of inner frame. I made notes to describe the colors of the dress on one: a mannerist sunburst or rainbow, outrageous, false-looking oranges, yellows and blues that shouldn't have worked, they were so lurid, so acidic. But that's just what they did: their job, the job of heating up the flesh tones so they looked a little feverish, a bit unwell.

I concentrated on the stomach, the upper abdomen, the triangle below the breastbone, the deep navel with a curve of indented flesh above it like an eyebrow, the belly, prosperous looking as a merchant's purse, almost androgynous, voluptuously underlined by a fold of skin just above the tuft of hair.

I wondered what I'd do to replicate the framing device of the candles. Perhaps I'd turn them into the arms of a bench. But I'd begin by concentrating on the greenish expanse of flesh emanating from darkness.

*    *    *

B was waiting for me at the Ritz. I moved my things from Helena's room to his. I'd spent so much time thinking about stomachs I was eager to attend to his. Rosso's Jesus isn't what you'd call hard-bodied, so it was an easy transition to B, who certainly isn't fat but who let his gym membership lapse years ago, if he ever had one. I licked the area around his navel; I made a circular path with my tongue until the hair lay flat like a newborn animal's. I loved the way his stomach rose and fell with his arousal; I reveled in the textural variety, the wet, animal fur, the hardness of his ribs, and then the cock, that miraculous combination of hard and soft.

I was trying not to feel like a nervous teenager at the prospect of introducing my boyfriend to my sister. After all, I told myself, even if she hated him, I wouldn't give him up. But actually, I wasn't exactly sure of that. I understood that to be the reason I hadn't introduced him to anybody. If I gave him up, I had to give up not only a lover, but a benefactor who gave me the freedom to do my work. In some ways, it was a diabolical knot, and once again I felt angry with him. It wasn't a good way to start the evening, moving from being loving toward his little paunch to berating him about exercising, as a way of expressing my unease with our bargain.

I wanted to call the dinner off. I suggested this in the elevator as the bell rang for the fourth floor and he told me I could do whatever I liked but he was surprised that I'd give in so easily to a failure of nerve.

"Failure of nerve?" I said to him. "What is this, fucking Mount Everest? Can you drop the Sir Edmund Hillary talk? Any minute now you'll be calling me 'old chap.' "

"Buck up, old chap. You don't want them saying you gave up so close to the top. After all, we're already on the mezzanine. And besides, the natives are there already. The ones who haven't died carrying your gear. The little one, with the diaper. Sam Jaffe, isn't that his name? Jewish fellow, Indian accent though."

"If you think you're distracting me by being funny you're doing a lousy job. There's my sister."

I hugged her. "Just once in my life, Helena, I'd like to get someplace before you do."

"It'll never happen. It's my rigorous scientific training. I learned to tell time at an early age. I can read the time on my watch at a glance. Is she still late all the time?" she asked B.

"Unless she's afraid not to be."

I sat stiffly while Helena did the equivalent of showing pictures of me on a bearskin rug. Then she asked B what I never do: she asked him about his work. He told her some of the things he told me, but since she wasn't so ready to call him a capitalist pig piece of shit, he could answer her more readily.

They talked about how they both felt they were in the vortex of the world, that they lived in the world, not just in a pocket of it, how things that happened in places they'd never thought of when they were children affected them directly, that they had a stake in great numbers of places.

I felt humbled that she'd allowed him to talk well about his work and I hadn't. But I also felt a little out of the conversation. They were standing in front of a map of the world moving pins, and I was in my studio, thinking of flesh tones and the place of triangles in compositional space.

"We have something else in common," Helena said. "We both think my sister's a great painter. Except that we're not allowed to use the word 'great.' She'll jump down our throats."

"We both think she's really good," B said.

"And a lot of fun and occasionally a tyrannical pain in the ass."

"Just go on as if I weren't here," I said. But naturally, I was enjoying it.

He ordered champagne and they toasted me.

"To Spent Men," B said.

"To My Sister. To Art and Pleasure."

"To Sisterhood and Work," I piped up, like the littlest Little Pepper.

We drank vintage champagne. Which was excellent. It was a good thing we drank the whole bottle, because the dinner was mediocre. I started to head for my sister's room. She had to remind me that I was with B. For a minute, I was a little disappointed, and a little worried about being disloyal, as though I'd deserted the female nest for the glamorous world of men.

When he went into the bathroom to take a shower, I called her up and whispered into the phone.

"So what did you think?"

"He's great. You're lucky."

"You don't think I'm a whore?"

"Monica, don't talk like that, he makes you laugh. He's got great hair."

"Yes, well, that's not everything."

"It's not nothing."

"Why should I listen to you? You liked Roger."

"*You* liked Roger for about twelve years. He was fine for what he was. He was the right person at the right time. And B is the right person for this time."

"I'm hanging up. He's getting out of the shower."

"I can't believe we're in our fifties and we're still whispering on the phone."

"When we stop, that will be a terrible moment."

We drove her to the airport, and I was reluctant, as I always am, to let her go. I would like to have everyone I love around me. Yet I was eager for B to go back to New York, because I could be alone for the whole month of September. I didn't have to teach. It was time I'd always longed for and hadn't been able to get.

The hyperclear September light sometimes made my eyes ache. I was overstimulated by the light, and overexcited about working. I found it hard to sleep. It was one of those times when everything I did was right. I was very pleased with the drawing of the Master figure superimposed over my painted one. Do you get the idea? It was as if a glass plate, with figures etched into it, were placed on top of my painting.

I got the fun of drawing, and the demands of it, with the voluptuousness of paint. In those months, I finished three paintings: after Carpaccio, after Mantegna, and after Rosso Fiorentino. Three paintings in two months; I'd never accomplished anything like that in my life.

*       *       *

You want to know what I was like to B while my work was so absorbing? I was like a wife with young children, taken up with something else, worn out by the end of the day. He came on Thursday night and stayed till Monday. I was reluctant to make love early in the morning. I wanted the part of my brain that was still rinsed in dream available to work. The best time for sex was the afternoon, when we came together a little sleepily, as a prelude to a nap. We almost had to pretend we didn't mean to do it. We'd lie down next to each other on our backs, maybe in our underwear, holding hands and looking at the ceiling as if we'd just been shipwrecked. I'd put my hand on his shoulder; he'd put his hand on my thigh. I'd be aroused by his chest hair, or the position of his feet. Those days when I lay beside him, I felt that I was lying in a mist; my eyes never felt completely open and I always fell asleep right after sex, and then awoke, not quite refreshed. He'd bring me coffee. He'd make dinner. I'd go back to work.

Dinner was something I felt I earned those days; sex was something I felt I'd stolen. From what? From time. From concentration. I would steal into sex as if it were a tepid, not-quite-clean pool; my skin would be coated, softened, but I felt a little weakened by it, as if I'd hit my head on an underwater rock.

I moved back to my apartment on the fifteenth of October. I decided it was time to go when I noticed I was wearing sweaters all the time, and I began to have thoughts about a winter coat. It was time to be home, to watch, through my window, the deep gold October light strike the river, to see what would happen to the zelkova tree in front of the yeshiva now that it was fall. I worked on another painting, the Sodoma. And then it was the fifteenth of November, time to start thinking about the holidays again, always a gruesome prospect.

"What does the Lone Ranger do on Thanksgiving?" Michael said.

He always called B the Lone Ranger, because he said he always felt he was hearing the sound of withdrawing hoofbeats, but never getting a glimpse of the man himself. He said he might have passed him on the street and not known who he was. Sometimes he called him "The Lone" or just "Lone," because the shorter form of address indicated they were making progress with intimacy.

I said I didn't know what he did on Thanksgiving and if there was one thing I didn't want to get involved in with someone I was fucking it was major holidays. I always went to my ex-husband's on Thanksgiving: Merrill just seemed the Thanksgiving type. Maybe it was all that Laura Ashley wallpaper in the bathrooms. Or the pressed wildflowers in oval frames.

I'd realized after one too many weepy sessions pulling a large stuffed turkey out of a hot oven that these birds and I were not in a good relation to one another and I blamed the birds. It was obvious that many people felt wretched on holidays, and I disagreed with Michael that the causes were to be found in childhood traumas. I thought it was much better to blame the birds. After all, I said to Michael, it's no accident, really, is it, that they're called fowl? As in foul play.

Three years ago, Michael decided that the day after Thanksgiving we'd have what we called the *Salon des Refusés*. People detached from traditional families, food that was seasonally inappropriate. For me, any food consisting largely of olive oil and garlic is a dispenser of good health. So our usual post-Thanksgiving meal was shrimp with garlic and parsley followed by pasta *con aglio ed olio*. Followed by a salad with a lemon and garlic dressing. Followed by strawberry sorbet and biscotti. Now, doesn't that sound more inviting than creamed onions?

Michael suggested that I invite B to the *Salon des Refusés* that year.

"I'm not ready," I said.

"You let him meet Helena."

"Helena's nicer than you."

"She's nicer than *you*. But I'm nicer than you too. She's actually not that much nicer than I. She just looks nicer."

"She lives four thousand miles away. And if she didn't like him, I wouldn't have to see her face all the time. Do you know how awful your face gets when you're pretending to like someone?"

So I didn't invite him. But after the party was over, I was sorry I hadn't. I let Michael go home halfway through the cleanup. Usually, he and I enjoyed it, draining the glasses of wine, deciding what to wrap up and what to throw away. I told Michael I was tired, that I'd finish the dishes in the morning.

But I wasn't tired. I was suffering from the wrongness of my decision. B was a man I liked. A mature woman shouldn't be afraid to introduce a man she likes to her friends. I was worrying about what I might lose. My work was going too well. It was flowing so easily, so beautifully, like a transparent river over a bed of whitish sand. I didn't want the risk of complicating boulders, or channels of hesitation or regret.

It was ridiculously warm for Thanksgiving. I opened a window and leaned out for a moment. I saw that a fly must have come in and was buzzing around the food. His movements sounded both torpid and desperate. What was he doing, this fly? Whatever it was, it was wrong. It was wrong for him to be in my apartment on the night after Thanksgiving, November 29.

The sound of the fly made me miserable. And the sight of him was worse; that sick iridescence, that failure to progress. I watched couples walking arm in arm past the monument on Riverside Drive. I felt the shame of being in a room full of wasted food, alone with the congealed butter and the clots of oiled parsley that clung to the china like a stubborn minor illness. And the fly.

The couples made me want to call B, but I knew I had no right. I kept cleaning till everything was done. I didn't want the dirty dishes to get in the way of my morning's work. After I got a morning's work done, I'd call him. I'd make him a wonderful dinner; I'd make sure he had a terrific night.

When I called him in the morning, I was alarmed at the sound of his voice. It was the kind of hello that can only be responded to by the phrase "What's wrong?"

"I threw out my back," he said.

"Well, that was careless of you. Can't you get another one?"

He was too drugged for the joke.

"I can't move much. I've got everything next to my bedside. I'll be all right."

It hadn't occurred to me to think he wouldn't be all right until he said that.

"Do you want me to come over?"

"I don't want to take you away from your work."

"Don't worry, I wouldn't dream of letting you do that. I suppose

you have some huddled mass around to buy your groceries and pick up
your prescriptions."

"Yes, the person I have to shave me."

"You hired a person to shave you?"

"I can't stand by the sink long enough to shave and I can't get in and
out of the shower by myself, so I hired someone."

"A nurse?"

"A valet."

"You hired a valet? From where?"

"An agency."

"You just called an agency and they sent you a valet? Who is he?"

"A very nice Englishman in his sixties."

"I want to know his name."

"Jenkins."

I said I'd bring him supper. It would be the first serious meal we'd
eaten in his house, the first thing I'd done for him that was anything
like a ministration. But I wanted to do it because I felt so bad about not
inviting him to the *Salon des Refusés*. It was easier to keep him sealed off
as my benefactor and someone I fucked when I was able to convince
myself that I didn't like him that much, that I wasn't really grateful to
him, that I was his newest risk/investment: cheaper and less stressful
than a plunge into the vanilla market. Only sex and money: hard-
edged things, words, ideas that didn't bleed into one another, didn't
make a mess. But now I was both grateful and fond: two words, pastel
and British sounding. Like a Constable landscape. But of course, Constable landscapes are wonderful, those feathery trees, those easy-on-
the-eye streams, those cows, dripping water from their tender
mouths, so restful, so restorative. But, sweet and calm as those words
seemed—grateful, fond—they were remarkably difficult to integrate
into my life.

Jenkins answered the door and the expression on his face made me
think I ought to look at the bottom of my shoes. I was hoping Jenkins
wouldn't be around for long. I was hoping Jenkins understood that his
tenure might have something to do with me. If he did, I had to respect

him for his refusal to be obsequious, or even normally pleasant. But I wondered if his avoidance of any attempt to make me feel at ease meant that he thought I was dispensable, one of his wealthy employer's many incomprehensible playthings, or if he thought that the force of his superiority would make as nothing the paltry vector whose source was what his employer might find between my thick, plebeian legs.

It became terribly important to me to set him straight, but I had no idea how this might happen.

"That will be all for tonight, Jenkins," B said, propped up on his pillows like a minor god. He looked a little stiff, a little stoned, a little uncomfortable, but he didn't seem to be in excruciating pain.

"Very good, sir," Jenkins said. I think he walked out backward, but I didn't want to look at him, so I'm not sure.

"I can't believe how easy your transition to *Upstairs, Downstairs* has been," I said.

"It's all in the tailoring."

He was looking very elegant in a navy silk bathrobe. The collar of his light blue striped pajamas was arranged over the bathrobe collar as if the bathrobe were a suit.

"How mobile are you?"

"Hardly at all."

"Has this happened to you before?"

"Once a year. I think it's stress-related. It happens when I've locked myself in front of the computer for longer than usual."

"What does your doctor say?"

"What doctor?"

"You haven't been to the doctor?"

"I never go to the doctor."

"You mean you have a valet but not an internist?"

"I don't like doctors. I'm normally very healthy. I just stockpile Valium in case my back goes out. And I retreat to bed."

"And call Jenkins."

"Or someone like him."

"Wouldn't a doctor be more productive?"

"If you go to doctors, they invariably tell you you're sick. They have a stake in it. I haven't been to one since college."

I told him that was the stupidest thing I'd ever heard and I was calling Michael to find the best person for backs.

"Michael's a psychiatrist. There's nothing wrong with my mind."

"You'd never convince anyone who heard what you've just been saying."

I sat on the bed and leaned over him to get to the phone. He took the receiver out of my hand and hung it up.

"I have a better idea for a cure. One that makes real use of my immobility."

He moved the blanket and lay back on his pillows.

"I'm not going to move," he said. "Everything's up to you. I'm completely at your mercy."

He was a little drowsy from the drugs. Something about his posture and his voice suggested bees buzzing above a clover field on a hot August day. He wasn't going to lift a finger for his own pleasure. Whatever I did, he wouldn't resist. There was something wounded about him, something resigned, but at the same time expectant, so he seemed like a child who knows his sickness is temporary and takes advantage while he can. He was determined not to touch me. He was almost forcing himself not to move his body at all, as if the greatest possible stillness would produce the greatest possible excitement.

I made the point of dividing him into zones, and I gave each zone a particular approach. He tried to keep inert, but I felt him begin to tense and I knew it was time to get to work. Everything had suddenly turned serious; a pilgrim's progress. His. There was a task at hand, or no, a goal, the Thoroughbred racing to the finish line. And then, across the finish line, the roar, then the full stop, then silence. And instead of prancing to the winner's circle for the floral tribute, a complete withdrawal into an oblivious, exclusive and excluding sleep.

Over the next few days, we amused ourselves playing World War I. Wounded British officer and dedicated Red Cross nurse. He'd wrap a towel around his cock and I'd pretend to change the bandage.

"By God, the Huns haven't shattered everything," I'd say, then take

him in my mouth, saying it was my contribution to the war effort. To
the Empire. He'd say that of course I understood he couldn't take me
back to Somerset because of his esteemed wife, Lady Bracknell, but
we'd meet in London from time to time, perhaps in tea rooms, perhaps
in Charing Cross Station.

It was fun for a while, playing the devoted nurse. Then I began to
suspect him of malingering. I think it happened when Jenkins had to go
back to Brighton for a funeral, and the shaving stopped. It's a thin line
between enjoying aristocratic indolence and letting yourself turn into
a bum, and by the third day's growth of beard, I felt he'd crossed it.
He'd turned from Ronald Colman in *The Light That Failed* to Walter
Huston in *The Treasure of the Sierra Madre*. I began to think he was enjoying lying back and being sucked, lying back and being brought ice
cream. The common theme was lying back.

You see, I believe that every man's dearest wish is to be served by
his mother. B had told me that his happiest moments in childhood were
when he was sick and his mother would play cards and checkers with
him. He talked about the marvelous feeling of sitting in the chair in his
bedroom watching her change the sheets, knowing that when he got
between them, they'd be wonderfully cool.

If he was changing from Ronald Colman to Walter Huston, I was
changing from Helen Hayes in *A Farewell to Arms* to Rosalind Russell in
*Sister Kenny*. The tender massages with a little detour below the waist-
band were becoming more deep muscle work laced with crisp exhor-
tations to try walking more than a few steps. When he'd lean on my
shoulder, I was tempted to run away and leave him in a smelly grizzled
heap on the bathroom floor.

After a week, I told him that if he wouldn't go to a doctor I wouldn't
visit him any more. He started looking craven, like a cornered animal,
and when I said I was going to call an orthopedist who was a good friend
of Michael's, he mumbled something that I didn't take as a no.

Stan Pearlman, the disc king, said he'd see us the next morning. I
began to realize that B was really afraid of going to the doctor. I figured
that out when he went limp in my mouth.

I told him I'd go with him to the doctor's, and after a few perfunc-
tory demurrals he seemed grateful, even pleased.

*        *        *

When I came by to get him in the morning, I called him my gallant doughboy as he tried, unsuccessfully, to get his pants on by himself. One leg at a time, I kept telling him.

He told me not to make him laugh when he was trying to walk because it hurt when he laughed.

I told him that excruciating pain was no excuse for losing your sense of humor.

He really was in pain. Every bump the taxi rode over made his eyes roll back in his head.

"Are you purposely aiming for potholes?" he asked the driver, in a fury.

The driver didn't even turn around. He had a Greek flag stuck in his dashboard.

When we got to the medical center I asked him if he wanted a wheelchair. He told me not to treat him like an invalid.

"I thought you liked being treated like an invalid."

"Only if I think it's attractive," he said. "Wheelchairs are not attractive."

I mentioned Jon Voigt and Jane Fonda in *Coming Home.*

"Jesus, I hated that movie. That was the stupidest movie ever made."

I told him I thought it had a long way to go to compete with *Francis the Talking Mule.* But he wasn't in the mood.

When we got to the doctor's waiting room he froze so dramatically that I thought he was having a back spasm.

"I can't believe this," he said.

"What?"

"It's my ex-wife."

There was only one woman in the waiting room. She wore a neck brace, not usually a positive fashion statement, but this woman was so overwhelmingly *groomed* that she made the neck brace seem like a cutting-edge accessory. I was pretty sure her very black hair was dyed, but if so it was skillfully and expensively done. Everything about the way she looked indicated a major capital outlay: her beige Gucci loafers, her Chanel bag, above all her quite alarming and I suppose admirable fingernails, the color of pearls but square cut at the top of their mandarin expanse. I couldn't imagine performing a single action with those nails. But I guess, like the mandarins, she intended to convey that message to the viewer. I use the word "viewer" deliberately, because it was impossible to assume anything but that those nails were meant to be seen, not used. I wondered what she did if she had to open packages or scratch her ear. Maybe her husband the periodontist had hired a package opener and an ear scratcher for her. People will do a lot in a depressed economy. But then B had hired Jenkins to shave him and buy him the right pajamas at Brooks Brothers. The ability to hire engenders thoughts of tasks that someone must be hired to perform.

B's wife, or the ex-Mrs. B, hadn't opened her mouth and already I'd decided that I didn't like her. That I was on his side. I understood, then, that he and I were a couple. And a fairly happy one. Certainly a sexually lively one. Nothing marks the death of desire like the moment when you find yourself thinking that the ex-wife had a point.

"What are you doing here?" she asked. I thought: if Brillo could talk, this is what it would sound like.

"Same thing as you," he said, not looking at her. I hadn't asked for details, but it was easy to see that this was not a divorce that could be characterized by the word "amicable." Have you ever noticed that there are some words that are used in one context only? Like "amicable" for divorce or "fluids" when you have a fever: force fluids.

"No, we're not here for the same reason," she said. "As you should perfectly well know. What you never really understood is that all my years of intensive dance training, all that stress, ruined my sixth cervical vertebra. But you haven't done any physical exercise since Little League."

"You're right, Natalie. You deserve medical treatment and I don't."

"I'm Natalie," she said. "I used to be married to him."

"This is Monica," he said. "She's my manicurist."

"No manicurist in the world would have nails like that," she said.

"Actually, I'm a painter," I said, with false brightness, masking my deep desire to flee. I hoped that the word "painter" would conjure images of spattered rags and full brushes, so I'd have some excuse for the state of my nails. The idea of artistic work cuts through a lot of obligations for the romantic imagination. But somehow, I couldn't think of Natalie as a romantic when it came to fingernails.

"You know," she said, "he has no talent. He likes to live through other people. Not that I know if you're talented or not. I used to be a dancer."

"Now," he said, "because of her fabulous diplomatic skills, she's a high-level negotiator at the UN."

"I happen to be a full-time homemaker," she said. "Not that you have any idea of a home."

I could have gone down on my knees to the nurse who appeared, called Natalie's name and led her off with a supportive arm around her waist, although she'd said her problem was a cervical vertebra.

"Lovely woman, your ex-wife," I said. "Sensitive creature. Kind of like a Fragonard."

"I've died and gone to hell," he said. "I'm about to see a doctor who's going to tell me I have ten minutes to live, and Natalie's lifted face will be before me for all eternity."

"I'm here, too."

"Oh, I forgot you're of the religion that invented Purgatory. Partial damnation."

"I'm going to choose to take that as a compliment."

"I mean it that way. How come you're friendly with your ex-husband?"

"Because I was happy to pass him on to someone else."

"And you didn't lose any money on the deal."

"How will you think of me, afterward? That I was a loss, or a drain? Or whatever word you use to indicate a fiscal catastrophe?"

"Please," he said. "I'm in great pain. I can't think about anything like that. Besides, whatever our arrangement, it won't involve my having to pay alimony because I made it impossible for you to find your true métier. Which in Natalie's case involved a shift from Martha Graham to step aerobics."

We spent the day taking medical tests. He was childish and rude to everyone but me; to me, he was silent. Stan, the disc man, told B he had a herniated disc. He didn't recommend surgery. Bed rest. Physical therapy.

When I got him back to his apartment, I'd used up the last of my meager store of appetite for nursing. I filled his refrigerator with food. I said I'd phone him and I'd see him the following evening. I couldn't wait to get away.

I wouldn't have liked anyone whose sickness was taking me away from my work, but it was exacerbated in this case because he was my lover. I kept thinking there was something unwomanly about this response, but I thought there was something unmanly about his lying around. I'm not big on lying around when something goes wrong; I firmly believe that lying around leads to more lying around. This is a legacy of my marriage, during which, in my memory, Roger spent most of the mid-eighties prone. I don't like inertia and I don't like compliance. Which is something of a problem, because I like getting my way. I guess what I mean is that I don't like the appearance of a too easy compliance. I like the spectacle, however false, of someone putting up a fight, then giving in because they see the justice of my claim. I don't want to think that they're going along with me because they have no other options. Sometimes I even got annoyed with B when I thought he was being too nice to me, when he was letting me ask for too much, or behave too badly.

I don't know what I wanted him to do, given his herniated disc. No, that's not true. I know exactly what I wanted him to do. I wanted him to be active. To *move*.

Don't think I was proud of all this. I would like to have that combination of discipline and generosity that would allow me to do without sleep so I could shift from artistic creation to nursing my lover without a second's hesitation. Simply to go from this to that because I wanted to do both.

But I couldn't. I was at that stage of making a painting that's so physical that the moral has no force in relation to it. When you're thinking about painting—no, not thinking, it's a much more physical thing—you're involved in the creation of shapes and color, and that relationship, in ideas of emptiness and fullness and the connections between the two, you're in a world that stops at the edge of the canvas, or does it? You enter a universe entirely absorptive, or centrifugal, pulling everything it needs into itself. I'm not saying this right because words don't serve; this isn't about language. It isn't a code for anything else, it's only itself, the thing and the appearance of the thing. Pulled as I was by the universe of my own canvas, how could I give it up to go with my lover to physical therapy, to be sure that he was really getting the abdominal exercises right?

And of course, the nature of my agreement with B was that nothing was meant to stop me from working full out, the way I wanted to, anytime and for as long as I liked. How could I put his suffering body in the center of our agreement?

It wasn't hard to silence the voice that said I should do exactly that. I told myself that if I weren't a woman, if the sex weren't good, I wouldn't have given a moment's thought to leaving my work so I could help him into the sitz bath.

I convinced myself that it was an act of virtue to turn a blind eye to his back trouble. Once again, just as money complicated some things, it made some things easier for both of us. He could hire a physical therapist to come to his house every day. He could pay someone; he didn't need me, and if he ran away with Jill the physical therapist from Boise, I'd just have to live with that.

I had a few tough minutes before I started work in the morning when I wrestled with the demons of female duty. But once I got to work, it was all over. And actually, it was better if I spent the night with him and I could leave after sex. His ardor made him seem vital, healthy, not pitiable. Able to look after himself. I accused myself of bad feminist consciousness—weren't we supposed to be in favor of men expressing their vulnerability?—for many of my thoughts during this period. I told myself I'd deal with it later, when I didn't have so much work.

And when my dealer wasn't about to pay a studio visit.

I'm not the kind of painter who's comfortable with somebody, particularly a dealer, paying a visit before I feel everything is up to scratch. I like Theresa to look at things before they're finished, and Nick, my friend who does figurative paintings too, and Adrienne, who works with stencil on wood, because they know how to look at work before it's finished, and we can all speak about things without making them seem fixed. I don't know if you understand how dangerous it is to think things are fixed before they are. How grateful I am to my friends to be able to speak in such a way that their words are authoritative but not finalizing. Too often speaking critically is like setting a seal. Sometimes I take my friends' directions, sometimes I don't. Sometimes I'm a little abusive first, but take the suggestions later.

I've been unbelievably lucky with my dealer. I first met Fanny Taylor in May of 1985 when my old dealer, the ever-popular buccaneer and drug addict Timothy Schwartz, had grown too difficult even for me. I have a couple of standards in a dealer; I don't think they're excessive but they prove to be met less frequently than you'd think. First, I want the dealer to understand my work. Second, I want the work hung properly. And third, I want to be paid. I guess Timothy understood my work—before he began spending five thousand dollars a weekend on cocaine. He hung it all right, although the space was pretty small for the number of paintings he felt he had to show—we disagreed about that, but I was younger then and more grateful. Now I'm almost never grateful about anything having to do with my work.

The real sticking point was that he didn't pay me. I didn't have expensive tastes in those years, but I did enjoy thinking it was OK to go to the dentist if one of my molars happened to abscess. Timothy kept getting vaguer and vaguer about his payment schedule. Finally, he did pay up, but I was sick of him. It was time to move on.

The way Fanny Taylor looks and moves and speaks may not be fair to other dealers. At first you think she's a little stoned because everything she does is just a bit slower than most people, particularly most New Yorkers. She's from New Zealand and her gestures always seem to come from some terribly distant and yet accessible place, like New Zealand. She makes you believe in the solar plexus. She's very tall and I always imagine her wearing velvet slippers, mustard-colored or wine-colored—the shade of something comestible—although I've never seen anything remotely like velvet slippers on her feet. She gives the sense of being simultaneously archaic and avant-garde. Partly it's her height—six-one, she tells me. And she's large-boned without being athletic. She's languid, but more efficient than anyone I know. Except Michael, and his efficiency always seems a little frantic, a little reproachful. Fanny's efficiency always seems like a wonderful accident, something she's let you in on because she thinks you'd find it fun. Everybody always wants more of Fanny in their lives, but she deflects greed, so no one ever fights over her. I forgot to tell you that she has these dimples. Two in her cheeks and one on her chin. And a little one at the tip of her rather long nose.

In '85 she was rolling her own cigarettes, taking the tobacco from a pouch that looked like it was made to hold florins or ducats or some tribute to some soon to be deposed—if not beheaded—potentate. Her eyes are very smoky, and the combination of her eyes and the physical smoke was a bit hypnotizing.

When she first came to look at my paintings she didn't say anything for a long time. In those years I was doing neorealist portraits, sort of Alice Neel, with a lot of California colors. A little Fairfield Porter. Maybe a little Diebenkorn. She loved the work, and she didn't try to conceal her enthusiasm. Two other dealers were interested in me, but it wasn't even close. I felt both safe with Fanny and excited by her; I trusted her, but I felt she'd make things happen if she could.

Up to the last one, my shows have sold respectably but not spectacularly. She never made me feel I was failing or disappointing her. She always made me feel that everything was proceeding according to an exact and particularly delightful plan.

I like Fanny so much that I've been careful not to make too close a friend of her. I always wanted us to feel that we could separate from each other without that sense of betrayal that's so poisonous in professional relations, particularly between women. When I called her to invite her for a studio visit, I hadn't seen her in fifteen months.

She came with a little bunch of chrysanthemums from her house in Connecticut. It had been so unseasonably warm that in the beginning of December there still hadn't been a killing frost. The flowers carried with them an aftertaste of fall, an unexpected, all the more valued, glow. They were so sure of themselves without being prim, so fixed without seeming rigid. I had exactly the right green Depression glass vase to put them in, and it was a pleasure to feel the cool water run over my hands, to put the geometric rightness of the flowers into the rather severe green glass. We were both very pleased with the arrangement.

We chatted about my children, her children, her new granddaughter, she was unabashed showing me pictures. I'm exactly the right person to show baby pictures to: I'm always interested in snapshots. She said she'd been too young when she had her own children, too interested in still having boyfriends when she was first married, so she hadn't been as good a mother as she ought to have been. Too much of her attention went into thinking about what she would wear to a party so she could flirt and then go home with someone without her husband discovering.

"But I'm perfect as a grandma," she said. "I worry much more about Matilda being in a plane crash than I did my own children. I guess I have a more realistic sense of mortality."

Fanny has a partner who's the money part of the deal; she leaves all the charm and intelligence to Fanny. I guess that's why the gallery works. I never deal with Phyllis; she just signs the checks.

She's signed the checks for twelve years, since 1985, when the booming eighties were winding down. I've shown with Fanny five times since then, four before the Spent Men show.

I'd told Fanny about the idea for Spent Men. And she loved it. She said she couldn't wait to see the work. But loving the idea and loving the work were two different things, as she and I both knew.

She started walking around quietly in that way that made me feel she was shod in velvet. She held her fingers in front of her as if she were still holding a cigarette. She looked for a long time. She told me to leave the room because I was making her nervous. I went into the kitchen and talked to Michael on the phone. I asked him to tell me the plot of every Cary Grant movie he'd ever seen, and then to tell me about every patient he'd saved from suicide. I told him to make them up if he ran out.

"Which, the movies or the suicides?"

"Both," I said. "She might be in there for a long time."

*      *      *

He was moving from a summary of *Father Goose* to a story about a window washer with a squeegee in his hand, whom he'd talked down from the twenty-eighth floor. I told him I didn't believe him. He said he absolutely meant it, on his honor as a professional. I asked him how the window washer was able to pay his fees. "Medicaid," he said, "this was the good old days." He was about to tell me how the guy had thrown his rubber safety belt out the window and seen it crash to the sidewalk when Fanny walked out.

"I don't know what to say."

"Say something," I said.

"It's the most exciting work I've seen for a long time. I knew the idea was great but the execution is a triumph. How far along are you?"

"There are the six you've seen and there are three others."

"Could you be ready to show in May?"

"May? It's December."

"Yes, I know, but I have an unexpected hole in my calendar. The wretched Don Roper has jumped ship to go to Mary Boone."

"I have to think about it."

"Not long, darling. If you don't want the spot I have to give it away rather soon. I'm perfectly happy for you to show next October, if it suits you better."

"Let me think about it a couple of days."

"I know, it's rather a lot to spring on you. But the work is so exciting that I want it out as soon as anything. But above all, don't rush it. October will be marvelous as well."

I was awfully excited by what Fanny had said. I'd like to think of myself as being impervious to praise, of just doing the work for its own sake, of saying no one's standards mattered but my own. But I wasn't that pure. I respected Fanny and I knew she wasn't my toughest critic, didn't look as closely as Theresa, wasn't as unvarnished in her comments as Adrienne. I also knew she was running a business and that her reputation was at stake in showing my work. What she said mattered in the public way that, although I wish it weren't, is important. Like the bubbles in champagne. You can't be nourished by champagne, but there's nothing like it to give you a sense of promise.

I phoned Theresa but she was at the periodontist and I knew she'd be too miserable to disturb the rest of the night. Then I realized I hadn't really wanted to call Theresa. I'd just done it because she was the one I always called about work. I realized that I really wanted to call B. That surprised me, and I had the impulse to resist; I didn't want him taking over my life. I tried Michael, he was with a patient. I took it as a sign from God. It's remarkable what you'll take as a sign from God when you're trying to find justification for doing what you want.

But be a little merciful with me. The relationship was complicated. I was thinking about showing him paintings for which he was not only the patron but the subject. And not only the subject of the painting but the object of my desire. Subject, object: even those words got mixed up. I think you can understand why I was looking for messages from the Divine. He'd watched me paint, but he hadn't seen anything finished. Why hadn't I shown him anything? I guess I felt no one painting was complete until the series was. I guess it's simple, I was scared.

I was tempted to forget being with anyone, go down to the liquor store, buy a bottle of Merlot and a bag of salted cashews, leave a message for Michael and sit in my bed with my quilt around me, eating and drinking till the phone rang. But that seemed like a posture of defeat rather than exaltation. It was a moment not for cowering and furtive consumption, but for exaltation and display.

But because I was so rattled by all the different things I was feeling I was a little nasty to B on the phone.

"I was wondering if you could leave the economic fate of the Americas for long enough to celebrate with me. Fanny's really pleased. She's ready for a show in May. I don't know if I can do it. I want you to look at the paintings. But of course I'm sure you have more important things to do."

"Yes, I was about to make a decision that could forestall a coup that will involve the lives of thousands. But I'll be right over."

"Is that true?"

"No, it's six o'clock. The market's closed."

"I thought you said there was always a market open somewhere."

"But not a market I can trade from."

I didn't know what he meant. I knew so little about what he did that I had no idea what, or where, the market was.

*    *    *

If it was hard for me to be around while Fanny was looking at the paintings, it was impossible with B. I put my running clothes on and went into the park with Mikey. I'd already run that morning, but it seemed like the only thing to do. My limbs were tight and resistant, my breath worked against me, there was no pleasure in the movement, no sense of overcoming gravity or odds. I had to talk to myself, like a Nike commercial; just do it, just do it. I practiced my old Catholic childhood trick of "offering it up." In Catholic lore, if you dedicated to God anything unpleasant or difficult, through some kind of economics none of us understood, you could release souls from Purgatory. There was a perversion of the bet: saying things to God like, "If I walk in the cold to Mass and don't complain to my mother, please make Frankie Gerardi ask me to the dance." Now I was saying: "If I run to the next tree, the show will be successful. I'll get a review in the *Times*."

I opened the door, gave Mikey a milk bone, took a cup of water, then another, trying to act natural in front of myself.

There was no putting it off. I had to find out what B thought of the paintings. When I went into the room, he was standing wiping his glasses on his shirt. His eyes were wet. He took me in his arms. Neither of us said anything.

I was embarrassed. Then I was terrified.

I was embarrassed because I never know what to do with my face when someone praises me. It's like being the one in the movie who's being sung to. There's the singer, looking perfectly all right, looking like a singer, concentrating on his vowel sounds or something sensible, and the poor fool who's being sung to always looks like a fool.

But why the terror? Simple fear of hubris, punishable by every nameable God? Fear of believing that you're really good and finding out later on that you're not and never were? Yes, that's it, isn't it: the worst of all fates, self-delusion.

Maybe I have trouble accepting praise because my hunger for it is so boundless and I'm always convinced that whatever praise I get will never be enough. At the same time, I'm convinced that no one's standards are the right ones, are high enough, in the same way I'm concerned that, when traveling, I might miss the important sights.

Whose words would I have believed? Irwin Panofsky's? Meyer Shapiro's? Why did it have to be a dead European-born male? Why did the horse of the horse's mouth always have to be a horse and not a mare? I revered Linda Nochlin, who'd written the essay "Why Are There No Great Women Artists?" but even if she'd told me my work was great, it wouldn't have carried the same weight. But I also wouldn't have believed her because she was Theresa's friend and I knew she was nice. Would I have believed Meyer Shapiro if he were Theresa's friend, and nice? He might have been perfectly nice, for all I know. But I thought of him as exacting. The only praise that really interested me, on the deepest level, the subcellar of the ego where the eyeless creatures breed, went something like this: "Every other living painter's work is shit. Yours, only yours, is gold."

"No no," I would have said. "You go too far."

But I would have loved it.


I wasn't with Meyer Shapiro, or Linda Nochlin, or even Theresa. I was with B. My lover was praising me and holding me. He wasn't saying much, only, "I'm very moved." And all I could think was: if he's wrong, I've lost so much.

I wanted to get away from him so I could remove myself from questions of response. Judgment/Failure. Judgment/Praise. At the same time, the smell of him, the wool of his sweater, itchy against my nose, his own smell mixed with the chemicals of his deodorant, reminded me of my connection to his body. It was a good thing, in the midst of embarrassment and fear, to feel the roughness of the wool and imagine the rough texture of his underarms, unbarbered, undomesticated, wilder than any other hair on his body, like a weed sprung up in a bed of cultivated flowers. I wanted to think of us as hungry animals, not lovers. I wanted anything that seemed to have nothing to do with the ideal.

"I can't do it by May. Fanny wants it by May and I can't do it. I still have to do the Bronzino and the Pontormo and the other Rosso, and finish the cloth on this Rosso, which I'll probably never get right. I can't do it. I have to call her right now and say I can't."

"Of course you can," he said, taking my hand and leading me over to the couch.

"If I do it, I can't do anything else. We can't go anywhere. We can't go out to dinner. And no sex."

He put his hand under my sweater.

"Just this last time," he said.

He unzipped my jeans.

"All right," I said. "Just this once."

For the next two weeks, I behaved erratically. I would overeat and then go days eating almost nothing. I wouldn't bathe, then I'd take four baths a day. I'd wear the same sweat pants days in a row, then try on every piece of clothing I owned, and ask him to take me someplace fancy for dinner. About sex, I was even more unpredictable. Some days I was an anchorite: I worked, I ran, I spoke to no one. Then I was too worn-out to do anything but sleep, or I'd be obsessed by the weather, overcome by it: a dull sky, a disturbing wind would absorb my concentration entirely. Some days I yearned for him with a hunger that was so much simpler than painting that I followed it like a blind animal following a scent. Some days he was the only one I could bear to see, and I would sleep with my legs around him the whole night.

I knew I wasn't looking well. I was gaining weight because I wasn't running regularly, and I was eating so oddly and so carelessly. Mikey looked awful too, because if I didn't run, he didn't run. I was spending too many hours sitting on the couch looking out the window. It was during this sluggish phase that he phoned and said I had to put everything down. Someone he knew, a client, had a friend who was a curator at the National Gallery in Washington and he could get us into the Vermeer show in the morning before the ordinary viewers arrived.

It was usually the case that when he offered me something that could only be had because of enormous privilege, privilege based on money, I objected out of egalitarian habit. All the people, I wanted to say, should have equal access to Vermeer. I should only be able to see the show in the morning if people in trailer parks and SROs could be given the same privilege. The problem was that the idea of looking at Vermeers in silence, without the crush of democratic others, seemed so desirable that even I thought it was ridiculous to object. I gave myself credit for having thought of the people in the trailer parks and SROs, and then asked what hotel we'd stay in, wondering if he'd find one with a pool and a Jacuzzi because my back and shoulder had been bothering me from all the hard work.

I don't know who he called to find the kind of place I wanted; I never knew exactly how he made these things happen. I guess I didn't want to know. But two hours after we got out of the cab at La Guardia, we were in an ultramodern lobby—you know how popular the concept of an atrium and lots of ferns is with a certain cohort of architects—where, half a level down, in a sunken piano bar, someone was playing Gershwin, badly, and above, huge arrangements of lilies spread their scent as you walked toward the elevator.

I'll never get over thinking of a hotel as an erotic place. Maybe you'd have to have been brought up in one, like Eloise, not to. There's something about the perfectly made king-size bed with the mint on the pillow that makes you want to eat the mint, roll around, mess up the bed. The crispness of the sheets, the endless multiplicity of the towels, the idea that someone is going to clean up, makes me feel like one of the English aristocracy at a weekend party at a country house in the twenties, you know, where everyone ends up with everyone else's spouse, so you can never tell about the purity of the bloodline.

We hung the little breakfast sign over the doorway: coffee and croissants at six. He answered the knock; it was pitch dark, and the waiter pretended not to see me in the bed, talking to B about the weather, congratulating him on having chosen the *New York Times* as his complimentary newspaper. We ate quickly. We couldn't ignore the supplication of the king-size bed. Flakes of croissant stuck to his buttocks. I licked them off. We were out of the hotel by 6:45.

And then, in the hush of a closed museum, where only a few others who had also paid hugely for the privilege tapped their expensive heels on the marble floors, I saw a miracle of light and composition, of order and astonishment, of beautiful painting on its own terms and for its own sake, the creation of an atmosphere that would bring consolation and hope for hundreds of years. All achieved by a man working on perspective and luminosity, holding a brush dipped in white to create the sheen of pearl, dipped in blue to make the envelope of a woman's dream, in red for the shock of a feathered hat, in yellow for the sunlight on a young girl's dress, or the band of the turban of a daughter who is leaving, leaving her father's regard for the regard of men, that rich, unknowable blackness in which she will disappear and not be followed.

I don't know if I was looking at it, or experiencing it, as an artist. The work was so complete in itself, so absolutely transparent, inviting the spectator in and yet forcing him back on himself, demanding that people come to it not as people who did things—bankers, surgeons— but as people who were things, had been born, saw, mourned, desired, and would die. It wasn't that I was thinking I would imitate his technique, the use of perspective, the underpainting, the opalescence of pearl or lip. He did make me think, of course, about the importance of emptiness, of uncrowded space, of the evocation of emptiness as a question of volume. But, do you understand, it wasn't that I would paint like Vermeer in the technical sense. What I wanted was more an example of something I would have to call moral; that sense of his getting out of the way of his own vision, of not coming between the spectator and what the spectator wanted to see, the graciousness of a withdrawal so complete that there was space between the viewer and the image that made room for the whole world. I was thinking about how to bring silence into my paintings. Of course I couldn't do it as he did; he was a man in seventeenth-century Holland; I am a woman in late-twentieth-century America. But in a different sense, I could follow his example, in ways I knew would have to come from the memory of what I'd seen.

I had three days of good work when we came back from the Vermeer, then it was time to go to Florida to see my mother for Christmas.

I was thinking of canceling, on account of work, but then I thought of a story someone had told me about Martha Stewart, how one Christmas she sent her husband and daughter away so she could finish a book and she spent the day eating liverwurst out of a tube and ironing all her linen napkins. I've always known one thing about myself: I don't want to be Martha Stewart.

I guess it's a sign of mental health that I could contemplate a visit to my mother without succumbing to a major ailment. For many years, I never went to Florida without swollen glands or stomach flu. Only recently have I begun to enjoy my mother; Helena could do it much earlier than I. Only recently have I realized that my mother and I have something very important in common: we're both interested in pleasure.

My mother had a gift for getting small doses of pleasure for herself, in a life that was made up primarily of hard work. Sitting on the fire escape on a sunny day, smoking a cigarette. Making lavender sachets for her underwear drawer. And one night a month, she went to the movies with her girlfriends.

My mother is what you might call an entertaining narcissist, and almost entirely without malice. When I was younger it pained me that she never seemed to fully grasp that I was in the world apart from her. Now it doesn't seem to matter quite so much.

She calls the senior citizens' complex where she lives the Reservation. She's one of the unusual ones among her friends because she has a beau. She's a very attractive woman, particularly her feet. Even at eighty-one, she has absolutely perfect feet, and she's very vain about them.

I think my mother and her boyfriend, Harry, are doing it, although of course she'd never admit to that. She only hints. Broadly. Once she complained about her ribs aching because of "the pressure of a man who tends to be large in the torso." She wasn't mentioning any names.

The good thing about Christmas is that Helena and Hans and their girls and my girls and I all stay at the most vulgar possible Holiday Inn; of course my mother doesn't have room for us. Hans is very nice about dealing with his children; I think he knows nobody else wants to talk to him as much as they want to talk to each other. But that's not fair; his English isn't good and none of us knows German. He's very handsome, though, and that allows my mother to sit herself in flattering lights and smile and offer him a lot of bite-size foods, like olives and peanuts, so she can make several trips and show off her figure.

I knew it would come: The Question. "I don't mean to pry, you know I never pry, but just out of curiosity, are you going out with anyone? Not that I ever really knew why you broke up with Roger. It wasn't my business, so I never asked."

A few years ago, I would have said, "That's actually not true, Mother, for the past five years you've asked about every two weeks. It's just that I've never told you."

But this time I answered her question. I told her I was going out with someone.

"Would you say he's serious?"

"About what?"

"You know, Monica, at your age, you don't have to get wise with me."

It struck me as noteworthy that in my mother's lexicon "wise" was always a put-down.

"I don't want to live with anyone again."

"You say that now. But it's nice to have someone when you get older."

"You don't live with Harry."

"Harry's married. Not in the physical sense, of course, he's never been interested in that with her, not for years, and he's a very healthy male animal, so who could blame him."

"Would you marry him if you could?"

"I don't want to take care of an old man."

"But you're an old woman."

"I've gotten used to my own way."

"See, Mom, you've come around to my point of view."

"I haven't come around to your point of view. The situations are entirely different."

My mother had never known exactly what to make of Sara, but she and Rachel always got along very well. Their relationship was based on cards; my mother is a demon cardplayer, which is remarkable when you consider that she's unable to balance a checkbook or remember anybody's name. Rachel learned bridge, poker and pinochle from my mother; since Rachel was the only one related by blood to share her interest, she quickly became the favorite.

My mother had given up cooking; she announced that, after my father died, she would bake but she would never again cook another major meal for anyone. So the house was full of Christmas cakes and cookies but nothing whose major ingredients weren't butter and sugar. We always went to the Red Lobster for Christmas dinner, because my mother knew the hostess. The food was awful, but at least it wasn't turkey.

I had trouble getting back to work after my Florida sojourn. I wanted to blame it on my mother and the Red Lobster; I tend to think that I can't be a daughter, a consumer of bad food and a painter at the same time. But it was simpler than that: I'd been interrupted, and this time it *was* like being interrupted at the edge of orgasm.

I phoned B as soon as I got home. I told him my refrigerator was empty, and asked if I could come to his place. I spent the first half hour complaining about not being able to work and telling him I had to leave.

"This kind of conversation is not interesting," he said. "Either leave or let me distract you with my voluptuary ardor."

"Be nice to me, I'm suffering."

"I was planning to be nice to you," he said, putting his hand on my stomach.

It was a good move. His fingers tracing my ribs made me want to stop thinking about artistic conflict and dive into that zone where I am not a person who produces, but a person who finds certain sensations irresistible.

"I want to be completely passive," I said. "I want you to start everything and do everything. Let's play Rick and Ilsa. I want you to do the thinking for both of us."

"You want me to put you on a plane with your husband and walk off with Claude Rains?"

"No, I just don't want to be in charge of anything."

"I'm wondering how long this will last. But anything for a change. Now, you do exactly as I say. Go into my bedroom and stand there."

I walked in like a good little soldier. Or like a good little first communion girl.

He turned on the overhead light.

"Isn't that awfully harsh?" I said.

"You're not in charge of anything. Sit on the edge of the bed."

He knelt in front of me.

"Lean on my shoulder," he said. "I'm going to take off your shoes and socks."

He unlaced my hiking boots. He took off my wool socks. My feet were chilly and he cradled them in his hands. He put them under his armpits to warm them. He told me to lie back on the bed. He unzipped my jeans. He slipped them off. He slipped off my underpants. He told me to leave my feet on the floor. He told me to keep my hands under my head and not to move them. He licked the insides of my calves, behind my knees, and then inside my thighs. But no further. I was sweating in my wool shirt, but he didn't move to take it off. He concentrated on my knees and feet.

I couldn't bear to be so untouched, so unattended. I reached for his head.

"I said keep your hands behind your head. You're not in charge of anything."

This time, with dry kisses, he traveled the length of my legs, then down again.

"Please, I can't wait," I said.

"You have to wait."

He still didn't take my shirt off, and the heat increased my sense of frustration. He refused to do anything but run his dry lips up and down my legs.

I was making sounds like a calf who can't quite find the teat. When I thought I couldn't bear another second of this, he moved his tongue up the inside of my leg, insinuated it, wet, flat, settled it on the necessary quarter inch, circled, traveled. He unzipped his jeans but didn't take them off; the material was rough against me. I was on the edge of the bed; my feet, still on the floor. Then there was no insinuation; entrance was what it was all about, and he came in hard, sharp bursts, unnuanced and without refinement.

I moved to the center of the bed.

"I didn't say you could do that," he said.

"Oh, fuck off, I'm back in charge now."

"How did you like your holiday?"

"It was very diverting," I said. "But I didn't get to suck you."

"You sound like you're a copilot going through the checklist. Extensive foreplay, check. Suck cock, check. Roger. Ready for takeoff. Over and out."

"What do you know about copilots? Did you ever make it with a stewardess?"

"No, I was afraid they'd give me drinks from those little bottles and their bed would be full of those fake pillows and those blindfolds for overseas flights."

"You may have missed something."

"Have you ever had a pilot?"

"I never wanted a pilot."

"What makes you think I wanted a stewardess?"

"Let's say it's a lucky guess."

He came in from the kitchen carrying a tray loaded with pastrami, cole slaw, potato salad, corned beef, chips, beer. I showed him how I could open a beer bottle with my teeth.

"That's impressive. But I always said you had a very talented mouth. Except when you're talking about artistic conflict."

"I'm not having artistic conflict," I said. "I'm leaving now. I'm dying to get back to work."

It was wonderful going out into the cold with my lips abraded from lovemaking and the salt of the unhealthy meal, standing on the corner exposed to the river and the wind when we'd been so cosseted by warmth and each other's bodies, so fattened by the spicy, fattening food. I was there, but I was in the room in front of my canvases. I knew exactly what needed to be done.

I don't remember doing anything that winter except working. I spent time with my dog; I saw my friends. Occasionally, I slept with B, but not so much as at other times. Time swallowed itself; I woke in dread and was free of it only when I was working.

I dreamed of holding brushes that made no mark. I dreamed the gallery caught fire; I dreamed no one came to the opening; I dreamed everyone in the world came to the opening and I was wearing only a bra.

Many mornings, the first words running through my head were

YOU'RE TRYING TO DO TOO MUCH. YOU'RE NOT GOING TO BE ABLE TO DO ANY OF IT. WHO DO YOU THINK YOU ARE?

In the palmy days before I actually began any of the paintings, when I was just planning and making sketches, I thought I had a wonderful idea. When I actually had to execute it—and the word's a good one, I did feel like I was murdering my beautiful idea—the amusement stopped. I tried to get the dopey fatigue into the third Rosso Fiorentino face, the Venetian one, where Jesus looks like a lounge lizard being taken down from the cross, his arm flopped over the man on the ladder trying to depose him. I replaced the man on the ladder with a bench. Even though it was freezing, I made B try to lounge on a park bench, his arm flopped over the back. It wasn't easy, that floppy arm. Or the blue of the night sky—how to make it cloudy but not muddy. And the pink of Jesus's loincloth, B's running shorts. I would have liked to make him sit on the bench in his running shorts, but even I'm not that exacting. Not in January.

I had to try to maintain Pontormo's hard-edged but uneasy sense of balance. I almost started smoking again because of the Mantegna legs and feet. The Bronzino went easily, and so did the Sodoma. The Carpaccios required a lot of reworking because they were the first ones. After I'd done two or three in the series—particularly after the ordeal of the Mantegna—I'd learned a lot.

I didn't thank B enough for posing for me. It took a great deal of time. It was uncomfortable. It might have been humiliating. Posed, he was my creature. But I couldn't afford to acknowledge the extent of my gratitude; it would have overwhelmed me. And I had too much work to do.

SPENT MEN wasn't going to be a huge show, but then Fanny's gallery wasn't huge. Nine paintings. Twenty-eight by eighteen, except for the Sodoma, which was small, and a series of red charcoal drawings after Pontormo, also small.

There's a point in the preparation for a show when you just have to give it up. When you know there might be more things you can do but you know you're not going to do them.

I knew that day had come on April 25 when I dressed to go to the gallery to talk with Jimmy, the young man who hangs paintings for Fanny.

I always felt a little unbalanced walking down Fifty-seventh Street on my way to Fanny's gallery. After you cross Fifth Avenue, heading east, Fifty-seventh becomes one of the most expensive streets in the world. It starts with Bergdorf, on the corner of Fifth, with mannequins in the window who look electrocuted, wearing clothes that seem unwearable or insane, and yet desirable at the same time. Not like Milan where you can't imagine anyone even buying the clothes. You can imagine someone buying the clothes at Bergdorf. Just not anyone you know.

Past Madison, all frivolity, all sense of play disappears. You're confronted with stores offering the possibilities of serious purchases, purchases made to last, purchases beyond fashion. In a row: Hermès, Burberrys, Chanel. And then the Fuller Building, where Fanny's gallery is, abode of so many galleries, suggesting a prosperity whose roots dip down to a more solid layer than even Hermès or Chanel.

I'm glad that Fanny's gallery is on Fifty-seventh Street in the Fuller Building, instead of down in Soho. There's something about the art deco bronze that makes me feel secure. All that stylization. All those symbols based on war or agriculture. Those ears of corn. Those axes. Sometimes I suspect that the design on the door of the Fuller Building has something to do with Fascist iconography. But I don't dwell on it.

And there really was a Fuller: a plaque in the lobby says the building is dedicated to George B. Fuller. I always mean to look him up. I keep wondering if he's the original Fuller Brush man, and if all this opulence, this bronze and marble, has its source in some little guy selling brooms door to door. But I don't think of myself as of the party of George B. Fuller. I think of myself as one of the workers on the bronze elevator doors: hoisting and lifting and building the cities of the future.

On the wall is a list of the galleries, including their permanent collections; and those are some pretty dazzling names: Dubuffet, Léger, Delaunay. But I think of us as all workers here; I have something in common with Léger, and we both have something in common with the bronze stevedores. We have nothing in common with the businessmen who buy the candy at the newsstand or the leather bags in the lobby shop. I got into a fight with one of them once, before my last show with Fanny, when I was feeling particularly on edge. Some poor teacher from the provinces, in washed-out corduroys, Adidas and a backpack, made the elevator stop at the second floor. Another one in a long Laura Ashley dress and identical Adidas made it stop on the third. "Oh, goody, gallery watchers," said the businessman in his three-hundred-dollar haircut.

"For Christ's sake," I said, "you should feel privileged to be able to work in a building with all this art instead of complaining about it. It's people like you who kill tourism in New York."

I thought the two women would be grateful, but they just looked embarrassed. Another of my mistakes based on too high an estimation of human nature.

After I'd worked with Jimmy on the hanging, there was nothing to do but wait. I couldn't stop thinking about the paintings, but I couldn't do anything to change them. And I didn't feel I could really start anything new until I'd seen this show through, at least until the opening. All the metaphors for showing your work, like giving birth or appearing naked on a lit-up stage, are inadequate. Although I've never appeared naked on a lit-up stage, I have given birth and it's nothing like that. With a painting you're about to show it's not as if you don't know what you're going to get, boy or girl, cherub or monster. And, I guess, if you appeared on a lit-up stage, you'd be doing it because you wanted to do it. The display would be the whole point of the deal. But showing your work is different because when you worked on it you weren't necessarily interested in people looking at it. You were just interested in making it.

After I've finished, it occurs to me that people looking at what I've done is somehow part of the process.

I often wonder what it would be like to paint and never have anybody see it. It seems like a terrific luxury. Because all the pleasure I get from the positive response to one of my paintings is nothing compared with the anguish I feel from one negative comment. It could come from the most ridiculous person in the world, some sixteen-year-old who strolled into the gallery while waiting for her hair appointment at Bergdorf's, or someone in the cleaning crew—anybody—and I'll believe it. Of course, it's worse if someone I respect says something negative. The difficult but crucial thing is to be open to criticism so that in case anybody says anything helpful you can take it in, but to have enough faith in what you've done not to let it affect you if it isn't helpful. Everybody tells you all those things about the critics who hated Manet, but they never tell you about the horrible reviews that have been written about horrible painters. The problem is that critics aren't 100 percent wrong. You can count on them to be moronic, but not exclusively.

That's the problem.

And in the weeks or nights before the opening you lie awake composing the most devastating reviews that have ever been written. I could hear the words: "Her reach exceeds her grasp, she ought to return to the pleasant figurative of her last show. I recall, particularly, some fine studies of her dog."

This opening was going to be even more difficult because along with my paintings, I was going to display B. I thought that since I would already be out of my mind with anxiety, I might as well go all the way and introduce B to my friends at the same time.

Maybe he was nervous, too, because he was unusually unsympathetic to my anxieties. He said, "I can't believe you. Having conversations with critics, people who aren't even in your zip code at the time, to say nothing of the same room. I think of you as being a strong person, someone who has confidence in herself. I don't think of you as being so formed by the opinions of others. The hypothetical opinions."

"What the hell do you know about it?" I shouted. "You never put yourself at risk like this. The risk of public humiliation. People telling you that what you need is vocational counseling."

"So because I haven't experienced exactly what you've experienced, I have no right to speak about it?"

"You have no right to speak about it unsympathetically. Do you know what I'd be allowed to do if I were one of those male painters? Do you know what you'd have to do? You'd be down at the precinct bailing me out of the clinker I'd gotten into when I punched out two cops in a drunken brawl. You'd be sitting with me in the doctor's office waiting for the results of my gonorrhea test. I'm getting up to make Ovaltine in the middle of the night and you're calling me weak-minded. Jesus Christ."

"All I'm saying is that you're not helping yourself."

"Oh, thanks, I thought I was."

An opening is Purgatory for me. I try to concentrate on the fact that a lot of people I'm very fond of are in the room. But I'm listening to their conversation in such a peculiar, distorted way; I'm trying to hear what they're saying about the work and not hear it at the same time, and above all I'm trying to pretend I'm not listening, so that I can trap them into an honest response. A lot of painters, some of whom are my friends, some of whom aren't, but we're on each other's opening lists, would be there. In some ways the criticism of other painters is the only criticism that really matters to me, because they're the only ones who know what it's like. Some people are there because they've bought my work in the past, or they've said they liked it. Or pretended to because they liked me. And friends of friends, there for God knows what reason.

And then there was B. He was looking as good that night as I'd ever seen him, wearing a new jacket, a beautiful silk tweed with a touch of violet in the weave. A light blue shirt with onyx cuff links. His new Italian loafers, which I'd smelled, inhaling them with pleasure and then putting them back in their pristine box. At least I didn't have to worry about Rachel saying, "Jesus, Mom, you've really got yourself a loser." Or a sad look in Sara's eyes. Or Michael saying he'd take him to the barber or shopping. Or Theresa making supportive statements about how appearance isn't everything. He looked terrific. He was mine.

I introduced him awkwardly, stupidly. "Well, you all know who this is, so say whatever it is you have to say." Then I stood there.

Michael said, "What we love most about you are your social graces."

"I can't deal with this," I said. "I'm going to talk to someone I don't know."

Which I think I did, though I don't have much memory of what I actually did or said that night. I was swept up in a whirl of elation and terror; I presented a false smile to everyone who told me how brilliant everything was, how courageous I was, how original. I didn't believe anything, but it felt good for a minute, like cool water on a third-degree burn. My sense of the horrible mistake I'd made felt like a burn; I had an enormous desire to put all the paintings under my arm, hail a cab, run home with them, and not let anybody look.

I couldn't help noticing Fanny's assistant, who walked around with a sheet of those red dots, stuck them, rather often, on the wall next to the paintings. At one point, Fanny came up to me and said, "You've sold out, darling, 100 percent. You're a terrific hit."

I ran over to Michael and B, who were talking about Joel McCrea and Preston Sturgess. "I've sold out," I said.

I was trying not to smile.

The two of them put their arms out at the same moment to embrace me. I didn't know where to go. Then B stepped back with a gesture that indicated I should go to Michael. I'd never liked him better than I did then, when I saw that he'd understood he should defer to Michael, how bad it would have been if, at that moment, he'd asserted primacy of place based on the fact that he was the man I slept with or lived off.

Michael had spent a fortune at Zabar's and we invited about twenty people to his apartment for an after-show party. Traditionally, you go out with your dealer and a few people, but I can't stand the anxiety of exclusion, so I refuse. I was still a little shell-shocked, and still worried that people weren't going to like B. I'd never seen him in a social setting; it had been a quality, or a condition of our love affair that we'd been alone. I had no idea how he'd behave. I knew that I found him intelligent, attractive and witty, but suppose I was wrong? There were a couple of tricky customers in the group, particularly Rachel, who wasn't, to begin with, well-disposed. He and Michael could talk about movies; he could talk about music to Sara, except that she was trying to appear invisible; Theresa gets along with everybody, and they could talk about art. I was just hoping nobody would bring up money; that was, once again, the problem. Most of the people I was close to felt money was tainted, and money was what he did.

At one point in the evening he and Rachel were talking. I think it had something to do with the international labor movement and the possibilities of global unionization. I was afraid to listen too closely. I could tell by her posture that she was trying not to like him, to resist him. I recognized the posture because it was one I so often adopted. But then I saw her laughing. I was dying to know what they were laughing at, I thought it was in my interest to find out.

"So what kind of lunatic would sign up for a cruise to relive the sinking of the *Titanic?*"

It turns out they'd both ripped out a full-page ad in *USA Today* (they both read it on a plane, they kept reassuring each other, they never would have bought it). They'd both sent away for a free invitation for a cruise around New York Harbor that took place on a replica of the *Titanic*. People were to arrive in period costumes. I kept trying to get details, but neither of them was particularly interested in talking to me. And I knew Rachel well enough; she was a tough sell, but once sold, she was a marshmallow. From now on she'd always take his side. I would never be able to criticize B to her.

I sat on the couch with my feet on the coffee table, which Michael would never have stood for if it weren't my big night. Sara sat next to me. On the chair across from us was Michael's new beau, a dermatologist. I knew he wouldn't last because he wasn't getting our jokes; he kept looking at us as if we were in a tennis match he couldn't keep track of. Champagne corks popped, and my friends kissed me. Sara put her head on my shoulder. Rachel said, "Well, I think I should toast my sister and myself for the future embarrassment we'll have to endure when people talk about us as the daughters of a woman who paints dirty pictures."

Nobody said anything about the fact that the man in the pictures was clearly B.

In the years since I'd been divorced, I'd gotten used to leaving parties by myself. Or with Michael. I wasn't accustomed to being toasted and then returning home for sex. And I wasn't accustomed at all to sharing B with the people I knew. Knowing my friends and family didn't hate him was a relief. I couldn't have taken the risk of finding out until I'd finished my paintings; I would have felt differently about him as a subject if he was someone I'd have to defend, even in my own mind, someone I'd have to silence my objections about.

At the same time, sharing him with other people, opening him up to the rest of my life, was a bit of a loss. Our secrecy had added a charge—the erotics of darkness, of concealment, a sense of steamy enclosure, like one of those French movies about adultery in the tropics. The thrill of secret vice, of course, was connected to money as well. Now we were opening ourselves to the light of day and there was the comparative letdown of wholesomeness. I was grateful that he could find a place in my life, proud of him, but also a little disappointed.

"I think we need to get away for a few days, to celebrate your success with a particular extravagance. How would you like to go to Rome for the weekend? I have a friend with an apartment that's nearly always empty because she lives with someone. But the apartment was her divorce present and she doesn't want to give it up."

"Rome for the weekend?"

"Or just for lunch. No work. No looking at paintings. I want us just to walk the streets and look at monuments and spaces. And the color of the walls. I want you to be just a girl on my arm. Do you think you can do that?"

"I think I'm up to it. A Roman bimbolina. I solemnly pledge."

We flew, first class. But I was too exhausted for airplane sex play; I fell asleep on his shoulder after the first glass of champagne. I was ready to do something I'd never done before: travel to Italy and not look at paintings that could help me with my work. There was a certain freedom in going to a city like Rome just for a weekend. It was so clear that you couldn't do it properly, couldn't see everything, couldn't see even the most important things. It was so obviously an enterprise of frivolity, a scandalous waste. We took the plane on Thursday night, and we'd be returning Tuesday afternoon. Four days in one of the world's great cities. You could do whatever you wanted. It was the only thing to do.

B's friend lived in the Nomentana where there were a lot of embassies. Not the most central neighborhood, but full of huge old plane trees and elegant art nouveau cafés. Scattered on the pavement of our courtyard were pinecones the size of toy footballs; the building was art deco, or Fascist, hard to tell, just like the Fuller Building. The terrace overlooked the always festive Roman roofs.

The apartment was so obviously not inhabited that it seemed unthinkable to even make morning coffee there. On the other hand, the bed was enormous and there was a mirror that covered the entire wall across from it. I could imagine it might be alarming if you woke suddenly in the middle of the night. But it had other possibilities.

We bathed in the tub with the green stain under the faucet, and we positioned ourselves in front of the mirror. It was shocking how big he looked in the mirror, much bigger than in real life, and how small my mouth looked. I felt a little sorry for myself. But I was actually rather moved by the curve of my breasts and shoulders, as if they belonged to somebody else.

I wasn't just moved, I was aroused. How can it be that I was aroused by the sight of myself, and by seeing a man I had looked at a hundred times? What did we see when we looked? Were we looking at each other as a couple, or as individuals? Were we looking at each other, or at ourselves? In the mirror, I was a stranger to myself, an actress skillfully and shockingly performing for my own eyes. My own, not his. Can it be true, what B had said about posing, that we really don't know what we look like, that our own aspect has the capacity to surprise, even excite us? Was I seeing my lover in a new way, or seeing a new lover? I don't know; I couldn't see my face, I wasn't focused on it. I had no face. I was featureless. And at what moment did I leave the scene? At what moment did the visible become nothing, did I pass through the visible to pure sensation? How did it happen that, my back against the red kilim thinly covering the gray white marble, I was everyone and no one, and that afterward, beneath him, I was almost ready to resent the weight and pressure of the body I had minutes before avidly followed? When did we grow informal, unworthy of regard, and only fit for sleep?

We bathed again, caught a taxi to the Pantheon, and had coffee in the café that was supposed to have the best in Rome. When it rained we took shelter in the Pantheon, that utterly unornamented tribute to the greatness of the Empire. The ceiling of the Pantheon is an open circle and the rain fell through it like a stream of water in a funnel. It wet the circle of stone immediately below it, but the water didn't seem to spread, and it was clear that it would do no damage. I was fascinated by the simplicity, the crudeness of that solution—a hole in the ceiling for light and air—by people of such obvious sophistication and mastery.

We walked to the Trevi Fountain. He told me he had an idea for a short film. He said I should look at all the people who had their pictures taken at the fountain. I did. Germans, Japanese, Americans, Africans, Latins, every single one of them did exactly the same thing: threw a coin over the shoulder, gave a sheepish grin, then widened it into a big smile for the camera. He said this proved something profound about human nature and one day he'd make a short film, he swore he would.

We walked in the dreamy green of the Borghese Gardens with the statues of historical figures no one could believe had ever inhabited solid earth. We listened to the fountains. At the top of the Pincio he pressed me up against the wall and kissed me, told me I was the sexiest thing that ever lived and it was too bad I had no mind. On our way to the Baths of Caracalla, he stopped at a barbershop.

"I've always wanted an Italian haircut," he said.

It was clearly a place where women weren't welcome. Men were draped in striped sheets that buttoned at the neck; they were reading God knows what magazines. Just like America, except their shoes were better.

I told him I'd come back in half an hour. He was standing on the sidewalk with his great new haircut, grinning.

"I've found out something terribly important," he said. "The slang for clitoris in Italian is *grillo*. Cricket."

"How did you happen to find that out? You go in to get a haircut and discover the Italian slang for clitoris? That doesn't happen to a lot of guys. They might learn the word for sideburns. Or for not too much around the ears. I hope you didn't make another stop between here and there."

"There was a guy in the barbershop who spoke a little English. He felt a burning need to tell me that he was really puzzled in New York by a sign that said Bar and Grill. He thought it was a place for a drink and some quick nooky, but he couldn't figure it out."

"I do like it," I said. "Chirping and hopping and making a cheerful noise around the house all night. Just singing away in its quiet little corner."

"All tucked in and happy," he said.

One evening as we were about to go to dinner, the phone rang. We didn't know whether to answer it; we were afraid it might be B's friend's ex-husband. But I'd given my number to Michael and to the girls; I always did. My greatest fear was that something would happen to them and I'd be unreachable, would innocently return home not knowing that the news of disaster was waiting for me the minute I turned my key in the lock. I answered the phone.

It was Fanny, and she couldn't keep the excitement out of her voice.

"How would you like to hear a rave from Michael Kimmelman?"

"Michael Kimmelman? In the *Times*? He's reviewing me? With how many other people?"

"No one but you, darling, you have four columns to yourself."

"And he liked it?"

"Just listen: 'In a time of postmodern ironic emptiness, this painter dares to combine wit and feeling, a line that takes its clarity from the Renaissance Masters, and its intelligence from the best feminist revelations of the seventies.'"

He went on to praise the Mantegna and the Rosso Fiorentino. My palette and my line. My exciting new vision.

"New," I said. "I've only been showing for fifteen years."

"Never mind," said Fanny. "I can't make room for all the people who want to get into the gallery. You're a smash hit."

"Are they looking because of the painting or because they're being prurient?"

"What do you care?"

"Of course I care. I can't stand that just anybody gets to go in and look at my paintings. Painters have to try out to be taken on by galleries. People should have to try out to come in and look."

"Well, it's not going to happen, love. You'll just have to learn to get used to your hordes."

When I told B, he lifted me up in the air and twirled me around. My first thought was that he was going to throw his back out. But he didn't. He threw me on the bed and covered me with kisses.

"How do you say champagne in Italian and where do we get some?"

"Champagne is champagne. I don't know. I don't even know where we could get the fucking article faxed to us. Not that I care that much. I mean Kimmelman, he hates a lot of people that I like. Who is he, after all, just a critic. Why should I care what he thinks?"

"Because all over New York people on buses are reading your name, and reading what a great painter you are."

"Well, that happens fifty times a year at least. It can't be true fifty times a year. And why all of a sudden is he paying attention to me? I haven't gotten that much better. I just thought of a good gimmick."

"You have gotten better. And why are you calling it a gimmick? Is the Blue Period a gimmick?"

"I hate the fucking Blue Period as you perfectly well know."

"You're clearly too insane to be cooped up. Let's go to Roselli's on the Piazza del Popolo. We'll have champagne and watch the world go by. Then I'll get you drunk and carry you home in my arms."

"We shouldn't do that. It will make the review seem too important."

"It is important. And it's wonderful. Can't you enjoy it even for a little while?"

"I'm afraid to," I said.

Which was partly true, though even as I lectured myself, little bumps of joy kept rising up like molehills in a level lawn. The *New York Times* was saying I was good. Everybody was reading it. Everyone I knew and people I didn't know. People who didn't believe in me and people who always had. What did it have to do with me? Nothing, really. But I felt, when I allowed myself to, like a big deal. I couldn't wait to get home.

I was a little hung over on the flight, so I just kept drinking till I felt sleepy. Thank God a car was waiting for us, and I could fall into bed once I got home. It wasn't till the next morning that I looked at my mail and listened to my phone machine. Which had, and I do not exaggerate though I'm often accused of it, twenty-eight messages. None of which I could exactly understand. The word "picket" kept recurring and I couldn't imagine which of the groups I belong to had organized a strike. It hardly seemed like Watson faculty behavior.

When I finally answered the phone it was Fanny. "Only in America. I'll never get used to how serious you all are."

I asked her to tell me what she was talking about.

"You haven't heard?"

"Nothing I can make sense of."

"I scarcely know where to begin. It seems you're being picketed by the religious right. They're accusing you of blasphemy. I don't know whether to recommend that you come down here or not. It does have a certain dreadful carnival air. But these people are not amused and they're not pleased. Of course, from a business point of view, it's heaven. The show is packed from opening till closing, when we have to throw people out. And everyone wants you for an interview. The *Times,* the *Voice, Art in America.* And Charlie Rose wants you on TV with a woman who organized the picket line. Come if you like but perhaps you should bring your dishy new boyfriend with you. He's rather broad-shouldered."

I wish I didn't have to admit this to you, but the first thing I felt when I heard that someone had accused me of blasphemy was guilt. When I was growing up, blasphemy was a big thing. I had a concept of the sacred and it never occurred to me, until accused, that I might be violating the sacred.

But was I really honest in saying that? Had I gotten off on being a smart-assed bad girl doing something naughty that might get me in trouble with the nuns? Michael would suggest that I did not give enough credit to my subconscious. Oh, I forgot, he keeps telling me, they've disinvented the subconscious. It never existed. It's the unconscious now. Or repression or whatever it is that makes you not know what you're doing when you mix up words or forget the keys to your hotel room on your wedding night.

Maybe I had offended some really sincere and decent people. I called B and tried to explain it to him. He couldn't stop laughing. I told him he lacked imagination. I mentioned some aunts of mine who were very kind but literal-minded. He said he'd be right over, that we'd beard the lion arm in arm.

I was cringing a little in the cab, prepared to apologize to my great-aunt Bettina, who'd been dead for twenty years. And then I saw the pickets, a ragged crew of seven women and two men, ill-dressed and middle-aged. I got out of the cab and saw who was carrying the biggest sign. All impulse to apologize vanished.

That person wasn't a stranger. It was Alice Marie Cusalito, who'd been Helena's and my archenemy at St. Augusta's—head prefect of Sodality, chief justice of Student Court, president of the Vocation Club and snitch extraordinaire.

She was supposed to have become a nun right after graduation, the only one in our class. She was dressed in a way that meant she possibly could still be a nun: a navy blue raincoat and beige flats and one of those terrible pocketbooks with two straps that she'd flung over her forearm— a real handicap if you're carrying a poster that says: "Stand up to visual blasphemy. Jesus is not a joke."

It's hard to know where to start with Alice Marie. A lot of water had gone under the bridge. I hadn't seen her in thirty-two years, since graduation, and at that time I was delighted to think I'd never see her again. Now I looked at her puddingy face, or maybe it wasn't a pudding, it was a failed pineapple upside-down cake. She'd always had bad hair—frizzy and wild in an age when the Jackie Kennedy flip was prized—and now it had gone gray. You couldn't say Alice Marie had fallen from a graceful youth, but however bad she'd looked at eighteen, at fifty she looked even worse. She was wearing glasses with steel blue frames and both her eyes and mouth looked grim. She wasn't fooling around. She meant business.

My last encounter with her was something of a struggle. I was president of our homeroom, and acknowledged by everyone in the school to be the one with artistic talent. So I had the final word on issues of classroom decoration. The other class officers and I had decided to decorate for spring using the words of the song we were all obsessed with: Simon and Garfunkel's "Scarborough Fair." There was a huge supply of precut green felt letters in the art nun's cupboard—nuns were very good at having endless supplies of things you wouldn't have thought of. We'd put yellow shelf paper on the bulletin boards and I'd done some apple blossoms—pink and white with black stems. They looked very good; the other people in the class thought I was a genius. Alice Marie was instructed to arrange the felt letters so that they spelled out the words: "Are you going to Scarborough Fair/Parsley, sage, rosemary and thyme." But when we walked into the classroom, we saw she'd arranged the letters to spell out: "It's nice to be important, but it's important to be nice."

I went into one of those rages that looms large in your personal history because they are, after all, unusual and because they help you understand people who go after their families with chain saws. I don't think I physically hurt Alice Marie, but I know I went for her person. The homeroom nun, who was really very nice and liked me, separated us and brought us over to the convent to calm down over a cup of tea. I would not apologize. I told her that Alice Marie had been clearly instructed by all the class officers and that she'd ignored our instructions. I may have used the words "overstepped her authority." I pointed out that she was lucky we let her do anything in the classroom because everybody thought she was such a creep, and that would teach me to do things out of the goodness of my heart. Sister Perpetua told me not to say things I'd later regret. I told her no one regretted the truth. Sister Perpetua told Alice Marie to express her point of view. She said that the message she put up was more important than the whim of the moment, some popular song that everyone would forget in a month. She asked Sister if she understood that songs were only in the top ten for a week or so. I said that had nothing to do with anything: she'd been given instructions. She said the way everything turned out it proved she'd been right, because some people had no idea how to be nice, ever.

Neither of us would apologize. We walked back into homeroom; there was a loud buzz that ended in silence the minute everyone saw Sister Perpetua's face. It was a facet of Catholic girls' schools in those days: the buzz of rumor, so that tales of Gothic intensity could be spread and believed in seconds, a roar that built up like a tidal wave, that could be silenced by the appearance of one of those white faces framed by a black veil.

Sister Perpetua asked Kathy Grogan, class vice-president and one of the kindest people who ever lived, if perhaps she'd stay after school and replace Alice Marie's message with the one the class had agreed on. Alice Marie sat down at her seat, heavily—she was always heavy, and we speculated that she wore at least a size-ten shoe—and she let out a righteous sigh. For the next three months, every time she looked at me she glared. Occasionally I was tempted to apologize for having gone for her throat, but she'd always do something—like taking advantage of her position as chief justice of Student Court to give my friend Diane Mulcahy a month's detention for getting into a car with a boy while still in her school uniform—and my resolve would harden.

And I guess it hadn't softened in thirty-two years because the first thing I could think of to say to her on the sidewalk on Fifty-seventh Street was, "Well, Alice Marie, I guess you're still busy with your old mission of harassing artists and obstructing their work."

She seemed to think there was only one possible response to my greeting: "What doth it profit a man to gain the whole world and suffer the loss of his immortal soul?"

I didn't think it was the moment to press for gender-inclusive language.

All this time, B was holding my arm, and as I hadn't had the chance to fill him in on my history with Alice Marie, he was understandably puzzled. He asked me if I wanted to talk to these people or if I was ready to go into the gallery. I said, quite loudly, that I wouldn't talk to those ignoramuses if they were the last people on earth.

I wasn't used to having to walk through crowds of people with my head down to avoid being recognized. I felt a little like one of those mafiosi who walks through a gauntlet of photographers with his rain-coat over his face. I was wishing I had a raincoat. I suppose it was my fault that I felt exposed; I didn't have to confront Alice Marie the minute I saw her. I could have kept my mouth shut; she might have been so busy chanting the mysteries of the rosary with her group as they walked in their little circle that she wouldn't have noticed me. I guess it's possible that she wouldn't have recognized me. But no, she'd been waiting for this moment for thirty-two years, since Sister Per-petua had told Kathy Grogan to change the green felt letters. She'd been waiting to pay me back.

I suppose there was something magnificent about such a patient revenge. Except that there was nothing magnificent about Alice Marie in her navy blue raincoat and beige flats. Whatever she did, her most salient quality was that she was annoying. Whatever she did, Alice Marie Cusalito was a fool.

I've often thought that the problem of foolishness is more meta-physically vexing than the problem of evil. Evil is a hard dark point, or a hypnotizing vortex; it's humbling; you can learn something from it, if it doesn't destroy you; you can pit yourself against it and be consumed or triumph. St. George and the Dragon. But foolishness is an unworthy adversary; it just smothers you in its wet thickness. Who could be interested in that? You can't imagine it inspiring centuries' worth of art. And yet, so many of us lose our lives to battling foolishness. Or being overwhelmed by it.

And I was feeling twice overwhelmed, as, after passing through the line of hostile pickets, I had to walk through a crowd of what would be called "fans." "I'm a fan" was the typical diction of an artsy cocktail party in New York. But what did that mean?

And who was I, the physical person, walking past people who made certain assumptions about me, had certain thoughts or beliefs about me, based on my work? Their idea of me had no more to do with who I really was than the ideas of the praying picketers. I gripped B's arm. At least I felt he knew me as a body, as someone who responded to touch and temperature, like any animal. Walking through those lines, I didn't feel like an animal, I felt like a symbol. Everybody's Rorschach.

Nothing being said seemed to have anything to do with me. Even though they were talking about me, I had nothing to do with it. I had lost myself to them. Or I would if I let myself. B's arm seemed necessary to me at that moment as it never had before.

And I felt an enormous need to hear my sister Helena's voice. The minute I got into the gallery I asked Fanny if I could call Geneva.

"You're not going to say hello? You're not going to try and help me understand all this?"

"I have to talk to my sister," I said.

"You'll want to take it in my office," she said. "It's the only quiet place. You've caused quite a buzz among your fans. They're not a quiet group of lookers. For one thing, there's a certain amount of laughing."

"With or at?"

"Not at, the ones who don't like it are outraged. Nobody's contemptuous."

I was hoping it was some normal time of day in Switzerland. I could never remember whether it was earlier or later than New York, and sometimes I woke Helena or Hans in the middle of the night. He was always polite. She wasn't. She'd say, "What planet are you on? It's four o'clock in the morning." So I was never afraid of making a mistake; she'd shout at me, get it over with, and be back to sleep in a flash. My sister and I are brilliant sleepers. We get it from our mother.

I called her office number, ready to interrupt her if she was in a meeting of world officials, but hoping I wouldn't have to. I asked her secretary, in French, if she was available. She answered me, in English, that the doctor would be right with me.

When I told her that Alice Marie Cusalito was leading a picket against my show, she made a noise that I'm sure no one in Switzerland had ever made. It was a particular whoop of Helena's—half cry of pain, half of joy at the insanity of the world. I couldn't believe that in that land of chocolate and cuckoo clocks and no war anybody made a noise like that.

"Listen, it's Friday. I'm getting on the plane in three hours. I have to be there."

"Oh, thank God, I was just about to beg you."

"I think she'll be really scared if she sees the two of us. Is she still a nun?"

"It's hard to tell. She has the shoes and the pocketbook. But sometimes they leave the order and keep the look."

"Pick me up at midnight on Swissair. I'm only staying for the weekend. Just enough to put the fear of God into that little snitch."

I almost felt a bit sorry for Alice Marie. You see, my sister and I have always been a formidable pair. A kind of tag team. Helena was, on the surface, a milder character. So she'd set up the victim. Then, when the victim was relaxing, I'd zoom in with my tank. We took no prisoners. There was no need to. Nothing, and nobody, was left standing.

B was looking at the show, walking around, just like anybody else. Except I kept wondering if, at some point, someone would shift her glance from the figure of the male to B and then say to her companion, "Am I crazy or is that the guy who . . ." But I didn't stay around to find out. As I've told you, I can't stand being near people who are looking at my work.

"I do think you need to see this," Fanny said.

It was a poster with a headline in large red letters that said: "The Catholic Defense League." The poster proclaimed that the Catholic Defense League was against "the proabortion, progay lifestyle, procontraceptive, proeuthanasia mentality." It went on to say, in bold blue letters this time, that "God is not mocked" and that "it's not all right to make fun of nuns, priests, bishops and the pope." It asked that people be on the lookout for the liberal media's assaults on traditional Catholic values. It urged people to call a toll-free number. It ended with more boldfaced red. "We have seen the enemy and they are legion."

I threw the poster on the floor. I don't know why anything connected to Alice Marie Cusalito brought out the primitive in me. I guess it's the smug self-righteous certainty, the imperviousness that comes with a taste for martyrdom.

"Am I supposed to understand this?" B said. "Why do I feel this is an invitation to a party I'm not invited to? It's not just that it's in some code I can't read."

"I feel exactly the same way," Fanny said. "Which is why I can't imagine they'll have much impact. How many of them can there be?"

"Don't underestimate them. They do a lot of damage. There are a lot of people out there who think the world's going to hell in a hand-basket. Or a wheelbarrow pushed by a black, gay, feminist, Jewish mil-lionaire. Their name is legion," I said. Then I realized I was quoting from their handout. I didn't know whether B or Fanny got the reference. When I asked, it turned out they didn't.

Maybe you won't either, so I'll tell. It comes from the place in the New Testament where Jesus drives the demons out of the afflicted man and sends them into a herd of swine, who go tumbling over a cliff into the sea. On their way over, they say their name. Legion. It always con-fused me when I was a kid, because the word "legion" was around quite a lot in those days. The American Legion. The Legion of Mary. But most important, the Legion of Decency, which determined what movies you were or were not allowed to see, under pain of hell. I don't remember the equivalent of G or PG, but I remember the bad ones. The equiva-lent of R was a category called MORALLY OBJECTIONABLE IN PART FOR ALL. You have to love a mind that makes up a category like that. Not completely morally objectionable, and not morally objec-tionable for some. It was a combination of democracy—the rules applied to everyone—and a veneer of sophistication: we're not saying every second of it is bad, but what kind of person wants a taint of moral objectionableness? But the really scary category, the word that even if you only saw it in print seemed to be accompanied by the tones of the March from Saul, was CONDEMNED. A movie called *The Moon Is Blue* was on the condemned list for about ten years. *La Dolce Vita* was con-demned. One Sunday every year, you had to stand up in church and take the Legion of Decency pledge, in which you had to promise not to see any movies that were morally objectionable in part or condemned. We all promised. Then something would be condemned, like Elizabeth Taylor in *Butterfield 8,* and we would all decide to risk our immortal souls. Just that once.

Things are so much easier for the right wing because they can use the words and images of the past. They can all assume an audience of people who know what they're talking about. It was the same way with the American flag during the Vietnam War. Next to the Red, White and Blue, the peace symbol just didn't cut it. Nobody ever wrote a song called "You're a Grand Old Peace Symbol."

I suppose what was driving Alice Marie and her friends crazy was that I was taking images that they thought of as theirs and using them in a way that they didn't like. In a way that they thought was downright evil. If I thought about it in that way, I could come to a calm understanding of what they were doing. But I didn't want to come to a calm understanding of what they were doing. I wanted to pound their heads on the pavement.

I needed my sister.

B asked me if I'd like him to drive me to the airport, since Helena's plane arrived at midnight, and since I'd have so much to say to her that the chances of my watching the road weren't terrific. I was grateful to him: Kennedy at midnight on Friday was nothing I looked forward to.

"Don't worry," he said, "the two of you don't have to talk to me. I'll wear a little cap and you can call me James."

"And then afterward I get to screw you in the backseat because I've been terrifically turned on by your tight Italian chauffeur's uniform— you know I have a thing for uniforms, and when you look in the rearview mirror, you'll see I have my skirt up around my neck, just to get your attention."

So we jumped into my bed before we left for the airport, and we were very quick, afraid to be caught, chauffeur and mistress. I called him James. He called me madam. He said, "Please, madam, keep it to yourself. Don't tell your husband or I could lose my job."

"So what does Alice Marie look like?" Helena said, walking out of the gate. She always started talking before she said hello.

"She looks like shit. She always looked like shit." I gave her the poster of the Catholic Defense League.

"You know, as a physician, I can tell you these people could be significantly helped by psychotropic drugs. But they'd have to be very carefully monitored. Daily blood tests. I'll draw the blood."

We didn't even pretend she was going to sleep on the foldout couch, because we had too much to talk about and I was looking forward to feeling like the little cub in the lair with the big cub. I don't know if you've had the experience of being able to completely trust a person, of knowing that that person will do absolutely anything for you, that their motives toward you are not mixed, that they want only your good. I wonder if you have to be a younger sister to have that feeling. Or maybe you have to be Helena's sister. I know Michael would tell me that all love has a component of aggression. I grant him that, with one exception. My sister and me.

"We have to be cool tomorrow," she said.

"I haven't exactly been cool."

"What a big surprise. But from now on you will be. Just stand next to me and be completely quiet. And don't try to hit her. I can do first aid, but I don't think it will help the cause."

"It's hard not to want to hit Alice Marie Cusalito."

"I know, baby. But think of restraint in service to the cause."

I got up early to buy croissants and oranges. Of the two of us, I'm the more domestic. Helena lets Hans decorate the house, so it looks like something out of a magazine no one I know would buy, and she occasionally cooks grilled cheese sandwiches.

"What will you wear?" she asked.

"I thought I'd wear my new black pant suit."

"Wrong, wrong, wrong. We need to wear pastels, both of us, preferably blue. We must look like children of Mary. I brought this suit with me."

She opened a complicated garment bag with about eighty-five zippers. She can't cook, but she's a brilliant packer. A sky blue suit came out of the bag as if it had just come from the dry cleaners.

"You must have something pastel," she said.

"I don't. The best I can do is black and white. At least that's somewhat clerical."

"No, we're going to buy you something pastel. Call B and tell him to meet us."

I said I was not wearing light blue. It was fine for her, but I'd look like a junior executive in telemarketing.

B sat on a chair at Ann Taylor like a reluctant husband. Helena would push me out of the dressing room wearing things I didn't recognize myself in. I was lucky to have him there, because he vetoed some things she was really pushing. He said I had to look at least recognizably like myself. Finally we agreed on a wheat-colored linen suit with a white linen underblouse. I told Helena she could take it right back to Switzerland with her after I'd worn it today.

"Think of it as a Catherine Deneuve look," B said.

"I hate Catherine Deneuve."

"Well, no man in the world agrees with you."

"The whole fucking bunch of you jerking off over *Belle de Jour*."

"It's a very sophisticated film," he said. "Great cinematography."

"Yes, that's really what you like about it. Don't give me that shit. I have no patience with women asking for debasement. Let them spend a day with Alice Marie Cusalito. Now, that's debasement."

"How about shoes?" Helena said. "Do you have any shoes that aren't butch or Norma Desmond?"

"I don't care what Alice Marie Cusalito does to me. I will not wear bone pumps."

"You need heels. Fairly high heels."

I let her talk me into a pair of plain black pumps. They made my legs look good, B really liked them. He, like Helena, thinks my shoes make too much of a statement.

I felt like an impostor in high heels and a short skirt. But I also felt somewhat authoritative, and protected by an outfit my sister had picked out.

I tried to focus on the brass door of the Fuller Building to give me some sense of equilibrium. But the minute I saw Alice Marie with her rosaries around her hand and her pocketbook straps over her wrist, everything was lost. I sprang out of the cab. Helena held me back. "I'll go first," she said.

When Alice Marie realized that Helena was with me, she lost her grim smugness; she was afraid. And something else. I realized that look around her mouth was an attempt to be ingratiating. Because she was trying to respond to Helena's smile. And Helena walked right up to her, sign and all, and gave her a hug.

"Alice Marie, how nice to see you. Are you still in the Order?"

Alice Marie hadn't caught on. She thought Helena was being friendly, maybe there just to catch up on old times because she'd missed the twenty-fifth reunion. That was Helena's power; she could smile at you and make you start thinking whatever she wanted.

"Actually, I left the Order seven years ago," Alice Marie said.

"Oh, how interesting," Helena said. "And are you married?"

"Actually, yes."

"And your husband is older?"

"How did you know?"

"Oh, Alice Marie, you know I was always good at guessing."

"Naturally, he wasn't married before."

"Oh, naturally. Was he a priest, then?"

"Whatever you heard, Helena, we both made the decision to change our vocations to lay ministries separate from our feelings to one another."

"I haven't heard anything, Alice Marie. I've lived in Europe for twenty years. I'm a doctor."

"I knew that from the alumni newsletter."

"Yes, my specialty is AIDS research."

That wasn't true, she was doing the Ebola virus. But it made Alice Marie look a little hunted.

"You know we pray every day for a cure for AIDS."

"That's good," I said, "because you do enough to help spread it."

Helena pinched me, hard.

"Well, it's very challenging work," Helena said. "And what's your work, aside from all this?"

"My husband and I run a natural family planning counseling center."

"Oh, yes, cervical mucus," said Helena, with a dazzling smile.

"And we help people understand how restraint within a marriage can actually strengthen a relationship, as a sign of mutual respect."

"I guess some couples just don't have enough respect for each other," Helena said. "Particularly those men."

"That's exactly it," said Alice Marie. "But you know, we can't get people to think that way. The contraceptive mentality. The abortion mentality."

"You have no children yourself, Alice Marie?"

"No, we haven't been blessed in that way. But I'm very close to some of my nieces."

Just then, I became aware of another group of pickets. They were carrying signs that said, "The right to choose. The right to see. The right to make art."

Visually, this was a very different group from the Catholic Defense League. They were all under twenty-five, all in black, all with very short hair. I sort of recognized the bottom half of someone's body as she came around the other side of a van carrying so many posters that the top half of her was invisible. I knew those feet; those were my old Doc Martens boots. Rachel had organized her friends from Brown to come and picket for her mom. Filial devotion takes many forms; this was a new one.

"What's the Brady Bunch outfit?" she said.

"Your aunt made me. She said I looked more threatening this way."

"Well, you're scaring the shit out of me."

"I adore you," I said, giving her a lot of kisses.

"I'm not doing this because you're my mother. I'm doing it as a matter of principle."

"I still adore you," I said.

"You're premenopausal," she said. "You could have another mood swing in a minute."

"Just come with me for a second," I said.

I took my daughter, with her dyed black buzz cut, plucked eyebrows, black jeans, black leather jacket with studs, pierced nose and lace-up boots, and teetered over on my pumps to the other picketers.

"Alice Marie," I said, "this is the daughter I was blessed with."

She turned away from me and said to Helena, "I never could communicate with Monica."

"I know what you mean," Helena said. "It's a funny thing about Monica. She's the kind of person who doesn't feel warmed when somebody tries to publicly humiliate her. She is just that kind of girl."

Finally, it occurred to Alice Marie that she'd been had. She got really red and her hair stood out even more. She looked literally shocked by Helena's words; she'd felt them as an electric charge.

"I guess I forgot what a big phony you always were, Helena," she said.

"You shouldn't let that kind of thing slip your mind, Alice Marie," Helena said. "Not in your position."

Helena and I linked arms and walked into the gallery. Rachel and her friends were shouting, "Freedom to choose, freedom to see." I was feeling much, much better.

But not for long. Helena left on Sunday night. All that next week I had to submit to interviews. And "submit" was the right word. Michael Kimmelman was fine, and he was the first. I thought it was sort of fun, getting to mouth off about myself to someone who was asking interesting questions. Then I had the *News* and the *Post,* who knew nothing about art and weren't sure whether they liked me better or Alice Marie. They thought they liked me, because I was better looking, but they didn't know who their readers would like. They remembered the fuss about Scorsese's *The Last Temptation of Christ.* They were waiting for a position from the archdiocese. Nothing official came, but a monsignor interviewed at the chancery said all people of goodwill would naturally be offended by such a cynical use of the image of Our Lord, as they would be of the cynical use of any figure central to any of the great religious traditions.

I told the reporter from the *Post* I didn't think the Jewish Defense League would go into high dudgeon about any paintings using Moses as their subject. She wrote that down really fast. Then she asked me if I thought Jesus had sex, if that was what I was saying. I said I had no way of knowing, but I hoped so. She wrote that down really fast. I told her that I wasn't painting the historical Jesus or the religious Jesus; rather, I was referring to a tradition in which the way to paint the idealized male was to paint him as Jesus or one of the saints, in the same way that to paint an idealized figure of a woman was to paint the Madonna.

The reporter (she seemed about sixteen to me) asked if I was planning to do a series of Madonnas. Maybe Madonnas in bikinis or something like that. I said no, never. I was not being disrespectful, first of all. I was enjoying incorporating the work of the Masters into my own work; I was enjoying painting vision. I should have said that to Kimmelman instead of the girl reporter from the *Post*. She didn't take a note when I said I was painting vision. I tried again. I said I was also making a comment about women looking at men, which I believed was different from the way men looked at women, and that this hadn't been well recorded in the history of art. She asked me if I thought men and women were different. I said yes, that women never forgot to put down the toilet seat. She wrote that down.

I made my really big mistake when she asked about the nature of the disagreement between the Catholic Defense League and myself.

"The nature of the disagreement is that the leader of that particular pack is still annoyed because she didn't even get nominated for senior class president at St. Augusta's High School and I won the election."

"Am I to understand that you knew each other before?"

So the *Post* printed the story under the headline "Matter of Principle or High School Feud?" And, of course, Alice Marie looked wounded and sincere and I looked like a smart-ass. She was talking about reverence for the sacred and I was talking about putting down the toilet seat.

The reporter from the *Voice* told me I was to understand that all her questions were coming from a Lacanian perspective and what did I have to say about the female gaze.

I said I was very supportive of lesbianism and that people's sexual orientation was up to them.

She looked at me like I needed a brain transplant. "G-A-Z-E," she said. "Surely you've read Lacan? I mean, you couldn't have done what you did if you hadn't read Lacan."

I said that actually I'd tried but hadn't got very far because I didn't like reading people who made me feel stupid.

I could hear her thinking that must mean I didn't read very much.

She kept asking me questions about phallocentrism and the construction of a new phallic center. When I heard "phallic center," all I could think of was a kind of gym for penises, penises playing racquetball and squash and tennis, older penises playing shuffleboard and checkers.

I thought she and I actually agreed about a lot of things, but her language only inspired me to be parodic.

*Newsday,* which covers Queens (where St. Augusta's is), had a special two-page spread about me in the Sunday Arts Section, with pictures of the school, Alice Marie's and my yearbook pictures, an interview with the school principal, who clearly thought this was only bad news for her and wanted to have nothing to do with it. She said that in the house of God there were many mansions, but you had to draw the line. Which I didn't get, but I figured she was trying not to dry up the pool of alumnae contributors, of whom I was not one.

Of course someone from the old neighborhood sent that article to my mother, who called me asking when I was ever going to learn to keep my big mouth shut, and thank God she was in Florida, where her daughter wasn't the talk of the town, and was I finally making money and did I still have that nice boyfriend.

"How do you know he's nice? You've never met him."

"Rachel likes him, so he must be nice."

"Rachel likes him? That's news to me."

"Rachel tells me many things that she doesn't share with you. She thinks of me as more understanding."

"Well, if you get any hot bulletins, count me in, Mom."

"I talked to our parish priest, just in case, about what you were doing, and he said he didn't think you were being irreverent, just looking at things in a new way."

"That was rather enlightened of him."

"He's a very cultured man but we all think he's a fairy."

"That's very enlightened of you."

"Oh, we'll defend him to the death. He's the best thing that happened in Star of the Sea since we installed central air."

After the *Newsday* piece, somebody pulled Alice Marie off the case, saying that dealing with the media was causing her too much stress. I think it was that she was too unphotogenic for *Time* and *Newsweek.* The

Catholic Defense League came up with one of those exceptionally well-groomed right-wingers whom I also recognized from high school. Perfect skin, perfect hair pulled back in a velvet bow, perfectly manicured nails with colorless polish. A calm, long-suffering tone. This type always repeated your first name a lot, which made it appear they thought you were a child, or not very bright, or maybe you'd forgotten what your name was. This version was called Regina McArdle and she was a lot more effective than Alice Marie. She didn't get red in the face, she didn't get flustered, she didn't lose her temper, she just sat back and looked rational so that everyone would think, seeing me next to her, that all my money was going to renovate some particularly industrial-looking former warehouse in Tribeca that never saw the light of day.

"We all like a laugh, but there are some of us who hold some things dear, and we're not afraid to stand up for them."

There was something about her that silenced me and drained all impulse to wit. I think it was those manicured nails, that velvet bow. I wondered where they found her and how much she was paid. She was worth every penny.

I became a new person for every interviewer. For the *Times,* I was a combination of seriousness and daring; for the *News* and the *Post,* I was full of one-liners; for the *Voice,* I became a wimpy middle-class feminist; for *Time* and *Newsday,* I was someone who couldn't stand up to someone with a manicure. I had become a public person; I felt that my real self had been scooped out, as if someone were making melon balls of me. Melon balls, that wholly frivolous invention of consumer culture. There's no need for them, no point to them, except presentation. I was being scooped out, shaped and presented. My insides on some luncheon table, and afterward nothing much left but a rind. And that rind was useless. For one thing, I was out so much, and talking so much, by the time my mind was clear, the sun had gone down and I was too tired to paint, or even draw. I didn't even want sex. There was so little of myself left, I didn't want what there was exposed or shared.

B was patient for a while. Then he took the low road. He got me a little tight. He bought a beautiful bottle of Pouilly-Fuissé—the bottle itself was beautiful, clear, except for the tiniest touch of sea green, and the label had red and black lettering that looked official and maybe bureaucratic, or no, ecclesiastical, like the lettering in my old missal. The wine, too, was almost colorless, almost nothing in it of yellow or amber; it was all about clarity. You knew it would be a clarifying experience, even if you didn't know quite what it would clarify, or what it was that needed clarification. He bought olive paste and crackers. We sat on my couch. He didn't approach me very seriously; we both had our feet on the coffee table, and occasionally we'd touch toes. He let me lounge. He let me sprawl. He waited for me to grow vague and forgetful, for the irritating shards and spurs to be smoothed out. He put on a tape of a woman from the Cape Verde Islands; everything in the music was a curve, everything was insinuating. She sang in Portuguese, so of course I couldn't understand, but you knew it was about sex whose only consequence would be the residue of longing after it was over. Then there would be a new lover, and the curve would begin again: desire, stretched out to the point of satisfaction, then an extended, if temporary, longing. It was sex you might disappear into; you might never find your way home, back to the mainland, money, property, what you had thought of as your life.

He stood in front of me, dancing by himself, his eyes closed, there for me to see him. He swayed his hips. He turned his back to me, so I would notice him all around. I could hear the woman singing "Pequeno, pequeno," little one, little one. That voice was urging me toward him, not urging, suggesting. But only if I wanted. What was will, though, in the face of my undulating brain and the undulant shadows of the music? And the curve of his body, and the curve his arm made, suggesting a place for me inside it. Suggesting that inside that curve was the only right place.

So I put myself there. I gave myself over to a series of undulating curves. I let him press me up against him and hold me as if we were locked, front to front, almost immobile, moving only slightly, the leeway between the lock and the lock's groove. I wanted to let him do whatever he wanted. He wanted to lead me into bed.

The room was dark. He drew the curtains, cutting the light from the street. He was invisible to me. For a moment, I couldn't remember what he looked like. The music kept insinuating. I didn't know what he was going to do. I heard him open a bottle. I heard him rubbing his hands together. Then I felt the oiled palms of his hands. Then he teased and tantalized, but only with his fingertips; I moved his hand lower. He said, "No, not yet, not yet. Shh."

Just before the point of outrage at deprivation, he approached, pinning my arms to the bed and following the curve of the music, of his arm, of my progress from reluctance to yearning, then to arrival.

The next day Fanny called to ask what I felt about being on television.

"You want me to go on TV with transsexual twins or orthodontists who are into leather? Or between the adopt-a-pet section and the weather? Forget it."

"Monica, this is serious. It's Charlie Rose."

"Charlie Rose? He's interested in me?"

"Everyone's interested in you, love. You're the talk of the town."

"Shit," I said.

"You can't tell me you're not enjoying it."

"I *can* tell you, Fanny, I am not enjoying it. I would like people to be writing intelligent, deeply felt, unreservedly laudatory things about my work. I would like sensitive buyers to pay exorbitant prices. But I don't see why my corporal presence is required."

"Think about it. You can't go on except with your corporal presence. But you should know that the Catholic Defense League is booked, with or without you."

I was feeling two things simultaneously, not, as you by now understand, an uncommon occurrence with me. But these two pulls were unusually equal. The first was a desire to ask B to take me somewhere remote, like Canada, someplace unfashionable and difficult, maybe Edmonton, Alberta, and just let me be alone and try to get back to work. The other was the street kid's instinct not to back away from a fight, especially when you knew it was the good fight. Alice Marie Cusalito was bad enough, but you had to feel a little sorry for her. She was born ugly, stupid and annoying. But Regina McArdle had all the advantages: perfect hair, perfect skin, good manners. She had no excuses. Her life could only be explained by a cold-hearted desire to deprive others of pleasure. She was the real monster; Alice Marie was just on the farm team. I couldn't let them get away with it. I didn't know who *they* were. But I thought it was worth giving up Edmonton, Alberta, to take up arms.

Theresa told me I had to get an outfit that made me look obviously different from Regina. Hipper but more richly human. "What you have to get across is that you present a deeper, fuller vision of life. Something artistic and maternal. She doesn't look maternal. She looks too tidy to ever have fucked. That's what you have to get across: they're against fucking."

"And I can do that with the right jacket?"

"You can't do it without one."

Theresa knew a Japanese woman who could look at you and invent the perfect thing for you to wear, make it up in your size in two days, and not charge you a fortune. B said money was no object, but when it came to clothing, I always thought there was a limit, and it wasn't the sky.

Theresa's friend Misako made me a pantsuit, light wool, grayish blue, a hint of lavender. The collar was a little clerical looking; it could have accommodated a Roman collar if I happened to want to slip one in. I had my hair cut, and I went to someone Fanny knew who did my makeup, a young Italian woman whom I trusted not to make me look like a transvestite. Since I wasn't going on *Geraldo,* I thought that was a good idea.

I insisted on having my claque accompany me. I wanted Michael there to keep me sane and make me laugh; Theresa to make me feel smart. I wanted Rachel to raise my moral ire, and Sara so that if everything turned out to be a complete disaster, there would be an endless well of comfort on which I could endlessly draw. I wanted B to make me feel that, even if I was a horrible failure on the show, someone still wanted my body. And I needed him to tell me I was more attractive than Regina McArdle, even if she could put her hair into one of those velvet bows and it wouldn't fall out during a nuclear attack.

*         *         *

Everyone in the studio looked under twenty-six. They were all wearing black jeans and white tee shirts or chinos and plaid shirts and Dock-Sides without socks. I had a two-minute conversation with a young assistant producer who wanted to make sure she had the facts right. I had a thirty-second consultation with a very overweight makeup woman who said my makeup was great, and that she thought I had a lot of guts, and good luck. Somehow, I didn't find that reassuring. Then we sat in the green room with Strobe Talbot, an expert on industrial safety, Edward Said, and a former senator, who kept saying he had no idea who any of us were. "Except for you, Strobe, everyone knows who you are."

Remarkably, Regina McArdle was late, and she was looking a little flustered. She'd brought her claque, too; her two preschool children, two of her seven, she seemed thrilled to add. This was particularly annoying because she looked thirty-two and was a size five in her straight navy blue skirt, white turtleneck and red blazer.

"Seven children," I said. "I guess natural family planning's been a great success in your house."

"All my children were wanted and planned for," she said.

"Wanted and planned for, you sound like a prochoice leaflet."

"I find it fruitless to dialogue with you," she said. "You purposely drag everything down."

Luckily, she was called into makeup. I was glad to see that *she* came out looking like a transvestite, but a censorious one.

We were all sitting in silence, each wishing to be home in bed eating Oreos and watching *Waterloo Bridge.* Or maybe I was projecting, and I was the only one wishing that.

A producer brought me an envelope. "This just came, International Federal Express, from a Doctor Szabo in Geneva."

Everybody looked alarmed, as if I'd just been given my life-saving heart medicine.

"I tore the house apart looking for this," Helena said in her note. "I knew I had it. I want you to wear it on television."

It was my Knights of Columbus Christian Doctrine Medal, which I'd won in a contest for knowing the answers to more catechism questions than anyone in the parish in 1960. I pinned it on the breast of my suit. No one dared ask me what it was.

Finally, after Edward Said and the former senator, Regina and I were called in. And there was Charlie, quite simply one of the handsomest men I'd ever seen. The American dream. The American God. And we were supposed to believe he read books, too?

He looked a little harried. I wasn't sure he really wanted us to be there.

"Well, Ms. Szabo, you've caused quite a stir," he said. But at least he seemed to be smiling. I thought he had beautiful hands. I was thinking of asking him if we could wait a minute and I could sketch them, maybe instead of talking.

"And you, Ms. McArdle, you see what Ms. Szabo is doing as offensive to your beliefs."

"We're not against artistic expression and we're not curtailing freedom. We're witnessing an offense to us as Catholics. We're the silent majority, Mr. Rose. You can say anything about a Catholic and get away with it."

"I wasn't saying anything about anyone. I was painting something that interested me."

"Let's save this for the camera," he said. And then he was looking somewhere that had nothing to do with us.

"Today on glamorous Fifty-seventh Street, in front of the Fuller Building, home of some of New York's most distinguished galleries: something unusual. A picket. A demonstration. Against what: an art show. An art show by a woman painter. An art show that uses the idea of Old Masters to say something about how we see today. For this artist, Monica Szabo: freedom of expression, the right to paint what she sees as she sees it. For this Catholic activist, Regina McArdle: blasphemy. Blasphemy. Not a word we hear much anymore. Care to tell us what that means?" he smiled. I noticed his teeth were a little small.

"Certainly, Mr. Rose," Regina said, folding her tiny manicured hands. "We of the Catholic Defense League are saying simply this: there are things we hold sacred. The image of Christ is one of them."

"Let's back up a little bit here. Ms. Szabo, may I call you Monica and Regina . . . would you care to tell us about the subject of your paintings?"

"Sure," I said, as if discussing my paintings before a million television viewers was something I just happened to be doing at this time, in this place. "It occurred to me that what is called the Deposition of Christ—that is, Christ after his death but before his burial—was a very popular motif. And as I looked at some of the art, it occurred to me that what was really being represented was not death but—"

He interrupted me, "But the little death. *La petite mort.*"

"Right, and that because of the conventions, it wouldn't have been possible to portray that directly. All art at that time was about sacred subjects, unless it was portraits of rulers, and you couldn't imagine doing a duke after—"

"After love," he interrupted. "No, they probably wouldn't have been available for a sitting then."

"Well, available or not, it wouldn't have exactly made them look like they'd be a good bet in the next battle against the neighboring city-state. But as I was saying—"

"You were saying that most of the art depicted sacred subjects."

"It occurred to me that these dead Christs had the repose, the heaviness of postcoital men, but unlike the Northern dead Christs, they didn't really look dead. Just worn out."

"Like they'd had too good a time the night before," he said.

"No, I must interrupt," said Regina. "You see, Mr. Rose, as a member of the liberal media you almost automatically fall into the trap of laughing at the sacred. I'd just ask you to reconsider your position."

"All right, all right. Good point. Good point. What would you like me to do?"

"I'd like you to think that this figure of Christ is the focus of the faith of many simple people and that it offends the simple people of this world to see their God mocked."

"I haven't noticed many of the simple people of the world in the Fifty-seventh Street galleries," I said. "And why do you assume I'm mocking? Why do you assume that the figure of Jesus is not as sacred to me as it is to you?"

"It couldn't possibly be," said Regina, reddening. Prettily, as I'm sure she'd been told.

"Why not? I don't know if you knew that I won the Knights of

Columbus Christian Doctrine Medal awarded at St. Hyacinth parish in June of 1960, at which time I knew more catechism than anyone else in the parish. And catechism is not something you forget."

"Knowledge is not faith."

"And faith is not knowledge, Ms. McArdle," I said. "Which is why it does no honor to the Catholic Church to speak in ignorance, ignoring the history of art and the history of thought, and scandalizing the world by reinforcing its prejudices that Catholics are a bunch of ill-educated, bigoted yahoos."

"There is worldly knowledge and knowledge of the spirit."

I think Charlie felt the boat was capsizing; he was trying to bail out.

"Now, both of you have values, and these values conflict. Would I be right in saying that?"

"You wouldn't be wrong," I said. "You could definitely begin there."

"But where do we go from there?" he asked. "OK: here we are. Free society. Rights of expression. Conflicting values. Whose rights prevail? Monica's: the right to express herself in art. Regina's: the right not to have what's dear to her mocked."

"I could understand it if I could be said to be mocking. All I'm saying is that, as an artist, the way I look at what's before my eyes is partly determined by what other artists have seen before me. I don't understand why that's a mockery."

"Regina, you want to respond to that?"

"All you have to do is look at the paintings and see the mockery."

"But that's in the eye of the beholder, isn't it, Regina?" said Charlie.

"That's relativism. We don't believe in relativism."

"You believe in?"

"The truth."

"And you believe in?"

"What I believe in won't fit into a sound bite, Charlie," I said, giving him what I hoped was a sincere, yet stunning, smile. "Which is why people like me often seem at a disadvantage to those whose beliefs are simple enough to be boiled down to half a sentence."

"The truth *is* simple," Regina said.

"I guess I'll close with a line right from the Bible," Charlie said.

"'What is truth?' But I recommend that, from an artistic point of view, you visit the Fanny Taylor Gallery on Fifty-seventh Street, see Monica Szabo's show, 'Spent Men,' and make up your own mind."

"Good television," he said, taking off his earphones.

I was still thinking of asking him if I might sketch his hands. But Strobe Talbot was standing behind me, ready to get into my seat.

Regina went out and fell into her husband's thousand-dollar suit. My claque didn't even try to be cool. Rachel lifted me off the ground, or tried to. She's bigger than me. But not that much.

By the time everything settled down, by the time I was no longer a media star—Regina made a few more appearances at right-wing venues but I wasn't going to be any part of that—I was due to pack up for the Cape.

I'd thought that since B's house was available to me all the time, I'd go up there in the spring. But the show had taken up all my attention, had consumed me from October to June, and I did feel consumed, the jaws or teeth of publicness having taken me up and left me on the ground again only out of boredom, because the season was over. In the fall there would be another victim, another pack of them.

There's something about going back to the same place every year that arouses your sense of mortality—and your sense of continuity. I guess it's a temperamental thing. My mother used to say, "For your sister, the glass is always half full, for you it's always half empty. I don't know which of you is more of a damn fool, but I know you're more of a pain in the ass on a rainy day."

Packing up gave me a sense of my longevity with B. It was our third summer on the Cape. We'd been lovers for almost two years. You could hardly say we were new at it.

But what was "it"? Sex, certainly. We knew each other's bodies very well. I knew that if I ran my tongue down his flanks he would flinch first, then moan. I knew the circumference of his biceps and his shoulders' span, the breadth of his back, the gradual narrowing to the waist, the swell of his buttocks and their heft as I grabbed them, the crease marking the transition to the legs, the varieties of hair—thick, sparse, rough, coarse, fine, bristly, kinky—the softness and hardness of the cock, its gradation of shading, darker at the tip and lighter at the root. We could still surprise each other, but surprise was not really the point. We were working in a form that had grown familiar: the Petrarchan sonnet, say, and the point was the small turn of phrase, the shocking break in rhythm that could cause a crash, a jet of flame burning through the surface to reveal the gold specks underneath.

We'd learned how, literally, to sleep with each other, intertwined or not, like animals conducive to each other's rest. I hadn't been living enough like an animal. An animal keeps to the task at hand. When it's looking for food, it looks for food; when it's running from an enemy, it runs; when it's trying to make a lair to have its pups, it finds the place. It doesn't get deflected. And I had been.

I felt that I'd been eating nothing but chemicals for months, that my cells swam in false and toxic substances. That instead of blood some olive-colored thickness filled my veins. I needed to cleanse myself. I'd do that by becoming more of an animal. B and I were driving in tandem to the Cape; he had his GTO and I had my rented van. I honked and signaled him to pull over as soon as we crossed the bridge.

"What's the matter?" he said.

"I need to smell your armpit."

"Right here on the side of the road?"

"Yes, right here. Right now. It's very important to my development as a human and an artist."

"OK, if a cop comes, you do the talking."

"There's nothing illegal about smelling someone's armpit on the side of the road."

"It's true," he said. "It's too unusual for anyone to have gotten around to making a law against it. Even the Puritans probably let it pass."

I wanted to rinse my mind, my consciousness, of everything I'd been through. So I spent a weekend being completely physical. We slept late and made love until the noon sun urged us to the water. We bought overpriced sandwiches to eat on the beach, sandwiches with names: the Lighthouse, the Cranberry Cove. We lay on the beach till suppertime. I read fashion magazines. I devoted myself to an article called: "An

Alphabet of New Accessories: What Spells You." We made elaborate recipes—cioppino, bouillabaisse—that required an enormous number of pots and dishes, and we left them in the sink till morning. Then he went back to New York.

The morning was gray and heavy, but the taste of sea moisture made it exciting nonetheless. I decided to walk to the bay through the woods. Mikey ran ahead of me; he was looking heraldic at the top of the dunes. I wanted to thank someone, but it seemed commonplace to invoke anything so up-market as the Deity. I would have liked a minor saint, a household god, to thank for the goodness of the day, the pleasure it had given me this early in the morning. The heavy air did something to the vegetation—bayberry, hog cranberry—so that it had a smell of hotness, fecundity, something female, sexual, a little dangerous, still healthy but on the just-pleasing side of fetid.

I sat on the little rise. The grayness of the day made the sky and the bay indistinguishable; a half dome of mist, punctuated only by the different texture of the water, ruffled on its surface by the light, warm breeze. The tide was low. A gull dipped stolidly, too bored to search for food. The swaying of the reeds was only just perceptible. I took my shirt off and enjoyed the sluggish breeze against my breasts. I lay back and let the sand abrade my back. My limbs were shamefully white from a whole year of city living. I looked up at the dull sky, which suggested nothing. And I thought of nothing but the pleasure of my senses. The most unbodily sensation that came to me was my love for my dog.

I took long walks, trying not to think about my work. But I was worried. I realized how torpidly my movements came, as if I were walking through water. I was very tired, worn-out, like an Oriental carpet whose pile is missing in some places, so you can't recognize the figures anymore.

I didn't realize quite how done up I was until my friend Adrienne told me she had Lyme disease. She described being in bed, taken over with fever, aches and fatigue. She said she was completely immobilized, could do nothing but give in to the disease.

I made understanding, sympathizing noises, as Adrienne talked, although I was really feeling jealous. Jealous of my friend's Lyme disease. It wasn't that I didn't want Adrienne to have the Lyme disease, if she wanted it, or that I felt there was a scarcity: not enough Lyme disease to go around. It was simply that she had something I wanted. I remembered being a child and having a high fever. I remember that feeling of being taken over. That was what I wanted: to be taken over by something so that no one could expect me to produce a thing. A condition that made a product, a production, any productivity unimaginable. Even to myself.

I allowed myself to feel fatigue, and at first I thought it was a mistake, because I often found myself in tears. When I asked myself why I was crying, I heard myself saying, "I'm so tired, I'm so tired."

When B came for the weekend, he found me crying.

"I'd ask what time of the month it is but you might stab me, and if you *are* premenstrual, they'd let you off on the PMS defense, so you'd be free to kill again."

He had his arms around me and I loved his being so much larger than I. I wanted to be a weak little animal burrowing into Mama or Papa Bear.

"I'm worn-out. Done up. Burnt out. All those phrases ending in words of two or three letters."

"Your life has been turned around. What you need is a Sabbath."

"What do you know about Sabbath? You're the most irreligious person I ever met."

"I'm capable of understanding things I'm not capable of doing. I remember an Israeli friend of mine, an academic, who had six children and was politically active. She was an observant Orthodox woman, and when I asked her how she did it all, she said it was because of the Sabbath. Twenty-four hours when she was forbidden to accomplish anything. But let's make it a week. One week: I forbid you to accomplish anything."

"It sounds a little terrifying."

"There's one possible exception."

"And that is?"

"It depends upon whether you call orgasm an accomplishment. Or a product."

\*    \*    \*

For seven days I didn't read anything serious. I didn't shop or cook. I didn't wash a dish or wipe a surface. He did everything.

"Think of me as your shabbes goy," he said.

I forbade myself to think of work, and the day opened before me like a toothless mouth. I made myself lie in the sun and I tried to concentrate on its goodness on my skin. When I began to think about what colors I would use for the dense blue of the water, I forced myself to think of something else. I didn't allow myself to carry a pad or pencil. I spent a lot of time asleep.

I ran more than usual, then worried that it could be called an accomplishment. Then remembering that I'd cut my runs short to get back to work, I decided they shouldn't be thought of in that way. I took several swims a day, as long as I wanted. I signed up for an Audubon Society nature walk, and looked at barn swallows and plovers through a sight, along with other earnest-minded tourists. I bought binoculars and a bird feeder and a bird identification book. Sometimes, I'd still find myself crying, but they were cleansing tears, like sweat.

I focused on B's body, its qualities of temperature and texture, its taking up of space, its place in the world, its place in the arousal and satiation of desire.

On the sixth day of my sabbatical, B told me Fanny had called.

"I'm sorry to interrupt your idyll but I have an offer you can't refuse. Or at least you must consider it."

"I'm already leaning toward refusal. Have you ever heard of Sabbath? This is my Sabbath."

"The point of Sabbaths is they have an end. Now, just listen. I have a client, also a friend, Peggy Riordan. She fell in love with the show, but she was out of town for the opening. She's heartbroken that everything's sold and that you have nothing else ready. So she'd like to speak to you about a commission."

"I've never done anything like that."

"There's nothing intrinsically wrong with it, my dear. The marvelous part is she's right there on the Cape with you and she wants you to come to lunch and talk to her. She can pay you well. Don't say anything about money. Not a word. You'll fall in love with her. And she can afford what you're worth now."

"What did I used to be worth?"

"The moon, but now you might get it."

Peggy Riordan phoned and asked me to lunch at her house in Chatham, the one place on the Cape where no one I ever knew lived. It's a little rich, a little overcivilized. On the other hand, it's five miles from the Stop & Shop, so I could easily go to lunch before my big weekly shopping, now that my Sabbath was over.

Chatham is much tidier than Wellfleet, and the landscape is quite different. I don't know what they did with all the scrub pines—they must have thought it gave the place too rough a look—but they seemed to have gotten rid of them and replaced them with oaks and larches. The small road I turned up for Peggy Riordan's house seemed more like an Irish lane than a Cape Cod road; there was no reminder of sand anywhere, and the houses were shielded from the road by a series of thick hedges. Not the tight hedges of the suburbs or the anal-retentive hedges of formal English gardens, but generous hedges, accommodating hedges, forgiving hedges.

The house was a Victorian, not a Cape Cod. A modest sprinkling of gingerbread hung from the roof, but not enough to suggest the lugubrious or overornamented. The door behind the screen was open and the wood border around the screen was too narrow to knock on. I knew I had to call out, but I couldn't think of a proper "o" sound to end my "Hello." I didn't want to sound like Bea Lillie; didn't want to sound like I was making a delivery from the Fulton Fish Market. I must have stood on the step long enough for someone to sense my presence, because as it turned out, no sound was required at all. From the dimness of the house, like a flower making itself visible in the gradual light of early morning, a woman approached the door.

I guess all of her life people have been comparing Peggy Riordan to a flower, and I could imagine that might get a little boring. But it seemed inevitable. She was—the word has unfortunate connotations but sometimes it's inevitable—pretty. She suddenly made sense of pastel fabrics; I was thinking I'd been unfair on my shopping expedition with Helena.

Peggy's shapes and textures were all flowerlike. Fanny had told me she was eighty but her skin made you think of petals, pink peonies, white peonies with a drop of pink in their whiteness. She was slender and upright and supple, she seemed to have not so much a spine as a stem. You could imagine undressing her and seeing white petals supported by a vertical greenness. Her eyes were really like forget-me-nots and whatever lipstick she was wearing should have been called English Rose. Her hair was still brown, and you knew it was natural because the shade was too soft to be dyed. It was as if she hadn't put enough stress on her body to use up any pigmentation in her hair, really remarkable hair in an old woman, because though it was pulled back, its waviness made the line around her face undulant, so there was no possibility of the severe.

She wore light blue loose-cut cotton pants and a slightly darker but still pastel cotton shirt with a white collar. Her espadrilles were a third, still darker pastel blue. Her smile made me feel at once welcome and shy because there was both welcome and shyness in it. She hadn't spoken yet, but I felt that, in comparison, whatever noise came out of my mouth would be too loud.

"Aren't you nice to come and see me. I could have come to you, but then I wanted to give you lunch. It's a privilege to feed someone who's provided you so much pleasure."

I think I blushed. I don't remember having blushed for thirty-five years. Maybe I wanted to do something pastel so I could go with the color scheme.

That sounds like I didn't like the sight of her. It's not true; I liked everything about her. I just felt maybe I wasn't good enough to be with her. No, that's not it, my fear wasn't of not being good enough. Not being nice enough was what I feared. Ever since I've met Peggy, I've tried not to say "fuck" in her presence. And it hasn't happened once. I'm always afraid it will.

She offered me a drink, wine or something nonalcoholic. She was drinking cranberry juice and it looked so pretty in the glass that I

wanted some, really desired some cranberry juice so I could drink it
with her and be like her.

In Peggy's house, everything was understated but nothing was makeshift
or unconsidered. For a beach house, it seemed a bit too carefully
designed; I couldn't imagine anybody walking into the rooms in a wet
bathing suit. I wouldn't have been surprised if there had been a special
little shed in the back for that. A shed for shedding. A shedding shed.

The slipcovers on the couch were a restful shade of apple green;
the wood of the furniture was oak; there were rag rugs on the floor, and
the room was full of books. I tried to see what art there was, realizing,
of course, that people didn't bring the art they really valued to their
beach houses. There were a few pleasant watercolors and a small oil of
the local dunes that I quite liked. But then I was drawn up short by a
pencil drawing that I knew was by Vuillard. I did a kind of flying leap
over to it; what he accomplished with a few lightly drawn lines—an old
woman sitting in front of a mantelpiece—was a masterpiece of economy. I think that's what I love most about drawing: its thrift.

"You weren't in the house a minute before you found the best thing
to look at," said Peggy.

I wanted to say that she was probably the best thing to look at,
because I was longing to sketch her, but instead I congratulated her on
having such a beautiful thing.

"I bring it with me everywhere, luckily it's small. I live in a few different places, and wherever I live I can't seem to be without it."

"Where do you live?"

"In the winter, Santa Fe, in the spring and late fall, New York and
sometimes Rome, and here for the summer. I know I'm very lucky.
And it's all rather a surprise. Prosperity came to me late in life. I don't
know why I'm telling you this right away. Probably my guilt about it all.
I suffer from Irish Catholic guilt about prosperity. But then you were
raised Catholic too."

"But my parents are Hungarian. It made me a little different from
my Irish friends. My mother, particularly, was pleasure-loving. Still is."

"That's a great gift. I had to learn to be easy about pleasure. I'm still learning, and, as I'm eighty, I may die without fully having the knack."

"Well, there's all kinds of pleasure. Your Vuillard gives you pleasure, I can see by the way you look at it, by the way you're attached to it."

"Oh, yes, I've always gotten pleasure from beautiful things, which was my parents' gift to me. My father was a public school art teacher, and my mother taught music. So you see it was all terribly genteel. No raised voices. Trips to the museum after Sunday Mass."

"It sounds OK to me. I don't think either of my parents ever went to a museum. That's not exactly right. My father knew museums were important, but he didn't quite know why, so he'd take my sister and me to the Met a few times a year. He'd sit in the lobby and read the newspaper. He'd tell us to find something good to look at and come back when we were finished."

"But that gave you a lot of freedom. My parents were very good at explaining things but I always felt I was running to catch up to them, and what I saw was never the real thing."

"Do you have that fear, too? Of missing the real thing?"

"Yes, it holds me back."

"I've missed a lot looking for the real thing."

"In myself, I always thought it was an excessive law-abidingness. But—and you'll forgive me for jumping from the work to the worker— I thought of you as more daring, more robust, than law-abiding."

"I'm afraid I'm a bad combination of obedience and rebellion. It's not a good mix."

"It's a wonderful mix for your work."

I couldn't understand why I was feeling so at ease with Peggy Riordan; we were having a real conversation, and we'd only just met. The Vuillard had done it.

"Would you mind if I sketched you while we talk?"

"How could I refuse? Even if I had the impulse to, I wouldn't, and as I don't have the impulse . . . well, you see we can just go ahead. There's no reason to think of it as anything but easy."

"I'll do it while we eat. I don't want you to pose. Just be yourself. That's a wholly unrealistic request, but, you know, as much as possible."

"It's hard to live and be looked at simultaneously."

"But you're a beautiful woman. You must always have been looked at."

"I was brought up not to acknowledge it, if it happened. And by the time I felt free to acknowledge it, it was hardly happening anymore."

"After a certain point women must stop giving off a particular scent and we become invisible. I mean, simply not looked at. I used to be able to get almost any man's eye if I looked at him in a particular way. Now it's about one in eight."

"For me, it's probably about one in eighty. And he might be wondering whether I dye my hair."

I asked if I could help her with lunch. Her kitchen was like an illustration from a Mother Goose: black and white diamond-shaped tiles, wooden cabinets with round wooden handles, the kind you don't have to worry about coming off in your hand, a white painted table with a blue tablecloth, and a bouquet of snapdragons in a red glass vase. Everything was very clean without giving the impression, as so many modern kitchens do, of a hospital. I knew that if I went into the cabinets, the shelf paper would be held down by tacks whose heads matched the paper.

She took cups of vichyssoise out of the refrigerator. She put them down on the white counter and sprinkled them with chives she'd cut up and left on the cutting board.

We walked through the swing door into the dining room, which was very much a separate entity, closed off by doors from both the kitchen and the living room. There were candles on the table in low silver holders and a tablecloth with embroidered daisies in yellows and pinks. Pink napkins of a rough-spun linen were in silver rings. It was an inspired combination of the formal and the informal, and I knew that, however hard I tried, I'd never come up to it.

"I've never commissioned a painting before. It's rather a new role for me, the patron."

"I've never had a painting commissioned."

"I don't want to tell you what to paint, that's not what I mean. It's simply that I was heartbroken when I talked to Fanny and everything was gone. Let's get vulgarities out of the way first: Fanny's made it clear to me that your price has risen since the show."

"Please talk to Fanny about that. I have a problem with money; I like it, but I think it's the root of all evil."

"I had that problem as well. Then suddenly I was left a very great deal of it. I had to change the way I thought. It's something I know about."

"Actually, I'd like to talk about it with you. It's very difficult to talk about money. Sex is nothing compared to that."

Then I felt uneasy, because I guessed that for her, sex probably wasn't easy to talk about. But she let it go.

I couldn't stop thinking about her in a kneeling position. In a prayerful position. There was something about her face that was saintly—I don't mean that it had any great moral qualities, only that it seemed to compose itself so that it was remarkably free of strain, like the faces of many Renaissance saints.

I was listening to what she said; I was enjoying her company; I was dying to know who'd left her the money, and how much, and when, but I was willing to wait. I told her I was, in principle, delighted to be doing a painting for her, but I had no ideas right then, I'd have to think. I wanted to tell her that I really liked her, but I knew that would be difficult for her. So I said, "Will you come to my house for dinner sometime? Or rather my friend's house. It's really his house but I live there quite a lot."

"I'd love to come, and may I bring my companion as well?"

I had no idea what she meant by a companion. It could be anything from a Henry James paid retainer to a lesbian lover. I didn't know whether to expect a distressed gentlewoman or Natalie Barney.

"Victor loves your work as well, and he'd be thrilled to meet you."

Victor. So she was part of an ordinary couple. I was a little disappointed.

On the drive home, and for some days after, I was thinking about Peggy Riordan's visible presentation. I was sketching her from memory. I was thinking about her beauty. It conformed to ordinary standards, not a special set invented for the old, but it was only tangentially connected to sex, like a dress in a closet that still bears a very faint trace of scent. I couldn't wait for B to arrive so I could talk about it. At the same time, I was glad he wasn't there, because I could get up early in the morning and drink coffee, stare at the trees and the water, and think about what might be shaping up into a very good idea.

*    *    *

This was the problem. I loved waking beside him in the morning; I loved turning and fitting into his body in the middle of the night. I liked sex in the morning, and I knew it was best for him. But if he was there, I couldn't have those early-morning hours to myself. He was a light sleeper. If he stayed in bed, I knew he was doing it to give me time to myself, and I felt every breath he took. So even trying not to, he stole my freedom. I'd been living in his house because he was gone during the week, and also because I wasn't working on anything. But now that ideas were coming, I was simultaneously longing to share them with him—just a little, then to cut him off when he was asking me something it would have been dangerous to talk about before I tried it out. And, of course, when I was excited about working, I was randy and frisky as a colt.

So there was no good combination. When I wasn't working, I wasn't happy, so I went to sex for consolation; I was probably more attentive but I wasn't as much good plain fun. When I was working, I was ardent, but resentful of the time taken from my work to feed that endlessly hungry little furnace. I was more playful, but less languorous; I wanted to get on with my work.

When I talk about how ideas come to me it sounds as if they came to me all at once. And this idea didn't come all at once; I didn't take a walk on the beach at sunset and say *Eureka*. What happened was that I kept sketching Peggy from memory. Then, partly because I genuinely liked her, and partly because I wanted to look at her again so I could draw her, I invited her to dinner. "You need to understand that I'm not ready to talk about a painting yet," I said. I kept thinking that she would have known a more graceful way of saying it, but I didn't, and it simply had to be said. Also I felt graceless saying, "Please bring your friend Victor." It was like talking to a first-grader, "And please bring your nice little friend Victor to the monkey bars." I hate those euphemisms.

I always forget how good B is socially, probably because most of the time we're not with people. I'm socially good in a limited range; I'm a good storyteller and I actually am interested in most people, but I'm not good at modulating my tone, and this anguished me a little with

Peggy. Twenty years ago, I wouldn't have been able to talk to her because at the time I thought you had to reveal everything about yourself to everyone you liked. Now I knew that I could enjoy Peggy and keep part of myself in shadow; it no longer seemed hypocritical to me, but still I wasn't very good at it. B was very good at talking to people entertainingly, and keeping things away from the personal. This was perfect for Peggy and Victor, who seemed somewhat younger than she, maybe seventy, but not nearly so well preserved, not nearly so good-looking. He was bald and I think he got his dentures on the GI Bill. He had a little pot that he seemed to push around at the front of his body like it was a bibelot—something fragile or breakable he'd been given that he didn't know quite how to transport.

I made a dish I'm certain of, a cold bluefish with green, yellow and red peppers, onions and garlic. It's very colorful and tasty, and it can be made ahead of time so you can talk to your guests. I served cold lentils with it, and a cucumber salad with lots of vinegar. It was a stimulating, rather than a soothing, meal. We talked about the art market and the publishing market. Victor had been a publisher; he'd had his own company, which specialized in travel books; he was able to get out in time, he said, before being swallowed by a conglomerate. He'd traveled all over the world; he spoke wonderfully about Angkor Wat, but not in that way that makes you think you're seeing your aunt Madeline's slides of her trip to Bermuda. He made it sound mysterious and tragic and impossible: my kind of dinner table talk. His conversation made you understand he was sexy, and of course I wondered whether he and Peggy had sex, although I couldn't imagine a way of finding out.

This is when my new idea came to me. I was drawing Peggy and I kept writing under the drawing the words "My patron." And I was thinking that she really wanted a dead Christ, and that I didn't want to do just another dead Christ like I'd done for the show. Gradually, the idea came to me of a triptych, because in Renaissance paintings, the figure of the patron, or the donor, is often the subject of one of the two wings. And Peggy was such a natural. Then I thought about what went in the other of the wings and that was where I got stumped. Sometimes you got the donor and the donor's wife, but Victor just wasn't going to make it as a subject for me.

The other traditional subject of the second wing is the patron saint, either of the donor's family or of the religious order that is going to house the picture. I tried to think of a modern equivalent of a patron saint: someone you go to for inspiration and protection. I was thinking of painting an angel, to suggest inspiration in the abstract. Not long before, I'd misinterpreted a title in Theresa's bookshelf. The book was called *A Passion for Wings,* and I thought it would be about wings, but it turned out to be about airplanes. But the misreading made me go back to the fabulous wings of Fra Angelico's angels—the stripes of dark red, sea green and peach, impregnable as armor, yet feathery and light at the same time. Something that made flight seem possible, but was sculptural as well. Then I realized that an angel on the other panel of a triptych would be impossible because if I really let myself go with the wings—which is what interested me—it would unbalance the composition, and the challenge of the triptych form was a challenge of balance. So I asked myself whom I went to for inspiration and protection. The answer was the artists of the past whose work I loved. But when I tried to find the equivalent of St. Dominic or St. Bonaventure in a Renaissance triptych, I couldn't think of *one*. I kept seeing a group, a community. The word "community," linked to the words "patron saint," evoked an old Catholic concept, the communion of saints. So then I thought of a group of the artists I loved on the other side of the triptych. I made lots and lots of drawings of groups—men, many more than women, whose work had inspired me, given me consolation and a sense of not being alone. I made drawings of Giotto, Bellini, Vermeer and others whose countenance I knew—Ingres, Corot, Berthe Morisot, Vuillard, Matisse and Gwen John. I had them kneeling in a cluster, their eyes fixed on the same point as the kneeling Peggy. I decided I'd do something larger than I'd customarily done. The middle panel would be eight by six, the two sides eight by four. It was possible that Peggy wouldn't want so big a painting. In that case, I'd have to thank her, but refuse the notion of a commission. I'd do the triptych anyway.

Luckily, there was one Renaissance painting of Christ that I'd wanted to work with, but hadn't gotten around to. I'd seen it once in a show in the National Gallery: Lelio Orsi's *The Dead Christ Flanked by Charity and Justice*. I was attracted to it by the tilt of the slab on which Christ was lying. Its downward slope would be an important compositional element and, as in the Mantegna, would require some foreshortening. But I'd also been attracted to the blue of the cloth on which Jesus lies and the whiteness of the legs, milky and somehow innocent. I'd been amused by the voluminousness of the loincloth, the curve of the chest, the tilted head. But I focused on the slope and the milky legs.

I realized that whether or not Peggy wanted to commission the painting, I'd have to get her permission to use her image on the triptych. It also occurred to me that if she wasn't commissioning it, she wouldn't want to be known as the donor. I hoped that even if she didn't want the painting for herself, she'd be willing to pose for me. I got myself in a panic; I needed to paint her, but suppose she didn't want her image set loose in the world? I was jealous of landscape painters; they didn't have to worry about getting permission from trees and rocks. Peggy Riordan owned her countenance; it was how she was known in the world and she determined what could be done with it. I wondered if Renaissance donors ever refused to allow their countenances to be used. In any case, I guess they could count on being idealized in a way that a modern sitter can't.

I was paralyzed by the idea of approaching Peggy. I asked B how I should do it. "Just be yourself," he said. I told him that was a stupid oversimplification. "Just be one of your selves then," he said. I told him that helped a lot.

Peggy invited me for tea, which she served in thin cups, with a plate of thin cookies that looked so good but so insubstantial I felt like eating fifty of them. But I knew that wasn't quite the thing. I told her that what I had to ask her was difficult and that she should feel absolutely free to refuse me. No, I take it back, I said. Not absolutely free. Luckily, she laughed.

I proposed my idea and to my astonishment she got up and put her arms around me, an embrace that was much more robust, much more off-balancing than anything I would have imagined of her. She said that nothing exciting had happened to her in years. She'd love to do it, she was absolutely at my service, and the size was no problem because she was moving in with Victor in the spring, and they were doing over his apartment on Park Avenue; it was a duplex with miles of wall space and they'd base everything on the new painting, which she knew would be a masterpiece.

If B or one of my friends had used the word "masterpiece" I would have told them to fuck off. As it was, I gently told her that that kind of language made me nervous. "Of course it will be a masterpiece," she said. "How could you fail, with this face." She tried to mug. She actually mugged pretty effectively, which was surprising because you would have thought anything smacking of low comedy would have been beyond her. But I found everything about her response surprising. So surprising that not until I was on my way home was I able to be astonished by the fact that at eighty, Peggy Riordan was shacking up.

It was a great change, painting Peggy after having spent all that time painting B. In one way, when I was painting him, there was less of a barrier between love and work. Both were centered on his body, and even though, when I was drawing or painting him, he wasn't exactly himself but my image of him, the focus of my mind was still his body. It was easy for me to spring from inefficient labor into desire and then into sexual action.

As I focused on Peggy's body, B's took a different place in my imagination. It wasn't banished; it wasn't even shoved to the side, although it was no longer center stage in quite the same way. But it was always present, pervasive, a stage backdrop that was neutral, yet absorptive, porous, responsive to different lights and different dramas.

But often when I was working on Peggy, I didn't think of him, or I thought of him a little guiltily, because I didn't miss him and I didn't miss sex. It didn't seem to matter to me if I never had sex again. But then the atmosphere would change; I could no longer stop the new, pervasive scent in the air, like cooking or flowers, and I would think of being with him as a delicious prospect, an avenue that opens up into a vista, leading to a grove of settled, generously leafy trees.

Ideally, I would have liked him at my beck and call, waiting in bed twenty-four hours a day, but willing to be ignored for days at a time. Ready at a moment's notice to respond with boundless energy, boundless enthusiasm, boundless imagination. Then ready to disappear.

Sometimes in the middle of the week I'd initiate phone sex. The first time was sort of accidental. I guess maybe serial killers say that too. I was lying in bed talking to him and I realized that my hand was traveling. Then I told him it was. I told him exactly what I was doing, my middle finger featherlight. I was touching myself but I was thinking of his hand, moving faster and faster. I've always found it exciting to watch a man with his hand moving so fast it's like he's running a race he can't possibly win, faster and faster, with a desperation that stimulates your vanity about your own sinuous languor in comparison with all that rush.

I began to notice that when I wanted him he wasn't as available as he had been, more involved in his work, of which I still had very little sense. He might have been an alchemist or a blacksmith for all the understanding I had of what he did. He wasn't even willing to take long weekends anymore; he flew up Friday night, and I would meet him, like the other wives. I wondered if everyone got in their cars and started feeling each other up before they were onto Route 6.

Our sex those nights felt like a solid meal after a hard day's work. Chili or beef stew. You were really hungry; you weren't doing it to satisfy a refined appetite, you wanted a lot and fast. Sometimes he'd apologize for being too quick. I don't think he understood that it can be very exciting when it happens like that. I was excited by his excitement, his amateur or adolescent failure of timing. I wouldn't have wanted it to happen all the time, but like anything else, male sensitivity can be misplaced or overused. So that you feel like you're involved in a terribly wholesome, labor-intensive enterprise, like weaving, or organic farming.

On Monday mornings, not quite so famished, we'd make love and swim and I would drive him to the ten o'clock plane, like the other wives, kissing him familiarly on his uxorious, wage-earning cheek.

Maybe some of them were worried that their husbands were going back to their mistresses in the city. I was not.

And just as I'd begun to be his lover before we got onto Route 6 the Friday night before, I began to be the artist-nun before I hit the highway on the day he left. I'd drive right down to Chatham to make Peggy's body the focus of my attention.

I was worried about her fatigue, and every ten minutes I asked her whether she was tired. I could see she didn't like that. "I'll tell you when I'm tired," she said. "I have a perfectly audible voice, I'm not so far gone as all that." And she was marvelously able to be still; she read; we played music, all the Schubert string quartets. We talked. In the weeks I was painting her I learned quite a lot about her life.

She was born in Brooklyn; her parents were, as she'd already told me, high school teachers of music and art. I don't think she liked her mother, though she would never have said as much, only that she believed her mother had some imaginary ailments, which her father might not have helped by being too understanding. She went to Catholic school all the way through college; she was interested in law, but it was unthinkable that she should go to law school. She didn't want to teach or nurse; nothing was said about her marrying, and no prospects suitable to the little family of three seemed to arise.

"And then I did that fatal thing so common for women like me. After college I went to Katherine Gibbs. Katy Gibbs. I learned to be an executive secretary. I learned shorthand and typing, how always to wear white gloves and the right hat. I learned posture and smiling and deference. I learned how not to let any man think I was smarter than he."

She worked, from the moment she left Katherine Gibbs, for one partner in a Madison Avenue law firm made up entirely of Irishmen and Jews. She worked for John Driscoll until she retired—rather early, she said—after John Driscoll died.

And then she told me how she got the money to buy the houses, to commission a painting at top dollar.

Peggy's revelation came about when I realized I wanted to paint her in a kneeling posture and we needed a prie-dieu.

"I wonder where we could go to rip off a prie-dieu," I said.

"Why not just ask to borrow one?"

"In the circles I move in, there's no one you could ask to borrow their prie-dieu. And if you could, what would've been done on it would've been so perverse you wouldn't want to put your knees near it."

I was worried that I'd misspoken, but she laughed.

It made me feel I could be playful with her.

"So, Peggy, do you know someone with a spare prie-dieu?"

"I do have friends who are priests, but they're in the city. I could call the priest in the church here, but he's rather a stick."

"How would you explain it?"

She looked impatient. "I wouldn't tell him the whole story, Monica. That's the error of your generation. The error of mine is thinking you can't even begin it."

"So you'd say . . ."

"That I needed to borrow a prie-dieu."

She called the stick, who wasn't unwilling, but all his prie-dieux happened to be nailed down. So Peggy agreed to do a tour of the churches on the lower Cape with me to look for a portable—and liftable—prie-dieu.

That's how we spent the next Sunday. We finally found one in an old Episcopal church. We agreed that if anyone asked I'd say I was an upholsterer. I'd say I was being paid by the vestry. I had no idea what a vestry was, but it sounded like it might carry weight.

But no one stopped us. I left a note on the floor saying, "This prie-dieu will be returned intact in two weeks." And I left an envelope with a hundred dollars. Then I walked—not ran—looking cool, and Peggy gunned the engine.

There was something about that exploit that she really loved. She kept telling me how much fun it was.

"It's only recently I've become un-law-abiding," she said. "Or I guess that's not true. I spent many years being un-law-abiding, but I was so covert about it that much of the pleasure was lost."

Then she told me some of her story.

"It's remarkable that I still go to church at all because this is such a damn Catholic story. A goddamn Catholic story." She didn't use the adjective as if it came to her easily. "And like most of the stupid things the Catholic Church does, it has to do with sex. I think that the final motivation I needed to become your patron—and don't misunderstand, I greatly admired your work whatever its associations—was to spit in the eye of that part of the Church that thinks sex is wicked and shameful. I bet you don't go to church because of something having to do with sex. Sometime, perhaps we'll talk more about it."

It was my turn to be the Prefect of Reserve.

"Actually, Peggy, I'd tell you every detail of my sexual life before I talked to you about my feelings on religion."

"And as you know I have no wish to hear every detail of your sexual life, you're probably quite safe."

I heard her story over several weeks, as I was painting her. It was remarkable because all the while she was kneeling at the prie-dieu in a traditional confessional posture.

When she began working for John Driscoll, she was twenty-five and he was thirty-seven. His wife had been in a mental hospital for ten years; they'd only been married for two when she tried to kill herself, and then became permanently unhinged. "Paranoid schizophrenic was the diagnosis," Peggy said. "But who knows what that meant in 1932?

"John was a very beautiful man, elegant and fine. He had beautiful hands and marvelous thick hair. Unusually red lips, unusually full for an Irishman. I was his mistress for forty years, until he died. His wife is still living.

"John and I went for decorous vacations to the Continent, where we could pretend to be married. I don't know what my parents thought; nothing was said of it. He was a very successful lawyer. Most of his clients were Irish Catholics, so he probably would have lost a fortune if he'd divorced a mad wife to marry me outside the Church. He never took the risk. We never spoke about it. It was painful for me to watch him escorting eligible women to charity affairs, everyone charitably understanding he wasn't available; everyone knew his tragedy and his devoutness. They didn't know that his greatest virtue was prudence. Heroic prudence. Who's the patron saint of that? Everyone thought we were both such good Catholics we'd never do anything like screw."

The way she used that word made it seem ugly, and I saw her bitterness.

"At least I think that—most of the time. Sometimes I think everyone knew everything all along, despite our care. I still have no idea what my parents thought."

At eighty, she was still worrying about what her parents had thought.

"He left me all his money when he died. So I've been able to live well. And I know he loved me. He simply wasn't able to take certain risks. And perhaps I wasn't either. But I had some things, important things. I had love. I had nice vacations, off-season always, so we wouldn't run into anyone we knew, but the best places. No children, but I mustn't have had a deep instinct or I would have done something about it. I didn't take communion for twenty years and I didn't go to confession. It was only in my late fifties that a wonderful priest told me to come back to the sacraments, that John and I were married in the eyes of God. Naturally he left the priesthood to get married himself. I wish I'd lived more as you do. I wish I had had your audacity. And I like to think, if I were your age, I would have."

"Of course you would have," I said.

"Maybe if I were your age, I'd have carried the prie-dieu."

Eventually, I found out about Victor. They met ten years ago; he was seventy-two, widowed. Yes, they were sexual. They'd been in love for years, but she was reluctant to give up her independence. I told her I could understand that.

"Last year, after almost a decade of pusillanimous cogitation, I decided that I would marry him. I was all ready to marry for the first time at age seventy-nine. Then our lawyer threatened to have me declared incompetent if I made that decision. It would spell financial ruin."

I told her I didn't understand.

"The truth, as you very well know, is that I'm eighty. And unless I die suddenly, I'll probably spend some time in a nursing home. Victor is seventy-two. Those eight years make a difference. If we marry, he's responsible for all my expenses should I require what they so euphemistically call long-term care. Now, Victor is very well off, and doesn't need my contribution to live well. But the thing is, we don't want all his assets given over to some nursing home. So you see, the law is turning me into an outlaw."

"I don't know whether you like being an outlaw or if you feel deprived of not ever having had the legal status of marriage."

"You see why I'm fond of you. Most people who know me would immediately assume the latter."

With Peggy and me, love happened slowly; it wasn't like my love affair with B, whom I was drawn to at first sight; I couldn't resist him anymore than I could have resisted an electric field. At first, I'd felt shy with Peggy, and inadequate, reserved. But I grew to love her because she gave me a sense of fineness—a word I hadn't had much access to, as if she'd introduced me to a new musical instrument. We rejoiced in the sight of each other; we were happy in each other's presence. We spoke on the phone every day; there were always things we wanted to say. We bought each other little gifts; fresh figs I saw in the market, a smoked fish paté. She bought me a bar of soap in the shape of a seashell and a soap dish made of blue glass she'd found in the flea market. She brought me snapdragons from her garden, because I'd said I liked them. I sent her drawings in the mail, the envelopes decorated in watercolor.

But the greatest gift I gave her was introducing her to Sara. I hadn't realized before how much Sara needed someone like Peggy. Someone with a palette similar to hers. The women in our family—me, my mother, Helena, Rachel—are all pretty high-colored. Matisse. Beethoven's Ninth. Ups and downs and indiscretions and bursts of enthusiasm and hard, vengeful aversions. In Peggy, Sara found a resonance. I don't know what they talked about, except that Peggy could speak to Sara about the technical aspects of music in a way that none of the rest of us could. But it wasn't so much what they talked about; it was more a matter of tone. Or a series of tones that they both inhabited or were enveloped by. Dove grays, ivories tinged with pink, gradual gestures, gentle fadings out. Words like "wistful," "somber," that had no place in the lexicon suggested by her family DNA. She'd gotten some of that sweetness from Roger, but Roger's was tinged by forgetfulness and an underlying torpor that had caused problems for her as a child.

Peggy entered her life at a time and in a way that could do Sara only good. And what did Peggy get? How can I answer fairly? She got my daughter's presence, and perhaps, the dream of a younger self, with the chance, this time, of its being done right.

When I left them alone together, I wanted to tiptoe, backward, as you do when you overhear a child creating a fantasy world. Yet I don't want to imply that what they had was childish or fantastical. Simply, it was tender, it was delicate, and it was rare.

I'm telling you this so that you understand that when Peggy made her extraordinary offer to me, although it was rather startling, it made a certain amount of emotional sense. It was an emotional gesture, a token of love. And because it was that, no rational argument against it held sway.

It was September, late enough in the season that Peggy and I felt alone on the Cape. The summer crowds had cleared out; the sky seemed larger, although tinged with melancholy. I wondered how acute that sense was for Peggy, but I didn't need to ask. I could tell when she said, "Isn't it like that wicked poison ivy to be the first plant to turn red and remind you of the end of things."

She'd asked me for supper. I suggested we go out so she didn't have to cook but she said she needed privacy. I asked her if anything was wrong. She said she hoped not, and when she heard the anxiety in my silence she said, "I believe it's the opposite of wrong, but we'll see soon enough."

We had a simple dinner of broiled cod, russet potatoes with butter and dill, a salad of romaine lettuce, cucumbers and cress. She said, "This is what I wanted for dessert. It's what I would have had if I were alone. I'd never have the nerve to give them to Victor."

She took two Klondike bars from the refrigerator, and we ate them, leaning over a plate. There was no elegant way to eat a Klondike bar, no way of dividing it up. We just ate them, not even trying to hide the greed that made us unable to talk.

"You're a genius," I said. "That's what's the matter with civilized society. Everybody would probably rather have a Klondike bar than biscotti and sauterne, but nobody feels free to do it."

"I believe I've had another idea that partakes of genius. Nothing to the Klondike bar, but what is. Put on your thinking cap, as my father would say, we have to be clear-headed. This is about money."

"Talk to Fanny."

"It's not about a painting. It's about something else."

I wanted to put my hand over her mouth or tell her I was feeling sick and had to go home immediately. My friendship with Peggy had been purely pleasurable. I knew enough about money to fear its muddying aspects.

"I've had a talk with my lawyer. When you have an estate of a certain size, lawyers travel to the Cape to see you. Perhaps that's not fair, this is the nephew of John's partner, and I've known him since he was a boy. It doesn't mean I like him, but I know he's clever about money.

"He's the one who figured out that Victor and I couldn't get married. As you very well pointed out, something in me was well served by that so I didn't object. But now I'm moving in with Victor and I have a huge apartment on Central Park West. It was John's. To tell you the truth I've never really liked it; eight rooms, and no good light in any of them. But I did like the neighborhood and there it was, when John died, a block away from Lincoln Center. At sixty-five, I thought it was time to move out of my parents' home.

"None of that matters. The point is, the other people on the floor, who do something for their money I probably don't want to know about, have always told me that if I want to sell they want to buy so they can have the whole bloody floor for their ill-behaved children and their twin mastiffs. Can you believe that? I dislike those dogs because I always have to be thinking of their penises."

"Peggy, I think I'm a bad influence on you. Do you talk this way to other people?"

"Of course not, I have more sense of decency than that. But don't try and distract me. The point is this: I have the house in Santa Fe and this one. Victor has Park Avenue and Trastevere. You see, he's almost entirely urban, it's why he doesn't come here much. I have, as they say, a healthy stock portfolio. I'm eighty years old. I have no children, and I dislike my relatives. Not to put too fine a point on it, there's no one I'm as fond of and admire as much as you. Except Victor. And I'm determined that a nursing home will get as little as possible. It is time for me to divest. I have to divest at least two years before I go into a nursing home for them not to claim those assets. So that, eventually, after they've taken what I have up to that point, I get to be called a pauper and go on Medicaid. Yes, it's possible to give your fortune to a nursing home if you live long enough. The earlier you divest the better, so they don't begin fussing, so they don't think I'm doing exactly what it is I'm doing. My proposition is this: while I'm healthy, I'd like to sign the Central Park West apartment over to you."

"Thanks, but I've already got an apartment."

"I understand that, Monica, you're not thinking well. The apartment can be sold to the drug dealers on the floor for two million dollars. You could do what you liked with that."

"I can't take it."

"Give me a good reason why."

"You might need it."

"I have more than I need."

"Give it to ghetto children or some worthy cause."

"I've already given an enormous amount to ghetto children and worthy causes. What I haven't had is the pleasure of a legacy. Will you deny me that? You've no good reason, and you know it."

"Peggy, you're making me feel a little sick. I think I have to go home and throw up for a few hours. I'll call you in the morning."

I paced up and down B's living room with Mikey. The moon was hidden behind the clouds; the sky was a royal blue with patches of pure blackness. I'd been given an extraordinary financial offer; the second in my life. I lay down and pulled the covers over my head, and must have drifted off to sleep, because I was startled by the phone's ring. And startled by the dreadful sound of B's voice; it was literally full of dread.

"What happened?" I asked.

"Something awful."

"Are you sick? Are you in the hospital?"

"No, I'm all right physically, but some Japanese cornered cocoa."

I was trying to make a visual image, some small man in glasses, bowing, trying to surround a huge mountain of chocolate powder.

"I don't understand," I said.

"Yoshimoro cornered cocoa. I've lost four million dollars. I'm wrecked."

I was terribly relieved that it was only money, so relieved that, despite what he'd said, I felt elation. And it was in a spirit of elation that I spoke. "Darling," I said. "This couldn't have come at a better time. Don't worry about being broke. I'm rich."

PART THREE

Looking back on it, I can see that euphoria might not have been the right response to the sentence "I lost four million dollars."

The euphoria didn't last. Because he really was shattered. I drove to New York immediately. When I went down to his apartment, and he answered the door, the sides of his face didn't match up; he held his body as if he'd been beaten. There was a sense of panic in the air, and doom, a panic and doom particularly connected to money. It must have been around on October 30, 1929. It must have been what led tycoons to jump from buildings.

I didn't know whether he wanted to be near me, whether my body would be a comfort to him or an abrasion. He was sitting in the dark, and the apartment felt overheated. I felt as if I were in one of those Berlin boardinghouses in the twenties with a bad gas stove giving off fumes that could only be toxic. One of those George Grosz rooms where the skin tones are navy blue and maroon and none of the lines are plumb.

I turned on a few lights; I opened the blinds. I looked in the refrigerator for food; I felt he needed to be taking in nourishment. There were eggs and butter and half a loaf of whole wheat bread, a single onion. I made him a buttery omelet, and slathered butter on the whole wheat toast. I must have been trying to create lubrication.

He ate silently, like a mental patient or a prisoner. As soon as he was finished, he said he was going into his room to lie down. I asked if he'd like me to join him. He shrugged. I took it for a yes.

We lay in the dark, and I could feel the wideness of his open eyes. I held his hand, and he squeezed mine halfheartedly. And then—I can't explain it—the charge of desire entered the room. Was it some old instinct of retrieval or healing? I must be honest: the erotic vector was operating in one direction only—from me to him.

Something about the stillness of his desolation made his body seem extraordinarily clean, luminous, like a pearl in black water. I was drawn to him as you would be drawn to moonlight on a dark patch of ground. I thought it possible that he'd consider a physical approach an invasion, so I moved a bit away from him. The few inches of blanket between us became fraught, electrified, as irresistible to try to breach as any other border zone. I turned to him. He did not turn to me in response. I kissed his hand, the vulnerable palm, place of the wounds in my dead Christs. I stroked his hair. I placed kisses, cooling as poultices, on his forehead. I didn't even approach his mouth. He responded to no part of it. I lay back in the darkness, shimmering with yearning.

If we hadn't had a life together, a history of desire and satisfaction, it might have ended there. A moment of unbalanced stasis, marked by the shame of going out to the cold air of the street with the fever sore of unmet lust. But his was a body that I knew.

And his wounded state wasn't shameful to me, simply another of his body's states, which I'd known: elated, weary, driven, playful, withdrawn, sluggish, exploratory, sated and insatiable, wild and at rest.

His body was the body of my partner. Partner as in a dance. And I wanted him. I had a deep impulse to repair the infliction of damage—like that of a bomb site—and to place myself in the broken structure. To cover over the fissure with rich earth. I took off my clothes; I could tell he didn't even notice. I put his hand between my legs. Slowly, stealthily, almost sleepily, his third finger made curves around the rim, circling then, peripheral, arousing me until I felt that my arousal made him suddenly alert. Memory took over; he reconsidered. He remembered a task or a skill he'd known before. He woke up. He watched me climb, approach, reach up and break my flight. And then he held me. He was not erect, but he was not alone.

That night he thought of my body as a miracle. He wasn't getting hard, but he would put his fingers and his mouth to me, over and over, as if he needed to drink me in to keep himself alive. After many hours, I'd come so much that my mouth felt dry, and all I wanted was long drinks of water. But as I moved to get a drink, he pulled me back. I tapped him with my fingertips as if he were a keyboard, not even trying to arouse him, but in a kind of whisper, a murmuring with no message. The aimlessness affected him, and he grew half hard in my hand, then slowly harder. It was a long time, a very long time, and then suddenly, boyishly, with only a soft cry, almost an apology, he left in my cupped hand a healthy residue. A mess.

In those days, we talked very little. We slept in patches, shallow tunnels of sleep where we would grope for each other, as if we were under water, then swim up to wakefulness. Each time I was with him, I felt I had to tear down screen after screen between us. And I knew, but did not know how, this had to do with money.

I made him go to the Cape with me. It was November and beginning to be cold. He'd light a fire, but he couldn't concentrate on anything very well, and it took a long time. When the sun was golden over the water, which was taking on its winter purple, he'd squint and cover his eyes as if the half light were all he could endure. I made soups all week; I even made bread. He didn't lift a hand to help me. When I invited him to go to the store with me, he'd say, "No thanks," and as I pulled out of the driveway, I could see him turning off the lights. It was darkening early, four-forty-five one day, four-forty-two the next, then four-twenty-five, four twenty. I felt the early darkness as a theft, but I could tell he saw it as a mercy.

The darkness and the heat of indoors made me feel avid for the November wind, the dried leaves scudding along the road, the few yellow ones left behind, stubbornly, hopelessly, on the almost-bare trees. The light would strike them with a lucidity that made me hungry; the open spaces that surrounded them made them a surface that accepted light, then bounced it off again into the air, which was beginning to be freezing. I would walk without him, letting the wind seep under the clothes I wore, purposely insufficient so I'd be just a little cold. I wanted to carry the cold back to the overheated house, the house that was like an incubator, where I would brood over my fledgling: damp, featherless, unable to bear the outside temperatures, the buffeting of this new season's wind.

I decided to work only on drawings so I could be available to B if he wanted to do anything. I'd never painted a group, and the multitude of the artists' bodies on their side of the triptych must not unbalance the kneeling Peggy. While I worked, he slept. When I cooked, he slept. When I ran, he slept. He took very long showers, often both a bath and a shower in one day. Sometimes I'd walk into the bathroom, afraid that he'd fallen asleep and drowned.

Sometimes he came, always in my hand, but often he didn't. Still he turned to my body with ardor; he became newly attentive to certain latitudes of skin; I could sense that what he wanted was to spend time attending to me, and I changed my focus. I became, not an attending body, but a body attended to. He never penetrated me in those weeks. Not even once.

It was as if I'd entered a sexual architecture without lines, without frames or stanchions or doorways or scaffolding. As I lay in bed, opening myself to his ministrations, to his imagination and his tenderness, I felt that I was swimming in a blue gray water. I had no responsibility except to my own pleasure. I could float in the grotto of my own arousal, watching, as if out of the corner of my eye, the colorful flashing tails of fish, at the deepest end.

Sometimes I didn't touch him, sometimes I did, and he was soft, baby soft, and I held on to him anyway, a light reminder, tentative and shy.

I saw myself removing all the barriers I'd thrown up between us to keep myself from feeling grateful and beholden. Holding what? Or whom? Not money, anymore. He could no longer give me money. And he couldn't give me an erect, penetrating penis.

For the first time, I asked him to tell me about his parents. I asked him about his childhood. And for the first time, I wanted to know who his friends were. I offered to meet his friends and his parents. I asked nothing about his work.

I knew that it was a double impotence that brought about in me such an impulse of tenderness. He couldn't penetrate me and he couldn't pay my bills. I could imagine giving him anything.

I was awash in a bath of what I can only call benevolence. Perhaps it was the physical unselfishness of his sexual attention. He was, in the most obvious sense, getting nothing from it, from me. It made me wish, with an unusual singleness of heart, to give him things. My body, with a kind of plainness I'd refused myself and him. I wanted him to be happy. Simply happy. I wanted to arrange my days to please him. If he wanted to be quiet, I was. If he wanted music, we had it. If there was a movie, we drove to it. You could hardly say I was working. I was absorbed and satisfied with my new full-time job: the profession of being WITH.

Sometimes I'd sneak out and talk to my friends on a pay phone. A kind of infidelity from all that benevolence. I asked Michael if he thought B needed antidepressants. He said no, that B was experiencing something situational and not inappropriate. I asked Theresa if she'd ever had a good time without penetration, and she said yes, sometimes surprisingly terrific, and what would men say if they knew that?

If men knew the ways that women talk to each other about sex, they might never come near us. It's nothing like the traditional notion of male locker-room talk. There is very little in bragging. Sometimes there are surprised congratulations. But most frequently, technical advice. Recipes. Absolutely crucial hints from Heloise, which more men have been helped by than they know, and are much better off not knowing about.

I phoned Peggy and said I needed to talk. She was distracted with moving, and with moving in for the first time at eighty with a man. But I needed her advice about money. I had asked her again if she meant her offer to let me have the apartment. She rather waspishly asked if I thought she was kidding. I asked if we could do it, and sell it quickly. I told her about my plan to give half the money to B. Cash. Ready cash. Cash now. I saw all that wood paneling, those beveled windows, transformed into a pile of coins, a pile of greenbacks. She said the neighbors were chomping at the bit; they couldn't wait to phone the contractors and start breaking down the walls between the apartments. I said my only problem was to talk him into taking the money. She said she was sure I'd think of something.

On November 23, we packed up the van and drove back to New York. We'd been alone for two weeks, he'd had my full share of what is now nauseatingly referred to as nurturing. But now it was over. I had to work.

When we got home, I seemed to travel down to his apartment more, although mine was much nicer. He kept saying he needed to be near his computer.

Every time I visited him, I brought food. I had an impulse to spend money on him, to lavish things on him. I didn't think he knew how to lavish things on himself, to comfort himself with those comforts money could buy.

If I'd been really low, a clothes-shopping trip would have given me a great temporary solace. A new pair of shoes—Italian, narrow-cut— would have made me feel life was full of possibilities I hadn't thought of. A French bra would have reinstated my sense of irony. A man-tailored jacket of excellent British tweed would have made me feel sensible and ready for a bracing uphill battle. A new haircut, a manicure, and for at least half an hour, I'd be the equal of anyone. But there was only one area of his body where a consumer outlay would be helpful to him: his stomach. I couldn't buy him a new sweater; he'd throw it, unopened, in a corner. But I could spend a fortune on filet mignon. When the butcher rang up a tab of fifty dollars for two steaks and a bottle of virgin olive oil, I felt the plutocrat's sexual thrill. Diamond Jim Brady. Only I was Diamond Lil. I'd wave my arms in their elaborate sleeves, and the orbit of the world would be changed.

Money and sex, sex and money. Men and women. Women and men. Having money after not having money. Not having money after having it. Money and fear, money and greed. Sometimes I wanted to sit with my head in my hands, holding the bones of my thin skull together so my brains wouldn't spill out from the force of all this focus on money. When I thought about money, I could see my brain turn from a healthy white, a cauliflower, something steady and stable, to a writhing mess of eels, blood red, or the color of intestines, the color of disease. Poussin to Francis Bacon, in one quick leap.

I had a lot of money that I didn't need. Two million dollars. I remembered a TV show that I was fascinated by as a child: *The Millionaire*. A plutocrat named John Beresford Tipton—whose face you never saw, you only heard his voice—gave away a million dollars a week, anonymously of course, to someone deserving. He was represented in the world, to the deserving one that is, by a suave emissary named Michael Anthony whose eyes suggested something of the hypercultivated mandarin. You wouldn't have been surprised to see him with long, useless fingernails.

It wasn't insignificant that we never saw the philanthropist's face, never knew anything of his life or his relations. How, in a half-hour TV show in the black and white 1950s, would it have been possible to portray the benefactor's intention, the gnawing of a minor but irrepressible avarice, the wave he must always push against; to keep everything for himself?

In this show, no one was made unhappy by his or her new money; no one's life ever got worse. I forgot to say that this was fiction. Because you read all the time about people whose marriages are ruined by the lottery, who become crack addicts, whose children end up in the streets, who die alone in mental hospitals or SROs. Or in their mansions, friendless, attended by servants who bilk them of every cent and pocket the jewelry before the corpse is cold. You heard of Howard Hughes and Doris Duke. But you never really believed it. You never thought it would happen to you, that kind of ruin or corruption. Or I never did.

And I never thought of money affecting my sex life. Particularly for the worse. When B was my benefactor, I wanted to hold part of myself back from him; it made our sex a bit theatrical, and the unnaturalness was probably exciting, like silk restraints, keeping you from something, you're not sure what, and not too much. I was occasionally aroused by my own resistance. Sex was like a wrestling match and the urge to use everything in my body to keep itself from being overwhelmed or overcome by something stronger than itself—the force of his money—gave the sex a hard industrial edge, like Léger's paintings of the workings of machines.

It was exactly the opposite of the endless benevolence I felt after he was broke. After that there was nothing I wanted to hold back.

I wanted to give him the money I soon would get from Peggy. It seemed right; it made me happy to be able to repay him in some way for the gift that had changed my life so dramatically. I kept telling myself that I didn't need Peggy's money; I owned an apartment, all I had to do was pay twelve hundred dollars a month maintenance. I had a sold-out show, a commission, a job at Watson I could go back to anytime. I had more money than I'd ever had, and even before that I'd lived perfectly well.

But I felt the tooth of greed, the first hint of the idea that there was no such thing as too much money, that there could never possibly be enough. I didn't see the money, but I heard it. Coins clinking down a well. I heard a voice saying, "You're ruined." The words were from the mouth of someone in a Cruikshank illustration of Dickens, or the Charnel House paintings of Géricault. I heard creditors on the phone, calling day and night, threatening me with jail. I heard the insults of the people who refused to hire me to work as a dishwasher; I heard the mad ravings of the woman I slept next to on the shelter floor.

And his reluctance to take money from me, his feeling that it was adding to his impotence, made it more tempting for me to forget the whole idea, to keep the money for myself. I decided that I needed to create a new set of images. Something that would always be in the front of my mind, projected on the dome-shaped bones of my forehead, so I could always call them up when indecision or reluctance struck. I had to be able to see myself as opulent, so words like "largesse" could surround and protect me, drown out the words "debt" and "ruin." So I spent a day looking at Sargent paintings at the Met.

I began with Madame X. I concentrated on her marble shoulders, powdered and violet-tinted, her sculpted dress, gleaming and yet granitic, her narrow waist—won by who knows what resistance to nature, what denial, what whalebone-induced pain. Did the purple light come from the straps made up of brilliants? From the lights on the diamonds holding up the granitic creation of the dress? No, that purple powder emanated from nothing but the white flesh itself, flesh that could be seen as an investment. Something money had been poured into. I asked Madame X to endow my flesh with the power of the voluptuary, with the force of abundance. It was so solid, yet so shimmering,

that flesh, nothing you could get lost in or swallowed up by. This was
the flesh B and I needed, and since his flesh was wounded now, the
power of Madame X would have to come from me. I would have to find
in myself the white body of the benefactor. When he put his lips to my
shoulder, he would taste cool whiteness, endlessly replenishable. The
spring and sheen made possible only by access to resources that could
be thought of as endless. I could present myself to him as Madame X,
then he would take my money.

Or perhaps I should be like Mrs. Phelps Stokes in the picture next
to Madame X (her hand on her hip, her boater at her side, her long
skirt, her cotton shirt, a bit mannish), looking ready for a gallop on one
of her Arabians, or a sail on one of her boats, or a trip to the Grand
Canyon. The curve of her hip suggests that prosperity can never be a
curse, always and only an opportunity.

In the background of the picture, Mr. Stokes—whom I'd read had
been put in at the last minute by Sargent because the Great Dane he
really wanted wasn't available—is looking a little petulant, a little
resistant. I thought of B. Maybe Mrs. was the one with the money.
Maybe Mr.'s crossed arms were a protest against being thought of as a
gigolo. Maybe those firmly planted legs and feet were insisting that he
would do only and exactly what he wanted to do.

There's no word attaching to a woman that has the status of "gigolo."
Nothing with that residue of loathsomeness, that whiff of the gutter or
the drain. The associations of "mistress," or even "kept woman," at least
suggest physical cleanliness. Rosy flesh, well tended for the purpose. If
there is depravity, it's not connected with ill health. "Gigolo" sounds
disease-bearing. And though the mistress may be indolent, the gigolo
is lazy.

This is what I was fighting against; this is why I was looking at the
Sargents. But if I'd found the necessary image for myself, I didn't find
what I needed for B. I moved to the Whistler side of the room. I looked
for one of those young men for whom the concept "earning a living"
was obviously beside the point. Sometimes they might make money,
sometimes they would "come into it." But however it arrived, they
would accept it without questioning its source; they would emerge
from their mauve or onyx backgrounds, in their dove gray toppers and

their morning coats, leaning on or against something (a cane, a mantel-piece), elegantly accepting the fact that they needed money, that it enhanced their stature, that the money itself, and not its source, was what made their position in the world.

I decided I wanted to buy B a shirt that Whistler's M. Duret, standing in the pink gray light, might have worn. Something Whistler himself might have worn, as he pictured himself in his engravings: the artist dandy, the spirited younger son. Something with a soft, pointed collar, something you could wear a tie with or not. Perhaps a light blue. No, white. I wouldn't tell B that I was giving him a costume for a part he'd be playing in my mind. I wouldn't tell him that it was all about inhabiting an image to cleanse the bad vapors that surround a man who takes money from a woman.

I wasn't sure what shirt size he wore, because I'd never bought him a shirt. My not knowing what size shirt he wore said a lot about how, or who, we were to each other.

He knew my sizes because he'd bought me things to wear. My body had been adorned by shirts and camisoles and pajamas he'd seen and imagined clothing me in. He had thought of my body in a way I hadn't thought of his, as a vessel, or the opposite of a vessel, because my body would be covered by what he saw, not containing it. Now I wanted to think of his body in this way, a combination of vision and expenditure. I wanted him to represent something that wasn't possible without his being dressed for the part. Dressed like a doll? I remembered the statue of the Infant of Prague in my parish church in Astoria. The statue had clothing, vestments that were changed according to the liturgical season: green for Pentecost, purple for Lent, white for Easter. Women fought over the honor of dressing the statue of the Baby Christ. Was that what I was doing with B? Dressing him like a doll?

I wouldn't accept that. If he could have the pleasure of adorning me, an homage to my allurements, a tribute to their range of possibility, then I would have the same. I would dress the languid boy he sometimes was. The languid boy destined—but not right now—to make a mark in the world. I would dress him for his period of wounded rest.

I phoned him, hoping he wasn't home. He wasn't. I let myself into his apartment, went into his closet and stole what looked like his best shirt. Then I took a cab back to a shop on Madison Avenue that sold only shirts. Right away, the presence of such established, such time-honored masculinity—a masculinity made possible by years and years of stocks and bonds and investments I couldn't even know the names of—made me feel pleasantly on edge. I was drawn by the sheer perfection of the form.

The salesman, a bald man with pale eyes, who wore a signet ring with a milky blue stone, asked me to describe what I wanted. I couldn't say: "I want a shirt from a Whistler painting." But I could do something else. I could draw it. The salesman was delighted with my sketch and asked if he could keep it if he could come up with a shirt that gave me pleasure. I felt a little shy, but pleased; he was shy and pleased too.

And he knew his business. He walked out from behind the green curtain, with a white cotton shirt of loose weave, a wing collar. He said it could be worn with or without a tie, but he suggested a loose-knit one, maybe a Prussian blue. He said everything connected with this shirt must be light; it was a shirt about lightness.

"I think you'll understand when I say every shirt is about something. Does that sound strange?"

"No," I said, "it sounds like you love your work."

"I do," he said, and when he took my credit card he looked at me intently. "You're that painter they made all that fuss about. Wow. And now I have a sketch from you. Next time you have a show, I'll come. Not that I could afford you."

I apologized.

"No," he said. "It's wonderful. You deserve it. Enjoy it. Enjoy everything while you can."

I took his words as a blessing and a warning. In the cab downtown, the shiny red shopping bag glowed like a ruby in my lap. I was feeling monumental as I walked into his building, holding my expensive shopping bag, my face flushed from the wind off the East River. But my monumentality was shaken when I walked into his apartment and saw B sitting in front of the computer, not alone. And I was really shaken when the man standing behind the computer turned grudgingly, unsmilingly toward me when I said hello.

*       *       *

The first thing I noticed about him was that he had unusually red lips, as if they were perpetually chapped, and his mouth was a more perfectly circular shape than I'd ever seen. This was probably because his mouth was never quite closed; he had an absolutely ordinary nose, but it didn't seem functional for breathing. He was holding an unlit cigar.

"Nice to meet you," he said, in a way that indicated I shouldn't believe him for a second.

"This is Jerry Weiss," B said. "I've known him since public school. He was the schoolyard bully. He looked out for me until I learned how to fight."

"You always held your own," he said. "Or at least you used to."

"Jerry's in the market, too. We used to work for the same firm."

"Till you decided to be the fucking Lone Ranger," Jerry said, flicking his cigar, which puzzled me, because it was still unlit. I was also amazed that he was calling B the same name that Michael had called him, and I wondered if his identity was so legible that perfect strangers could come up with the same reading.

"This guy is what you'd call a real mess right now," he said, cocking his head toward B. "I mean, I would refer to this individual right now as a hundred percent mess."

"I think I hear your mother calling you, Jerry. I definitely heard her lift up the window and shout your name. You better go."

"I'm not going, buddy, and there's one very good reason for it. I think this lady needs to know some things, and you're probably too much of a gentleman to tell her. It's not my problem, being a gentleman."

"No, Jerry, it's never been your problem."

"This guy was doing very well for himself. Very well. And then the art thing comes along. He buys these paintings. Good, I said, art is a good investment. You can be pretty sure the value goes up, unless you're a real asshole and buy at asshole prices, which he wasn't doing. So I was all for it. And even this thing with you in the beginning. I thought, what the fuck, he's got plenty of money, if he wants to be an asshole, let him enjoy it. But then it wasn't funny, because in this game, you can't start fucking around. Taking long vacations, not paying attention, taking off in the middle of the day to hold somebody's hand. I mean, it just doesn't work. I'm happy for you, you got a good deal for yourself, but you need to know, the guy is wrecked and it's your fault."

"That's enough, Jerry," B said, with more force than I'd seen in him since he lost his money. "What happened to me has nothing to do with Monica. A lot of guys in soft markets took a beating because of Yoshimoro."

"Yeah, but I've never seen you taken for an asshole like this."

"It happens to everybody."

"But in this day and age, a quick comeback isn't so easy. You're fucked, buddy. I can help you, but basically, you're fucked."

"I know this is going to come as a shock to you, Jerry, but actually, I don't need your help. And I don't need it because of Monica. Her financial position has improved dramatically, and she's giving me a million start-up capital."

"Bullshit," he said. "What's she doing, fucking the fucking Salomon Brothers?"

"No," I said. "Not even one of them. As a matter of fact, he's made a very sound financial investment. As a result of his backing, I've had a very successful show and I've got a very wealthy patron who's given me an extremely generous commission. I can come up with this start-up money because of her. So maybe he wasn't such a complete asshole."

"He was an asshole. He let himself be pussy-whipped. First by you, then by Yoshimoro. You're really giving him a million bucks start-up?"

"Yes, I am," I said, trying to look like Deborah Kerr.

"And he's taking it? From someone he's fucking?"

"I think it's time for you to leave, Jerry," said B.

"Why is it that I feel that everyone from your past should go through a metal detector? He wouldn't happen to be your ex-wife's brother? I guess you're taking me up on my offer."

"I guess I have to if I don't want to look like I was too much of a pussy to take a dare. I always told you, everything I need to know I learned in the schoolyard."

"Not everything you need to know. Just everything you *do* know."

"If we're going to be partners, you have to be more respectful."

"I was thinking of less," I said.

He put his arms around me. "I'm scared," he said. "I think I've never been so scared."

"I know," I said. I didn't know whether he wanted to go to bed or not, whether sex right now would seem like another test, another responsibility. I decided to cook the steaks.

From that time on, he didn't want to think about much but commodities and making money. The simplest way to put it is he had no time for me.

If you'd asked me, I would have said I understood; that he was under enormous pressure, that the stakes were terribly high, that his self-confidence had taken a near-mortal blow, that when I'd been absorbed in my work, I'd kept him at a distance. Of course I would have said I understood. My mind was a heroine, one of those long-suffering Eakins women, sad-eyed and infinitely patient. But my body was one of Käthe Kollwitz's starving workers. I thought of the word "starveling" in relation to myself. The purple-dusted Madame X had shrunk, her marble bosom was pitiful now, her hands chapped, red and raw. I felt pathetic to myself.

Of course, I kept wondering whether Jerry Weiss was right, whether it was my fault that B had lost everything. This made me feel he should leave me alone. Every time I thought that way, I convinced myself that no one like Jerry Weiss could possibly be right about anything. He couldn't even light his cigar.

I made myself go back to work. I was at the point in the triptych where I had to concentrate on the fabric, the white sheet on which Jesus lies, which drapes his body from stomach to upper thigh, so that it begins as a pallet cover and ends up looking like hot pants. I'd been pleased to think about working on the Lelio Orsi because I was interested in the problem of whiteness, as I'd work it out in the linen of the fabric. I'd been looking at Mondrian's whitenesses, in the combinations of greens and purples, the underhints of blue that made up white. I was very interested in limiting my palette; the original was quite spare. Jesus lay on a slab in an outcropping of barren rock. White and gray, emptiness and bareness, and in the foreground, a few isolated flowers, hard fixed points of dazzling red and blue.

But it was difficult for me to call up my excitement for whiteness and grayness, barrenness and emptiness when I was feeling like a starveling. The feeling took root in my stomach; I ate sugary foods until my mouth was sore, and then, sick with self-loathing, I'd lie on the couch and do the crossword puzzle, which I'm not good at and don't enjoy.

I'd look at the painting and the sheer size of the canvas would daunt me. I'd set myself to do a little task, one inch of beautiful paint, but I couldn't, because all I could think of was the Whistler shirt, abandoned in the closet like my unloved, neglected self.

So when a man named Vladimir Sokolov wrote to ask me if he could interview me in connection with his work at the University of Tallahassee, he was on exchange from the University of Moscow, deeply involved in a project called "Fundamentalism(s) and the Culture(s) of High Art," of course I said yes, he should come. I was longing for distraction, and he'd be bound to have something interesting to say about the Hermitage, or the Russian Mafia, or even the free market. Or different kinds of vodka, for all I cared.

He explained in his letter that he was preparing to start a Department of American Studies at the University of Moscow. He had written a book about American musical theater, but recently the collision of "religious and secular realms in the world of art" had struck him.

I phoned him in Tallahassee and he said he'd come the following weekend.

"I very much look forward to seeing your work. Your ideas are full of daring, very daring woman's view. I wish I could see some of original work. The reproductions in *New York Times* are very interesting."

I told him I'd try to provide him with some transparencies and slides.

"It's an honor, believe me, an honor I did not expect to have, to come close to the process of a living artist."

I was prepared to like him.

He arrived in a snowstorm, wearing a fur hat. I guess he was making a point, but it didn't seem so at the time; it was winter, he was Russian, his hat was made of fur. His eyes were slanty and they gave the impression of darting and at the same time being very still, like certain kinds of water. They were the eyes of a young French girl: Berthe Morisot's portraits of her daughter.

He spent a long time wiping his boots on the outside mat, and then he stopped and asked if I'd like him to take them off.

"Not at all, I'm not that fastidious."

"Fastidious. An excellent word. But I assume your abode is of aesthetic importance to you, and a violation could cause you pain."

"I had two kids, and I got over it," I said. "Anyway, come in, you don't want to stand in the vestibule."

"What is it, 'vestibule'?"

I laughed. "It just means hallway. Sorry."

"No, no, not to be sorry. A new word is always a gift."

He walked around the living room. "Magnificent," he said. "But I am always breathtaken by the grandeur of American urban apartments. In Moscow such space and such light, unthinkable."

I felt like apologizing. Or confessing. I offered him coffee.

I brought the coffee out with a few Milano cookies. They were what was left over from a binge I'd had when I couldn't bring my attention to the flowers in the foreground of Peggy's painting and B couldn't take his attention from cocoa. I was shocked to see how few cookies were left in the bag. Five. Five out of how many? Fifteen? Twenty? I'd bought them just the day before. I comforted myself with the idea that I hadn't finished the whole bag. I told myself that five cookies on a plate didn't look ungenerous.

"What are these marvelous biscuits?" he asked. "Have you made them yourself?"

"Oh, no, I don't bake. I cook, I like cooking but I don't bake. My father was a baker, and the standard's just too high. Besides, there's something too domestic about baking."

He was writing things down in a little loose-leaf black leather notebook, maybe six by eight inches. I was wondering if it came from Russia or here. I asked him what he was writing.

"Oh, you see, I am particularly interested in you as specimen of contemporary woman artist. The conflicts. The discoveries. In my country, the whole relation of women to paid work under the Soviet system creates different sets of problems. Soviet women were overworked, overexploited; they look upon the ability to stay home, to be supported, as a kind of liberation. To bake biscuits, particularly in a kitchen like yours, with a ceiling like the blue of heaven, would seem to them like heaven."

I didn't know whether or not to feel censured. I was thinking how annoyed B would be with the way the conversation was going. All that emphasis on European suffering.

"I don't think I'm a specimen of anything."

"Dear lady, you feel attacked." He took my hand. "The last thing I would do is attack you. You must forgive me because some things in your country are difficult to understand. Pardon me if I've overstepped some boundary, but what I find particularly fascinating about you is that you are so obviously womanly, and this is not, of course, a gift all artists have."

"You'd be afraid to say male artists aren't manly."

"You see, this territory is for me dangerous. I seem always to be giving offense. Can you believe me that I was trying to compliment?"

I noticed that in the space between his moustache and his beard, his lips were very full. And he was fixing me with those Berthe Morisot eyes, which he knew very well how to make work for him. But I just didn't feel like fighting. I was enjoying myself; he was making me feel attractive. And since for so long I had felt I couldn't compete with the coffee market—B didn't even laugh when I found him a '78 of "They've Got an Awful Lot of Coffee in Brazil"—it was a feeling I couldn't help but enjoy.

I gave him the slides and the transparencies and I said I'd do some errands while he was looking at them. When he heard my key in the door, he jumped up from his seat as if he'd been caught in the middle of a theft. He came over to me and took my hand. "You must allow me an old-fashioned gesture. But I've been so moved—no, more than moved—delighted, exhilarated by your work that I feel need."

He kissed my hand.

I was quite flustered; responding to hand-kissing wasn't something we'd been taught at St. Augusta's. And he was looking into my eyes and saying, "Fascinating, fascinating."

He asked me if I had been a founding member of the women's movement. I tried to explain the nuances of the term "founding member," and although I'd been a feminist since the late sixties, I couldn't credit myself with having had any influence. He asked me about Ti-Grace Atkinson. I could hardly remember who she was. He asked me if I felt angry about the Catholic Church's treatment of women, and I said it was terrible. He asked me if I considered myself a member of the avant-garde. I said probably not, I was probably too old, believed too deeply in good painting, and lived too far uptown.

He took a rather yellowish index card from his jacket pocket and began reading from it. "This is quoted from Russian architect, dating from early years of this century. He says as follows, 'The role of women in the arts is significant, and will become even more so when women themselves become fully conscious of it, when they are fully aware of their own strength, and cease imitating the work of men. They must stop being ashamed of their own feminine souls and sympathies and use all their strength to reveal their beauty of spirit, which is finer and more sensitive than that of men.' "

"Those terms are wrong," I said. "We've got beyond thinking we're finer and more sensitive than men. For one thing, it's the kind of idea that can be used against us."

"Would you say you were making a statement?"

"No, I'd just say I had the itch to paint a particular thing."

"You use the expression 'had the itch.' Is the desire to paint something you feel in a bodily way?"

"Yes, I would say so."

"Do you think you feel it in a particularly female anatomical way?"

"I don't know, I've never had a male anatomy."

"And that is fortunate for us all. For I must say there is something—and of course, this is, once again, minefield I step into—so female about your vision of these men. And yet you are looking as informed artist."

"Bingo," I said.

"Pardon?" he said.

"Never mind, Vladimir. It would take too long."

He asked me about Jesse Helms and the religious right and then about Robert Mapplethorpe. I said I had very little interest in Robert Mapplethorpe.

He said, "Like all true artists, you have your strong opinions. You use what is useful to you, you dismiss the rest. But there again, and you will forgive me if I misstep or misspeak, a very female audacity about it. You remind me of the manifestos of the avant-garde women artists of earlier in this century. Goncharova, Popva, Rosanova. If you will allow me, I will send you translation. Like them, mixed up in you is great talent and intelligence, and underneath a female self-confidence."

I knew that what he was saying was probably largely bullshit. I wasn't sure whether it was simply a geographical reflex—everyone knew Russians overstated, it had something to do with the size of the country. And in my experience most European men flirted instinctively; it meant no more than that they smoked instinctively; it meant nothing, or it meant something. Whatever happened, they'd say it was because you'd made something of it. But like all people who were good at flirting, he presented me with an appealing version of myself, something I'd hoped for but wouldn't dare to claim. I liked the woman he'd created, the one sitting in my seat—it didn't matter whether she was real or not.

But even as I was enjoying the theater created by his flirtation, even as I saw myself enlarged and enhanced in the flattering theatrical light, I was wishing that, at my age, I wasn't still susceptible to it. There was something slightly pathetic about my excitement. I knew that as a prize, Vladimir's value was mixed. He was good-looking; he was, if not intelligent, then learned, the way so many Europeans are—capable of making a wide range of references. On the other hand, his flirtation was so reflexive as to be stripped of patina. What he said had clearly been said before, and with some frequency.

"You know," he said, "there's something Russian about you. Your eyes, I think. You have Russian eyes."

"My family would hate to hear you say that. We're Hungarian; we haven't felt good about the Russians since '56."

"Please, please, it pains my heart to hear you confusing the Russians with Stalinists. We are country with history, literature, way of life; we cannot be reduced to the tyrannous tragedy of a few years. No one has suffered more than we; don't punish us further."

"I don't mean to be punitive."

"I was seven years old when Stalin died," he said. "And I don't know if you can understand, but it was like having a father die. I remember all of us, in the classroom, seven-year-olds weeping. We felt very frightened, as if there were no one to take care of us."

I thought to myself, If I slept with him, I'd have a lover who wept at Stalin's death as a child. I kept thinking how enjoyable it would be to say that sentence to Michael.

As I thought that, the face of B loomed up, an apparition, only partly believable, like the Wizard of Oz in front of the curtain. I had to bring him into the room more fully. I told Vladimir that a friend of mine owned four paintings I'd done before the last show, and that it might possible for him to see them while he was in New York. He said he'd be most grateful. I phoned B and explained what was happening.

"A Russian? For a Russian magazine? Some guy who smokes his cigarettes sideways telling you how brilliant you are and how much he's suffered? You must be absolutely beside yourself."

"I would think you'd want to enhance my international reputation."

"Right, there's a big art-buying market in Russia now. They don't even have enough rubles to buy Kleenex."

"It would be a real relief if you could think of anything in terms other than financial. Just for a holiday."

"Well, you know I'm just not pure like you and the Russian. I'm just down here trying to recoup my fucking four million dollars. And trying to do something with your amazing gift. Which, by the way, was amazing. And I'm being a shit. All right. But I won't have dinner with him. Bring him for coffee, bring some dessert with you. I'll show him what I have."

"Do me a favor and take the garbage out first."

"If I get around to it," he said. "If you make it too pleasant for him, next thing you know he'll try to defect. Or talk you into marrying him so he can get a green card."

I invited Vladimir for dinner, and said I would just run out to the bakery for a dessert, which we'd take down to my friend. I gave him copies of all the interviews.

"This is very kind, this is astonishingly kind. In return, allow me to give you a small gift. I guess not the biggest surprise in world, a Russian brings you a bottle of vodka."

I got two small glasses from the cupboard.

He poured the vodka and gave me one glass. "I must toast a woman of many powers."

He made sure his fingers brushed against mine as he handed me the glass.

I bought a strawberry cheesecake at Greenberg's and stopped for a bottle of Frascati, which I realized was probably superfluous, since the vodka had already fuzzied my brain. I could tell this because when I tried to figure out how many quarters I should give the clerk along with my ten-dollar bill—the wine had come to $10.80—it seemed a real intellectual challenge.

I got home and took my coat and hat off in the hallway. I could see he was looking at me, so I did it slowly; I made it something of a striptease.

"You were wonderfully amusing in some of the interviews," he said.

"I have a hard time keeping my mouth shut. I can't say I was an absolute model of prudence."

"Prudence is virtue for the timid, and you are in nothing timid. That's what's wonderful about you; you're always so strongly what you are. You see, for myself, I've lived much of my life as if I were sleepwalking. But you, even when you're asleep you're probably awake."

"I'm a very sound sleeper. You don't know me very well."

"I'm hoping this will change."

He poured us two more glasses of vodka. They're small, I kept telling myself. I asked him if he was married. He was, his wife was a doctor; he traveled a lot so they had an open marriage. "To me," he said, "fidelity is like saying that *War and Peace* is the greatest novel in the world so you'll only read *War and Peace*."

I was longing to ask him how *War and Peace* felt about this, but I decided not to.

He had two children, teenagers. "They are in love with rock and roll," he said. "Now, of course I understand this, how could I not, I who've devoted my professional life to the study of American culture. But when I see my daughters, two years ago playing with dolls, now dressed up like prostitutes and singing words I wouldn't even dare say, it causes me difficult."

"I went through it with my girls, particularly my daughter Rachel. She used to listen to some hair-raising stuff. I guess you'd call it rock and roll, but it's not what I listened to. At the age when I was singing, 'We'll have fun, fun, fun till her daddy takes the T-bird away,' she was singing, 'Let's get buck naked and fuck.'"

"How wonderfully you say the word 'fuck.' What freedom, what a natural expression for you. Would you say you'd been influenced by the sexual liberation of the sixties?"

"No, saying 'fuck' just came to me naturally. I didn't need a movement."

I offered him more salad. I couldn't remember if I'd put the oil in or not. I remembered the lemon, but after that, I'd lost track.

I brought out the cheesecake. He asked for a glass of milk to drink with it.

"I find it so endearing, this American milk drinking. I feel so purified when I drink it, like child. We would always read about American mothers giving their children milk and cookies, and to us it was exotic, luxurious. What did you think about Russia?"

"We thought you were trying to kill us."

The phone rang and it was B, grumpy, asking if we were going to come down after all. I hadn't realized that it was ten o'clock. I told him we'd get right in a taxi. Then I remembered I'd said we'd bring dessert, and

I'd already served the cheesecake to Vladimir. It sat on the table, violated, half consumed, staring at me with censure and reproach. I put it in the refrigerator without wrapping it, just to get it out of sight.

"Listen, Vladimir," I said, "you'll have to keep a secret for me. And you'll have to eat another dessert. I told my friend I'd bring the dessert to his house, and I forgot and served it here. So we'll have to buy another and not say anything. Will you do that for me?"

He put his finger on his lips and then on mine. "You can trust me. Silent as tombs."

B wasn't looking his best. I was pretty sure he hadn't been out all day; he was wearing gray sweats and he hadn't shaved. His hair was standing up; I know when he's nervous he plays with it, twisting tufts of it like Buckwheat. He was making no effort to play the gracious host.

He nodded at Vladimir, kissed me and showed Vladimir the paintings. It's always odd for me to see old work, a style I've stopped working in is like a child I've given up for adoption. I can't afford to think about it anymore, and besides, it doesn't really interest me.

"What a fascinating route this fascinating woman has taken," Vladimir said.

"Absolutely fascinating," said B. "That's the fascinating thing about her, how fascinating she is."

"Shall we have coffee?" I asked.

Vladimir asked B what his business was.

"Commodities."

Vladimir asked him if he thought of art as a commodity.

"Absolutely," he said. "I put it somewhere between microchips and pork bellies."

"I'm sorry if I seem to be insulting you but in my country, where there is nothing like an 'art market,' the idea of artists' value being tied to money is foreign. It's something I must force myself to understand."

"Yes, well, we have had the commoditization of art, but we haven't had gulags. You win some, you lose some."

"Vladimir's working in the American Studies Department of Tallahassee University," I said.

"So how do you like Florida?"

"Not as exciting as New York, of course, but perhaps more of the real America."

"There is no one real America," said B.

"But surely there's something distinctive, some essence, some consciousness you'd call American. Monica, for example, her work seems distinctly American. It could only have happened in America, after the women's movement. It has distinctly American audacity, playfulness, but mastery of form as well. Like a pedigree dog that still loves to wag its tail."

"I don't think she'd say that a consciousness of being American has been important to her. Her major influences are all European. What she mainly feels about being American is embarrassment."

"It must be exciting to have relationship with artist of this caliber, to see creative spirit take flight," Vladimir said.

"Yes," said B. "I often feel that a lot of my job with her is air-traffic control."

I felt like I was watching a tennis match that was being played for my benefit, and to the victor, I'd be the trophy. I also felt like a saloon girl in Dodge City; I was hearing a tinkly piano playing "O, Dem Golden Slippers" and I was seeing one cowboy throw another through swinging doors. All for me! I can't say that I was comfortable, but I was having a good time.

I said I'd get the coffee. I wanted to see what they'd do left alone.

When I came in, B was looking quite cheery. And, I was sorry to see, Vladimir was looking extremely pleased with himself. I was hoping they'd be a little more bloodied.

"Your friend has kindly asked to see a copy of my dissertation," Vladimir said.

"Yes," B said, really beaming. "I think Monica would like to hear the subject."

"It's on American musical theater."

"Oh," I said. "I love musical theater."

"So perfectly American," said Vladimir, "in its innocence, its hopefulness. Last true populist medium."

"Tell her what your thesis is about," B said.

"It's focusing on the important impact on the American musical of *You're a Good Man, Charlie Brown*."

"That's very interesting," I said, smiling, and suddenly feeling I'd had much too much vodka, and that my head was aching terribly.

"If I understand Vladimir's thesis," B went on, putting his hand on Vladimir's shoulder, "*You're a Good Man, Charlie Brown* represents the American zeitgeist far more than *Oklahoma!, Carousel* or *Guys and Dolls.* Am I right about that, Vladimir?"

"Exactly. You see, Charlie Brown is American everyman. Is innocent. In tradition of *Billy Budd.* And Lucy is woman representing the blessings and curses of civilization."

"Did you say you had a chapter on Charlie Brown and Billy Budd?"

"Yes, if I may say, is the keystone of the project."

I couldn't pay much attention to what the two men were saying. B was asking Vladimir something about stagecraft. Vladimir knew he'd lost me. He said he'd have to be on his way to Brooklyn.

"But you're staying here, darling, of course," B said.

He'd never called me darling in his life. He stood next to me at the door like the biggest, fattest cat who'd ever swallowed a canary.

He closed the door; I could hear Vladimir's disappointed Slavic steps down the hall, like the defeated tread of Ivan Denisovich.

But B wasn't defeated at all. He went over to his CD rack and put on a Donna Summer disc and pulled me to dance. I wanted not to want to. I wanted to tell him how badly we'd both behaved to Vladimir. But the saloon girl didn't feel like making a moral point to the winning cowboy. Donna Summer, who I think has had a conversion experience and is now singing to Jesus, was in her former incarnation on B's sound system, singing, "Do it to me again and again," and the pulse was cheap and irresistible. We did do it on the couch, as if we couldn't wait to get into the bedroom, taking off only as few clothes as we needed to. He was in his socks; I was in my socks; I was hot in my sweater and the drawstring of his sweatshirt hood pressed into my cheek. But there was nothing to complain about. I started singing, "My boyfriend's back." He told me to hold that thought.

*      *      *

I GUESS IT's naive to think that his victory over Vladimir, and then our mutual victory on the couch, made it possible for B to make the move the next day that earned him 60 percent on his coffee trade. It's naive in the same way that most ideas about inspiration are naive, in the way that associating the different periods in Picasso's development with the different women he was involved with at the time is naive, or saying that he painted two paintings on one day—one of Dora, one of Marie-Thérèse—because he was confused about his relationships. A lot of guys are confused about their relationships, a lot of guys go through a lot of women, and they're not Picasso. And the two paintings he did on that one day are simply the fruit of God knows how many days and months of work, of failure and false starts and dread and emptiness. Nevertheless, something in it isn't absolute nonsense, some accident, some quickening of the blood that's not connected to dogged effort. Whatever the case, the next day B made a trade that earned 60 percent. I asked him about it, because for the first time I was actually interested. Of course, when he told me, I couldn't pay attention for very long. Or that's not it, I did pay attention, I was trying, but the way he used words made it impossible for pictures to come into my mind. I kept thinking of mountains of coffee, and harvests, and things I *could* make pictures of, and that wasn't the point, the point was not the objects in themselves, but what they made happen.

"That loss took my confidence, so I was trading too conservatively, and the only way I can get out is to get back my old sense of the pleasure of risk. Of course, it's your money I'm risking. Right now, you're virtually my only client. Almost all my old clients pulled out on me. This is a business with no loyalty."

"That's where I come in."

"Right, as long as no one's using words like 'samizdat,' I'm safe."

"Nothing happened," I said.

"Of course not, I know how to protect my investment."

I should have been insulted when he put his hand on my crotch. I wasn't.

*      *      *

Working on the triptych was pleasing, but frightening. In enlarging my scale, I was changing something in my relation to life. I wasn't reducing the scale of things anymore, I was entering into it. I was transferring rather than interpolating. It was a little more like living than doing smaller work, but it was alarming because the joy of limits wasn't so available to me. I was doing the kneeling saints in charcoal: the knee of Matisse, the shoulder of Ingres. I was putting people into relationship with each other and with space. I was at the terrifying point of putting the first marks down, the marks that I knew weren't final, weren't irrevocable, but which implied so much. It was like diving into a very cold lake; you could get out, you didn't have to stay there until your blood froze or your heart stopped beating. On the other hand, it might be exhilarating. You had to dive in to find out. You had to make those first marks.

Unlike other work, it was quick, you couldn't go back and fine-tune it; it was done, and it was over. Then I just had to leave it, and go back and look the next day. I literally had to force myself to close the door and not look, at least for some hours. There were hours when the main occupation was the occupation of not looking. It made me— unlike those periods in which I was focused on the small areas of the canvas—eager for company. B wasn't available, my kids were in school. Michael and Theresa were working during the days. I took to visiting Peggy, who was trying to settle into her Park Avenue duplex—the kind of place I never thought I'd go to for a visit to a friend.

When I was younger, the formality of Peggy's apartment might have made it impossible for me to have a friendship with her. I would have felt I had to tell her that the Audubon prints that dominated the living room were Victor's taste and not hers, that she should assert herself more. I would have told myself I couldn't relax on that furniture. But somehow I liked Peggy too much for all that. She was my patron and my subject; she was the mother superior I adored, straight from *The Nun's Story,* and the cultivated mother I never had. And she was full of surprises.

She told me, one morning, that my Sara had spent the weekend there.

"My Sara?" I said. It's a way of talking about children that I've always loathed, although I do fall into it: my Sara, like my poodle, my Mercedes, my Degas. Colette was once said to have slapped her little daughter when she fell and cut her lip. "How dare you ruin my master-piece," she said to the child. I don't know if I believe that story. But it's always scared me, that motherhood red-in-tooth-and-claw aspect, and I felt it when I said "my Sara." I was hurt that she'd come to the city without seeing me. But, of course, I never wanted to show Peggy my more primitive side, so I said, "Odd that she didn't call," in my Mrs. Miniver voice.

"No, she didn't call. And of course it made her feel a bit wretched. But she was here to talk about you, about why she's afraid to talk to you."

"Me?" I bellowed: the mother bear who's just noticed her cub's not under her armpit.

"She's asked me to speak to you for her. It's not a strategy I usually approve of, but Sara has a way of getting around me. You can feel free to shout at me; Sara warned me of that; it's a side of you I haven't seen but am prepared to believe. I'm simply going to hope that you under-stand that I understand the nature of the problem, and I'm on no one's side."

"What problem? What side?"

"There are some things in life that Sara wants that she thinks you don't entirely approve of."

"Sara's never done anything I didn't approve of. What is it? She's becoming a Jesus freak. She's becoming a Republican."

"She wants to get married."

I suppose that, of the options that had run through my mind, mar-riage was among the least horrifying. But not by much.

"She's too young. And I don't know him. Who the hell is he? And what does she think this is, 1959? Is she pregnant? I can help her, for God's sake, she doesn't have to get married."

"She's not pregnant. His name is Jeremy Todd. He's graduating in Environmental Science from the University of Massachusetts in June. He's very handsome, intelligent, idealistic. You might actually like him."

"Environmental Science. No sense of humor. She'll start wearing those Birkenstocks, or those sandals made out of tires. Why's she getting married? She hasn't even lived."

"She wants to live rather differently from you. She thinks of herself as quite different from you."

"Well, of course she is, she always has been. I've always understood that."

"She wants to get married and live in the country and teach music to preschool children. Jeremy's been offered a job directing a nature study center in Montana and she could run the children's education part of the program."

"Montana. Isn't that where all those Mormons are?"

"That's Utah, Monica. We're talking about another style of life. This is not a tragedy."

"It just sounds so boring. It's asking so little from life. It's so unadventurous."

"Looked at another way, it's of use. She'd be living in a beautiful place, she'd be with a man she loves, and she'd be happy."

"Why does she have to get married?"

"She likes the 'death do us part' part."

"What does she know about it?"

"Probably about as much as any of us, I would think."

"Peggy, you sound like a romance novel. I thought you had more sense."

"I think I've told you all the facts. I think it's time you talked to Sara. Perhaps you should give yourself a few days to turn things over in your mind."

"Turn things over" was not a good way of describing it. That was much too calm, as if I were holding a stone, then moving it to look at its underside. I took a long walk with Michael and asked him if it was my fault: if, because I'd left her father I'd given her a longing for stability that resulted in this foolishness. As always, I feared I'd spent too much time on my work, and she'd felt abandoned and bereft and was making up for it now.

"You're acting like she's fifteen and she's dropping out of high school to get a job at the lipstick counter at Kmart."

"Environmental Science," I said. "Marriage at twenty-two. She's probably doing it because Rachel's out of the country. Rachel would have a fit. You know, there's a lot of funny things between twins that are very mysterious."

"Maybe it doesn't have to do with Rachel. Or with you. Maybe she just thinks it's a good idea."

"Well, it isn't a good idea, so it must have to do with something."

"You're making a terrific amount of sense."

"It's just rebellion, of a particularly self-destructive kind."

"Monica, you might try meeting the guy. But before you call your daughter, do me a favor and go down to B's. Tell him to involve you in a long carnal swoon. Then get on the phone after you're a little more serene."

"Carnal swoon comes a long way after the coffee market these days."

"As I recall, there was a time when it came a long way after Carpaccio and Mantegna."

"Not that long."

"Call him."

"Well, I will. He makes me feel better."

"You say that as if it's not very much."

"I know it's very much. I just don't like to think about it."

I guess he wanted me too, he didn't even say that I should wait until the market closed in Bangladesh or the cocoa prices came out of Tokyo. But he did want me to come down to his place so he could be near his computer in the morning. It was all right with me; it would be helpful for me to look at the charcoal sketch on the canvas after walking in the door from the outside world.

He'd ordered Chinese food. We ate it, coating our tongues and arteries with salty, death-inducing food, and told each other the details of the last couple of days. I didn't tell him about Sara; I didn't want to lose the erotic tone set by the spareribs. I could tell this was going to be comfort sex, familiar, absorbing, distracting, a tourist activity where the real world and what was disturbing about it could be left behind. But the comfort of it all, and its release, allowed me to cry, lying in his arms. It began with a simple physical feeling of emptying myself out, but then the weeping just continued, and I wept all the tears I'd been wanting to about my daughter.

I'd never cried like that in front of him, uncontrollable, extravagant tears that felt like a physical debility. My breath wasn't mine; it no longer came easily; it was something to be sought after, grasped. I didn't know if he'd understand. He didn't have children. And I knew my response was excessive. Michael was right; she wasn't dropping out of high school; she wasn't joining a religious cult; she wasn't taking crack. But I was losing her. And, more than any relationship in my life, the one with Sara had provided me with a steady love, always at hand, always nourishing, like bread or warm milk. I accused myself of having robbed her of something by taking the nourishment she offered so easily. I told myself, over the years, that the nourishment had gone both ways; it had always seemed easy to give her what she asked for, and she'd never seemed reluctant to ask. But now I wondered what hesitancies I hadn't seen, what hungers I'd ignored because the ribs seemed covered with healthy flesh. Rachel's rages and frustrations were always so clear; she adored me; she hated me; I was ridiculous; I was a power freak. We were completely different; we were exactly alike. She was a master of drawn-out, intricate punishments and highly ornamental, equally drawn-out reconciliations. But Sara had been the child of my simple heart; and now I felt I was losing her. How could I explain that to my childless lover? He couldn't possibly understand.

But he did. "It was always easy for you to love Sara. Now, for the first time, she's making it hard. You must feel like a displaced person. Like you've been turned from the hearth where you could always count on warming yourself."

I just kept crying and nodding. He never had any tissues in his bedroom. He gave me his undershirt to blow my nose in.

"Why don't you make a really elaborate meal for them. Something that takes a lot of effort, to show them you want to welcome him. You can invite Peggy and Victor. And I'll be there, so I can stand on a chair and pull you off the ceiling in case you try to take off."

"All right," I said. "God is my copilot. I'll call her in the morning."

*     *     *

We both cried on the phone. I told her I was sorry I was so overbearing. I told her I never meant to be a steamroller. I told her I knew she wasn't me, that she was her own person, that she was different and it was fine.

"It's not that I'm not a feminist, Mom. I can't explain it to you right now. But I love him. I know you might think that's a crock, that society is doing it to me. I don't think it is. We want to live in a simple way; I like nature; I like working with children; I'd like to have them relatively soon. There's nothing I want to do that takes years and years of training; I'm already trained for my work. There doesn't seem to be any good reason not to do what we want."

"But this is the first serious relationship you've had. Maybe you should travel first, meet other people, see other places, other ways of living."

"You did that, Mom, and then you married Dad. It didn't seem to accomplish much."

"I suppose there's no one right way of doing it," I said.

"I know you don't believe that, but thanks for saying it anyway. And thanks for the dinner. I really appreciate it. I love you. And I want you to know Jeremy. He's kind of different from the people you usually like. He's pretty quiet; he doesn't tell a lot of jokes. But give him a chance, OK?"

"Of course I will, sweetheart," I said, with a terrible foreboding in my heart.

It was one of those times when I regretted turning my other bedroom into a studio. Where would my daughter and her boyfriend sleep? If the girls were alone, they'd be on the foldout love seats in the living room. But that would be sexually inhibiting, I could see that, and I didn't want Sara to think I was being sexually inhibiting. When I'd chosen the apartment, my daughters' sex lives were pretty far from my mind. I suppose I could have sent them to Roger and Merrill in Hastings, but the point of this visit was to make them feel welcomed, and that didn't seem like a welcoming gesture. I asked B if I could go home with him after the party. Sara and Jeremy would probably like the idea of having an abode to themselves; it would feel like playing house. But when I thought of that, I criticized myself for thinking of them as children. I tried to remember that when Michelangelo was their age, he'd already done monumental sculpture. Not that Michelangelo was a helpful role model for two people who wanted to teach children at a nature center.

I would cook the food that Sara most liked. Carrot ginger soup, salmon with parsley sauce, garlic mashed potatoes. For dessert: profiteroles. Certainly she'd see that all that preparation was an indication of love, and more than love, goodwill.

I was facing the fact that my daughter was doing something that, not only would I not have done, I would never have wished to have done, and more than that, something I found embarrassing. Of course it would have been infinitely worse if she'd done something life threatening, but at least it would have had a sort of glamour. Both of us could have been bathed in a tragic light. We might have been operatic. But now we were just standing in separate fields; she was swaying gently to folk tunes and I was knocking myself out to some kind of relentless march that urged me to follow in the footsteps of people I'd never laid eyes on—mostly men and mostly dead.

Peggy and Victor and B arrived first; Sara and Jeremy were late, but they were taking the train from Springfield, and I knew it was often delayed. Still, we all had a sense of making conversation that was somewhat false, like the initial small talk at the beginning of a play when everyone's waiting for the star to walk into the drawing room.

It was sleeting, so I was convinced they were lying dead of exposure. When the bell rang, they were over an hour late. They were almost invisible, wrapped in serious-looking parkas that could have been dwellings rather than clothing. Sara hugged me, but nervously, perfunctorily. "This is Jeremy," she said, looking at her feet in their Nordic socks.

I know I have a habit of saying that people look like they've been done by certain painters or that they've sprung from certain paintings, but there's no question that Bellini's risen Christ was standing in my foyer with the sleet melting into his long, golden hair. I remember that Bellini Christ particularly well; it's in the Kimble Museum in Fort Worth, and once it saved my life. We'd gone to a particularly excruciating extended family reunion of Roger's. God knows why I agreed to it; I guess the marriage was in trouble. I'd had one too many conversations with people who said, "I just don't get modern art," or people who wanted to talk to me about their paintings of cowboys and horses.

That was when I saw the Bellini risen Christ, standing against that sky with its romantic clouds—blues, pinks, grays, blacks, browns— remarkable for a Renaissance painter. And the shocking matte of Jesus' chest: a boy's chest, hairless, whitish, yellowish, actually tallow-colored, with a sexy girlish slit indicating the penetration of the spear. He's holding his hand up in a gesture of blessing; his eyes are a little vague, a little dopey, as anyone's might be if they'd just risen from the dead. His lips are slightly parted, his beard is young and tentative, the chin might be a little weak. He suggests the weakness after death, but also the benevolence of someone who's been purged of all impulse to violence. And there he was, standing in my foyer, the boy my daughter was planning to build her life with.

Sara positioned herself next to Peggy as if Peggy's was the only safe zone in the room. She gave me darting glances, like a frightened animal; I didn't know if she was afraid I'd say "cocksucker" or start defending people who wore mink coats, so I disappeared into the kitchen.

Peggy and Victor had done a good ten minutes on Amtrak's record of delays, railway travel past and present—I think they were moving to the illustrious journeys of the Trans-Siberian—and I could hear B manfully trying to talk to Jeremy about toxic waste. But I didn't hear Jeremy saying anything. I called out to Sara to sit people around the table. I called B to help me serve the soup.

"I don't feel I've made a lot of headway with the swain," he said.

"You were trying with toxic waste."

"I always get confused between toxic waste and global warming. One of them I believe in and one I don't. No, I remember. It's global warming I don't believe in. Or maybe it's just that I don't care about it."

"How can you not care about global warming?"

"Because I know it's not my fault."

He carried the soup and placed one bowl before Peggy and one before Sara.

"Is that the ginger carrot soup you always make, Mom?" Sara said, looking a little desperate.

"Yes, I made it because I know you like it."

"It's the one with the chicken stock."

"Yes."

"Well, Jeremy can't eat it. He's vegetarian. I forgot to tell you. It's just that everyone we know is vegetarian, and I never think I have to mention it."

I thought of the fifty-dollar salmon, voluptuously lying, like an odalisque, in its parsley bed. It was crying out to me; its reproaches were the only things I could hear, since I couldn't bear to process the words Sara had just spoken.

My inability to process those words, to relax and call up a rational and effective response, led me to a sentence that was probably the worst of any I could have said. The only thing I could think of was how hard I'd worked, and that everything was ruined. I turned to Sara, and all I could muster was the desire to blame. "I can't believe you'd do something like this," I said.

She burst into tears. Jeremy sprang to the space behind her chair, as if I'd launched a javelin into her breast and it was up to him to pull it out.

Everyone kept mentioning the names of foods that Jeremy could eat. Potatoes, people kept saying. Bread, salad, cheese. Sara sobbed and sobbed. I stood in the middle of the room with a soup ladle in my hand, as if I'd just been shot.

Jeremy rementioned the names of the foods that had just been called up. Potatoes, bread, salad, cheese. "Don't worry," he said. "It's totally cool."

Then I heard a sound that was so unexpected, so entirely out of place, that at first I couldn't recognize it. Then I placed it. It was B, laughing.

"Jeremy," he said. "There are a lot of ways to describe this situation, but 'totally cool' is probably the last."

Then a miracle happened. Jeremy laughed too. Peggy laughed and so did Victor. Only Sara and I weren't laughing. She was sobbing, and I was standing still.

"Now listen, Jeremy," B said. "This is one of those nightmares that will pass into family lore as a great story. If you can just thrust yourself into the future, you'll see how much fun you'll have over it one day. And just to make it a better story, let's do something extravagant. Think, Jeremy. You're back in the past now. You're a little boy. You have one recurrent fantasy. It's about a food that you'd like more than anything to have as your main course for dinner. You want it in a soup bowl. Mounds of it. Mountains of it. What is it, Jeremy, what is this magic food that you've wanted in just this way all your life?"

"Ice cream," Jeremy said.

"Absolutely. Now, I happen to know that Monica's work is going slowly at the moment. Which means I'll bet any money that the freezer is stocked with Ben and Jerry's Cherry Garcia, Häagen-Dazs Swiss Chocolate Almond, and just to clear the palate, Sharon's Coconut Sorbet. Oh, and I forgot. She bought Breyer's vanilla for the profiteroles. Would that be a safe bet, Monica?"

"See for yourself," I said. I was beginning to think I might, one day, be able to move again. Sara had stopped crying.

B returned to the table with his arms full of containers of ice cream, a scoop, and a dark blue bowl. "You've died and gone to heaven, Jeremy," he said. "Help yourself."

Jeremy filled his plate. People ate their soup. When they finished, Jeremy still had ice cream in his bowl. I brought the now-silent salmon to the table. After I'd served everyone, I kissed the top of Jeremy's golden Bellini head.

"Welcome to the family, Jeremy," I said. "I'd like to say this is an unusual kind of occurrence, but that wouldn't be truth in advertising. Sara's not like me. She's a very nice person, and very steady."

"Sara said you were totally cool."

B laughed again. I wasn't sure if it was a kindly sound coming from his mouth. "Probably, that's not an absolutely apt description of Monica either," he said.

"And actually," Jeremy said, "Sara *is* really nice, but she's not steady. We all think of her as an incredible flake."

From the way Sara threw her napkin across the table at him, I had the idea that they were having a good time in bed.

SPENDING    –  269  –

Soon after dinner, they claimed to be tired, but I figured that what they really wanted was to talk about the evening and have sex. Peggy was helping me clear the dishes. B and Victor seemed absorbed in talk.

"Peggy," Victor said. "Come and tell me what you think."

Nobody called for me, so I just stood in the kitchen loading the dishwasher like Cinderella. But I could hear them using words that gave me no incentive to join them. Words like "percentage of the gross," words that made scraping the dead gray salmon skin into the rubbish seem, in comparison, great fun. They all looked very satisfied with themselves by the time they remembered I was still in the kitchen, and we all left together—they to go to the East Side, B and I to go downtown.

It was cold, but it had stopped sleeting and the black night seemed festal, punctuated by the white lights of urban celebration and the red and green functionality of the traffic lights—all wrong because white should be functional, red and green celebratory. I looked out at his costly view, the Fifty-ninth Street Bridge spanning the river with so much ornate hope in progress. There was a thin film of sweat covering the hair on B's chest and belly; he'd overdressed and I could smell the kind of sweat that comes from exertionless heat, flowing neither from activity nor anxiety, a simple declarative sentence from the body: I am hot.

"Do you know the movie *The Producers?*" he said.

"Of course I do. And if I were you, I wouldn't consider sleeping with anyone who didn't."

"I think I might be signing up for the Zero Mostel role."

"What did you have in mind?"

"You remember, his scheme is to make money by romancing rich old widows. Of course, he wants his investment to fail and I'm not that complicated. Ordinary success would be fine with me. But Victor and Peggy want to introduce me to their friends, who have too much money by half, according to Victor, and involve them in my rehabilitation. I'm supposed to charm them, they're supposed to give me their money to invest. Peggy's going to set up a series of 'little luncheons.'"

"Are Peggy and Victor going to invest in you, too?"

"They are. I'm a little scared, but I've got some of my nerve back.

And besides, I have a new ace in the hole. A partner on the ground. Someone who has insider information about coffee crops."

"Who?"

"I happen to know a young woman who's doing her anthropological thesis on coffee growers in Brazil. I've hired her as a consultant. She's giving me the coffee growers' ideas about next year's crop."

"You may not hire my daughter as a consultant. Besides, I don't believe you. She wouldn't do it. She thinks you're an exploitative capitalist pig."

"No, she thinks I'm a decent guy in a corrupt situation. And she's convinced herself that she's beating the system."

"You're using my daughter as an inside trader, you're using my friends to pimp for you. Isn't this a little collaborative for the Lone Ranger?"

"Listen, kemo sabe, you might be the best thing that happened to me in a long time. Of course I'm not sure about that." He put his arms around me. "I am sure about that, but I don't want you to get a swelled head." On that note, he moved my hand down to the front of his jeans.

That night, we lay in each other's arms, and what we did was born of fondness. We were saying, with each gesture, each contact of fingers or lips, of limb on limb, or skin against skin: how fond I am of you. You are a person I like. A desire to please was born of a circle outside the rapt sphere of desire, born of acts performed outside the bed, acts performed clothed, acts of thoughtfulness, of understanding. In our explorations we were patient that night, and we were surprised to see the sun; we had spent hours, and now they were gone. The sun streamed in slats onto the light wood floor, and we were saying to each other, with our bodies, thank you for your goodness, in this bed and out.

He was trying to prepare himself for his new role as courtier to the elderly rich. I told him he needed a new suit for it; I told him I wanted to buy it. I said I had to pay for it so it would be a talisman, a second skin to protect, encourage, arouse him.

He'd always bought his suits at the same place: Gossarts on Chambers Street, where the salesmen looked anxious and disappointed, like Daumier's law clerks. But they knew their business, showed him only the right zone of the right rack. They knew what colors went with what, what shirt went with what tie. They told him about shoes. There was something very sexy about seeing him disappear behind curtains and then reappear adorned, expectant, boyish, waiting for my approval. I wondered if all those stage door Johnnies felt this way when they took Nellie Melba for a fitting, or some far less stellar courtesan who might have to sell the dresses one day when her figure had gone. I was proud of him; he was mine; he said he'd only buy the suit I most liked, and the salespeople looked at us skeptically: we seemed a little old for such amorous deference. They probably thought I was the second wife.

They didn't blink when I said it would go on my credit card; they didn't wink at B, they didn't say "Nice work if you can get it." But that was the tune in the air. And we held hands, walking in the snow all the way home, under the decorations of Chinatown, knowing that in a minute we'd be in each other's arms, under his gray quilt for half an hour before I went back uptown and he went back to his computer.

I was involved in a kind of activity that was a calm completion. I had this thing that I had made, that I was making, that I could go back to; it always interested me, and when I'm interested I'm never frightened. I didn't have the anxiety of making a mark where nothing was; something was there, it just needed fixing. I had the serenity of the artisan; something needed to be done, and I understood that I could do it. It might be something about the relationship among the shapes, something that needed refining or something that needed rethinking. When I'm at this stage in a painting—and it was particularly true of the triptych because it was so big—it's like walking through a scene from my own life. There is no sense of escape or isolation. Whatever I'm doing is simply the thing that's required. I look at the whole painting, and it's scary. But then I look at one part only and I'm not scared of the rest. It's like a hunger for a particular food, but a hunger without despair, because you know you've eaten the food before and you'll eat it again. It's a pleasure, but a simple one, not like eating chocolate, like eating an egg, a normal thing that seems easy and good. Like walking on a street you know, you're open and taking things in, it's a nice day, you're not making more of it than it is.

Sometimes, I'll go away and I'll come back to the painting and realize that the relatively small thing made a very great change, and that's an enormous pleasure. I don't have to tell myself how great I am. Praising myself, judging myself, would be like talking to myself on the street when I just want to shut up and walk. Or getting back to food, this kind of work is like making a tomato sauce or putting a salad together, it has that kind of plainness. You know what you're doing, and that it's going to be good, but you aren't saying, "Aren't I marvelous?" You're just doing it.

And the calm of that, the pleasure of that, that point of certainty carries me through anything that might be difficult in the rest of my life.

Often, just as I'm coming to the end of one of these periods, new ideas for paintings begin to drift—not push, just gently insinuate themselves—into my brain. As I was finishing the flowers in the grass of the middle section of the triptych, a new series of images came floating up. Like the white breast of a backstroke swimmer, breaking the surface of a lake.

The images came to me on the day I took Peggy to the Russian baths. It's a challenge to make you understand the very odd conjunction between these two things: Peggy, who's bordering on the hyper-refined, and the Russian baths, which are probably just this side of being closed down by the board of health. But I happened to mention them on one of our double dates—she and B and Victor and I were spending a lot of time together in B's Zero Mostel phase; Peggy was very interested in the financial details of B's work. I couldn't pay attention, except for the parts that had to do with Rachel. The good thing was that B spoke to Rachel every two days, and he often waited till I was around to call her. I didn't bother to ask her about her political misgivings, but with Rachel you usually didn't have to express your reservations, she was always there with a preemptive strike.

"Don't even bother to ask if I've been co-opted by capitalism. It's just very interesting, and as a social scientist, it's giving me a whole new insight."

I asked her if she was getting enough protein and if her stomach was giving her any trouble.

"Yes, no, and I'm using condoms. And I'm in love."

"Who are you in love with?"

"Well, I'm not going to bother talking about it, in case it's all over soon. So just relax. Do you know that's the sentence I've said most frequently since I could talk, 'Relax, Mom'?"

When she was talking to B, I could hear him laughing a lot, also tapping things into his computer. Then he'd tell Peggy something about Pedro and rainfall when we were having dinner, and I was happy to be the bimbo, thinking about the fabric on the prie-dieu in Peggy's part of the triptych. During one of the dinners, when I was thinking of velvet and they were talking about "shorts" or "falls," the Russian baths came up. I described the scene: the brownstone on East Tenth Street, the lobby, then the curtain, behind which there were beat-up lockers and bunks that could have been in a gulag, people sleeping, snoring gently, while others got dressed in front of them, the radiant rooms, the saunas, the ice pool, the steam room, the masseuses with two words of English, the branches you could be beaten with, the mud massages, the Dead Sea salts. Peggy said she'd been to something like it in Russia, and would I take her for her birthday, which was coming up.

Peggy asked for very little, so I said fine, but I had to warn her it might be rough.

"There are all these fat hairy guys with wet bathing suits sticking to them ogling the women. I'm not sure it's exactly your thing."

"I shudder to think what you imagine 'my thing' is. Something involving white gloves and tea out of thin cups and little sandwiches."

"There's a big gap between the Cosmopolitan Club and the Russian baths."

"Good," she said. "Let's bridge it. Aren't there days for women only?"

"Yes, but everyone's nude on those days."

"Well, that's all right, isn't it?" she said.

She asked me how I got there, and I said I usually went by subway, but we could take a cab. She said she wanted to go by subway. She said she'd meet me at the platform of the R and N on Forty-second Street, a place so insalubrious that I got there twenty minutes early so there wouldn't be a risk of Peggy being alone for a second.

A saxophonist was playing for money, and I was happy standing on the gum-encrusted platform listening to "It Never Entered My Mind," followed by "I've Got a Crush on You." I called B from a pay phone so he could hear, and we sang to each other, "You may not be an angel/'Cause angels are so few/But until the day that one comes along/I'll string along with you."

I could tell that Peggy rarely took the subway. She walked down the ramp, grim-faced, clutching her handbag in a way that suggested to any potential thief that she was carrying the Hope Diamond. But when she saw me, she didn't look grim, she smiled so triumphantly (had Victor warned her not to take the subway? Was this the smile of the transgressor/survivor?), she was so much the naughty girl gamely risking smudging her pinafore, that I wanted to put her right into a taxi and send her home to Park Avenue. I was rattled by her thinking of me as her sidekick in a series of schoolgirl pranks: the two leading characters in a British series who'd giggle over our narrow escapes as we toasted crumpets, illegally, in our dormitory room.

Everything we passed on the way from the subway to the baths delighted her: a dismantled intaglio billiard table being delivered to "Blatt Billiard," which abutted onto "McDermott Cues." Grace Church, with its signs, "Private Garden" and "Chantry." She loved the bad murals on Tenth Street. A cross-eyed Billie Holiday, next to lions, which in turn were next to green, gelatinous or cucumbery-looking monsters with long tongues. She liked a china goose in an antique store called Troubles, and a terra-cotta urn of primroses in a florist's shop that looked like a suburban living room.

There was nothing picturesque about the Russian baths, nothing floral or inventive, nothing that couldn't withstand high temperatures and a lot of damp.

We paid our money, left our valuables in boxes at the desk, then went behind the navy blue curtain. I didn't think there was a good way of saying, "So, Peggy, how do you feel about being naked in front of strangers at your age?" There was nothing to do but take my own clothes off, make casual conversation about my moisturizer, and try to keep my eyes fixed on nothing, as if there were nothing to see.

The Russian baths provided secondhand-looking surgical gowns for people to use as cover-ups. I chose the lime green, Peggy the faux rose. It didn't matter; both were hideous. I tried to point out that the brass banister seemed a genuine art deco piece.

"It's pretty rough," I said.

"You've told me that, Monica. Believe me, you haven't been guilty of false witness. Not against this neighbor."

We walked downstairs to the main bath area. The first thing we saw was a woman floating on her back in the ice pool. She wasn't young, sixty-five at least; her hair was long and gray; it spread behind her so that she looked mythic, particularly since I knew how cold the water was: a Lorelei, with no susceptibility to hypothermia. Floating, too, but almost separate from her body, were her breasts, relaxed, rose-mouthed animals, demanding nothing. We took off our surgical gowns. It was ridiculous to pretend not to be looking. Still, I hesitated. I was afraid of finding Peggy not beautiful. But she was lovely. She was certainly not young, although her breasts, because they were small, had been spared the ravages of gravity that certain of our larger neighbors' hadn't been.

She was dignified in her nakedness, her flesh suggested a reserve not of renunciation, but of self-regard. Her legs were marked by blue and reddish veins, but they were straight and strong, as was her narrow but proud back. Her neck was girlish; in the damp, her hair formed into a coquette's curls.

We went into the steam room first. One of the things I like about the baths is that you are so busy feeling the intense sensation of heat that you don't want to talk. Peggy and I sat in silence. After a few minutes, she said she'd had enough and was going outside; I said I wasn't quite ready, and we waved at each other as she walked out the door, formally, like diplomats.

She was sitting at the edge of the pool, resting, when I left the steam room. A few feet from her sat a black woman, her feet in the cold water, her head on her arms. She looked as if all she wanted in this world was rest, and for a minute she'd found it. When she stood I saw that she wore a silver chain around her waist; the chain's links were scallop shells.

"Shall we go to the Radiant Room?" I asked.

"It sounds like something out of the *Arabian Nights*," she said.

"Scheherazade would have hired a decorator."

Women sat on benches, or lay on them in the cell-like grotto, with its dripping stone walls. One woman did *grands pliés;* one shaved her legs; one spread pink lotion on her knees and elbows. Incessantly running spouts filled white plastic buckets. Periodically, a woman would stand, move to the middle of the grotto floor, and pour a bucket of water over her head. Peggy did it too, then laughed, and sat down with an unself-conscious plop.

"I like it here," she said. "I like it very much. It's comfortable and safe."

As she said that, a woman walked in wearing a checkered towel around her head as a turban. And it came to me, as it had come to me seeing B sitting on the chair the night he reminded me of the Carpaccio, that I was seeing a version of something I'd seen before. It was Ingres's *Turkish Bath*. But this was different. This was a woman's world. A world in which the nakedness of bodies was not about being seen, but about the body's own well-being. The nakedness of women, removed from the pleasure of men.

And unlike the Ingres harem, there was a great variety of bodies, some young with long legs and firm breasts, bodies that you understood were desirable by anybody, man or woman, whose currency was noticeable even in the milky neutrality of the grotto. But even among them the range was great: breasts were globes or pears, they pointed out or flipped up. But then, there were the other women, the majority of them, who weren't young, or thin, or fit, whose buttocks hung or were too flat, whose breasts were worn from childbirth or fatigue or time. You could look at them and divide the women in two: the desirable, the undesirable. But it seemed to me there were far more interesting ways to see them.

You could see them as the metaphors their bodies were, by what, in their nakedness, they seemed to suggest. Some were queens and some were generals, some were—they couldn't help it—courtesans. Some were abbesses, some, in the orderliness of their nudity, were social workers or secretaries. There were birds and cats and bears. There were those who frolicked and those who lolled and those who perched, ready to spring. There were the adorned, the woman with her belt of shells, another, with the uncared-for feet of someone who thinks herself unloved, who nevertheless wore ankle bracelets fit for Matisse's Arab girls. All of them, in their variety, represented something more interesting than what we'd been told were the desires of men.

It came to me then: I wanted to paint groups of women's bodies, relaxed, unself-conscious. I wanted to grant to all their nudity the attentiveness of voluptuous paint. I wanted to grant this to the nudity of bodies not usually seen in art. I wouldn't do it as Lucien Freud had—although I admire him—the skin suggesting underlying disease just as his rotting couches did, his subjects miserable under the harsh, yellow light of Holland Park, London W. 12. I wanted to use paint as Vuillard did on his ceilings, on the pages of his books: opulently, lovingly, but restfully, a mixture of movement and repose. I would paint the women in the grotto seen through the white outline of Ingres's *Turkish Bath*. I would resee the bodies of women, as one of them. Perhaps I'd put myself in. Perhaps I'd do myself from the back, placed like Ingres's woman. I'd wear the checkered turban myself. I would paint women, looking, not as a desiring man, but as a painter who was one of them.

By the time Peggy and I were dressed and walking to the subway, I had to apologize to her, because I couldn't talk. All I could do was think of my new painting: *After Ingres: The Russian Baths*. If I recalled the Ingres painting in the Louvre, it was circular. That would be something new for me; that would be something to think about, to work on, a new set of problems to solve. That night I told B that in September we would have to go to Paris. But it would be my treat.

By the time I'd put the last touches on the triptych, the new ideas about female nudes were pushing against my brain. The triptych and the *After Ingres* were fighting each other for space.

It was during this period, a period marked for me by calm (I was finishing the last part of the triptych) and excitement (keeping the *After*

*Ingres* ideas at bay), that B made what everyone, even I, called his big score. It had to do with my daughter Rachel. It had to do with my daughter Rachel's Brazilian boyfriend, Pedro. It had to do with Pedro's grandfather, who according to Rachel (and Rachel somehow convinced B) was a genius. Pedro's grandfather could tell from the way the bark looked on the coffee tree (or maybe it was the buds, or maybe it was the early leaves, I can't remember, nobody seemed able to tell me in their frenzy) that it was going to be an especially bad crop: I think it had something to do with a frost and a bad rain. I don't know how Pedro's grandfather could tell, or why B believed him, but he did. And B had to do something that was something like buying low and selling high, something to do with anticipating rather than responding. Something to do, it seemed to me, with playing chicken.

Everybody else's sources figured out it was going to be a bad crop about two weeks later than Pedro's grandfather had. Which means the supply will be low, so prices will be high. A natural disaster is always a good thing for the futures market. So two weeks after B had bought a huge amount of coffee low, he was able to sell it very high.

This is what I think happened.

All I know is that he made me come down to his apartment. The floor was covered with paper. I could smell his sweat in the room. His hair was soaking wet and standing out as if he'd been electrocuted. The phone kept ringing. He kept whooping and dancing. My daughter called and he told her he loved her, he told her she was brilliant, that Pedro's grandfather was brilliant, that he'd pay for a new tractor, or a new school, or whatever it was they wanted. He'd earned back his money. He was a player, again.

He took me and Victor and Peggy to a Jewish-Italian restaurant, where he'd reserved a table for us on the back porch, glassed-in now, the windows only partly open, spring air thrusting in, frightening us all, because we were afraid of a too-early hope, afraid of the inevitable disappointment: days and days of rain that would chill our bones like February. B sat and served us, not like a player, but a host. He insisted we share everything. He divided the sautéed artichokes, the tomatoes and mozzarella, the grilled vegetables, the salmon carpaccio, thin, with its adorning capers. He divided gnocchi, mushroom ravioli, asparagus risotto, penne arrabbiata. He cut saltimbocca into quarters, and put on each plate a piece of striped bass with a topping of tomatoes and zucchini. He insisted we have zabaglione and strawberries for dessert, and grappa to finish the meal, which he poured from a belly-shaped bottle, pointing out to us what he called "its superior, its truly superior glug, glug."

And in his bed, he was my host, endlessly generous, telling me, "No, you mustn't sleep, just stay awake, just stay awake for this." And when I said I couldn't, when I'd fall over the edge of sleep, I'd feel his hands, appreciative, simply praising, and when I opened my eyes he'd say, "Sleep if you like, I just can't get enough of touching you."

And then, how could I sleep?

Soon after that, I understood that the triptych was finished, or at least that I wasn't going to work on it anymore.

My first feeling was fear that the whole labor—in the case of this painting, almost a year's work—could have been for nothing.

The moment you finish a painting is the death of hope. The death of possibilities. You've sent it out into the world. It's not like sending a child out into the world because when the child leaves you her fate isn't fixed—she has the autonomy to change her fate. The frustration and the consolation of motherhood is that the child isn't your creation. You just, sometimes, falsely think she is.

That's why the sense of responsibility to a painting is so different from the sense of responsibility to a child. If you don't saturate the canvas with everything you saw, if you haven't used all your skill to create that impossible congruence of form and vision, then it simply won't be in the world. It's possible not to care about that, to say that the world doesn't need your vision, that there's more than enough expression, God knows, even enough beauty, in the world already. But if, through some accident, you feel the urgency of making that connection between your vision and its form, if you feel that, however superfluous a job it is, it's your job, you simply have to do it as well as you can, attending to every line and surface, and then to the way they all relate. You absorb your inevitable sense of failure. And then you say: it's finished. There's nothing more for me to do.

I left the painting alone for three days. Those days were very physical. I ran in the morning and the evening with the dog; I brushed him thoroughly in the park. I had my hair cut and my legs waxed. I had a manicure. I spent every night with B. On the fourth morning, after a long night of sex that made my calves feel tight and my thighs stretched, my ribs feel bruised and my tongue long for the taste of citrus, I took a long bath in Dead Sea salts. I brushed my hair and pinned it up and opened the door to see my painting.

At first I thought it was so good I was afraid. I admired myself as if I'd caught a glimpse of myself reflected in a store window and was surprised at the allure of the woman I saw. Jesus' tilted body, the nuance of gray, the whiteness of the cloth, the brilliant points of color in the flowers, all came together. The wings of the triptych commented on the central panel with the poignancy I'd hoped for: the kneeling Peggy was upright, a chaste, chastening commentary on the man's sprawling isolation. I had done it. I had done what I set out to do.

But this was a commissioned work, created to please one person, the person who'd paid me. And that person had become a friend. Suppose she didn't like it? What would happen to our friendship? Would we go on like mature adults after a failed love affair, aware that this must have happened to others before us? Or would our friendship, too, become a failure, marked by disappointment on her side and shame on mine?

I didn't sleep the night before Peggy's visit. I stayed in my apartment alone. I sat at the window, watching the light on the monument, the reassuring moonlight casting feathery shadows of new leaves on the pavement.

In the morning I dressed in black cotton pants, a boat-necked white tee shirt, black sandals, no socks, no jewelry. I wanted to be as unadorned as possible.

Both Peggy and I knew better than to try for small talk. I opened the door of the studio and left her alone. I sat on the couch with my hands folded, concentrating on not letting them unclasp. I closed my eyes, then opened them. Closed them again. Was tempted by the oblivion of sleep. Forced my eyes open. Read the titles of my books on the shelves. Closed my eyes. Invited Mikey onto the couch, a blandishment he wouldn't fall for.

I turned the TV to the Weather Channel. There were storms in Mississippi. Colorado was unseasonably dry. Madrid was rainy, seventy-eight degrees, but Moscow was fifty. I saw an advertisement for a video called *Great Storms and Other Weather Disasters*. I copied the 800 number.

Then Peggy came out and took my hands. She looked older to me, weaker. Her face was white.

"Well, my dear," she said. "You've done it."

We sat on the couch and held each other's hands. Then she got up to leave.

She said she'd phone me in the morning. When she left, I took my clothes off, dropped them in a pile beside my bed, slipped in between the covers so that they made a sheath for my body.

When I woke up, three hours later, I was very lonesome for B. I wanted to show him the triptych.

I felt grateful to him, a gratitude I found impossible to express. We'd never been good at the kind of direct communication of feeling you'd expect in people who'd been together as we had for three years. I think it was because of the money. Initially, it had made me self-protective; perhaps it had made him unwilling to assert what could be interpreted as a claim. And we'd just got into the habit of not saying things.

Now it was time to say things and I didn't have the voice or the language for it. I knew that the triptych was the end of "Spent Men." And although I couldn't say the work was due to him—it was my idea and I made the paintings—it was certainly connected to him. He provided the money that gave me the time to work without the pressure of earning a living. He gave me the image of himself to reproduce. He posed for me. He allowed me to look at him as an object. He gave me his time. He gave me his desire and his sexual attention, and those things made me feel livelier than I had in years.

I suppose I could simply have said all this to him, as I've said it to you. But, you see, I couldn't. I didn't have the habit, or the skill.

When he looked at my paintings, he expressed a part of himself that didn't seem to find a place in the rest of his life. He cried, not like one of those characters Alan Alda plays who thinks crying is a breakthrough; I'd see the tears beginning in B's eyes and he'd walk somewhere—you could tell he was wishing he could get to Nepal or somewhere inaccessible in the Himalayas—so I wouldn't be able to see him. This time, when he looked at the triptych, he took me in his arms and kissed the top of my head. "I can't believe someone I could describe as my girlfriend did that," he said. "I feel like the boyfriend of the girl singer in one of those big bands. You do this thing, everyone looks at you, everyone praises you, and then you come home with me."

"Sometimes I do, and only if the drummer's not good-looking."

You see, I wasn't very good at saying things to him. Or hearing them.

A few nights after he saw the triptych, B asked if I'd make dinner for him, just something quiet and simple and restful. He said he wanted to talk to me about something. Of course all I could imagine was a cancer diagnosis.

I made fettuccine Alfredo, because I thought it would be soothing and I didn't know what he'd be able to eat in the future. I was trying to be calm.

He didn't say anything during the dinner, and I didn't bring up Sloan Kettering at all. Then over coffee he said, "Some important things have happened."

The word "biopsy" shimmered in the air.

"I've worked hard, I've worked very hard, and I've had some good luck. I've made some good trades, and I've recouped my losses."

"You're not dying?" I said.

"Why would you think I was dying?"

"Why wouldn't I?"

"I've decided to make some changes. I'm fifty; that's old for a futures trader. But I love trading; it's what I'm good at. It makes me feel part of the world. I don't want to be so unattentive that I'm not doing

my job, but I don't want to live like a lunatic anymore. So I've decided
to take on a partner. One of the young guys on the floor. He's honest,
he's hungry, he has a sense of humor. I think it's worth a try. And I'm
moving the operation out of my apartment. I think I was too isolated.
I'm renting space in the office of a Futures Clearing Market, down in
the World Trade Center."

I told him that since I had no idea what his work life was about, I
didn't know what to say, but it sounded like a good idea. I asked him if
I could help decorate his office.

"There's nothing to decorate. I'm sitting in a huge room, in the
middle of a hundred people."

I asked him if I could see where he worked. I asked if I could see the
commodities market, so I could make an image of it.

"Yes, but you can't talk about it. You can look, then you have to
shut up."

A week later, he said he was settled in his new office, and I could
come down the next day, if I wanted.

"But no comments afterward."

"Why?"

"You'll see. I have to work here. I have to do this. It won't help me
to know what you think."

Clearing market. Trading house. I didn't know what to imagine. I knew
it would be frantic; I knew it wouldn't be civilized and decorous, like
Degas's cotton traders, half asleep in their frock coats and top hats, fingering their fleecy product, holding their newspapers in their relaxed
but businesslike hands.

I was looking forward to being in the World Trade Center. I like
anything surrounded by water. I like high places made of glass.

As soon as I got out of the subway, I knew I was in a self-contained
universe. There were shops whose signs were geared to the financial
workers. One said, "Money can buy happiness." I followed the arrows
to the World Financial Center, where Arlon, Inc., is. The World Financial Center. Even the words sounded momentous to me, as if all the
money in the world was emanating from the ground under my feet. I
heard the sound of coins dropping into tills, the sound of vaults open-

ing and closing. But there was nothing I could make myself see, because in front of my eyes were only the muffled feet of worried-looking men and women making their way over the quarter mile of red carpet.

I came to the World Financial Center 3. I wasn't allowed to go further. A guard phoned B's extension. Even before he did, I had to show my driver's license. I didn't know what that was supposed to accomplish.

When I got off the elevator, he was there.

In the waiting room of Arlon, Inc., was a video screen with a sign next to it. "We encourage you to use this interactive system to peruse our art collection. And please type in any comments you have." On the screen was what looked like a tepee in flames, and a quotation, presumably from the artist, "I make art out of rage." I was longing to type in my comment, but B said he'd kill me if I went anywhere near the screen.

The room where he worked was a maze of interconnected desks, beside which mostly men, mostly young men, but a few young women (two-liter bottles of Poland Spring Water at their polished fingertips), stared at computer screens and spoke on phones. Some of them spoke on two phones at once. One for each ear.

"What are they doing?" I asked.

"Making trades. Talking to a client on one phone, and then to the floor to make the bid."

"Do you do that?"

"Sure."

"I never thought I'd have been intimate with someone who talked on two phones at once."

He sat at the edge of one of the rows of desks. On his computer screen was a series of graphs, red and blue lines crisscrossing each other, like someone's EKG, then bars going up and down, pulsing vertically, then yellow bars moving in and out and pulsing horizontally. He tried to tell me what each of them meant. Each pulse indicated a price change. The prices seemed to change every second.

"Ten seconds is a long time in a trade."

"Oh," I said, thinking of how long it could take to properly fill a quarter inch on a canvas. I remembered I wasn't allowed to make comments.

He introduced me to Jason, his new partner. Jason, I thought, looked around twelve, and I reckoned that his glasses probably set him back five hundred dollars, to say nothing of his haircut.

"You're Rachel's mom," he said.

I couldn't believe I was hearing the word "mom" in this place, where it seemed unlikely that anyone had ever come from a family or lived in one.

"How do you know Rachel?"

"We talk on the phone."

"Jason's going down to Brazil to visit next week."

"You've never met Rachel?"

"We've talked on the phone."

"You've never seen Rachel?"

"It's cool. B told me about the buzz cut."

The blinds were drawn in the room, but I had a sense that behind them the view was terrific.

"What's behind the blinds?" I asked.

B drew them, exposing sparkling water, surrounding the Statue of Liberty.

"Why are those blinds closed?" I asked.

"Marty Klingerman doesn't like the glare on his screen. And Marty's the biggest trader in the room."

"Marty should have his head examined," I said.

"I thought you weren't making any comments."

"That wasn't a comment. It was a diagnosis."

"I'm taking her down to the floor, Jason," B said.

"Nothing much is happening, but go for it. Nice meeting you," he said.

"Did you have to hire someone who says 'Go for it'?" I said on the elevator. "Did you have to hire someone who's going to visit my daughter in Brazil for the weekend?"

"He's a very sweet boy."

"Mmm," I said.

We walked across the plaza to another building. It was ten minutes to twelve; the air in the lobby was saturated with the grease from the french fries the delivery men—who were not allowed past the velvet ropes—were holding patiently in stained paper bags. B had the woman guard, a black woman with striped nails that must have been four inches long, call his friend Tom, a floor trader. B was not a floor trader, so he couldn't get up without Tom.

Men emerged from the elevator wearing blue badges. I couldn't help reading the badge of one who bumped into me. It said "Jaws."

"What are those badges?"

"They're people's code names," he said.

"Interesting," I said, noting another one, which said "Dagr." But then I saw one that said "Viol." I wondered if it was for violin or viola, if it belonged to someone who didn't want to lose the sense of his better self. I thought of suggesting to him that compared to Jaws and Dagr, he wasn't making himself look very daunting. Then I wondered if it was supposed to be short for "Violent," or if he meant "Vile," but he just couldn't spell.

When we got off the elevator, I heard a sound that can only be described as bedlam. A roar doesn't do it justice. A roar would sound too natural, too animal, it would suggest something of the organic. There was nothing natural or organic about "the floor." There were no windows, there was almost no air because bodies were pressed so close together. The red carpeting was blanketed with strips of discarded white paper. There were hardly any women. Men, mostly in shirt sleeves, but some with jackets, were pushing and shoving and shouting. Some were making hand signals like interpreters for the deaf.

B explained that some people liked to shout their bids and some liked to use signals.

I asked why there were so few women.

"Size can count here," he said. "Pushing helps."

He showed me the declivities in the floor. "Each market has what's called a pit, where the traders stand to make the bids."

"Stand," again, was too polite a word for it. They pushed. They jostled. People were knocked over and got up, people were elbowed and elbowed back. They cursed and grunted and shouted and jumped and jabbed. B pointed out a very large fellow standing at the edge of the pit.

"Some of the brokers hire big guys to push them back into the pit in case they get pushed out. If you're not standing in the pit, your bid doesn't count."

"You mean that's a real job?" I said. "You mean somebody gets a W2 with that written on it? Pit pusher?"

"No comments," he said.

On the walls, bulletin boards like those announcing arrivals and departures at airports flickered constantly with the changing prices. On top of that, the news of the world raced by in green letters. "Talks on Chinese software piracy continue," "Yeltsin predicted winner," "African drought."

"People make decisions based on what they see up there," he said. "A good trader is looking at lots of things at once. The boards, the other traders, the news. See that guy, he made $170,000 in an hour on yen this morning."

"Maybe he'll take us out for sushi," I said.

"No comments," he said.

I tried to be calm, but the hysteria in the room made me feel anxious. Then I had an idea. I took a small sketch pad from my bag. I drew men jabbing their fingers in the air, men pushing, men falling to their knees, men throwing back their heads to take gulps of coffee, men using inhalers or nasal sprays.

"Are you paying attention?" he said, seeing my drawing.

"I'm paying attention to the look of it. Although the light stinks."

"They're into available light," he said.

"Do you really work here?"

"I did when I was younger. I got started here. I loved it for a while. Then it gets to be too much and you want to move upstairs. But, you see, it's in my blood."

I think I saw part of it. I understood that he liked being at the center, in a place where things happened in seconds yet had consequences thousands of miles away. And I understood the joy of time eating itself like a snake eating its own tail, and losing yourself in work you were born to.

"I'm a trader," he said. "That's what I do."

"That's not all you do," I said.

"It's what I do for a living."

"Then there's living."

"This is the place I feel most alive."

"Thanks a lot," I said.

"I didn't say happiest," he said. "If I said that, you'd need to worry. And you don't need to worry. As a matter of fact, will you come to Washington with me, for a long weekend? We can go to the same shameless hotel we went to before. There's an old lady, one of Victor's friends, whom I'm trying to seduce. She's invited me to her George-town house for lunch. We haven't had much time for each other."

"No, it's that you haven't had much time for me."

"It would kill you to put it tactfully?"

"It would kill me to put it untruthfully."

"OK, Diogenes. You'll have me all to yourself. It'll be Jason's first chance to run the ship. I think it's called the *Argo*. I'll try not to phone him every five minutes. It will be up to you to distract me."

He hadn't said, "Come away with me," but it was what I heard, what I needed to hear: something overheated, melodramatic even, just to set the right tone for the journey I thought we ought to take.

All these months, between the disappearance of a fortune and the regaining of it, I'd lost him to work in a way that, even when I was at my most absorbed, he hadn't lost me. There's some scientific experiment about men and women blinking, or men and women staring, that shows that the way the sexes literally look is different. Apparently, women look to the right and the left much more than men. When I'm working, my gaze is glued to what's in front of it. But when I put the brush or the pencil down, I want life. I remember that I have a body, that it wants to be fed, bathed, fucked. Some days maybe I don't wash my hair or go running. But I wouldn't do it for two months. B would. A lot of men would.

He'd become nothing but an eye glued to a computer screen. How could he respond to me when he had to be anticipating trends every ten seconds? No, less than ten seconds; as he'd pointed out, in the pit ten seconds is a long time.

I wanted to make a point that the space we'd be inhabiting in Wash-ington would be the receptacle for a different kind of time. A cloisonné box, even a bit overornamented. I decided I'd bedeck our hotel room lavishly with flowers. More roses than anyone would have imagined buying. I asked them to make sure our room had a CD player so I could play the Telemann violin fantasies we'd listened to the first week we were lovers, the sound track to the film of my orgasmic life. I also brought along the complete works of Frank Sinatra.

When we walked into the hotel room, I was overwhelmed by the scent of roses. I couldn't believe that four dozen roses had such a presence; the entire space seemed to be covered with them. I was waiting for him to thank me. He was looking around, with an expression that seemed to me at the same time expectant and disappointed.

Finally he said, "What do you think of all the flowers?"

"I hope you like them," I said.

"Of course I like them, that's why I ordered them," he said.

"You didn't order them, I did."

"Let's count these roses," he said.

We counted. There were ninety-six roses. Eight dozen.

"Welcome to the O. Henry hour," he said. There was a knock on the door and the bellman arrived with four bottles of champagne. Each of us had ordered two, the kind we knew we liked: Brut Reserve.

"Do you think this means we've been together too long?" I asked.

"Not long enough," he said.

He opened the champagne. I put on the Frank Sinatra. We danced and sipped. We lay down on the bed. He closed his eyes. In a minute, he was asleep. It wasn't exactly what I'd planned.

Because, let's face it, it's a big difference between a man and a woman: you can't just fuck a man without his will. A randy man could, theoretically, fuck a sleeping woman and she might wake up in the middle and decide she liked what was happening. But all I could do was try to coax him awake. Which I decided to do.

It was a pretty straightforward procedure. If only painting was this easy! You have an idea, you do what you think needs to be done, and it happens. Not this horrible gap between the idea and its appearance, the shadow between the thing and the idea of the thing. I put his cock, which was sweet, like a sleeping puppy, into my mouth, and soon I had a tense hound, straining at the leash. I think he was pretending to be asleep so I'd keep going and he could just lie there, but then I felt his hips move and I knew I had him.

Had him where I wanted him and where I would have him. What an odd verb for sex: to have. Possession. Holding. Completion. End of change.

I lowered myself onto him and fed a breast into his mouth. I kept thinking of the word "breadfruit," because it sounded like such a simple food, so nourishing, so unchallenging, and my breasts felt white and substantial, and completely good. I looked down at his face. What did his face show? Effort and enjoyment, the enjoyable effort of postponed pleasure, the race against time, the arrow toward the bull's-eye, the runner toward the pot of gold. I sat above him like a goddess, like a colossus; I could do anything, and everything was up to me. I didn't moan, I roared; I sounded, to myself, imperial. His moan was, in comparison, polite and tidy, like a thank-you note, or a permission slip. I could collapse on top of him. Our work was done.

We slept. We drank champagne. We ordered club sandwiches from room service and didn't finish them. We were hungry for each other, and not easily replenished. I saw the digital clock at 5:15 A.M., I think. After that, we both slept until nine.

I woke first and showered. He pulled me down to him: he was hot; the hair around his cock was damp and matted. I lowered my clean body onto his dirty one; my inside was warm, and he had sluiced it with his attentions. He flipped me onto my back and held my wrists on the pillow. He didn't wait for me. Afterward, I could see he was worn-out; so I was patient. I let him take a shower, then I walked into the bathroom. I dried off his back. I dried his hair and guided his head down, fixing the bath mat so his knees wouldn't be sore against the tiles.

We craved the outside world; we craved air. There were two shows I wanted to see in the National Gallery, one of ancient Mexican art, the art of the Olmec people, and one of Corot and Italian landscape. We walked to the museum, and went to the Mexican show first.

Having felt so recently colossal myself, I was really in the mood for those colossal heads, dug up centuries later from the Mexican sands. Heads only, but the size of giants, almost expressionless, impervious to supplication, or appeasement, mercy or remorse. An aspect of being human utterly removed from any narrative, from the sense of the importance of a particular life history beginning with an individual birth and ending with an individual death. Yet even in this impersonal vision, there was a touch of personality. Some heads looked younger than others, some more joyous or more despairing. And there were small, beautiful ceramic figures, made for use: funerary objects. Art for something, not for itself. Baby gods, acrobats. Technically, I was excited by the ornamentation of matte surfacing, red designs incised into the clay. They were doing what I'd been trying to do: presenting two visions, one seen through the other. The overlaying design and the shape of the face. Ornament and icon. Both present, at the same moment, to be seen.

We crossed from the East Wing to the West Wing, from the unencumbered modern openness of Pei's space, past the cheerful man-made waterfall, to the nineteenth-century probity, solidity, gift of a government you were supposed to believe you could always count on. We heard our heels as we walked on the marble floors, beneath the small panes of glass in the domed ceilings, past the gentle plash of the fountains surrounded by miniature geraniums. In moving from the expanse of the East Wing, perfect for housing Calder's mobiles, to this, we were moving in time only seventy-five years, but the aesthetic gap was as enormous as the one between the fourth-century B.C. Olmec civilization and the Romantic vision of Corot and his predecessors.

A quotation from Corot at the beginning of the show moved me with its simplicity: "I have only one goal in life which I want to pursue devotedly: it is to make landscapes."

I loved the modesty and the plainness of that statement. It was what I loved most in an artist: the sense of doing the task for its own sake, and the absorption of the life into the task. Corot lived at a time when landscape painting wasn't an honored genre. He painted pictures that wouldn't be sold, wouldn't even be exhibited. He was doing it for himself, for the sake of doing it, for the sake of recording what he'd seen.

I was completely happy in the museum, walking with my B, then walking without him. We'd been together for three years; he knew how I liked to look, making a sweeping first trip, letting my eyes flick over everything, and allowing paintings to attach themselves to my vision. Then I would go back to revisit. I did it that way because I was afraid of missing something, of being hypnotized by one painting, and missing out on something incredible. B just stopped as long as he liked at whatever painting took his fancy and then moved on to the rest. So we rarely walked next to each other when we were looking at paintings; we were like children engaging in what preschool teachers called parallel play. Sometimes, though, we'd find ourselves before the same picture at the same time, as we did in front of the cloud studies by a Belgian painter named Denis. They were wonderful cloud studies, called oil sketches, to distinguish them from the honorific "paintings." Nearly the whole canvas was cloud, with only a thin strip of green across the bottom border, marking vegetative life. Obviously the nonsky world did not compel Denis. He was interested in the play of color and light through cloud, and only that; there's no evidence of wind, no sense of movement. Only an absorption in three objects of concentration: color, light and cloud.

I've seen shows that were undeniably fuller of greatness than this little one. But perhaps because of its limitedness, this made me eager to paint. It's very odd that sometimes paintings that are merely very good, and not great, create in me an itch to paint that more obvious masterpieces don't. Several paintings in this show had this effect. One was by a German, odd because in the foreground of a mountain scene there were three quite detailed leaf studies. And that riveted me, including two different perspectives in one work, two points of interest, two different ways of focusing, two different levels of completion. A couple of views through windows made me think of the issue of a frame within a frame, something seen through something else. The formal problem and its possibilities, of course, of borders. I thought of the beautiful edges of Diebenkorn.

And another painting, called *The Artist in His Room in the Villa Medici, Rome,* made me excited about the possibilities of different sorts of objects in a room. The artist, in his loose eighteenth-century coat, is in a room in Rome, the room he's allowed to inhabit on account of winning a distinguished prize. He's reading a letter from home. The room is austere; it contains only what he needs for painting and for reading: allegorical objects, a helmet and feathers, a guitar. His easel and paints are on a shelf above the bed, and next to them, only one book. But through the window, which is draped on top, as if he believes the higher part of his mind shouldn't be concerned with landscapes, is the prospect of the inviting Campagna. The room is full of emptiness and muted light. The painter is painting space.

I was very excited by everything. The monumental, personalityless, colossal heads. The playful terra-cotta acrobats. Questions of borders, questions of embellishment, questions of focus. All these artists giving us their version of what it was like to be alive in the world.

I wanted to explain that to B, but I simply took his hand. I told him I was happy to be with him. I told him I wanted to go back to the hotel. I told him I wanted to go right to bed.

In bed he was discursive in his movements, concentrating on the area around my clavicle, the little declension in the middle of my neck, tracing it with his fingers first and then his tongue, following it in a straight line to my navel, and slowly opening my legs and tracing a straight path between them, as if he were making his way along a dark road.

As we packed the next day, I said, "I want to have a party. We have a lot to celebrate. Three years of a love affair. The end of a series of paintings. The end of a big painting. Your score. Your new partnership. Rachel back home. Sara about to leave, God help us, for a new life."

"Great idea," he said. "You do all the work and I'll pay for everything."

"Fine," I said. "But did it ever occur to you that it's no threat to your masculinity to help me with a party?"

"Masculinity has nothing to do with it. I'd be happy to do all the cooking myself, if you weren't involved. It's just that being anywhere near the kitchen where you're cooking for more than two is like taking out citizenship in a totalitarian state. Which I, as a loyal American, simply cannot do."

*    *    *

He was right, but he probably hadn't gone far enough in what he said. I wasn't just the head of a totalitarian state when I was arranging a party: I was conquering an empire. I was Napoleon, striding across Europe, stealing, with a humble melancholy, the treasures of each land where I planted my imperial, triumphant flag.

For a week, I covered the dining table with cookbooks, like a general spreading out battle plans and maps. How extravagantly the titles beguiled me; with what false promise of easy colonization and surrender did they call out their names: *The Splendid Table: 500 Years of Eating in Northern Italy, The Silver Palate, The Complete Book of Fish and Shellfish, The Cuisine of the Sun, The Cuisine of the Rose, Sinful Desserts.* More modestly the richer, older countries, knowing that they needed no extravagant claims, breathed quietly: James Beard, Julia Child. And joining them with its already ravaged landscape, besmirched with spilled gravies, the stains of custards or stocks, the *Joy of Cooking,* acquired in college when I was cooking for the love of men.

But now, there was no single, identifiable mouth that my imagination yearned to please. I was creating a celebration in praise of prosperity. It had to be opulent, extravagant, an obvious tribute to a generous claque of gods. So I sat with my cookbooks spread out: the general now conquering hero who is offered, as spoils, the most inventive and most submissive of the eager harem. Try me, cried the Fava Beans with Peccorino. No, me, insisted the Sweet Fennel in Garlic. How could I not consider Priest Stranglers—twisted pasta with clams and squid—particularly since the writer, neglecting to explain what priest is being strangled and why, assures me that much of the work can be done ahead of time. So as I thought of twisting the raw pasta into the shape for going round the priest's neck, I had memories of Parma violets, of Stendhal, the Parma Baptistry, octagonal, with its olive and rose-colored frescoes, and the town square where I heard, while I contemplated the Baptism of St. John, the sound of a rock band getting ready for that evening's concert.

Considering fish, I chose a three-colored seafood terrine. The author said that you could puree one batch of seafood in the food processor, divide it into thirds, then color one third with blanched and pureed watercress, another with saffron, and leave the last third alone. "But this approach always seems a little phony," said the cool voice, "so I make each layer with a different fish, so each has a subtle flavor." How could I resist this challenge, issued in the tone of the bluestocking, understanding, willing always to accompany her charges, but not, God forbid, not ever, to lower her standards?

Next I imagined Provençal Roast Tomatoes, and was in the country of the troubadours, the country of Matisse, endless sunshine, endless days of easy inspiration and unqualified, uncomplicated loves. And planning Potatoes Femme Boulanger, I thought of the Pagnol film with the beautiful cruel young wife and the obese devoted baker husband: how could I fail to serve my guests a dish of forgiveness, a dish of consolation, a dish without recrimination or remorse?

And dependable, from Poland, the ham I've done for years, glazed in honey, mustard, ground pepper, the cloves that bruise my finger as they penetrate the recalcitrant hide, little nails with their elaborate heads and tender points.

For dessert: some I'd make myself—plum tart with almond cream, fruit salad marinated in vermouth—and some I would buy, too complicated for my skills.

And so, on June 14, two days before the party, in white pants, striped tee shirt, light blue sandals, purple sunglasses (to show that, though I'm playful, I might nevertheless be fierce), I set out across New York like Stanley across Africa.

The two stops I needed to make that day couldn't be planned with efficiency. I needed to go downtown to the Polish butcher for the ham, Korowicki's on First Avenue and Eighth Street, where the red-faced butchers made you want to buy not only the ham you came in for but pounds of sausages you know you shouldn't dream of eating and fancy pots of mustard you'll never use. And I had to go to the Upper East Side, to the fancy Italian bakery.

I went downtown first, got the ham, brought it back and put it in the refrigerator. Before I set out for the East Side, I decided to take a quick look at my painting. It was all right. I still liked it. I went out into the street knowing it wasn't visible, this sense of accomplishment, this

sense of satisfaction. No one knew about it, above all the shopkeepers
with whom I dealt. It was important to me that they both liked and
respected me as a charming woman, as a knowledgeable and demanding consumer, as they pressed the coins into my hand, passed me the
parcels wrapped in white or brown paper. And important that they
didn't know the real truth about me: I was a painter who had done the
thing she meant to do.

No, they didn't know about it in the nearly terrifying Italian bakery, a minor branch (no one doubts that it is minor) of the original in
Milan. The window was full of elaborate cakes with white icing and
pink and violet flowers, cakes surrounded by leaves and baskets full of
the newest strawberries. The baskets and the leaves looked edible, as if,
putting them in your mouth, you'd crush against your palate only tenderness. This was the trick of the establishment; to make the merely
decorative look edible and the edible look merely decorative. I wanted
their fruit tartlets like dolls hats, the tiny cream puffs you could wear
as rings, the petits fours you could string together as a necklace. I
ordered them, a huge number it seemed, requesting that they be delivered to my apartment in two days. The lively salesgirls with their dark
skins and light blue eyes or blondeness vying with surprising darkness
looked like models, but they were polite and impassive, and the order
that I thought of as so extravagant caused in them no pause or comment. I treated myself to a cappuccino, the best, the most Milanese in
New York, standing at a zinc bar and looking at the varieties of bottles
stacked on the shelves against the mirrored walls, liquors or liqueurs I
always longed to have in my cabinet—Calvados, grappa, Punt e Mes—
but somehow never did.

The Italian bakery was only a block away from the Met, so I
stopped in for one look at a fourteenth-century Lombard relief of the
Crucifixion of Christ. I needed the sight of those bodies, electric with
the power of their gestures: kissing, strangling, jostling, falling to their
knees. As I spent the day cooking I wanted in the back of my mind the
image of bodies in groups so magnificently realized.

Home again, I coated the ham in its glaze and put it in the oven. I
went to Citarella for the fish; in the window, a display made of crabs'
claws, oysters, clams, mussels, arranged in the shape of a daisy. I made

the aspic and the fish mousse, then I hid the magazines and the unopened mail and washed the serving dishes.

I went to sleep at nine and woke at six. Because I knew what happened to time on the day of a party. It collapses upon itself, there is never enough of it. At eight o'clock in the morning, I hit the streets.

I began with Mr. Kim because he was my friend and knew how to relax me, and I wanted something of his to be at the party. I bought a pound of ginger sweets. It was early but people were out on Broadway, young lovers, shocked by the light, longing for their barely relinquished indolence, their postcoital coil. Runners, with and without hand weights, pumped by me, breathing hard. Two Latino boys played "Guantanamera" on a steel drum by the Eighty-sixth Street subway entrance. I gave them money because I knew no one else would; I wanted to tell them it was a mistake, no one wanted music so early, no one but me, I was having a party: I'd pay for their songs.

At 8:25, Fairway was full of energetic elders ready to run their shopping carts into my heels. They sniffed, they squeezed, they pinched and they disparaged; nothing pleased them: they had seen too much. Into my cart I piled arugula, melons—casaba, Persian, honeydew, the humble cantaloupe. I planned my still life; a fan spreading out from a center of ruby strawberries. I bought scallions. But not garlic, because Sara's Jeremy had brought me, straight from California, many brown bags of gourmet garlic, with names like Leningrad Red. His father, former Unitarian minister, had turned into a professional garlic grower. Sara talked me into having Jeremy as my sous-chef and bottle washer. "He's incredibly calming, Mom. You'll see him at his best."

"But he won't see me at my best."

"Jeremy doesn't care about things like bad behavior. He just watches."

I agreed, although I thought it was mad, until I came home and saw beautifully chopped piles of garlic and parsley.

Sara was right: this boy knew how to take orders. He didn't seem to mind having commands barked at him, he didn't seem to need to hear "please" like those other pathetic weaklings, those whiners, who complained about my tone. He knew how to work almost silently, except for singing angelically, songs by Handel and by Berlioz. He was such a good influence that I didn't scream at B when he called and asked if everything was under control, a word choice I would ordinarily think of as grounds for justifiable homicide.

Then it happened. The moment that always happened when I prepared for a party, the fever, the whirligig. All at once, I was in the middle of the battle; I was the general who had to be everywhere: loading the cannon, providing the infantry with rifles, the cavalry with fresh horses, forcing between the gibbering lips of a hysterical sergeant the flask from my hip pocket, hoisting the wounded and the dead. I was the general, surveying the expanse, whispering to myself: "What was I imagining with my maps, my battle plans? Nothing is worth this human outlay."

Everything had to be done at once, and it was too much, it was impossible. I thought to myself what I always think at such moments: why have I done this, no one likes parties, no one needs them, no one will enjoy herself, particularly me. I'm stupid, I'm a victim, the victim of a patriarchal illusion I've chosen to sacrifice myself to, I could be painting, what's the matter with me, don't I respect myself, why am I giving myself over to this monster—what's it called, a party?—which no one will like, no one has ever liked. Let me lie down on Broadway and let a bus roll over me, anything so I can stop doing all this and not have to appear tonight in front of guests. Let some disaster happen, war, kidnaping, so that from far off, I'll hear the benevolent, desired voice of someone, some utter stranger, saying, "Sorry, the party's off. The hostess is, unfortunately, dead."

But then everything was done. I looked with quiet pleasure at my serving dishes, some my grandmother's, some from my mother's wedding set, some brought home from happy travels, the white, pure white ellipse of my favorite pasta bowl. My silver—not matching—gleaned from flea markets and rainy days in the broth-colored air of filthy moldering shops. It was all mine: the tablecloth with its pattern of peach and russet tulips, the glass bowls of roses, the pitcher that would (soon but not now) be filled with water and ice.

I stood back. I surveyed. It would never be better than this. People would come. The hordes would break into my treasure. They'd violate the perfect circle of the aspic, smash the scallop design of the three-colored fish mousse, individual rotini would fall to the peach and russet cloth like ragged urchins falling to their death off a rotten Neapolitan pier. Some of B's friends would be boring, or wouldn't like me; someone might get into a fight or some couple would disappear into the bedroom. Anything could happen after the guests came in the door and ruined the perfect landscape I'd made. It was time to leave it; to bathe and groom myself so that, fragrant, dressed in a light green silk skirt, a sleeveless Nile-colored tunic, gold sandals, my toenails polished, cherry, no, rose red, I would be able, fear in my heart, and swallowing foreboding, to stand at the door and say to these, my guests, my enemies, "Welcome, so glad you're here."

B arrived; the party would begin, officially, in forty-five minutes. I had told him not to come too early but early enough. He was right on time; he knew better than to expose himself to the war of nerves I could be trusted to wage. Then the servers he hired arrived, the ones who would also clean up. I showed them the kitchen. B and I sat on the couch. Michael arrived. "Thank God," said B, embracing him, "reinforcements." Rachel came, my tanned daughter with the scarlet buzz cut, straight from Brazil and ready to pick something off one of my fruit arrangements. I hugged her, felt her new, coffee-picking muscles, grabbed her forearms as she approached a piece of cantaloupe and said, "Touch that and I'll cut your arm off at the shoulder."

Then they trickled in, my guests, and became indistinguishable, one undulating sea mammal, all mouth and tail swishing through the ocean I'd made, My party. It spoke to me, occasionally, this creature, and I answered, but no one really listened. Certainly I didn't. What I liked was the look of them, their clothes, mostly light-colored, summery. Theresa's hair was caught up in a tortoiseshell clip; she wore bright yellow silk trousers and a magenta Chinese jacket. Fanny wore white; I knew she'd leave without a wrinkle or a smudge and would have eaten everything and talked to everyone. Sara sat on the couch with Peggy; Jeremy brought them plates of food. Sara's hair was rippling, night-colored, and as she bent toward Peggy's smooth chestnut skull, their foreheads nearly touched. Someone I didn't know——one of B's friends, one of their dates——had a long tanned arm that was nothing but a stem for displaying her six Bakelite bracelets, candy rings: lemon, strawberry, lime.

I was happy, looking at everyone pretending to talk. I swam in and out of the sea of my creation. Mine, I said, all this is mine. My friends, my children, my dealer, my patron, my ex-husband. And my lover, who seemed to be toasting me, toasting the painting, displayed like the guest of honor, on the dining-room wall. He lifted his glass, "To love and work," he said. Was that what he said? He'd never said he loved me before. Was that what he was saying? I didn't drink, I allowed myself to be drunk to. And I thought, well, yes, there is something to all of it, this thing of being man and woman, for all its famous problems, all its varieties of grief.

"And here's to money," shouted the dreadful Jerry Weiss, who, earlier in the party, said he was sorry for having called me a pussy. Or implied it. I wanted to say, "I'm sorry I didn't call you a dick," but I said, "Oh, Jerry, forget it, that's all right." Because that's what parties are for.

Then they were all gone. The servers turned into cleaners and put everything away. It wasn't dark yet; the river hoarded up the day's last sun. B and I stood by the window.

"Thank you," I said. "For everything."

"We have a good time together," he said. "That's not so common after all."

He took me into bed. I looked at his body, stretched, alert beside me. Nothing had started; it was the second before the beginning. I wasn't doing anything, just looking. And thinking: this is a body of someone I know well.

Now I'll tell you something you've probably wanted to know. I'll tell you his real name. When I tell you, you'll know why I never did before.

It's Bernie. Bernard. Or as his mother says, BerNARD.

What kind of name is that for the hero of a great love affair? What kind of name is that to be calling out in a paroxysm of inextinguishable passion? Bernie.

He leaves in the morning. Can I explain to you the infinite voluptuousness of the sound of the door's click when you're still in bed and the lover, whom you know will soon be back, goes out, without you, to the world? And you lie, the sheets light on your recently caressed, caressive skin, and you know the whole day is ahead of you. And it's yours.

Today I'll pack the van and drive up to the Cape until October. Tomorrow I'll unpack. The next day I'll begin my new project: *After Ingres.* On the weekend, B will join me.

Some nights I'll wish he were there. Some nights I'll wish I didn't have to sleep alone.

But not every night. And certainly not every morning.

I know you understand. If you didn't understand, there'd be no reason for me to have been talking to you all this time.